Whiteladies by Margaret Oliphant

Margaret Oliphant Wilson was born on April 4th, 1828 to Francis W. Wilson, a clerk, and Margaret Oliphant, at Wallyford, near Musselburgh, East Lothian.

Her youth was spent in establishing a writing style and by 1849 she had her first novel published: Passages in the Life of Mrs. Margaret Maitland.

Two years later, in 1851 Caleb Field was published and also an invitation to contribute to Blackwood's Magazine; the beginning of a life time business relationship.

In May 1852, Margaret married her cousin, Frank Wilson Oliphant. Their marriage produced six children but, tragically, three died in infancy. When her husband developed signs of the dreaded consumption (tuberculosis) they moved to Florence, and then to Rome where, sadly, he died.

Margaret was naturally devastated but was also now left without support and only her income from writing to support the family. She returned to England and took up the burden of supporting her three remaining children by her literary activity.

Her incredible and prolific work rate increased both her commercial reputation and the size of her reading audience. Tragedy struck again in January 1864 when her only remaining daughter Maggie died.

In 1866 she settled at Windsor to be closer to her sons, who were being educated at near-by Eton School.

For more than thirty years she pursued a varied literary career but family life continued to bring problems. Cyril Francis, her eldest son, died in 1890. The younger son, Francis, who she nicknamed 'Cecco', died in 1894.

With the last of her children now lost to her, she had little further interest in life. Her health steadily and inexorably declined.

Margaret Oliphant Wilson Oliphant died at the age of 69 in Wimbledon on 20th June 1897. She is buried in Eton beside her sons.

Index of Contents

CHAPTER I

It was an old manor-house, not a deserted convent, as you might suppose by the name. The conventual buildings from which no doubt the place had taken its name, had dropped away, bit by bit, leaving nothing but one wall of the chapel, now closely veiled and mantled with ivy, behind the orchard, about a quarter of a mile from the house. The lands were Church lands, but the house was a lay house, of an older date than the family who had inhabited it from Henry VIII.'s time, when the priory was destroyed, and its possessions transferred to the manor. No one could tell very clearly how this transfer was made, or how the family of Austins came into being. Before that period no trace of them was to be found. They sprang up all at once, not rising gradually into power, but appearing full-blown as proprietors of the manor, and possessors of all the confiscated lands. There was a tradition in the family of some wild, tragical union of an emancipated nun with a secularized friar—a kind of repetition of Luther and his Catherine, but with results less comfortable than those which followed the marriage of those German souls. With the English convertites the issue was not happy, as the story goes. Their broken vows haunted them; their possessions, which were not theirs, but the Church's, lay heavy on their consciences; and they died early, leaving descendants with whose history a thread of perpetual misfortune was woven. The family history ran in a succession of long minorities, the line of inheritance gliding from one branch to the other, the direct thread breaking constantly. To die young, and leave orphan children behind; or to die younger still, letting the line drop and fall back upon cadets of the house, was the usual fate of the Austins of Whiteladies—unfortunate people who bore the traces of their original sin in their very name.

Miss Susan Austin was, at the moment when this story begins, seated in the porch of the manor, on a blazing day of July, when every scrap of shade was grateful and pleasant, and when the deep coolness of the old-fashioned porch was a kind of paradise. It was a very fine old house, half brick, half timber; the eaves of the high gables carved into oaken lace-work; the lattice casements shining out of velvet clothing of ivy; and the great projecting window of the old hall, stepping out upon the velvet lawn, all glass from roof to ground, with only one richly-carved strip of panelling to frame it into the peaked roof. The door stood wide open, showing a long passage floored with red bricks, one wall of which was all casement, the other broken by carved and comely oaken doors, three or four centuries old. The porch was a little wider than the passage, and had a mullioned window in it, by the side of the great front opening, all clustered over with climbing roses. Looking out from the red-floored passage, the eye went past Miss Susan in the porch, to the sweet, luxuriant greenness of the lime-trees on the farther side of the lawn, which ended the prospect. The lawn was velvet green; the trees were silken soft, and laden with blossoms; the roses fluttered in at the open porch window, and crept about the door. Every beam in the long passage, every door, the continuous line of casement, the many turns by which this corridor led, meandering, with wealth of cool and airy space, toward the house, were all centuries old, bearing the stamp of distant generations upon the carved wood and endless windings; but without, everything was young and sunny,—grass and daisies and lime-blossoms, bees humming, birds twittering, the roses waving up and down in the soft wind. I wish the figure of Miss Susan had belonged to this part of the landscape; but, alas! historical accuracy forbids romancing. She was the virtual mistress of the house, in absence of a better; but she was not young, nor had she been so for many a long day.

Miss Susan was about sixty, a comely woman of her age, with the fair hair and blue eyes of the Austins. Her hair was so light that it did not turn gray; and her eyes, though there were wrinkles round them, still preserved a certain innocence and candor of aspect which, ill-natured people said, had helped Miss Susan to make many a hard bargain, so guileless was their aspect. She was dressed in a gray gown of woollen stuff (alpaca, I think, for it is best to be particular); her hair was still abundant, and she had no cap on it, nor any covering. In her day the adoption of a cap had meant the acceptation of old age, and Miss Susan had no intention of accepting that necessity a moment before she was obliged to do so. The sun, which had begun to turn westward, had been blazing into the drawing-room, which looked that way, and Miss Susan had been driven out of her own chair and her own corner by it—an unwarrantable piece of presumption. She had been obliged to fly before it, and she had taken refuge in the porch, which faced to the north, and where shelter was to be found. She had her knitting in her hands; but if her countenance gave any clue to her mind's occupation, something more important than knitting occupied her thoughts. She sat on the bench which stood on the deepest side between the inner and the outer entrance, knitting silently, the air breathing soft about her, the roses rustling. For a long time she did not once raise her head. The gardener was plodding about his work outside, now and then crossing the lawn with heavy, leisurely foot, muffled by the velvet of the old immemorial turf. Within there would now and then come an indistinct sound of voice or movement through the long passage; but nothing was visible, except the still gray figure in the shade of the deep porch.

By-and-by, however, this silence was broken. First came a maid, carrying a basket, who was young and rosy, and lighted up the old passage with a gleam of lightness and youthful color.

"Where are you going, Jane?" said Miss Susan.

"To the almshouse, please," said Jane, passing out with a curtsey.

After her came another woman, at ten minutes' interval, older and staider, in trim bonnet and shawl, with a large carpet-bag.

"Where are you going, Martha?" said the lady again.

"Please, ma'am, to the almshouse," said Martha.

Miss Susan shrugged her shoulders slightly, but said no more.

A few minutes of silence passed, and then a heavy foot, slow and solemn, which seemed to come in procession from a vast distance, echoing over miles of passage, advanced gradually, with a protestation in every footfall. It was the butler, Stevens, a portly personage, with a countenance somewhat flushed with care and discontent.

"Where are you going, Stevens?" said Miss Susan.

"I'm going where I don't want to go, mum," said Stevens, "and where I don't hold with; and if I might make so bold as to say so, where you ought to put a stop to, if so be as you don't want to be ruinated and done for—you and Miss Augustine, and all the house."

"'Ruinated' is a capital word," said Miss Susan, blandly, "very forcible and expressive; but, Stevens, I don't think we'll come to that yet awhile."

"Going on like this is as good a way as any," grumbled the man, "encouraging an idle set of good-for-nothings to eat up ladies as takes that turn. I've seen it afore, Miss Austin. You gets imposed upon, right hand and left hand; and as for doing good!—No, no, this ain't the way."

Stevens, too had a basket to carry, and the afternoon was hot and the sun blazing. Between the manor and the almshouses there lay a long stretch of hot road, without any shade to speak of. He had reason, perhaps, to grumble over his unwilling share in these liberal charities. Miss Susan shrugged her shoulders again, this time with a low laugh at the butler's perturbation, and went on with her knitting. In a few minutes another step became audible, coming along the passage—a soft step with a little hesitation in it—every fifth or sixth footfall having a slight pause or shuffle which came in a kind of rhythm. Then a tall figure came round the corner, relieved against the old carved doorway at the end and the bright redness of the brick floor; a tall, very slight woman, peculiarly dressed in a long, limp gown, of still lighter gray than the one Miss Susan wore, which hung closely about her, with long hanging sleeves hanging half way down the skirt of her dress, and something like a large hood depending from her shoulders. As the day was so warm, she had not drawn this hood over her head, but wore a light black gauze scarf, covering her light hair. She was not much younger than her sister, but her hair was still lighter, having some half visible mixture of gray, which whitened its tone. Her eyes were blue, but pale, with none of the warmth in them of Miss Susan's. She carried her head a little on one side, and, in short, she was like nothing in the world so much as a mediæval saint out of a painted window, of the period when painted glass was pale in color, and did not blaze in blues and rubies. She had a basket too, carried in both her hands, which came out of the long falling lines of her sleeves with a curious effect. Miss Augustine's basket, however, was full of flowers—roses, and some long white stalks of lilies, not quite over, though it was July, and long branches of jasmine covered with white stars.

"So you are going to the almshouses too?" said her sister. "I think we shall soon have to go and live there ourselves, as Stevens says, if this is how you are going on."

"Ah, Susan, that would indeed be the right thing to do, if you could make up your mind to it," said her sister, in a low, soft, plaintive voice, "and let the Church have her own again. Then perhaps our sacrifice, dear, might take away the curse."

"Fiddlesticks!" said Miss Susan. "I don't believe in curses. But, Austine, my dear, everybody tells me you are doing a great deal too much."

"Can one do too much for God's poor?"

"If we were sure of that now," said Miss Susan, shaking her head; "but some of them, I am afraid, belong to—the other person. However, I won't have you crossed; but, Austine, you might show a little moderation. You have carried off Jane and Martha and Stevens: if any one comes, who is to open the door?"

"The doors are all open, and you are here," said Miss Augustine calmly. "You would not have the poor suffer for such a trifle? But I hope you will have no visitors to disturb your thoughts. I have been meditating much this morning upon that passage, 'Behold, our days are as a weaver's shuttle.' Think of it, dear. We have got much, much to do, Susan, to make up for the sins of our family."

"Fiddlesticks," said Miss Susan again; but she said it half playfully, with tones more gentle than her decided expression of face would have prophesied. "Go away to your charities," she added. "If you do harm, you do it in a good way, and mean well, poor soul, God knows; so I hope no mischief will come of it. But send me Stevens home as soon as may be, Austine, for the sake of my possible meditations, if for nothing else; for there's nobody left in the house but old Martin and the boy, and the women in the kitchen."

"What should we want with so many servants?" said Miss Augustine with a sigh; and she walked slowly out of the porch, under the rose-wreaths, and across the lawn, the sun blazing upon her light dress and turning it into white, and beating fiercely on her uncovered head.

"Take a parasol, for heaven's sake," said Miss Susan; but the white figure glided on, taking no notice. The elder sister paused for a moment in her knitting, and looked after the other with that look, half tender, half provoked, with which we all contemplate the vagaries of those whom we love, but do not sympathize with, and whose pursuits are folly to us. Miss Susan possessed what is called "strong sense," but she was not intolerant, as people of strong sense so often are; at least she was not intolerant to her sister, who was the creature most unlike her, and whom she loved best in the world.

The manor-house did not belong to the Misses Austin, but they had lived in it all their lives. Their family history was not a bright one, as I have said; and their own immediate portion of the family had not fared better than the previous generations. They had one brother who had gone into the diplomatic service, and had married abroad and died young, before the death of their father, leaving two children, a boy and a girl, who had been partially brought up with the aunts. Their mother was a Frenchwoman, and had married a second time. The two children, Herbert and Reine, had passed half of their time with her, half with their father's sisters; for Miss Susan had been appointed their guardian by their father, who had a high opinion of her powers. I do not know that this mode of education was very good for the young people; but Herbert was one of those gentle boys predestined to a short life, who take little harm by spoiling. He was dying now at one-and-twenty, among the Swiss hills, whither he had been taken, when the weather grew hot, from one of the invalid refuges on the Mediterranean shore. He was perishing slowly, and all false hope was over, and everybody knew it—a hard fate enough for his family; but there were other things involved which made it harder still. The estate of Whiteladies was strictly entailed. Miss Susan and Miss Augustine Austin had been well provided for by a rich mother, but their French sister-in-law had no money and another family, and Reine had no right to the lands, or to anything but a very humble portion left to her by her father; and the old ladies had the prospect before them of being turned out of the house they loved, the house they had been born in, as soon as their nephew's feeble existence should terminate. The supposed heir-at-law was a gentleman in the neighborhood, distantly related, and deeply obnoxious to them. I say the supposed heir—for there was a break in the Austin pedigree, upon which, at the present time, the Misses Austin and all their friends dwelt with exceeding insistance. Two or three generations before, the second son of the family had quarrelled with his father and disappeared entirely from England. If he had any descendants, they, and not Mr. Farrel-Austin, were the direct heirs. Miss Susan had sent envoys over all the known world seeking for these problematic descendants of her granduncle Everard. Another young Austin, of a still more distant stock, called Everard too, and holding a place in the succession after Mr. Farrel-Austin, had gone to America even, on the track of some vague Austins there, who were not the people he sought; and though Miss Susan would not give up the pursuit, yet her hopes were getting feeble; and there seemed no likely escape from the dire necessity of giving up the manor, and the importance (which she did not dislike) of the position it gave her as virtual mistress of a historical house, to a man she disliked and despised, the moment poor Herbert's breath should be out of his body. Peacefully, therefore, as the scene had looked before the interruptions above recorded, Miss Susan was not happy, nor were her thoughts of a cheerful character. She loved her nephew, and the approaching end to which all his relations had long looked forward hung over her like a cloud, with that dull sense of pain, soon to become more acute, which impending misfortune, utterly beyond our power to avert, so often brings; and mingled with this were the sharper anxieties and annoyances of the quest she had undertaken, and its ill success up to this moment; and the increasing probability that the man she disliked, and no other, must be her successor, her supplanter in her home. Her mind was full of such thoughts; but she was a woman used to restrain her personal sentiments, and keep them to herself, having been during her long life much alone, and without any companion in whom she was accustomed to confide. The two sisters had never been separated in their lives; but Augustine, not Susan, was the one who disclosed her feelings and sought for sympathy. In most relations of life there is one passive and one active, one who seeks and one who gives. Miss Augustine was the weaker of the two, but in this respect she was the more prominent. She was always the first to claim attention, to seek the interest of the other; and for years long her elder sister had been glad to give what she asked, and to keep silent about her own sentiments, which the other might not have entered into. "What was the use?" Miss Susan said to herself; and shrugged her shoulders and kept her troubles, which were very different from Augustine's in her own breast.

How pleasant it was out there in the porch! the branches of the lime-trees blown about softly by the wind; a daisy here and there lifting its roguish saucy head, which somehow had escaped the scythe, from the close-mown lawn; the long garlands of roses playing about the stone mullions of the window, curling round the carved lintel of the door; the cool passage on the other side leading into the house, with its red floor and carved doors, and long range of casement. Miss Susan scarcely lifted her eyes from her knitting, but every detail of the peaceful scene was visible before her. No wonder—she had learned them all by heart in the long progress of the years. She knew every twig on the limes, every bud on the roses. She sat still, scarcely moving, knitting in with her thread many an anxious thought, many a wandering fancy, but with a face serene enough, and all about her still. It had never been her habit to betray what was in her to an unappreciative world.

She brightened up a little, however, and raised her head, when she heard the distant sound of a whistle coming far off through the melodious Summer air. It caught her attention, and she raised her head for a second, and a smile came over her face. "It must be Everard," she said to herself, and listened, and made certain, as the air, a pretty gay French air, became more distinct. No one else would whistle that tune. It was one of Reine's French songs—one of those graceful little melodies which are so easy to catch and so effective. Miss Susan was pleased that he should whistle one of Reine's tunes. She had her plans and theories on this point, as may be hereafter shown; and Everard besides was a favorite of her own, independent of Reine. Her countenance relaxed, her knitting felt lighter in her hand, as the whistle came nearer, and then the sound of a firm, light step. Miss Susan let the smile dwell upon her face, not dismissing it, and knitted on, expecting calmly till he should make his appearance. He had come to make his report to her of another journey, from which he had just returned, in search of the lost Austins. It had not been at all to his own interest to pursue this search, for, failing Mr. Farrel-Austin, he himself would be the heir-at-law; but Everard, as Miss Susan had often said to herself, was not the sort of person to think of his own advantage. He was, if anything, too easy on that head—too careless of what happened to himself individually. He was an orphan with a small income—that "just enough" which is so fatal an inheritance for a young man—nominally at "the Bar," actually nowhere in the race of life, but very ready to do anything for anybody, and specially for his old cousins, who had been good to him in his youth. He had a small house of his own on the river not far off, which the foolish young man lived in only a few weeks now and then, but which he refused to let, for no reason but because it had been his mother's, and her memory (he thought) inhabited the place. Miss Susan was so provoked with this and other follies that she could have beaten Everard often, and then hugged him—a mingling of feelings not unusual. But as Everard is just about to appear in his own person, I need not describe him further. His whistle came along, advancing through the air, the pleasantest prelude to his appearance. Something gay and free and sweet was in the sound, the unconscious self-accompaniment of a light heart. He whistled as he went for want of thought—nay, not for want of thought, but because all the movements of his young soul were as yet harmonious, lightsome, full of hope and sweetness; his gay personality required expression; he was too light-hearted, too much at home in the world, and friendly, to come silent along the sunshiny way. So, as he could not talk to the trees and the air, like a poetical hero in a tragedy, Everard made known his good-will to everything, and delicious, passive happiness, by his whistle; and he whistled like a lark, clear and sweet; it was one of his accomplishments. He whistled Miss Susan's old airs when she played them on her old piano, in charming time and harmony; and he did not save his breath for drawing-room performances, but sent before him these pleasant intimations of his coming, as far as a mile off. To which Miss Susan sat and listened, waiting for his arrival, with a smile on her face.

CHAPTER II

"I have been waiting for you these fifteen minutes," she said.

"What—you knew I was coming?"

"I heard you, boy. If you choose to whistle 'Ce que je desire' through St. Austin's parish, you may make up your mind to be recognized. Ah! you make me think of my poor children, the one dying, the other nursing him—"

"Don't!" said the young man, holding up his hand, "it is heart-breaking; I dare not think of them, for my part. Aunt Susan, the missing Austins are not to be found in Cornwall. I went to Bude, as you told me, and found a respectable grocer, who came from Berks, to be sure, and knew very little about his grandfather, but is not our man. I traced him back to Flitton, where he comes from, and found out his pedigree. I have broken down entirely. Did you know that the Farrel-Austins were at it too?"

"At what?"

"This search after our missing kinsfolk. They have just come back, and they look very important; I don't know if they have found out anything."

"Then you have been visiting them?" said Miss Susan, bending her head over her knitting, with a scarcely audible sigh; it would have been inaudible to a stranger, but Everard knew what it meant.

"I called—to ask if they had got back, that was all," he said, with a slight movement of impatience; "and they have come back. They had come down the Rhine and by the old Belgian towns, and were full of pictures, and cathedrals, and so forth. But I thought I caught a gleam in old Farrel's eye."

"I wonder—but if he had found them out I don't think there would be much of a gleam in his eye," said Miss Susan. "Everard, my dear, if we have to give up the house to them, what shall I do? and my poor Austine will feel it still more."

"If it has to be done, it must be done, I suppose," said Everard, with a shrug of his shoulders, "but we need not think of it until we are obliged; and besides, Aunt Susan, forgive me, if you had to give it up to—poor Herbert himself, you would feel it; and if he should get better, poor fellow, and live, and marry—"

"Ah, my poor boy," said Miss Susan, "life and marriage are not for him!" She paused a moment and dried her eyes, and gulped down a sob in her throat. "But you may be right," she said in a low tone, "perhaps, whoever our successors were, we should feel it—even you, Everard."

"You should never go out of Whiteladies for me," said the young man, "that you may be sure of; but I shall not have the chance. Farrel-Austin, for the sake of spiting the family generally, will make a point of outliving us all. There is this good in it, however," he added, with a slight movement of his head, which looked like throwing off a disagreeable impression, and a laugh, "if poor Herbert, or I, supposing such a thing possible, had taken possession, it might have troubled your affection for us, Aunt Susan. Nay, don't shake your head. In spite of yourself it would have affected you. You would have felt it bitter, unnatural, that the boys you had brought up and fostered should take your house from you. You would have struggled against the feeling, but you could not have helped it, I know."

"Yes; a great deal you know about an old woman's feelings," said Miss Susan with a smile.

"And as for these unknown people, who never heard of Whiteladies, perhaps, and might pull down the old house, or play tricks with it—for instance, your grocer at Bude, the best of men, with a charming respectable family, a pretty daughter, who is a dress-maker, and a son who has charge of the cheese and butter. After all, Aunt Susan, you could not in your heart prefer them even to old Farrel-Austin, who is a gentleman at least, and knows the value of the old house."

"I am not so sure of that," said Miss Susan, though she had shivered at the description. "Farrel-Austin is our enemy; he has different ways of thinking, different politics, a different side in everything; and besides—don't laugh in your light way, Everard; everybody does not take things lightly as you do—there is something between him and us, an old grievance that I don't care to speak of now."

"So you have told me," said the young man. "Well, we cannot help it, anyhow; if he must succeed, he must succeed, though I wish it was myself rather for your sake."

"Not for your own?" said Miss Susan, with restrained sharpness, looking up at him. "The Farrel-Austins are your friends, Everard. Oh, yes, I know! nowadays young people do not take up the prejudices of their elders. It is better and wiser, perhaps, to judge for yourself, to take up no foregone conclusion; but for my part, I am old-fashioned, and full of old traditions. I like my friends, somehow, reasonably or unreasonably, to be on my side."

"You have never even told me why it was your side," said Everard, with rising color; "am I to dislike my relations without even knowing why? That is surely going too far in partisanship. I am not fond of Farrel-Austin himself; but the rest of the family—"

"The—girls; that is what you would say."

"Well, Aunt Susan! the girls if you please; they are very nice girls. Why should I hate them because you hate their father? It is against common-sense, not to speak of anything else."

There was a little pause after this. Miss Susan had been momentarily happy in the midst of her cares, when Everard's whistle coming to her over the Summer fields and flowers, had brought to her mind a soft thought of her pretty Reine, and of the happiness that might be awaiting her after her trial was over. But now, by a quick and sudden revulsion this feeling of relief was succeeded by a sudden realization of where Reine might be now, and how occupied, such as comes to us all sometimes, when we have dear friends in distress—in one poignant flash, with a pain which concentrates in itself as much suffering as might make days sad. The tears came to her eyes in a gush. She could not have analyzed the sensations of disappointment, annoyance, displeasure, which conspired to throw back her mind upon the great grief which was in the background of her landscape, always ready to recall itself; but the reader will understand how it came about. A few big drops of moisture fell upon her knitting. "Oh, my poor children!" she said, "how can I think of anything else, when at this very moment, perhaps, for all one knows—"

I believe Everard felt what was the connecting link of thought, or rather feeling, and for the first moment was half angry, feeling himself more or less blamed; but he was too gentle a soul not to be overwhelmed by the other picture suggested, after the first moment. "Is he so very bad, then?" he asked, after an interval, in a low and reverential tone.

"Not worse than he has been for weeks," said Miss Susan, "but that is as bad as possible; and any day— any day may bring—God help us! in this lovely weather, Everard, with everything blooming, everything gay—him dying, her watching him. Oh! how could I forget them for a moment—how could I think of anything else?"

He made no answer at first, then he said faltering, "We can do them no good by thinking, and it is too cruel, too terrible. Is she alone?"

"No; God forgive me," said Miss Susan. "I ought to think of the mother who is with her. They say a mother feels most. I don't know. She has other ties and other children, though I have nothing to say against her. But Reine has no one."

Was it a kind of unconscious appeal to his sympathy? Miss Susan felt in a moment as if she had compromised the absent girl for whom she herself had formed visions with which Reine had nothing to do.

"Not that Reine is worse off than hundreds of others," she said, hastily, "and she will never want friends; but the tie between them is very strong. I do wrong to dwell upon it—and to you!"

"Why to me?" said Everard. He had been annoyed to have Reine's sorrow thrust upon his notice, as if he had been neglecting her; but he was angry now to be thus thrust away from it, as if he had nothing to do with her; the two irritations were antagonistic, yet the same. "You don't like painful subjects," said Miss Susan, with a consciousness of punishing him, and vindictive pleasure, good soul as she was, in his punishment. "Let us talk of something else. Austine is at her almshouses, as usual, and she has left me with scarcely a servant in the house. Should any one call, or should tea be wanted, I don't know what I should do."

"I don't suppose I could make the tea," said Everard. He felt that he was punished, and yet he was glad of the change of subject. He was light-hearted, and did not know anything personally of suffering, and he could not bear to think of grief or misfortune which, as he was fond of saying, he could do no good by thinking of. He felt quite sure of himself that he would have been able to overcome his repugnance to things painful had it been "any good," but as it was, why make himself unhappy? He dismissed the pain as much as he could, as long as he could, and felt that he could welcome visitors gladly, even at the risk of making the tea, to turn the conversation from the gloomy aspect it had taken. The thought of Herbert and Reine seemed to cloud over the sunshine, and take the sweetness out of the air. It gave his heart a pang as if it had been suddenly compressed; and this pain, this darkening of the world, could do them no good. Therefore, though he was fond of them both, and would have gone to the end of the world to restore health to his sick cousin, or even to do him a temporary pleasure, yet, being helpless toward them, he was glad to get the thoughts of them out of his mind. It spoilt his comfort, and did them no manner of good. Why should he break his own heart by indulging in such unprofitable thoughts?

Miss Susan knew Everard well; but though she had herself abruptly changed the subject in deference to his wishes, she was vexed with him for accepting the change, and felt her heart fill full of bitterness on Reine's account and poor Herbert's, whom this light-hearted boy endeavored to forget. She could not speak to him immediately, her heart being sore and angry. He felt this, and had an inkling of the cause, and was half compunctious and half disposed to take the offensive, and ask, "What have I done?" and defend himself, but could not, being guilty in heart. So he stood leaning against the open doorway, with a great rosebranch, which had got loose from its fastenings, blowing in his face, and giving him a careless prick with its thorns, as the wind blew it about. Somehow the long waving bough, with its many roses, which struck him lightly, playfully, across the face as he stood there, with dainty mirth and mischief, made him think of Reine more than Miss Susan's reminder had done. The prick of the branch woke in his heart that same, sudden, vivid, poignant realization of the gay girl in contrast with her present circumstances, which just a few minutes before had taken Miss Susan, too, by surprise; and thus the two remained, together, yet apart, silent, in a half quarrel, but both thinking of the same subject, and almost with the same thoughts. Just then the rolling of carriage wheels and prance of horses became audible turning the corner of the green shady road into which the gate, at this side of the town, opened—for the manor-house was not secluded in a park, but opened directly from a shady, sylvan road, which had once served as avenue to the old priory. The greater part of the trees that formed the avenue had perished long ago, but some great stumps and roots, and an interrupted line of chance-sown trees, showed where it had been. The two people in the porch were roused by this sound, Miss Susan to a troubled recollection of her servant-less condition, and Everard to mingled annoyance and pleasure as he guessed who the visitors were. He would have been thankful to any one who had come in with a new interest to relieve him from the gloomy thoughts that had taken possession of him against his will, and the new comers, he felt sure, were people whom he liked to meet.

"Here is some one coming to call," cried Miss Susan in dismay, "and there is no one to open the door!"

"The door is open, and you can receive them here, or take them in, which you please; you don't require any servant," said Everard; and then he added, in a low tone, "Aunt Susan, it is the Farrel-Austins; I know their carriage."

"Ah!" cried Miss Susan, drawing herself up. She did not say any more to him—for was not he a friend and supporter of that objectionable family?—but awaited the unwelcome visitors with dignified rigidity. Their visits to her were very rare, but she had always made a point of enduring and returning these visits with that intense politeness of hostility which transcends every other kind of politeness. She would not consent to look up, nor to watch the alighting of the brightly-clad figures on the other side of the lawn. The old front of the house, the old doorway and porch in which Miss Susan sat, was not now the formal entrance, and consequently there was no carriage road to it; so that the visitors came across the lawn with light Summer dresses and gay ribbons, flowery creatures against the background of green. They were two handsome girls, prettily dressed and smiling, with their father, a dark, insignificant, small man, coming along like a shadow in their train.

"Oh, how cool and sweet it is here!" said Kate, the eldest. "We are so glad to find you at home, Miss Austin. I think we met your sister about an hour ago going through the village. Is it safe for her to walk in the sun without her bonnet? I should think she would get a sunstroke on such a day."

"She is the best judge," said Miss Susan, growing suddenly red; then subduing herself as suddenly, "for my part," she said, "I prefer the porch. It is too warm to go out."

"Oh, we have been so much about; we have been abroad," said Sophy, the youngest. "We think nothing of the heat here. English skies and English climate are dreadful after the climate abroad."

"Ah, are they? I don't know much of any other," said Miss Susan. "Good morning, Mr. Farrel. May I show you the way to the drawing-room, as I happen to be here?"

"Oh, mayn't we go to the hall, please, instead? We are all so fond of the hall," said Sophy. She was the silly one, the one who said things which the others did not like to say. "Please let us go there; isn't this the turn to take? Oh, what a dear old house it is, with such funny passages and turnings and windings! If it were ours, I should never sit anywhere but in the hall."

"Sophy!" said the father, in a warning tone.

"Well, papa! I am not saying anything that is wrong. I do love the old hall. Some people say it is such a tumble-down, ramshackle old house; but that is because they have no taste. If it were mine, I should always sit in the hall."

Miss Susan led the way to it without a word. Many people thought that Sophy Farrel-Austin had reason in her madness, and said, with a show of silliness, things that were too disagreeable for the others; but that was a mere guess on the part of the public. The hall was one of the most perfectly preserved rooms of its period. The high, open roof had been ceiled, which was almost the only change made since the fifteenth century, and that had been done in Queen Anne's time; and the huge, open chimney was partially built up, small sacrifices made to comfort by a family too tenacious of their old dwelling-place to do anything to spoil it, even at the risk of asthma or rheumatism. To tell the truth, however, there was a smaller room, of which the family now made their dining-room on ordinary occasions. Miss Susan, scorning to take any notice of words which she laid up and pondered privately to increase the bitterness of her own private sentiments toward her probable supplanters, led the way into this beautiful old hall. It was wainscoted with dark panelled wood, which shone and glistened, up to within a few feet of the roof, and the interval was filled with a long line of casement, throwing down a light which a painter would have loved upon the high, dark wall. At the upper end of the room was a deep recess, raised a step from the floor, and filled with a great window all the way up to the roof. At the lower end the musicians' gallery of ancient days, with carved front and half-effaced coats-of-arms, was still intact. The rich old Turkey carpet on the floor, the heavy crimson curtains that hung on either side of the recess with its great window, were the most modern things in the room; and yet they were older than Miss Susan's recollection could carry. The rest of the furniture dated much further back. The fire-place, in which great logs of wood blazed every Winter, was filled with branches of flowering shrubs, and the larger old-fashioned garden flowers, arranged in some huge blue and white China jars, which would have struck any collector with envy. Miss Susan placed her young visitors on an old, straight-backed settle, covered with stamped leather, which was extremely quaint, and very uncomfortable. She took herself one of the heavy-fringed, velvet-covered chairs, and began with deadly civility to talk. Everard placed himself against the carved mantel-piece and the bank of flowers that filled the chimney. The old room was so much the brighter to him for the presence of the girls; he did not care much that Sophy was silly. Their pretty faces and bright looks attracted the young man; perhaps he was not very wise himself. It happens so often enough.

And thus they all sat down and talked—about the beautiful weather, about the superiority, even to this beautiful weather, of the weather "abroad;" of where they had been and what they had seen; of Mrs. Farrel-Austin's health, who was something of an invalid, and rarely came out; and other similar matters, such as are generally discussed in morning calls. Everard helped Miss Susan greatly to keep the conversation up, and carry off the visit with the ease and lightness that were desirable, but yet I am not sure that she was grateful to him. All through her mind, while she smiled and talked, there kept rising a perpetual contrast. Why were these two so bright and well, while the two children of the old house were in such sad estate?—while they chattered and laughed what might be happening elsewhere? and Everard, who had been like a brother to Herbert and Reine, laughed too, and chattered, and made himself pleasant to these two girls, and never thought—never thought! This was the sombre under-current which went through Miss Susan's mind while she entertained her callers, not without sundry subdued passages of arms. But Miss Susan's heart beat high, in spite of herself, when Mr. Farrel-Austin lingered behind his daughters, bidding Everard see them to the carriage.

"Cousin Susan, I should like a word with you," he said.

CHAPTER III

The girls went out into the old corridor, leaving the great carved door of the dining-hall open behind them. The flutter of their pretty dresses filled the picturesque passage with animation, and the sound of their receding voices kept up this sentiment of life and movement even after they had disappeared. Their father looked after them well pleased, with that complacence on his countenance, and pleasant sense of personal well-being which is so natural, but so cruel and oppressive to people less well off. Miss Susan, for her part, felt it an absolute insult. It seemed to her that he had come expressly to flaunt before her his own happiness and the health and good looks of his children. She turned her back to the great window, that she might not see them going across the lawn, with Everard in close attendance upon them. A sense of desertion, by him, by happiness, by all that is bright and pleasant in the world, came into her heart, and made her defiant. When such a feeling as this gets into the soul, all softness, all indulgence to others, all favorable construction of other people's words or ways departs. They seemed to her to have come to glory over her and over Herbert dying, and Reine mourning, and the failure of the old line. What was grief and misery to her was triumph to them. It was natural perhaps, but very bitter; curses even, if she had not been too good a woman to let them come to utterance, were in poor Miss Susan's heart. If he had said anything to her about his girls, as she expected, if he had talked of them at all, I think the flood must have found vent somehow; but fortunately he did not do this. He waited till they were out of the house, and then rose and closed the door, and reseated himself facing her, with something more serious in his face.

"Excuse me for waiting till they had gone," he said. "I don't want the girls to be mixed up in any family troubles; though, indeed, there is no trouble involved in what I have to tell you—or, at least, so I hope."

The girls were crossing the lawn as he spoke, laughing and talking, saying something about the better training of the roses, and how the place might be improved. Miss Susan caught some words of this with ears quickened by her excited feelings. She drew her chair further from the window, and turned her back to it more determinedly than ever. Everard, too! he had gone over to the prosperous side.

"My dear cousin," said Mr. Farrel-Austin, "I wish you would not treat me like an enemy. Whenever there is anything I can do for you, I am always glad to do it. I heard that you were making inquiries after our great-uncle Everard and his descendants, if he left any."

"You could not miss hearing it. I made no secret of it," said Miss Susan. "We have put advertisements in the newspapers, and done everything we possibly could to call everybody's attention."

"Yes; I know, I know; but you never consulted me. You never said, 'Cousin, it is for the advantage of all of us to find these people.'"

"I do not think it is for your advantage," said Miss Susan, looking quickly at him.

"You will see, however, that it is, when you know what I have to tell you," he said, rubbing his hands. "I suppose I may take it for granted that you did not mean it for my advantage. Cousin Susan, I have found the people you have been looking for in vain."

The news gave her a shock, and so did his triumphant expression; but she put force upon herself. "I am glad to hear it," she said. "Such a search as mine is never in vain. When you have advantages to offer, you seldom fail to find the people who have a right to those advantages. I am glad you have been successful."

"And I am happy to hear you say so," said the other. "In short, we are in a state of agreement and concord for once in our lives, which is delightful. I hope you will not be disappointed, however, with the result. I found them in Bruges, in a humble position enough. Indeed, it was the name of Austin over a shop door which attracted my notice first."

He spoke leisurely, and regarded her with a smile which almost drove her furious, especially as, by every possible argument, she was bound to restrain her feelings. She was strong enough, however, to do this, and present a perfectly calm front to her adversary.

"You found the name—over a shop door?"

"Yes, a drapery shop; and inside there was an old man with the Austin nose as clear as I ever saw it. It belongs, you know, more distinctly to the elder branch than to any other portion of the family."

"The original stock is naturally stronger," said Miss Susan. "When you get down to collaterals, the family type dies out. Your family, for instance, all resemble your mother, who was a Miss Robinson, I think I have heard?"

This thrust gave her a little consolation in her pain, and it disturbed her antagonist in his triumph. She had, as it were, drawn the first blood.

"Yes, yes; you are quite right," he said; "of a very good family in Essex. Robinsons of Swillwell—well-known people."

"In the city," said Miss Susan, "so I have always heard; and an excellent thing, too. Blood may not always make its way, but money does; and to have an alderman for your grandfather is a great deal more comfortable than to have a crusader. But about our cousin at Bruges," she added, recovering her temper. How pleasant to every well-regulated mind is the consciousness of having administered a good, honest, knock-down blow!

Mr. Farrel-Austin glanced at her out of the light gray eyes, which were indisputable Robinsons', and as remote in color as possible from the deep blue orbs, clear as a Winter sky, which were one of the great points of the Austins; but he dared not take any further notice. It was his turn now to restrain himself.

"About our cousin in Bruges," he repeated with an effort. "He turns out to be an old man, and not so happy in his family as might be wished. His only son was dying—"

"For God's sake!" said Miss Susan, moved beyond her power of control, and indeed ceasing to control herself with this good reason for giving way—"have you no heart that you can say such words with a smile on your face? You that have children yourself, whom God may smite as well as another's! How dare you? how dare you? for your own sake!"

"I don't know that I am saying anything unbecoming," said Mr. Farrel. "I did not mean it. No one can be more grateful for the blessings of Providence than I am. I thank Heaven that all my children are well; but that does not hinder the poor man at Bruges from losing his. Pray let me continue: his wife and he are old people, and his only son, as I say, was dying or dead—dead by this time, certainly, according to what they said of his condition."

Miss Susan clasped her hands tightly together. It seemed to her that he enjoyed the poignant pang his words gave her—"dead by this time, certainly!" Might that be said of the other who was dearer to her? Two dying, that this man might get the inheritance! Two lives extinguished, that Farrel-Austin and his girls might have this honor and glory! He had no boys, however. His glory could be but short-lived. There was a kind of fierce satisfaction in that thought.

"I had a long conversation with the old man; indeed, we stayed in Bruges for some days on purpose. I saw all his papers, and there can be no doubt he is the grandson of our great-uncle Everard. I explained the whole matter to him, of course, and brought your advertisements under his notice, and explained your motives."

"What are my motives?—according to your explanation."

"Well, my dear cousin—not exactly love and charity to me, are they? I explained the position fully to him."

"Then there is no such thing as justice or right in the world, I suppose," she cried indignantly, "but everything hinges on love to you, or the reverse. You know what reason I have to love you—well do you know it, and lose no opportunity to keep it before me; but if my boy himself—my dying boy, God help me!—had been in your place, Farrel-Austin, should I have let him take possession of what was not his by right? You judge men, and women too, by yourself. Let that pass, so far as you are concerned. You have no other ground, I suppose, to form a judgment on; but you have no right to poison the minds of others. Nothing will make me submit to that."

"Well, well," said Mr. Farrel-Austin, shrugging his shoulders with contemptuous calm, "you can set yourself right when you please with the Bruges shopkeeper. I will give you his address. But in the meantime you may as well hear what his decision is. At his age he does not care to change his country and his position, and come to England in order to become the master of a tumble-down old house. He prefers his shop, and the place he has lived in all his life. And the short and the long of it is, that he has transferred his rights to me, and resigned all claim upon the property. I agreed to it," he added, raising his head, "to save trouble, more than for any other reason. He is an old man, nearly seventy; his son dead or dying, as I said. So far as I am concerned, it could only have been a few years' delay at the most."

Miss Susan sat bolt upright in her chair, gazing at him with eyes full of amazement—so much astonished that she scarcely comprehended what he said. It was evidently a relief to the other to have made his announcement. He breathed more freely after he had got it all out. He rose from his chair and went to the window, and nodded to his girls across the lawn. "They are impatient, I see, and I must be going," he went on. Then looking at Miss Susan for the first time, he added, in a tone that had a sound of mockery in it, "You seem surprised."

"Surprised!" She had been leaning toward the chair from which he had arisen without realizing that he had left it in her great consternation. Now she turned quickly to him. "Surprised! I am a great deal more than surprised."

He laughed; he had the upper hand at last. "Why more?" he said lightly. "I think the man was a very reasonable old man, and saw what his best policy was."

"And you—accepted his sacrifice?" said Miss Susan, amazement taking from her all power of expression;—"you permitted him to give up his birthright? you—took advantage of his ignorance?"

"My dear cousin, you are rude," he said, laughing; "without intending it, I am sure. So well-bred a woman could never make such imputations willingly. Took advantage! I hope I did not do that. But I certainly recommended the arrangement to him, as the most reasonable thing he could do. Think! At his age, he could come here only to die; and with no son to succeed him, of course I should have stepped in immediately. Few men like to die among strangers. I was willing, of course, to make him a recompense for the convenience—for it was no more than a convenience, make the most you can of it—of succeeding at once."

Miss Susan looked at him speechless with pain and passion. I do not know what she did not feel disposed to say. For a moment her blue eyes shot forth fire, her lips quivered from the flux of too many words which flooded upon her. She began even, faltering, stammering—then came to a stop in the mere physical inability to arrange her words, to say all she wanted, to launch her thunderbolt at his head with the precision she wished. At last she came to a dead stop, looking at him only, incapable of speech; and with that pause came reflection. No; she would say nothing; she would not commit herself; she would think first, and perhaps do, instead of saying. She gave a gasp of self-restraint.

"The young ladies seem impatient for you," she said. "Don't let me detain you. I don't know that I have anything to say on the subject of your news, which is surprising, to be sure, and takes away my breath."

"Yes, I thought you would be surprised," he said, and shook hands with her. Miss Susan's fingers tingled—how she would have liked, in an outburst of impatience which I fear was very undignified, to apply them to his ear, rather than to suffer his hand to touch hers in hypocritical amity! He was a little disappointed, however, to have had so little response to his communication. Her silence baffled him. He had expected her to commit herself, to storm, perhaps; to dash herself in fury against this skilful obstacle which he had placed in her way. He did not expect her to have so much command of herself; and, in consequence, he went away with a secret uneasiness, feeling less successful and less confident in what he had done, and asking himself, Could he have made some mistake after all—could she know something that made his enterprise unavailing? He was more than usually silent on the drive home, making no answer to the comments of his girls, or to their talk about what they would do when they got possession of the manor.

"I hope the furniture goes with the house," said Kate. "Papa, you must do all you can to secure those old chairs, and especially the settee with the stamped leather, which is charming, and would fetch its weight in gold in Wardour street."

"And, papa, those big blue and white jars," said Sophy, "real old Nankin, I am sure. They must have quantities of things hidden away in those old cupboards. It shall be as good as a museum when we get possession of the house!"

"You had better get possession of the house before you make any plans about it," said her father. "I never like making too sure."

"Why, papa, what has come over you?" cried the eldest. "You were the first to say what you would do, when we started. Miss Susan has been throwing some spell over you."

"If it is her spell, it will not be hard to break it," said Sophy; and thus they glided along, between the green abundant hedges, breathing the honey breath of the limes, but not quite so happy and triumphant as when they came. As for the girls, they had heard no details of the bargain their father had made, and gave no great importance to it; for they knew he was the next heir, and that the manor-house would soon cease to be poor Herbert's, with whom they had played as children, but whom, they said constantly, they scarcely knew. They did not understand what cloud had come over their father. "Miss Susan is an old witch," they said, "and she has put him under some spell."

Meanwhile Miss Susan sat half-stupefied where he had left her, in a draught, which was a thing she took precautions against on ordinary occasions—the great window open behind her, the door open in front of her, and the current blowing about even the sedate and heavy folds of the great crimson curtains, and waking, though she did not feel it, the demon Neuralgia to twist her nerves, and set her frame on an edge. She did not seem able to move or even think, so great was the amazement in her mind. Could he be right—could he have found the Austin she had sought for over all the world; and was it possible that the unrighteous bargain he had told her of had really been completed? Unrighteous! for was it not cheating her in the way she felt the most, deceiving her in her expectations? An actual misfortune could scarcely have given Miss Susan so great a shock. She sat quite motionless, her very thoughts arrested in their course, not knowing what to think, what to do—how to take this curious new event. Must she accept it as a thing beyond her power of altering, or ought she to ignore it as something incredible, impossible? One thing or other she must decide upon at once; but in the meantime, so great was the effect this intimation had upon her mind, she felt herself past all power of thinking. Everard coming back found her still seated there in the draught in the old hall. He shut the door softly behind him and went in, looking at her with questioning eyes. But she did not notice his look; she was too much and too deeply occupied in her own mind. Besides, his friendship with her visitors made Everard a kind of suspected person, not to be fully trusted. Miss Susan was too deeply absorbed to think this, but she felt it. He sat down opposite, where Mr. Farrel-Austin had been sitting, and looked at her; but this mute questioning produced no response.

"What has old Farrel been saying to you, Aunt Susan?" he asked at last.

"Why do you call him old Farrel, Everard? he is not nearly so old as I am," said Miss Susan with a sigh, waking up from her thoughts. "Growing old has its advantages, no doubt, when one can realize the idea of getting rid of all one's worries, and having the jangled bells put in tune again; but otherwise—to think of others who will set everything wrong coming after us, who have tried hard to keep them right! Perhaps, when it comes to the very end, one does not mind; I hope so; I feel sore now to think that this man should be younger than I am, and likely to live ever so much longer, and enjoy my father's house."

Everard sat still, saying nothing. He was unprepared for this sort of reply. He was slightly shocked too, as young people so often are, by the expression of any sentiments, except the orthodox ones, on the subject of dying. It seemed to him, at twenty-five, that to Miss Susan at sixty, it must be a matter of comparatively little consequence how much longer she lived. He would have felt the sentiments of the Nunc Dimittis to be much more appropriate and correct in the circumstances; he could not understand the peculiar mortification of having less time to live than Farrel-Austin. He looked grave with the fine disapproval and lofty superiority of youth. But he was a very gentle-souled and tender-hearted young man, and he did not like to express the disapproval that was in his face.

"We had better not talk of them," said Miss Susan, after a pause; "we don't agree about them, and it is not likely we should; and I don't want to quarrel with you, Everard, on their account. Farrel thinks he is quite sure of the estate now. He has found out some one whom he calls our missing cousin, and has got him to give up in his own favor."

"Got him to give up in his own favor!" repeated Everard amazed. "Why, this is wonderful news. Who is it, and where is he, and how has it come about? You take away one's breath."

"I cannot go into the story," said Miss Susan. "Ask himself. I am sick of the subject. He thinks he has settled it, and that it is all right; and waits for nothing but my poor boy's end to take possession. They had not even the grace to ask for him!" she cried, rising hastily. "Don't ask me anything about it; it is more than I can bear."

"But, Aunt Susan—"

"I tell you we shall quarrel, Everard, if we talk more on this subject," she cried. "You are their friend, and I am their—no; it is they who are my enemies," she added, stopping herself. "I don't dictate to you how you are to feel, or what friends you are to make. I have no right; but I have a right to talk of what I please, and to be silent when I please. I shall say no more about it. As for you," she said, after another pause, with a forced smile, "the young ladies will consult with you what changes they are to make in the house. I heard them commenting on the roses, and how everything could be improved. You will be of the greatest use to them in their new arrangements, when all obstacles are removed."

"I don't think it is kind to speak to me so," said Everard, in his surprise. "It is not generous, Aunt Susan. It is like kicking a fellow when he is down; for you know I can't defend myself."

"Yes, I suppose it is unjust," said Miss Susan, drying her eyes, which were full of hot tears, with no gratefulness of relief in them. "The worst of this world is that one is driven to be unjust, and can't help it, even to those one loves."

CHAPTER IV

Everard Austin remained at Whiteladies for the rest of the afternoon—he was like one of the children of the house. The old servants took him aside and asked him to mention things to Miss Susan with which they did not like to worry her in her trouble, though indeed most of these delicacies were very much after date, and concerned matters on which Miss Susan had already been sufficiently worried. The gardener came and told him of trees that wanted cutting, and the bailiff on the farm consulted him about the laborers for the approaching harvest. "Miss Susan don't like tramps, and I don't want to go against her, just when things is at its worst. I shouldn't wonder, sir," said the man, looking curiously in Everard's face, "if things was in other hands this time next year?" Everard answered him with something of the bitterness which he himself had condemned so much a little while before. That Farrel-Austin should succeed was natural; but thus to look forward to the changing of masters gave him, too, a pang. He went indoors somewhat disturbed, and fell into the hands of Martha and Jane fresh from the almshouse. Martha, who was Miss Susan's maid and half-housekeeper, had taken charge of him often enough in his boyish days, and called him Master Everard still, so that she was entitled to speak; while the younger maid looked on, and concurred—"It will break my lady's heart," said Martha, "leaving this old house; not but what we might be a deal more comfortable in a nice handy place, in good repair like yours is, Master Everard; where the floors is straight and the roofs likewise, and you don't catch a rheumatism round every corner; but my lady ain't of my way of thinking. I tell her as it would have been just as bad if Mr. Herbert had got well, poor dear young gentleman, and got married; but she won't listen to me. Miss Augustine, she don't take on about the house; but she's got plenty to bother her, poor soul; and the way she do carry on about them almshouses! It's like born natural, that's what it is, and nothing else. Oh me! I know as I didn't ought to say it; but what can you do, I ask you, Master Everard, when you have got the like of that under your very nose? She'll soon have nothing but paupers in the parish if she has her way."

"She's very feeling-hearted," said Jane, who stood behind her elder companion and put in a word now and then over Martha's shoulder. She had been enjoying the delights of patronage, the happiness of recommending her friends in the village to Miss Augustine's consideration; and this was too pleasant a privilege to be consistent with criticism. The profusion of her mistress's alms made Jane feel herself to be "feeling-hearted" too.

"And great thanks she gets for it all," said Martha. "They call her the crazy one down in the village. Miss Susan, she's the hard one; and Miss Augustine's the crazy one. That's gratitude! trailing about in her gray gown for all the world like a Papist nun. But, poor soul, I didn't ought to grudge her gray, Master Everard. We'll soon be black and black enough in our mourning, from all that I hear."

Again Everard was conscious of a shiver. He made a hasty answer and withdrew from the women who had come up to him in one of the airy corridors upstairs, half glass, like the passages below, and full of corners. Everard was on his way from a pilgrimage to the room, in which, when Herbert and he were children, they had been allowed to accumulate their playthings and possessions. It had a bit of corridor, like a glazed gallery, leading to it—and a door opened from it to the musicians' gallery of the hall. The impulse which led him to this place was not like his usual care to avoid unpleasant sensations, for the very sight of the long bare room, with its windows half choked with ivy, the traces of old delights on the walls—bows hung on one side, whips on the other—a heap of cricket-bats and pads in a corner; and old books, pictures, and rubbish heaped upon the old creaky piano on which Reine used to play to them, had gone to his heart. How often the old walls had rung with their voices, the old floor creaked under them! He had given one look into the haunted solitude, and then had fled, feeling himself unable to bear it. "As if I could do them any good thinking!" Everard had said to himself, with a rush of tears to his eyes—and it was in the gallery leading to this room—the west gallery as everybody called it—that the women stopped him. The rooms at Whiteladies had almost every one a gallery, or an ante-room, or a little separate staircase to itself. The dinner-bell pealed out as he emerged from thence and hurried to the room which had been always called his, to prepare for dinner. How full of memories the old place was! The dinner-bell was very solemn, like the bell of a cathedral, and had never been known to be silent, except when the family were absent, for more years than any one could reckon. How well he recollected the stir it made among them all as children, and how they would steal into the musicians' gallery and watch in the centre of the great room below, in the speck of light which shone amid its dimness, the two ladies sitting at table, like people in a book or in a dream, the servants moving softly about, and no one aware of the unseen spectators, till the irrepressible whispering and rustling of the children betrayed them! how sometimes they were sent away ignominiously, and sometimes Aunt Susan, in a cheery mood, would throw up oranges to them, which Reine, with her tiny hands, could never catch! How she used to cry when the oranges fell round her and were snapped up by the boys— not for the fruit, for Reine never had anything without sharing it or giving it away, but for the failure which made them laugh at her! Everard laughed unawares as the scene came up before him, and then felt that sudden compression, constriction of his heart—serrement du cœur, which forces out the bitterest tears. And then he hurried down to dinner and took his seat with the ladies, in the cool of the Summer evening, in the same historical spot, having now become one of them, and no longer a spectator. But he looked up at the gallery with a wistful sense of the little scuffle that used to be there, the scrambling of small feet, and whispering of voices. In Summer, when coolness was an advantage, the ladies still dined in the great hall.

"Austine, you have not seen Everard since he returned from America," said Miss Susan. "How strong and well he looks!"—here she gave a sigh; not that she grudged Everard his good looks, but the very words brought the other before her, at thought of whom every other young man's strength and health seemed cruel.

"He has escaped the fate of the family," said Miss Augustine. "All I can pray for, Everard, is that you may never be the Austin of Whiteladies. No wealth can make up for that."

"Hush, hush!" said Miss Susan with a smile, "these are your fancies. We are not much worse off than many other families who have no such curse as you think of, my dear? Are all the old women comfortable—and grumbling? What were you about to-day?"

"I met them in chapel," said the younger sister, "and talked to them. I told them, as I always do, what need we have of their prayers; and that they should maintain a Christian life. Ah, Susan, you smile; and Everard, because he is young and foolish, would laugh if he could; but when you think that this is all I can do, or any one can do, to make up for the sins of the past, to avert the doom of the family—"

"If we have anything to make up more than others, I think we should do it ourselves," said Miss Susan. "But never mind, dear, if it pleases you. You are spoiling the people; but there are not many villages spoiled with kindness. I comfort myself with that."

"It is not to please myself that I toil night and day, that I rise up early and lie down late," said Miss Augustine, with a faint gleam of indignation in her eyes. Then she looked at Everard and sighed. She did not want to brag of her mortifications. In the curious balance-sheet which she kept with heaven, poor soul, so many prayers and vigils and charities, against so many sinful failings in duty, she was aware that anything like a boast on her part diminished the value of the compensation she was rendering. Her unexpressed rule was that the, so to speak, commercial worth of a good deed disappeared, when advantage was taken of it for this world; she wanted to keep it at its full value for the next, and therefore she stopped short and said no more. "Some of them put us to shame," she said; "they lead such holy lives. Old Mary Matthews spends nearly her whole time in chapel. She only lives for God and us. To hear her speak would reward you for many sacrifices, Susan—if you ever make any. She gives up all—her time, her comfort, her whole thoughts—for us."

"Why for us?" said Everard. "Do you keep people on purpose to pray for the family, Aunt Augustine? I beg your pardon, but it sounded something like it. You can't mean it, of course?"

"Why should not I mean it? We do not pray so much as we ought for ourselves," said Miss Augustine; "and if I can persuade holy persons to pray for us continually—"

"At so much a week, a cottage, and coals and candles," said Miss Susan. "Augustine, my dear, you shall have your way as long as I can get it for you. I am glad the old souls are comfortable; and if they are good, so much the better; and I am glad you like it, my dear; but whatever you think, you should not talk in this way. Eh, Stevens, what do you say?"

"If I might make so bold, ma'am," said the butler, "not to go against Miss Augustine; but that hold Missis Matthews, mum, she's a hold—"

"Silence, sir!" said Miss Susan promptly, "I don't want to hear any gossip; my sister knows best. Tell Everard about your schools, my dear; the parish must be the better with the schools. Whatever the immediate motive is, so long as the thing is good," said this casuist, "and whatever the occasional result may be, so long as the meaning is charitable—There, there, Everard, I won't have her crossed."

This was said hastily in an undertone to Everard, who was shaking his head, with a suppressed laugh on his face.

"I am not objecting to anything that is done, but to your reasoning, which is defective," he said.

"Oh, my reasoning! is that all? I don't stand upon my reasoning," said Miss Susan. And then there was a pause in the conversation, for Miss Susan's mind was perturbed, and she talked but in fits and starts, having sudden intervals of silence, from which she would as suddenly emerge into animated discussion, then be still again all in a moment. Miss Augustine, in her long limp gray dress, with pale hands coming out of the wide hanging sleeves, talked only on one subject, and did not eat at all, so that her company was not very cheerful. And Everard could not but glance up now and then to the gallery, which lay in deep shade, and feel as if he were in a dream, seated down below in the light. How vividly the childish past had come upon him; and how much more cheerful it had been in those old days, when the three atoms in the dusty corner of the gallery looked down with laughing eyes upon the solemn people at table, and whispered and rustled in their restlessness till they were found out!

At last—and this was something so wonderful that even the servants who waited at table were appalled—Miss Augustine recommenced the conversation. "You have had some one here to-day," she said. "Farrel-Austin—I met him."

"Yes!" said Miss Susan, breathless and alarmed.

"It seemed to me that the shadow had fallen upon them already. He is gray and changed. I have not seen him for a long time; his wife is ill, and his children are delicate."

"Nonsense, Austine, the girls are as strong and well as a couple of young hoydens need be." Miss Susan spoke almost sharply, and in a half-frightened tone.

"You think so, Susan; for my part I saw the shadow plainly. It is that their time is drawing near to inherit. Perhaps as they are girls, nothing will happen to them; nothing ever happened to us; that is to say, they will not marry probably; they will be as we have been. I wish to know them, Susan. Probably one of them would take up my work, and endeavor to keep further trouble from the house."

"Farrel's daughter? you are very good, Austine, very good; you put me to shame," said Miss Susan, bending her head.

"Yes; why not Farrel's daughter? She is a woman like the rest of us and an Austin, like the rest of us. I wish the property could pass to women, then there might be an end of it once for all."

"In that case it would go to Reine, and there would not in the least be the end of it; quite the reverse."

"I could persuade Reine," said Miss Augustine. "Ah, yes; I could persuade her. She knows my life. She knows about the family, how we have all suffered. Reine would be led by me; she would give it up, as I should have done had I the power. But men will not do such a thing. I am not blaming them, I am saying what is the fact. Reine would have given it up."

"You speak like a visionary," said Miss Susan sighing. "Yes, I daresay Reine would be capable of a piece of folly, or you, or even myself. We do things that seem right to us at the moment without taking other things into consideration, when we are quite free to do what we like. But don't you see, my dear, a man with an entailed estate is not free? His son or his heir must come after him, as his father went before him; he is only a kind of a tenant. Farrel, since you have spoken of Farrel—I would not have begun it— dare not alienate property from Everard; and Everard, when it comes to him, must keep it for his son, if he ever has one."

"The thing would be," said Miss Augustine, "to make up your mind never to have one, Everard." She looked at him calmly and gravely, crossing her hands within her long sleeves.

"But, my dear Aunt Augustine," said Everard, laughing, "what good would that do me? I should have to hand it on to the next in the entail all the same. I could not do away with the estate without the consent of my heir at least."

"Then I will tell you what to do," said Miss Augustine. "Marry; it is different from what I said just now, but it has the same meaning. Marry at once; and when you have a boy let him be sent to me. I will train him, I will show him his duty; and then with his consent, which he will be sure to give when he grows up, you can break the entail and restore Whiteladies to its right owner. Do this, my dear boy, it is quite simple; and so at last I shall have the satisfaction of feeling that the curse will be ended one day. Yes; the thing to be done is this."

Miss Susan had exclaimed in various tones of impatience. She had laughed reluctantly when Everard laughed; but what her sister said was more serious to her than it was to the young man. "Do you mean to live forever," she said at last, "that you calculate so calmly on bringing up Everard's son?"

"I am fifty-five," said Miss Augustine, "and Everard might have a son in a year. Probably I shall live to seventy-five, at least,—most of the women of our family do. He would then be twenty, approaching his majority. There is nothing extravagant in it; and on the whole, it seems to me the most hopeful thing to do. You must marry, Everard, without delay; and if you want money I will help you. I will do anything for an object so near my heart."

"You had better settle whom I am to marry, Aunt Augustine."

Everard's laughter made the old walls gay. He entered into the joke without any arrière pensée; the suggestion amused him beyond measure; all the more that it was made with so much gravity and solemnity. Miss Susan had laughed too; but now she became slightly alarmed, and watched her sister with troubled eyes.

"Whom you are to marry? That wants consideration," said Miss Augustine. "The sacrifice would be more complete and satisfying if two branches of the family concurred in making it. The proper person for you to marry in the circumstances would be either—"

"Austine!"

"Yes! I am giving the subject my best attention. You cannot understand, no one can understand, how all-important it is to me. Everard, either one of Farrel's girls, to whom I bear no malice, or perhaps Reine."

"Austine, you are out of your senses on this point," said Miss Susan, almost springing from her seat, and disturbing suddenly the calm of the talk. "Come, come, we must retire; we have dined. Everard, if you choose to sit a little, Stevens is giving you some very good claret. It was my father's; I can answer for it, much better than I can answer for my own, for I am no judge. You will find us in the west room when you are ready, or in the garden. It is almost too sweet to be indoors to-night."

She drew her sister's arm within hers and led her away, with peremptory authority which permitted no argument, and to which Augustine instinctively yielded; and Everard remained alone, his cheek tingling, his heart beating. It had all been pure amusement up to this point; but even his sense of the ludicrous could not carry him further. He might have known, he said to himself, that this was what she must say. He blushed, and felt it ungenerous in himself to have allowed her to go so far, to propose these names to him. He seemed to be making the girls endure a humiliation against his will, and without their knowledge. What had they done that he should permit any one even to suggest that he could choose among them? This was the more elevated side of his feelings; but there was another side, I am obliged to allow, a fluttered, flattered consciousness that the suggestion might be true; that he might have it in his power, like a sultan, to choose among them, and throw his princely handkerchief at the one he preferred. A mixture, therefore, of some curious sense of elation and suppressed pleasure, mingled with the more generous feeling within him, quenching at once the ridicule of Miss Augustine's proposal, and the sense of wrong done to those three girls. Yes, no doubt it is a man's privilege to choose; he, and not the woman, has it in his power to weigh the qualities of one and another, and to decide which would be most fit for the glorious position of his wife. They could not choose him, but he could choose one of them, and on his choice probably their future fate would depend. It was impossible not to feel a little pleasant flutter of consciousness. He was not vain, but he felt the sweetness of the superiority involved, the greatness of the position.

When the ladies were gone Everard laughed, all alone by himself, he could not help it; and the echoes took up the laughter, and rang into that special corner of the gallery which he knew so well, centring there. Why there, of all places in the world? Was it some ghost of little Reine in her childhood that laughed? Reine in her childhood had been the one who exercised choice. It was she who might have thrown the handkerchief, not Everard. And then a hush came over him, and a compunction, as he thought where Reine was at this moment, and how she might be occupied. Bending over her brother's death-bed, hearing his last words, her heart contracted with the bitter pang of parting, while her old playfellow laughed, and wondered whether he should choose her out of the three to share his grandeur. Everard grew quite silent all at once, and poured himself out a glass of the old claret in deep humiliation and stillness, feeling ashamed of himself. He held the wine up to the light with the solemnest countenance, trying to take himself in, and persuade himself that he had no lighter thoughts in his mind, and then having swallowed it with equal solemnity, he got up and strolled out into the garden. He had so grave a face when Miss Susan met him, that she thought for the first moment that some letter had come and that all was over, and gasped and called to him, what was it? what was it? "Nothing!" said Everard more solemnly than ever. He was impervious to any attempt at laughter for the rest of the evening, ashamed of himself and his light thoughts, in sudden contrast with the thoughts that must be occupying his cousins, his old playmates. And yet, as he went home in the moonlight, the shock of that contrast lessened, and his young lightness of mind began to reassert itself. Before he got out of hearing of the manor he began to whistle again unawares; but this time it was not one of Reine's songs. It was a light opera air which, no doubt, one of the other girls had taught him, or so, at least, Miss Susan thought.

CHAPTER V

In all relationships, as I have already said—and it is not an original saying—there is one who is active and one who is passive,—"L'unqui baise et l'autre qui tend la joue," as the French say, with their wonderful half-pathetic, half-cynic wisdom. Between the two sisters of Whiteladies it was Augustine who gave the cheek and Susan the kiss, it was Augustine who claimed and Susan who offered sympathy; it was Augustine's affairs, such as they were, which were discussed. The younger sister had only her own fancies and imaginations, her charities, and the fantastic compensations which she thought she was making for the evil deeds of her family, to discuss and enlarge upon; whereas the elder had her mind full of those mundane matters from which our cares spring—the management of material interests—the conflict which is always more or less involved in the government of other souls. She managed her nephew's estate in trust for him till he came of age,—if he should live to come of age, poor boy; she managed her own money and her sister's, which was not inconsiderable; and the house and the servants, and in some degree the parish, of which Miss Susan was the virtual Squire. But of all this weight of affairs it did not occur to her to throw any upon Augustine. Augustine had always been spared from her youth up—spared all annoyance, all trouble, everybody uniting to shield her. She had been "delicate" in her childhood, and she had sustained a "disappointment" in youth—which means in grosser words that she had been jilted, openly and disgracefully, by Farrel-Austin, her cousin, which was the ground of Susan Austin's enmity to him. I doubt much whether Augustine herself, whose blood was always tepid and her head involved in dreams, felt this half so much as her family felt it for her—her sister especially, to whom she had been a pet and a plaything all her life, and who had that half-adoring admiration for her which an elder sister is sometimes seen to entertain for a younger one whom she believes to be gifted with that beauty which she knows has not fallen to her share. Susan felt the blow with an acute sense of shame and wounded pride, which Augustine herself was entirely incapable of—and from that moment forward had constituted herself, not only the protector of her sister's weakness, but the representative of something better which had failed her, of that admiration and chivalrous service which a beautiful woman is supposed to receive from the world.

It may seem a strange thing to many to call the devotion of one woman to another chivalrous. Yet Susan's devotion to her sister merited the title. She vowed to herself that, so far as she could prevent it, her sister should never feel the failure of those attentions which her lover ought to have given her—that she should never know what it was to fall into that neglect which is often the portion of middle-aged women—that she should be petted and cared for, as if she were still the favorite child or the adored wife which she had been or might have been. In doing this Susan not only testified the depth of her love for Augustine, and indignant compassion for her wrongs, but also a woman's high ideal of how an ideal woman should be treated in this world. Augustine was neither a beautiful woman nor an ideal one, though her sister thought so, and Susan had been checked many a time in her idolatry by her idol's total want of comprehension of it; but she had never given up her plan for consoling the sufferer. She had admired Augustine as well as loved her; she had always found what she did excellent; she had made Augustine's plans important by believing in them, and her opinions weighty, even while, within herself, she saw the plans to be impracticable and the opinions futile. The elder sister would pause in the midst of a hundred real and pressing occupations, a hundred weighty cares, to condole with, or to assist, or support, the younger, pulling her through some parish imbroglio, some almshouse squabble, as if these trifling annoyances had been affairs of state. But of the serious matters which occupied her own mind, she said nothing to Augustine, knowing that she would find no comprehension, and willing to avoid the certainty that her sister would take no interest in her proceedings. Indeed, it was quite possible that Augustine might have gone further than mere failure of sympathy; Susan knew very well that she would be disapproved of, perhaps censured, for being engrossed by the affairs of this world. The village people, and everybody on the estate, were, I think, of the same opinion. They thought Miss Susan "the hard one"—doing her ineffable injustice, one of those unconsidered wrongs that cut into the heart. At first, I suppose, this had not been the state of affairs—between the sisters, at least; but it would be difficult to tell how many disappointments the strong and hard Susan had gone through before she made up her mind never to ask for the sympathy which never came her way. This was her best philosophy, and saved her much mortification; but it cost her many trials before she could make up her mind to it, and had not its origin in philosophy at all, but in much wounding and lacerating of a generous and sensitive heart.

Therefore she did not breathe a word to her sister about the present annoyance and anxiety in her mind. When it was their hour to go upstairs—and everything was done like clock-work at Whiteladies—she went with Augustine to her room, as she always did, and heard over again for the third or fourth time the complaint of the rudeness of the butler, Stevens, who did not countenance Augustine's "ways."

"Indeed, he is a very honest fellow," said Miss Susan, thinking bitterly of Farrel-Austin and of the last successful stroke he had made.

"He is a savage, he is a barbarian—he cannot be a Christian," Miss Augustine had replied.

"Yes, yes, my dear; we must take care not to judge other people. I will scold him well, and he will never venture to say anything disagreeable to you again."

"You think I am speaking for myself," said Augustine. "No, what I feel is, how out of place such a man is in a household like ours. You are deceived about him now, and think his honesty, as you call it, covers all his faults. But, Susan, listen to me. Without the Christian life, what is honesty? Do you think it would bear the strain if temptation—to any great crime, for instance—"

"My dear, you are speaking nonsense," said Miss Susan.

"That is what I am afraid of," said her sister solemnly. "A man like this ought not to be in a house like ours; for you are a Christian, Susan."

"I hope so at least," said the other with a momentary laugh.

"But why should you laugh? Oh, Susan! think how you throw back my work—even, you hinder my atonement. Is not this how all the family have been—treating everything lightly—our family sin and doom, like the rest? and you, who ought to know better, who ought to strengthen my hands! perhaps, who knows, if you could but have given your mind to it, we two together might have averted the doom!"

Augustine sat down in a large hard wooden chair which she used by way of mortification, and covered her face with her hands. Susan, who was standing by holding her candle, looked at her strangely with a half smile, and a curious acute sense of the contrast between them. She stood silent for a moment, perhaps with a passing wonder which of the two it was who had done the most for the old house; but if she entertained this thought, it was but for the moment. She laid her hand upon her sister's shoulder.

"My dear Austine," she said, "I am Martha and you are Mary. So long as Martha did not find fault with her sister, our good Lord made no objection to her housewifely ways. So, if I am earthly while you are heavenly, you must put up with me, dear; for, after all, there are a great many earthly things to be looked after. And as for Stevens, I shall scold him well," she added with sudden energy, with a little outburst of natural indignation at the cause (though innocent) of this slight ruffling of the domestic calm.

The thoughts in her mind were of a curious and mixed description as she went along the corridor after Augustine had melted, and bestowed, with a certain lofty and melancholy regret, for her sister's imperfections, her good-night kiss. Miss Susan's room was on the other side of the house, over the drawing-room. To reach it she had to go along the corridor, which skirted the staircase with its dark oaken balustrades, and thence into another casemented passage, which led by three or four oaken steps to the ante-room in which her maid slept, and from which her own room opened. One of her windows looked out upon the north side, the same aspect as the dining-hall, and was, indeed, the large casement which occupied one of the richly-carved gables on that side of the house. The other looked out upon the west side, over the garden, and facing the sunset. It was a large panelled room, with few curtains, for Miss Susan loved air. A shaded night-lamp burned faintly upon a set of carved oaken drawers at the north end, and the moonlight slanting through the western window threw two lights, broken by the black bar of the casement, on the broad oak boards—for only the centre of the room was carpeted. Martha came in with her mistress, somewhat sleepy, and slightly injured in her feelings, for what with Everard's visits and other agitations of the day, Miss Susan was half an hour late. It is not to be supposed that she, who could not confide in her sister, would confide in Martha; but yet Martha knew, by various indications, what Augustine would never have discovered, that Miss Susan had "something on her mind." Perhaps it was because she did not talk as much as usual, and listened to Martha's own remarks with the indifference of abstractedness; perhaps because of the little tap of her foot on the floor, and sound of her voice as she asked her faithful attendant if she had done yet, while Martha, aggrieved but conscientious, fumbled with the doors of the wardrobe, in which she had just hung up her mistress's gown; perhaps it was the tired way in which Miss Susan leaned back in her easy chair, and the half sigh which breathed into her good-night. But from all these signs together Martha knew, what nothing could have taught Augustine. But what could the maid do to show sympathy? At first, I am sorry to say, she did not feel much, but was rather glad that the mistress, who had kept her half an hour longer than usual out of bed, should herself have some part of the penalty to pay; but compunctions grew upon Martha before she left the room, and I think that her lingering, which annoyed Miss Susan, was partly meant to show that she felt for her mistress. If so, it met the usual recompense of unappreciated kindness, and at last earned a peremptory dismissal for the lingerer. When Miss Susan was alone, she raised herself a little from her chair and screwed up the flame of the small silver lamp on her little table, and put the double eyeglass which she used, being slightly short-sighted, on her nose. She was going to think; and she had an idea, not uncommon to short-sighted people, that to see distinctly helped her faculties in everything.

She felt instinctively for her eyeglass when any noise woke her in the middle of the night; she could hear better as well as think better with that aid. The two white streaks of moonlight, with the broad bar of shadow between, and all the markings of the diamond panes, indicated on the gray oaken board and fringe of Turkey carpet, moved slowly along the floor, coming further into the room as the moon moved westward to its setting. In the distant corner the night-light burned dim but steady. Miss Susan sat by the side of her bed, which was hung at the head with blue-gray curtains of beautiful old damask. On her little table was a Bible and Prayer Book, a long-stalked glass with a rose in it, another book less sacred, which she had been reading in the morning, her handkerchief, her eau-de-cologne, her large old watch in an old stand, and those other trifles which every lady's-maid who respects herself keeps ready and in order by her mistress's bedside. Martha, too sleepy to be long about her own preparations, was in bed and asleep almost as soon as Miss Susan put on her glasses. All was perfectly still, the world out-of-doors held under the spell of the moonlight, the world inside rapt in sleep and rest. Miss Susan wrapped her dressing-gown about her, and sat up in her chair to think. It was a very cosey, very comfortable chair, not hard and angular like Austine's, and everything in the room was pleasant and soft, not ascetical and self-denying. Susan Austin was not young, but she had kept something of that curious freshness of soul which some unmarried women carry down to old age. She was not aware in her innermost heart that she was old. In everything external she owned her years fully, and felt them; but in her heart she, who had never passed out of the first stage of life, retained so many of its early illusions as to confuse herself and bewilder her consciousness. When she sat like this thinking by herself, with nothing to remind her of the actual aspect of circumstances, she never could be quite sure whether she was young or old. There was always a momentary glimmer and doubtfulness about her before she settled down to the consideration of her problem, whatever it was—as to which problem it was, those which had come before her in her youth, which she had settled, or left to float in abeyance for the settling of circumstances—or the actual and practical matter-of-fact of to-day. For a moment she caught her own mind lingering upon that old story between Augustine and their cousin Farrel, as if it were one of the phases of that which demanded her attention; and then she roused herself sharply to her immediate difficulty, and to consider what she was to do.

It is forlorn in such an emergency to be compelled to deliberate alone, without any sharer of one's anxieties or confidante of one's thoughts. But Miss Susan was used to this, and was willing to recognize the advantage it gave her in the way of independence and prompt conclusion. She was free from the temptation of talking too much, of attacking her opponents with those winged words which live often after the feeling that dictated them has passed. She could not be drawn into any self-committal, for nobody thought or cared what was in her mind. Perhaps, however, it is more easy to exercise that casuistry which self-interest produces even in the most candid mind, when it is not necessary to put one's thoughts into words. I cannot tell on what ground it was that this amiable, and, on the whole, good woman concluded her opposition to Farrel-Austin, and his undoubted right of inheritance, to be righteous, and even holy. She resisted his claim—because it was absolutely intolerable to her to think of giving up her home to him, because she hated and despised him—motives very comprehensible, but not especially generous, or elevated in the abstract. She felt, however, and believed—when she sat down in her chair and put on her glasses to reflect how she could baffle and overthrow him—that it was something for the good of the family and the world that she was planning, not anything selfish for her own benefit. If Augustine in one room planned alms and charities for the expiation of the guilt of the family, which had made itself rich by church lands, with the deepest sense that her undertaking was of the most pious character—Susan in another, set herself to ponder how to retain possession of these lands, with a corresponding sense that her undertaking, her determination, were, if not absolutely pious, at least of a noble and elevated character. She did not say to herself that she was intent upon resisting the enemy by every means in her power. She said to herself that she was determined to have justice, and to resist to the last the doing of wrong, and the victory of the unworthy. This was her way of putting it to herself—and herself did not contradict her, as perhaps another listener might have done. A certain enthusiasm even grew in her as she pondered. She felt no doubt whatever that Farrel-Austin had gained his point by false representations, and had played upon the ignorance of the unknown Austin who had transferred his rights to him, as he said. And how could she tell if this was the true heir? Even documents were not to be trusted to in such a case, nor the sharpest of lawyers—and old Mr. Lincoln, the family solicitor, was anything but sharp. Besides, if this man in Bruges were the right man, he had probably no idea of what he was relinquishing. How could a Flemish tradesman know what were the beauties and attractions of "a place" in the home counties, amid all the wealth and fulness of English lands, and with all the historical associations of Whiteladies? He could not possibly know, or he would not give them up. And if he had a wife, she could not know, or she would never permit such a sacrifice.

Miss Susan sat and thought till the moonlight disappeared from the window, and the Summer night felt the momentary chill which precedes dawn. She thought of it till her heart burned. No, she could not submit to this. In her own person she must ascertain if the story was true, and if the strangers really knew what they were doing. It took some time to move her to this resolution; but at last it took possession of her. To go and undo what Farrel-Austin had done, to wake in the mind of the heir, if this was the heir, that desire to possess which is dominant in most minds, and ever ready to answer to any appeal; she rose almost with a spring of youthful animation from her seat when her thoughts settled upon this conclusion. She put out her lamp and went to the window, where a faint blueness was growing—that dim beginning of illumination which is not night but day, and which a very early bird in the green covert underneath was beginning to greet with the first faint twitter of returning existence. Miss Susan felt herself inspired; it was not to defeat Farrel-Austin, but to prevent wrong, to do justice, a noble impulse which fires the heart and lights the eye.

Thus she made up her mind to an undertaking which afterward had more effect upon her personal fate than anything else that had happened in her long life. She did it, not only intending no evil, but with a sense of what she believed to be generous feeling expanding her soul. Her own personal motives were so thrust out of sight that she herself did not perceive them—and indeed, had it been suggested to her that she had personal motives, she would have denied it strenuously. What interest could she have in substituting one heir for another? But yet Miss Susan's blue eyes shot forth a gleam which was not heavenly as she lay down and tried to sleep. She could not sleep, her mind being excited and full of a thousand thoughts—the last distinct sensation in it before the uneasy doze which came over her senses in the morning being a thrill of pleasure that Farrel-Austin might yet be foiled. But what of that? Was it not her business to protect the old stock of the family, and keep the line of succession intact? The more she thought of it, the more did this appear a sacred duty, worthy of any labor and any sacrifice.

CHAPTER VI

The breakfast-table was spread in the smaller dining-room, a room furnished with quaint old furniture like the hall, which looked out upon nothing but the grass and trees of the garden, bounded by an old mossy wall, as old as the house. The windows were all open, the last ray of the morning sun slanting off the shining panes, the scent of the flowers coming in, and all the morning freshness. Miss Susan came downstairs full of unusual energy, notwithstanding her sleepless night. She had decided upon something to do, which is always satisfactory to an active mind; and though she was beyond the age at which people generally plan long journeys with pleasure, the prick of something new inspired her and made a stir in her veins. "People live more when they stir about," she said to herself, when, with a little wonder and partial amusement at herself, she became conscious of this sensation, and took her seat at the breakfast-table with a sense of stimulated energy which was very pleasant.

Miss Augustine came in after her sister, with her hands folded in her long sleeves, looking more than ever like a saint out of a painted window. She crossed herself as she sat down. Her blue eyes seemed veiled so far as external life went. She was the ideal nun of romance and poetry, not the ruddy-faced, active personage who is generally to be found under that guise in actual life. This was one of her fast-days—and indeed most days were fast-days with her. She was her own rule, which is always a harsher kind of restraint than any rule adapted to common use. Her breakfast consisted of a cup of milk and a small cake of bread. She gave her sister an abstracted kiss, but took no notice of her lively looks. When she withdrew her hands from her sleeves a roll of paper became visible in one of them, which she slowly opened out.

"These are the plans for the chantry, finished at last," she said. "Everything is ready now. You must take them to the vicar, I suppose, Susan. I cannot argue with a worldly-minded man. I will go to the almshouses while you are talking to him, and pray."

"The vicar has no power in the matter," said Miss Susan. "So long as we are the lay rectors we can build as we please; at the chancel end at least."

Augustine put up her thin hands, just appearing out of the wide sleeves, to her ears. "Susan, Susan! do not use those words, which have all our guilt in them! Lay rectors! Lay robbers! Oh! will you ever learn that this thought is the misery of my life?"

"My dear, we must be reasonable," said Miss Susan. "If you like to throw away—no, I mean to employ your money in building a chantry, I don't object; but we have our rights."

"Our rights are nothing but wrongs," said the other, shaking her head, "unless my poor work may be accepted as an expiation. Ours is not the guilt, and therefore, being innocent, we may make the amends."

"I wonder where you got your doctrines from?" said Miss Susan. "They are not Popish either, so far as I can make out; and in some things, Austine, you are not even High Church."

Augustine made no reply. Her attention had failed. She held the drawings before her, which at last, after many difficulties, she had managed to bring into existence—on paper at least. I do not think she had very clear notions in point of doctrine. She had taken up with a visionary mediævalism which she did not very well understand, and which she combined unawares with many of the ordinary principles of a moderate English Church-woman. She liked to cross herself, without meaning very much by it, and the idea of an Austin Chantry, where service should be said every day, "to the intention of" the Austin family, had been for years her cherished fancy, though she would have been shocked had any advanced Ritualists or others suggested to her that what she meant was a daily mass for the dead. She did not mean this at all, nor did she know very clearly what she meant, except to build a chantry, in which daily service should be maintained forever, always with a reference to the Austins, and making some sort of expiation, she could not have told what, for the fundamentals in the family. Perhaps it was merely inability of reasoning, or perhaps a disinclination to entangle herself in doctrine at all, that made her prefer to remain in this vagueness and confusion. She knew very well what she wanted to do, but not exactly why.

While her sister looked at her drawings Miss Susan thought it a good moment to reveal her own plans, with, I suppose, that yearning for some sort of sympathy which survives even in the minds of those who have had full experience of the difficulty or even impossibility of obtaining it. She knew Augustine would not, probably could not, enter into her thoughts, and I am not sure that she desired it—but yet she longed to awaken some little interest.

"I am thinking," she said, "of going away—for a few days."

Augustine took no notice. She examined first the front elevation, then the interior of the chantry. "They say it is against the law," she remarked after awhile, "to have a second altar; but every old chantry has it, and without an altar the service would be imperfect. Remember this Susan; for the vicar, they tell me, will object."

"You don't hear what I say, then? I am thinking of—leaving home."

"Yes, I heard—so long as you settle this for me before you go, that it may be begun at once. Think, Susan! it is the work of my life."

"I will see to it," said Miss Susan with a sigh. "You shall not be crossed, dear, if I can manage it. But you don't ask where I am going or why I am going."

"No," said Augustine calmly; "it is no doubt about business, and business has no share in my thoughts."

"If it had not a share in my thoughts things would go badly with us," said Miss Susan, coloring with momentary impatience and self-assertion. Then she fell back into her former tone. "I am going abroad,

Austine; does not that rouse you? I have not been abroad since we were quite young, how many years ago?—when we went to Italy with my father—when we were all happy together. Ah me! what a difference! Austine, you recollect that?"

"Happy, were we?" said Augustine looking up, with a faint tinge of color on her paleness; "no, I was never happy till I saw once for all how wicked we were, how we deserved our troubles, and how something might be done to make up for them. I have never really cared for anything else."

This she said with a slight raising of her head and an air of reality which seldom appeared in her visionary face. It was true, though it was so strange. Miss Susan was a much more reasonable, much more weighty personage, but she perceived this change with a little suspicion, and did not understand the fanciful, foolish sister whom she had loved and petted all her life.

"My dear, we had no troubles then," she said, with a wondering look.

"Always, always," said Augustine, "and I never knew the reason, till I found it out." Then this gleam of something more than intelligence faded all at once from her face. "I hope you will settle everything before you go," she said, almost querulously; "to be put off now and have to wait would surely break my heart."

"I'll do it, I'll do it, Austine. I am going—on family business."

"If you see poor Herbert," said Augustine, calmly, "tell him we pray for him in the almshouses night and day. That may do him good. If I had got my work done sooner he might have lived. Indeed, the devil sometimes tempts me to think it is hard that just when my chantry is beginning and continual prayer going on Herbert should die. It seems to take away the meaning! But what am I, one poor creature, to make up, against so many that have done wrong?"

"I am not going to Herbert, I am going to Flanders—to Bruges," said Miss Susan, carried away by a sense of the importance of her mission, and always awaiting, as her right, some spark of curiosity, at least.

Augustine returned to her drawings; the waning light died out of her face; she became again the conventional visionary, the recluse of romance, abstracted and indifferent. "The vicar is always against me," she said; "you must talk to him, Susan. He wants the Browns to come into the vacant cottage. He says they have been honest and all that; but they are not praying people. I cannot take them in; it is praying people I want."

"In short, you want something for your money," said her sister; "a percentage, such as it is. You are more a woman of business, my dear, than you think."

Augustine looked at her, vaguely, startled. "I try to do for the best," she said. "I do not understand why people should always wish to thwart me; what I want is their good."

"They like their own way better than their good, or rather than what you think is for their good," said Miss Susan. "We all like our own way."

"Not me, not me!" said the other, with a sigh; and she rose and crossed herself once more. "Will you come to prayers at the almshouse, Susan? The bell will ring presently, and it would do you good."

"My dear, I have no time," said the elder sister, "I have a hundred things to do."

Augustine turned away with a soft shake of the head. She folded her arms into her sleeves, and glided away like a ghost. Presently her sister saw her crossing the lawn, her gray hood thrown lightly over her head, her long robes falling in straight, soft lines, her slim figure moving along noiselessly. Miss Susan was the practical member of the family, and but for her probably the Austins of Whiteladies would have died out ere now, by sheer carelessness of their substance, and indifference to what was going on around them; but as she watched her sister crossing the lawn, a sense of inferiority crossed her mind. She felt herself worldly, a pitiful creature of the earth, and wished she was as good as Augustine. "But the house, and the farm, and the world must be kept going," she said, by way of relieving herself, with a mingling of humor and compunction. It was not much her small affairs could do to make or mar the going on of the world, but yet in small ways and great the world has to be kept going. She went off at once to the bailiff, who was waiting for her, feeling a pleasure in proving to herself that she was busy and had no time, which is perhaps a more usual process of thought with the Marthas of this world than the other plan of finding fault with the Marys, for in their hearts most women have a feeling that the prayer is the best.

The intimation of Miss Susan's intended absence excited the rest of the household much more than it had excited her sister. "Wherever are you going to, miss?" said cook, who was as old as her mistress, and had never changed her style of addressing her since the days when she was young Miss Susan and played at house-keeping.

"I am going abroad," she answered, with a little innocent pride; for to people who live all their lives at home there is a certain grandeur in going abroad. "You will take great care of my sister, and see that she does not fast too much."

It was a patriarchal household, with such a tinge of familiarity in its dealings with its mistress, as—with servants who have passed their lives in a house—it is seldom possible, even if desirable, to avoid. Stevens the butler stopped open-mouthed, with a towel in his hand, to listen, and Martha approached from the other end of the kitchen, where she had been busy tying up and labelling cook's newly-made preserves.

"Going abroad!" they all echoed in different keys.

"I expect you all to be doubly careful and attentive," said Miss Susan, "though indeed I am not going very far, and probably won't be more than a few days gone. But in the meantime Miss Augustine will require your utmost care. Stevens, I am very much displeased with the way you took it upon you to speak at dinner yesterday. It annoyed my sister extremely, and you had no right to use so much freedom. Never let it happen again."

Stevens was taken entirely by surprise, and stood gazing at her with the bewildered air of a man who, seeking innocent amusement in the hearing of news, is suddenly transfixed by an unexpected thunderbolt. "Me, mum!" said Stevens bewildered, "I—I don't know what you're talking about." It was an unfair advantage to take.

"Precisely, you," said Miss Susan; "what have you to do with the people at the almshouses? Nobody expects you to be answerable for what they do or don't do. Never let me hear anything of the kind again."

"Oh," said Stevens, with a snort of suppressed offence, "it's them! Miss Austin, I can't promise at no price! if I hears that old 'ag a praised up to the skies—"

"You will simply hold your tongue," said Miss Susan peremptorily. "What is it to you? My sister knows her own people best."

Upon this the two women in attendance shook their heads, and Stevens, encouraged by this tacit support, took courage.

"She don't, mum, she don't," he said; "if you heard the things they'll say behind her back! It makes me sick, it does, being a faithful servant. If I don't dare to speak up, who can? She's imposed upon to that degree, and made game of as your blood would run cold to see it; and if I ain't to say a word when I has a chance, who can? The women sees it even—and it's nat'ral as I should see further than the women."

"Then you'll please set the women a good example by holding your tongue," said Miss Susan. "Once for all, recollect, all of you, Miss Augustine shall never be crossed while I am mistress of the house. When it goes into other hands you can do as you please."

"Oh, laws!" said the cook, "when it comes to that, mum, none of us has nothing to do here."

"That is as you please, and as Mr.—as the heir pleases," Miss Susan said, making a pause before the last words. Her cheek colored, her blue eyes grew warm with the new life and energy in her. She went out of the kitchen with a certain swell of anticipated triumph in her whole person. Mr. Farrel-Austin should soon discover that he was not to have everything his own way. Probably she would find he had deceived the old man at Bruges, that these poor people knew nothing about the true value of what they were relinquishing. Curiously enough, it never occurred to her, to lessen her exhilaration, that to leave the house of her fathers to an old linen-draper from the Low-Countries would be little more agreeable than to leave it to Farrel-Austin—nay, even as Everard had suggested to her, that Farrel-Austin, as being an English gentleman, was much more likely to do honor to the old house than a foreigner of inferior position, and ideas altogether different from her own. She thought nothing of this; she ignored herself, indeed, in the matter, which was a thing she was pleased to think of afterward, and which gave her a little consolation—that is, she thought of herself only through Farrel-Austin, as the person most interested in, and most likely to be gratified by, his downfall.

As the day wore on and the sun got round and blazed on the south front of the house, she withdrew to the porch, as on the former day, and sat there enjoying the coolness, the movement of the leaves, the soft, almost imperceptible breeze. She was more light-hearted than on the previous day when poor Herbert was in her mind, and when nothing but the success of her adversary seemed possible. Now it seemed to her that a new leaf was turned, a new chapter commenced.

Thus the day went on. In the afternoon she had one visitor, and only one, the vicar, Mr. Gerard, who came by the north gate, as her visitors yesterday had done, and crossed the lawn to the porch with much less satisfaction of mind than Miss Susan had to see him coming.

"Of course you know what has brought me," he said at once, seating himself in a garden-chair which had been standing outside on the lawn, and which he brought in after his first greeting. "This chantry of your sister's is a thing I don't understand, and I don't know how I can consent to it. It is alien to all the customs of the time. It is a thing that ought to have been built three hundred years ago, if at all. It will be a bit of bran new Gothic, a thing I detest; and in short I don't understand it, nor what possible meaning a chantry can have in these days."

"Neither do I," said Miss Susan smiling, "not the least in the world."

"If it is meant for masses for the dead," said Mr. Gerard—"some people I know have gone as far as that—but I could not consent to it, Miss Austin. It should have been built three hundred years ago, if at all."

"Augustine could not have built it three hundred years ago," said Miss Susan, "for the best of reasons. My own opinion is, between ourselves, that had she been born three hundred years ago she would have been a happier woman; but neither she nor I can change that."

"That is not the question," said the vicar. He was a man with a fine faculty for being annoyed. There was a longitudinal line in his forehead between his eyes, which was continually moving, marking the passing irritations which went and came, and his voice had a querulous tone. He was in the way of thinking that everything that happened out of the natural course was done to annoy him specially, and he felt it a personal grievance that the Austin chantry had not been built in the sixteenth century. "There might have been some sense in it then," he added, "and though art was low about that time, still it would have got toned down, and been probably an ornament to the church; but a white, staring, new thing with spick and span pinnacles! I do not see how I can consent."

"At all events," said Miss Susan, showing the faintest edge of claw under the velvet of her touch, "no one can blame you at least, which I think is always a consolation. I have just been going over the accounts for the restoration of the chancel, and I think you may congratulate yourself that you have not got to pay them. Austine would kill me if she heard me, but that is one good of a lay rector. I hope you won't oppose her, seriously, Mr. Gerard. It is not masses for the dead she is thinking of. You know her crotchets. My sister has a very fine mind when she is roused to exert it," Miss Susan said with a little dignity, "but it is nonsense to deny that she has crotchets, and I hope you are too wise and kind to oppose her. The endowment will be good, and the chantry pretty. Why, it is by Sir Gilbert Scott."

"No, no, not Sir Gilbert himself; at least, I fear not," said Mr. Gerard, melting.

"One of his favorite pupils, and he has looked at it and approved. We shall have people coming to see it from all parts of the country; and it is Augustine's favorite crotchet. I am sure, Mr. Gerard, you will not seriously oppose."

Thus it was that the vicar was taken over. He reflected afterward that there was consolation in the view of the subject which she introduced so cunningly, and that he could no more be found fault with for the new chantry which the lay rector had a right to connect with his part of the church if he chose—than he could be made to pay the bills for the restoration of the chancel. And Miss Susan had put it to him so delicately about her sister's crotchets that what could a gentleman do but yield? The longitudinal line on his forehead smoothed out accordingly, and his tone ceased to be querulous. Yes, there was no doubt she had crotchets, poor soul; indeed, she was half crazy, perhaps, as the village people thought, but a good religious creature, fond of prayers and church services, and not clever enough to go far astray in point of doctrine. As Mr. Gerard went home, indeed, having committed himself, he discovered a number of admirable reasons for tolerating Augustine and her crotchets. If she sank money enough to secure an endowment of sixty pounds a year, in order to have prayers said daily in her chantry, as she called it, it was clear that thirty or forty from Mr. Gerard instead of the eighty he now paid, would be quite enough for his curate's salary. For what could a curate want with more than, or even so much as, a hundred pounds a year? And then the almshouses disposed of the old people of the parish in the most comfortable way, and on the whole, Augustine did more good than harm. Poor thing! It would be a pity, he thought, to cross this innocent and pious creature, who was "deficient," but too gentle and good to be interfered with in her crotchets. Poor Augustine, whom they all disposed of so calmly! Perhaps it was foolish enough of her to stay alone in the little almshouse chapel all the time that this interview was going on, praying that God would touch the heart of His servant and render it favorable toward her, while Miss Susan managed it all so deftly by mere sleight of hand; but on the whole, Augustine's idea of the world as a place where God did move hearts for small matters as well as great, was a more elevated one than the others. She felt quite sure when she glided through the Summer fields, still and gray in her strange dress, that God's servants' hearts had been moved to favor her, and that she might begin her work at once.

CHAPTER VII

Susan Austin said no more about her intended expedition, except to Martha, who had orders to prepare for the journey, and who was thrown into an excitement somewhat unbecoming her years by the fact that her mistress preferred to take Jane as her attendant, which was a slight very trying to the elder woman. "I cannot indulge myself by taking you," said Miss Susan, "because I want you to take care of my sister; she requires more attendance than I do, Martha, and you will watch over her." I am afraid that Miss Susan had a double motive in this decision, as most people have, and preferred Jane, who was young and strong, to the other, who required her little comforts, and did not like to be hurried, or put out; but she veiled the personal preference under a good substantial reason which is a very good thing to do in all cases, where it is desirable that the wheels of life should go easily. Martha had "a good cry," but then consoled herself with the importance of her charge. "Not as it wants much cleverness to dress Miss Augustine, as never puts on nothing worth looking at—that gray thing for ever and ever!" she said, with natural contempt. Augustine herself was wholly occupied with the chantry, and took no interest in her sister's movements; and there was no one else to inquire into them or ask a reason. She went off accordingly quite quietly and unobserved, with one box, and Jane in delighted attendance. Miss Susan took her best black silk with her, which she wore seldom, having fallen into the custom of the gray gown to please Augustine, a motive which in small matters was her chief rule of action;—on this occasion, however, she intended to be as magnificent as the best contents of her wardrobe could make her, taking, also, her Indian shawl and newest bonnet. These signs of superiority would not, she felt sure, be thrown away on a linen-draper. She took with her also, by way of appealing to another order of feelings, a very imposing picture of the house of Whiteladies, in which a gorgeous procession, escorting Queen Elizabeth, who was reported to have visited the place, was represented as issuing from the old porch. It seemed to Miss Susan that nobody who saw this picture could be willing to relinquish the house, for, indeed, her knowledge of it was limited. She set out one evening, resolved, with heroic courage, to commit herself to the Antwerp boat, which in Miss Susan's early days had been the chief and natural mode of conveyance. Impossible to tell how tranquil the country was as she left it—the laborers going home, the balmy kine wandering devious and leisurely with melodious lowings through the quiet roads. Life would go on with all its quiet routine unbroken, while Miss Susan dared the dangers of the deep, and prayer bell and dinner bell ring just as usual, and Augustine and her almshouse people go through all their pious habitudes. She was away from home so seldom, that this universal sway of common life and custom struck her strangely, with a humiliating sense of her own unimportance—she who was so important, the centre of everything. Jane, her young maid, felt the same sentiment in a totally different way, being full of pride and exultation in her own unusualness, and delicious contempt for those unfortunates to whom this day was just the same as any other.

Jane did not fear the dangers of the deep, which she did not know—while Miss Susan did, who was aware what she was about to undergo; but she trusted in Providence to take care of her, and smooth the angry waves, and said a little prayer of thanksgiving when she felt the evening air come soft upon her face, though the tree-tops would move about against the sky more than was desirable. I do not quite know by what rule of thought it was that Miss Susan felt herself to have a special claim to the succor of Providence as going upon a most righteous errand. She did manage to represent her mission to herself in this light, however. She was going to vindicate the right—to restore to their natural position people who had been wronged. If these said people were quite indifferent both to their wrongs and to their rights, that was their own fault, and in no respect Miss Susan's, who had her duty to do, whatever came of it. This she maintained very stoutly to herself, ignoring Farrel-Austin altogether, who might have thought of her enterprize in a different light. All through the night which she passed upon the gloomy ocean in a close little berth, with Jane helpless and wretched, requiring the attention of the stewardess, Miss Susan felt her spirit supported by the consciousness of virtue which was almost heroic: How much more comfortable she would have been at home in the west room, which she remembered so tenderly; how terrible was the rushing sound of waves in her ears, waves separated from her by so fragile a bulwark, "only a plank between her and eternity!" But all this she was undergoing for the sake of justice and right.

She felt herself, however, like a creature in a dream, when she walked out the morning of her arrival, alone, into the streets of Bruges, confused by the strangeness of the place, which so recalled her youth to her, that she could scarcely believe she had not left her father and brother at the hotel. Once in these early days, she had come out alone in the morning, she remembered, just as she was doing now, to buy presents for her companions; and that curious, delightful sense of half fright, half freedom, which the girl had felt thrilling her through while on this escapade, came back to the mind of the woman who was growing old, with a pathetic pleasure. She remembered how she had paused at the corner of the street, afraid to stop, afraid to go on, almost too shy to go into the shops where she had seen the things she wanted to buy. Miss Susan was too old to be shy now. She walked along sedately, not afraid that anybody would stare at her or be rude to her, or troubled by any doubts whether it was "proper;" but yet the past confused her mind. How strange it all was! Could it be that the carillon, which chimed sweetly, keenly in her ears, like a voice out of her youth, startling her by reiterated calls and reminders, had been chiming out all the ordinary hours—nay, quarters of hours—marking everybody's mealtimes and ordinary every-day vicissitudes, for these forty years past? It was some time before her ear got used to it, before she ceased to start and feel as if the sweet chimes from the belfry were something personal, addressed to her alone. She had been very young when she was in Bruges before, and everything was deeply impressed upon her mind. She had travelled very little since, and all the quaint gables, the squares, the lace-makers seated at their doors, the shop-windows full of peasant jewellery, had the strangest air of familiarity.

It was some time even in the curious bewildering tumult of her feelings before she could recollect her real errand. She had not asked any further information from Farrel-Austin. If he had found their unknown relation out by seeing the name of Austin over a shop-door, she surely could do as much. She had, however, wandered into the outskirts of the town before she fully recollected that her mission in Bruges was, first of all, to walk about the streets and find out the strange Austins who were foreigners and tradespeople. She came back, accordingly, as best she could, straying through the devious streets, meeting English travellers with the infallible Murray under their arms, and wondering to herself how people could have leisure to come to such a place as this for mere sight-seeing. That day, however, perhaps because of the strong hold upon her of the past and its recollections, perhaps because of the bewildering sense of mingled familiarity and strangeness in the place, she did not find the object of her search—though, indeed, the streets of Bruges are not so many, or the shops so extensive as to defy the scrutiny of a passer-by. She got tired, and half ashamed of herself to be thus walking about alone, and was glad to take refuge in a dim corner of the Cathedral, where she dropped on one knee in the obscurity, half afraid to be seen by any English visitor in this attitude of devotion in a Roman Catholic church, and then sat down to collect herself, and think over all she had to do. What was it she had to do? To prevent wrong from being done; to help to secure her unknown cousins in their rights. This was but a vague way of stating it, but it was more difficult to put the case to herself if she entered into detail. To persuade them that they had been over-persuaded, that they had too lightly given up advantages which, had they known their real value, they would not have given up; to prove to them how pleasant a thing it was to be Austins of Whiteladies. This was what she had to do.

Next morning Miss Susan set out with a clear head and a more distinct notion of what she was about. She had got used to the reiterations of the carillon, to the familiar distant look of the quaint streets. And, indeed, she had not gone very far when her heart jumped up in her breast to see written over a large shop the name of Austin, as Farrel had told her. She stopped and looked at it. It was situated at a bend in the road, where a narrow street debouched into a wider one, and had that air of self-restrained plainness, of being above the paltry art of window-dressing, which is peculiar to old and long-established shops whose character is known, where rich materials are sold at high prices, and everything cheap is contemned. Piles of linen and blankets, and other unattractive articles, were in a broad but dingy window, and in the doorway stood an old man with a black skullcap on his head, and blue eyes, full of vivacity and activity, notwithstanding his years. He was standing at his door looking up and down, with the air of a man who looked for news, or expected some incident other than the tranquil events around. When Miss Susan crossed the narrow part of the street, which she did with her heart in her mouth, he looked up at her, noting her appearance; and she felt sure that some internal warning of the nature of her errand came into his mind. From this look Miss Susan, quick as a flash of lightning, divined that he was not satisfied with his bargain, that his attention and curiosity were aroused, and that Farrel-Austin's visit had made him curious of other visits, and in a state of expectation. I believe she was right in the idea she thus formed, but she saw it more clearly than M. Austin did, who knew little more than that he was restless, and in an unsettled frame of mind.

"Est-ce vous qui êtes le propriétaire?" said Miss Susan, speaking bluntly, in her bad French, without any polite prefaces, such as befit the language; she was too much excited, even had she been sufficiently conversant with the strange tongue, to know that they were necessary. The shopkeeper took his cap off his bald head, which was venerable, with an encircling ring of white locks, and made her a bow. He was a handsome old man, with blue eyes, such as had always been peculiar to the Austins, and a general resemblance—or so, at least, Miss Susan thought—to the old family pictures at Whiteladies. Under her best black silk gown, and the Indian shawl which she had put on to impress her unknown relation with a sense of her importance, she felt her heart beating. But, indeed, black silk and India shawls are inconvenient wear in the middle of Summer in the Pays Bas; and perhaps this fact had something to do with the flush and tremor of which she was suddenly conscious.

M. Austin, the shopkeeper, took off his cap to her, and answered "Oui, madame," blandly; then, with that instant perception of her nationality, for which the English abroad are not always grateful, he added, "Madame is Inglese? we too. I am Inglese. In what can I be serviceable to madame?"

"Oh, you understand English? Thank heaven!" said Miss Susan, whose French was far from fluent. "I am very glad to hear it, for that will make my business so much the easier. It is long since I have been abroad, and I have almost forgotten the language. Could I speak to you somewhere? I don't want to buy anything," she said abruptly, as he stood aside to let her come in.

"That shall be at the pleasure of madame," said the old man with the sweetest of smiles, "though miladi will not find better damask in many places. Enter, madame. I will take you to my counting-house, or into my private house, if that will more please you. In what can I be serviceable to madame?"

"Come in here—anywhere where we can be quiet. What I have to say is important," said Miss Susan. The shop was not like an English shop. There was less light, less decoration, the windows were half blocked up, and behind, in the depths of the shop, there was a large, half-curtained window, opening into another room at the back. "I am not a customer, but it may be worth your while," said Miss Susan, her breath coming quick on her parted lips.

The shopkeeper made her a bow, which she set down to French politeness, for all people who spoke another language were French to Miss Susan. He said, "Madame shall be satisfied," and led her into the deeper depths, where he placed a chair for her, and remained standing in a deferential attitude. Miss Susan was confused by the new circumstances in which she found herself, and by the rapidity with which event had followed event.

"My name is Austin too," she said, faltering slightly. "I thought when I saw your name, that perhaps you were a relation of mine—who has been long lost to his family."

"It is too great an honor," said the old shopkeeper, with another bow; "but yes—but yes, it is indeed so. I have seen already another gentleman, a person in the same interests. Yes, it is me. I am Guillaume Austin."

"Guillaume?"

"Yes. William you it call. I have told my name to the other monsieur. He is, he say, the successive—what you call it? The one who comes—"

"The heir—"

"That is the word. I show him my papers—he is satisfied; as I will also to madame with pleasure. Madame is also cousin of Monsieur Farrel? Yes?—and of me? It is too great honor. She shall see for herself. My grandfather was Ingleseman—trés Inglese. I recall to myself his figure as if I saw it at this moment. Blue eyes, very clear, pointed nose—ma foi! like the nose of madame."

"I should like to see your papers," said Miss Susan. "Shall I come back in the evening when you have more time? I should like to see your wife—for you have one, surely? and your children."

"Yes, yes; but one is gone," said the shopkeeper. "Figure to yourself, madame, that I had but one son, and he is gone! There is no longer any one to take my place—to come after me. Ah! life is changed when it is so. One lives on—but what is life? a thing we must endure till it comes to an end."

"I know it well," said Miss Susan, in a low tone.

"Madame, too, has had the misfortune to lose her son, like me?"

"Ah, don't speak of it! But I have no son. I am what you call a vile fee," said Miss Susan; "an old maid—nothing more. And he is still living, poor boy; but doomed, alas! doomed. Mr. Austin, I have a great many things to speak to you about."

"I attend—with all my heart," said the shopkeeper, somewhat puzzled, for Miss Susan's speech was mysterious, there could be little doubt.

"If I return, then, in the evening, you will show me your papers, and introduce me to your family," said Miss Susan, getting up. "I must not take up your time now."

"But I am delighted to wait upon madame now," said the old man, "and since madame has the bounty to wish to see my family—by here, madame, I beg—enter, and be welcome—very welcome."

Saying this he opened the great window-door in the end of the shop, and Miss Susan, walking forward somewhat agitated, found herself all at once in a scene very unexpected by her, and of a kind for which she was unprepared. She was ushered in at once to the family room and family life, without even the interposition of a passage. The room into which this glass door opened was not very large, and quite disproportionately lofty. Opposite to the entrance from the shop was another large window, reaching almost to the roof, which opened upon a narrow court, and kept a curious dim day-light, half from without, half from within, in the space, which seemed more narrow than it need have done by reason of the height of the roof. Against this window, in a large easy chair, sat an old woman in a black gown, without a cap, and with one little tail of gray hair twisted at the back of her head, and curl-papers embellishing her forehead in front. Her gown was rusty, and not without stains, and she wore a large handkerchief, with spots, tied about her neck. She was chopping vegetables in a dish, and not in the least abashed to be found so engaged. In a corner sat a younger woman, also in black, and looking like a gloomy shadow, lingering apart from the light. Another young woman went and came toward an inner room, in which it was evident the dinner was going to be cooked.

A pile of boxes, red and blue, and all the colors of the rainbow, was on a table. There was no carpet on the floor, which evidently had not been frotté for some time past, nor curtains at the window, except a melancholy spotted muslin, which hung closely over it, making the scanty daylight dimmer still. Miss Susan drew her breath hard with a kind of gasp. The Austins were people extremely well to do—rich in their way, and thinking themselves very comfortable; but to the prejudiced English eye of their new relation, the scene was one of absolute squalor. Even in an English cottage, Miss Susan thought, there would have been an attempt at some prettiness or other, some air of nicety or ornament; but the comfortable people here (though Miss Susan supposed all foreigners to be naturally addicted to show and glitter), thought of nothing but the necessities of living. They were not in the least ashamed, as an

English family would have been, of being "caught" in the midst of their morning's occupations. The old lady put aside the basin with the vegetables, and wiped her hands with a napkin, and greeted her visitor with perfect calm; the others took scarcely any notice. Were these the people whose right it was to succeed generations of English squires—the dignified race of Whiteladies? Miss Susan shivered as she sat down, and then she began her work of temptation. She drew forth her picture, which was handed round for everybody to see. She described the estate and all its attractions. Would they let this pass away from them? At least they should not do it without knowing what they had sacrificed. To do this, partly in English, which the shopkeeper translated imperfectly, and partly in very bad French, was no small labor to Miss Susan; but her zeal was equal to the tax upon it, and the more she talked, and the more trouble she had to overcome her own repugnance to these new people, the more vehement she became in her efforts to break their alliance with Farrel, and induce them to recover their rights. The young woman who was moving about the room, and whose appearance had at once struck Miss Susan, came and looked over the old mother's shoulder at the picture, and expressed her admiration in the liveliest terms. The jolie maison it was, and the dommage to lose it, she cried: and these words were very strong pleas in favor of all Miss Susan said.

"Ah, what an abominable law," said the old lady at length, "that excludes the daughters!—sans ça, ma fille!" and she began to cry a little. "Oh, my son, my son! if the good God had not taken him, what joy to have restored him to the country of his grandfather, to an establishment so charming!"

Miss Susan drew close to the old woman in the rusty black gown, and approached her mouth to her ear.

"Cette jeune femme-là est veuve de voter fils?"

"No. There she is—there in the corner; she who neither smiles nor speaks," said the mother, putting up the napkin with which she had dried her hands, to her eyes.

The whole situation had in it a dreary tragi-comedy, half pitiful, half laughable; a great deal of intense feeling veiled by external circumstances of the homeliest order, such as is often to be found in comfortable, unlovely bourgeois households. How it was, in such a matter-of-fact interior, that the great temptation of her life should have flashed across Miss Susan's mind, I cannot tell. She glanced from the young wife, very soon to be a mother, who leant over the old lady's chair, to the dark shadow in the corner, who had never stirred from her seat. It was all done in a moment—thought, plan, execution. A sudden excitement took hold upon her. She drew her chair close to the old woman, and bent forward till her lips almost touched her ear.

"L'autre est—la même—que elle?"

"Que voulez-vous dire, madame?"

The old lady looked up at her bewildered, but, caught by the glitter of excitement in Miss Susan's eye, and the panting breath, which bore evidence to some sudden fever in her, stopped short. Her wondering look turned into something more keen and impassioned—a kind of electric spark flashed between the two women. It was done in a moment; so rapidly, that at least (as Miss Susan thought after, a hundred times, and a hundred to that) it was without premeditation; so sudden, that it was scarcely their fault. Miss Susan's eyes gleaming, said something to those of the old Flamande, whom she had never seen before, Guillaume Austin's wife. A curious thrill ran through both—the sting, the attraction, the sharp movement, half pain, half pleasure, of temptation and guilty intention; for there was a sharp and stinging sensation of pleasure in it, and something which made them giddy. They stood on the edge of a precipice, and looked at each other a second time before they took the plunge. Then Miss Susan laid her hand upon the other's arm, gripping it in her passion.

"Venez quelque part pour parler," she said, in her bad French.

CHAPTER VIII

I cannot tell the reader what was the conversation that ensued between Miss Susan and Madame Austin of Bruges, because the two naturally shut themselves up by themselves, and desired no witnesses. They went upstairs, threading their way through a warehouse full of goods, to Madame Austin's bedroom, which was her reception-room, and, to Miss Susan's surprise, a great deal prettier and lighter than the family apartment below, in which all the ordinary concerns of life were carried on. There were two white beds in it, a recess with crimson curtains drawn almost completely across—and various pretty articles of furniture, some marqueterie cabinets and tables, which would have made the mouth of any amateur of old furniture water, and two sofas with little rugs laid down in front of them. The boards were carefully waxed and clean, the white curtains drawn over the window, and everything arranged with some care and daintiness. Madame Austin placed her visitor on the principal sofa, which was covered with tapestry, but rather hard and straight, and then shut the door. She did not mean to be overheard.

Madame Austin was the ruling spirit in the house. It was she that regulated the expenses, that married the daughters, and that had made the match between her son and the poor creature downstairs, who had taken no part in the conversation. Her husband made believe to supervise and criticise everything, in which harmless gratification she encouraged him; but in fact his real business was to acquiesce, which he did with great success. Miss Susan divined well when she said to herself that his wife would never permit him to relinquish advantages so great when she knew something of what they really implied; but she too had been broken down by grief, and ready to feel that nothing was of any consequence in life, when Farrel-Austin had found them out. I do not know what cunning devil communicated to Miss Susan the right spell by which to wake up in Madame Austin the energies of a vivacious temperament partially repressed by grief and age; but certainly the attempt was crowned with success.

They talked eagerly, with flushed faces and voices which would have been loud had they not feared to be overheard; both of them carried out of themselves by the strangely exciting suggestion which had passed from one to the other almost without words; and they parted with close pressure of hands and with meaning looks, notwithstanding Miss Susan's terribly bad French, which was involved to a degree which I hardly dare venture to present to the reader; and many readers are aware, by unhappy experience, what an elderly Englishwoman's French can be. "Je reviendrai encore demain," said Miss Susan. "J'ai beaucoup choses à parler, et vous dira encore à votre mari. Si vous voulez me parler avant cela, allez à l'hôtel; je serai toujours dans mon appartement. Il est pas ung plaisir pour moi de marcher autour la ville, comme quand j'étais jeune. J'aime rester tranquil; et je reviendrai demain, dans la matin, á votre maison ici. J'ai beaucoup choses de parler autour."

Madame Austin did not know what "parler autour" could mean, but she accepted the puzzle and comprehended the general thread of the meaning. She returned to her sitting-room downstairs with her head full of a hundred busy thoughts, and Miss Susan went off to her hotel, with a headache, caused by a corresponding overflow in her mind. She was in a great excitement, which indeed could not be quieted by going to the hotel, but which prompted her to "marcher autour la ville," trying to neutralize the undue activity of her brain by movement of body. It is one of nature's instinctive ways of wearing out emotion. To do wrong is a very strange sensation, and it was one which, in any great degree, was unknown to Miss Susan. She had done wrong, I suppose, often enough before, but she had long outgrown that sensitive stage of mind and body which can seriously regard as mortal sins the little peccadilloes of common life—the momentary failures of temper or rashness of words, which the tender youthful soul confesses and repents of as great sins. Temptation had not come near her virtuous and equable life; and, to tell the truth, she had often felt with a compunction that the confession she sometimes made in church, of a burden of guilt which was intolerable to her, and of sins too many to be remembered, was an innocent hypocrisy on her part. She had taken herself to task often enough for her inability to feel this deep penitence as she ought; and now a real and great temptation had come in her way, and Miss Susan did not feel at all in that state of mind which she would have thought probable. Her first sensation was that of extreme excitement—a sharp and stinging yet almost pleasurable sense of energy and force and strong will which could accomplish miracles: so I suppose the rebel angels must have felt in the first moment of their sin—intoxicated with the mere sense of it, and of their own amazing force and boldness who dared to do it, and defy the Lord of heaven and earth. She walked about and looked in at the shop-windows, at that wonderful filagree work of steel and silver which the poorest women wear in those Low Countries, and at the films of lace which in other circumstances Miss Susan was woman enough to have been interested in for their own sake. Why could not she think of them?—why could not she care for them now?—A deeper sensation possessed her, and its first effect was so strange that it filled her with fright; for, to tell the truth, it was an exhilarating rather than a depressing sensation. She was breathless with excitement, panting, her heart beating.

Now and then she looked behind her as if some one were pursuing her. She looked at the people whom she met with a conscious defiance, bidding them with her eyes find out, if they dared, the secret which possessed her completely. This thought was not as other thoughts which come and go in the mind, which give way to passing impressions, yet prove themselves to have the lead by returning to fill up all crevices. It never departed from her for a moment. When she went into the shops to buy, as she did after awhile by way of calming herself down, she was half afraid of saying something about it in the midst of her request to look at laces, or her questions as to the price; and, like other mental intoxications, this unaccomplished intention of evil seemed to carry her out of herself altogether; it annihilated all bodily sensations. She walked about as lightly as a ghost, unconscious of her physical powers altogether, feeling neither hunger nor weariness. She went through the churches, the picture galleries, looking vaguely at everything, conscious clearly of nothing, now and then horribly attracted by one of those terrible pictures of blood and suffering, the martyrdoms which abound in all Flemish collections. She went into the shops, as I have said, and bought lace, for what reason she did not know, nor for whom; and it was only in the afternoon late that she went back to her hotel, where Jane, frightened, was looking out for her, and thinking her mistress must have been lost or murdered among "them foreigners." "I have been with friends," Miss Susan said, sitting down, bolt upright, on the vacant chair, and looking Jane straight in the face, to make sure that the simple creature suspected nothing. How could she have supposed Jane to know anything, or suspect? But it is one feature of this curious exaltation of mind, in which Miss Susan was, that reason and all its limitations is for the moment abandoned, and things impossible become likely and natural. After this, however, the body suddenly asserted itself, and she became aware that she had been on foot the whole day, and was no longer capable of any physical exertion. She lay down on the sofa dead tired, and after a little interval had something to eat, which she took with appetite, and looked on her purchases with a certain pleasure, and slept soundly all night—the sleep of the just. No remorse visited her, or penitence, only a certain breathless excitement stirring up her whole being, a sense of life and strength and power.

Next morning Miss Susan repeated her visit to her new relations at an early hour. This time she found them all prepared for her, and was received not in the general room, but in Madame Austin's chamber, where M. Austin and his wife awaited her coming. The shopkeeper himself had altogether changed in appearance: his countenance beamed; he bowed over the hand which Miss Susan held out to him, like an old courtier, and looked gratefully at her.

"Madame has come to our house like a good angel," he said. "Ah! it is madame's intelligence which has found out the good news, which cette pauvre chérie had not the courage to tell us. I did never think to laugh of good heart again," said the poor man, with tears in his eyes, "but this has made me young; and it almost seems as if we owed it to madame."

"How can that be?" said Miss Susan. "It must have been found out sooner or later. It will make up to you, if anything can, for the loss of your boy."

"If he had but lived to see it!" said the old man with a sob.

The mother stood behind, tearless, with a glitter in her eyes which was almost fierce. Miss Susan did not venture to do more than give her one hurried glance, to which she replied with a gleam of fury, clasping her hands together. Was it fury? Miss Susan thought so, and shrank for a moment, not quite able to understand the feelings of the other woman who had not clearly understood her, yet who now seemed to address to her a look of wild reproach.

"And my poor wife," went on the old shopkeeper, "for her it will be an even still more happy—Tu es contente, bien contente, n'est-ce pas?"

"Oui, mon ami," said the woman, turning her back to him, with once more a glance from which Miss Susan shrank.

"Ah, madame, excuse her; she cannot speak; it is a joy too much," he cried, drying his old eyes.

Miss Susan felt herself constrained and drawn on by the excitement of the moment, and urged by the silence of the other woman, who was as much involved as she.

"My poor boy will have a sadder lot even than yours," she said; "he is dying too young even to hope for any of the joys of life. There is neither wife nor child possible for Herbert." The tears rushed to her eyes as she spoke. Heaven help her! she had availed herself, as it were, of nature and affection to help her to commit her sin with more ease and apparent security. She had taken advantage of poor Herbert in order to wake those tears which gave her credit in the eyes of the unsuspecting stranger. In the midst of her excitement and feverish sense of life, a sudden chill struck at her heart. Had she come to this debasement so soon? Was it possible that in such an emergency she had made capital and stock-in-trade of her dying boy? This reflection was not put into words, but flashed through her with one of those poignant instantaneous cuts and thrusts which men and women are subject to, invisibly to all the world. M. Austin, forgetting his respect in sympathy, held out his hand to her to press hers with a profound and tender feeling which went to Miss Susan's heart; but she had the courage to return the pressure before she dropped his bond hastily (he thought in English pride and reserve), and, making a visible effort to suppress her emotion, continued, "After this discovery, I suppose your bargain with Mr. Farrel-Austin, who took such an advantage of you, is at an end at once?"

"Speak French," said Madame Austin, with gloom on her countenance; "I do not understand your English."

"Mon amie, you are a little abrupt. Forgive her, madame; it is the excitation—the joy. In women the nerves are so much allied with the sentiments," said the old shopkeeper, feeling himself, like all men, qualified to generalize on this subject. Then he added with dignity, "I promised only for myself. My old companion and me—we felt no desire to be more rich, to enter upon another life; but at present it is different. If there comes an inheritor," he added, with a gleam of light over his face, "who shall be born to this wealth, who can be educated for it, who will be happy in it, and great and prosperous—ah, madame, permit that I thank you again! Yes, it is you who have revealed the goodness of God to me. I should not have been so happy to-day but for you."

Miss Susan interrupted him almost abruptly. The sombre shadow on Madame Austin's countenance began to affect her in spite of herself. "Will you write to him," she said, "or would you wish me to explain for you? I shall see him on my return."

"Still English," said Madame Austin, "when I say that I do not understand it! I wish to understand what is said."

The two women looked each other in the face: one wondering, uncertain, half afraid; the other angry, defiant, jealous, feeling her power, and glad, I suppose, to find some possible and apparent cause of irritation by which to let loose the storm in her breast of confused irritation and pain. Miss Susan looked at her and felt frightened; she had even begun to share in the sentiment which made her accomplice so bitter and fierce; she answered, with something like humility, in her atrocious French:

"Je parle d'un monsieur que vous avez vu, qui est allez ici, qui a parlé à vous de l'Angleterre. M. Austin et vous allez changer votre idées,—et je veux dire à cet monsieur que quelque chose de différent est venu, que vous n'est pas de même esprit que avant. Voici!" said Miss Susan, rather pleased with herself for having got on so far in a breath. "Je signifie cela—c'est-à-dire, je offrir mon service pour assister votre mari changer la chose qu'il a faites."

"Oui, mon amie," said M. Austin, "pour casser l'affaire—le contrat que nous avons fait, vous et moi, et que d'ailleurs n'a jamais été exécuté; c'est sa; I shall write, and madame will explique, and all will be made as at first. The gentleman was kind. I should never have known my rights, nor anything about the beautiful house that belongs to us—"

"That may belong to you, on my poor boy's death," said Miss Susan, correcting him.

"Assuredly; after the death of M. le propriétaire actuel. Yes, yes, that is understood. Madame will explain to ce monsieur how the situation has changed, and how the contract is at least suspended in the meantime."

"Until the event," said Miss Susan.

"Until the event, assuredly," said M. Austin, rubbing his hands.

"Until the event," said Madame Austin, recovering herself under this discussion of details. "But it will be wise to treat ce monsieur with much gentleness," she added; "he must be ménagé; for figure to yourself that it might be a girl, and he might no longer wish to pay the money proposed, mon ami. He must be managed with great care. Perhaps if I were myself to go to England to see this monsieur—"

"Mon ange! it would fatigue you to death."

"It is true; and then a country so strange—a cuisine abominable. But I should not hesitate to sacrifice myself, as you well know, Guillaume, were it necessary. Write then, and we will see by his reply if he is angry, and I can go afterward if it is needful."

"And madame, who is so kind, who has so much bounty for us," said the old man, "madame will explain."

Once more the two women looked at each other. They had been so cordial yesterday, why were not they cordial to-day?

"How is it that madame has so much bounty for us?" said the old Flemish woman, half aside. "She has no doubt her own reasons?"

"The house has been mine all my life," said Miss Susan, boldly. "I think perhaps, if you get it, you will let me live there till I die. And Farrel-Austin is a bad man," she added with vehemence; "he has done us bitter wrong. I would do anything in the world rather than let him have Whiteladies. I thought I had told you this yesterday. Do you understand me now?"

"I begin to comprehend," said Madame Austin, under her breath.

Finally this was the compact that was made between them. The Austins themselves were to write, repudiating their bargain with Farrel, or at least suspending it, to await an event, of the likelihood of which they were not aware at the time they had consented to his terms; and Miss Susan was to see him, and smooth all down and make him understand. Nothing could be decided till the event. It might be a mere postponement—it might turn out in no way harmful to Farrel, only an inconvenience. Miss Susan was no longer excited, nor so comfortable in her mind as yesterday. The full cup had evaporated, so to speak, and shrunk; it was no longer running over. One or two indications of a more miserable consciousness had come to her. She had read the shame of guilt and its irritation in her confederate's eyes; she had felt the pain of deceiving an unsuspecting person. These were new sensations, and they were not pleasant; nor was her brief parting interview with Madame Austin pleasant. She had not felt, in the first fervor of temptation, any dislike to the close contact which was necessary with that homely person, or the perfect equality which was necessary between her and her fellow-conspirator; but to-day Miss Susan did feel this, and shrank. She grew impatient of the old woman's brusque manner, and her look of reproach. "As if she were any better than me," said poor Miss Susan to herself. Alas! into what moral depths the proud Englishwoman must have fallen who could compare herself with Madame Austin! And when she took leave of her, and Madame Austin, recovering her spirits, breathed some confidential details—half jocular, and altogether familiar, with a breath smelling of garlic—into Miss Susan's ear, she fell back, with a mixture of disdain and disgust which it was almost impossible to conceal. She walked back to the hotel this time without any inclination to linger, and gave orders to Jane to prepare at once for the home journey. The only thing that did her any good, in the painful tumult of feeling which had succeeded her excitement, was a glimpse which she caught in passing into the same lofty common room in which she had first seen the Austin family. The son's widow still sat a gloomy shadow in her chair in the corner; but in the full light of the window, in the big easy chair which Madame Austin had filled yesterday, sat the daughter of the house with her child on her lap, leaning back and holding up the plump baby with pretty outstretched arms. Whatever share she might have in the plot was involuntary. She was a fair-haired, round-faced Flemish girl, innocent and merry. She held up her child in her pretty round sturdy arms, and chirruped and talked nonsense to it in a language of which Miss Austin knew not a word. She stopped and looked a moment at this pretty picture, then turned quickly, and went away. After all, the plot was all in embryo as yet. Though evil was meant, Providence was still the arbiter, and good and evil alike must turn upon the event.

CHAPTER IX

"Don't you think he is better, mamma—a little better to-day?"

"Ah, mon Dieu, what can I say, Reine? To be a little better in his state is often to be worst of all. You have not seen so much as I have. Often, very often, there is a gleam of the dying flame in the socket; there is an air of being well—almost well. What can I say? I have seen it like that. And they have all told us that he cannot live. Alas, alas, my poor boy!"

Madame de Mirfleur buried her face in her handkerchief as she spoke. She was seated in the little sitting-room of a little house in an Alpine valley, where they had brought the invalid when the Summer grew too hot for him on the shores of the Mediterranean. He himself had chosen the Kanderthal as his Summer quarters, and with the obstinacy of a sick man had clung to the notion. The valley was shut in by a circle of snowy peaks toward the east; white, dazzling mountain-tops, which yet looked small and homely and familiar in the shadow of the bigger Alps around. A little mountain stream ran through the valley, across which, at one point, clustered a knot of houses, with a homely inn in the midst. There were trout in the river, and the necessaries of life were to be had in the village, through which a constant stream of travellers passed during the Summer and Autumn, parties crossing the steep pass of the Gemmi, and individual tourists of more enterprising character fighting their way from this favorable centre into various unknown recesses of the hills. Behind the chalet a waterfall kept up a continual murmur, giving utterance, as it seemed, to the very silence of the mountains. The scent of pine-woods was in the air; to the west the glory of the sunset shone over a long broken stretch of valley, uneven moorland interspersed with clumps of wood. To be so little out of the way—nay, indeed, to be in the way—of the Summer traveller, it was singularly wild and quaint and fresh. Indeed, for one thing, no tourist ever stayed there except for food and rest, for there was nothing to attract any one in the plain, little secluded village, with only its circle of snowy peaks above its trout-stream, and its sunsets, to catch any fanciful eye. Sometimes, however, a fanciful eye was caught by these charms, as in the case of poor Herbert Austin, who had been brought here to die. He lay in the little room which communicated with this sitting-room, in a small wooden chamber opening upon a balcony, from which you could watch the sun setting over the Kanderthal, and the moon rising over the snow-white glory of the Dolden-horn, almost at the same moment. The chalet belonged to the inn, and was connected with it by a covered passage. The Summer was at its height, and still poor Herbert lingered, though M. de Mirfleur, in pleasant Normandy, grew a little weary of the long time his wife's son took in dying; and Madame de Mirfleur herself, as jealous Reine would think sometimes, in spite of herself grew weary too, thinking of her second family at home, and the husband whom Reine had always felt to be an offence. The mother and sister who were thus watching over Herbert's last moments were not so united in their grief and pious duties as might have been supposed. Generally it is the mother whose whole heart is absorbed in such watching, and the young sister who is to be pardoned if sometimes, in the sadness of the shadow that precedes death, her young mind should wander back to life and its warmer interests with a longing which makes her feel guilty. But in this case these positions were reversed. It was the mother who longed involuntarily for the life she had left behind her, and whose heart reverted wistfully to something brighter and more hopeful, to other interests and loves as strong, if not stronger, than that she felt in and for her eldest son. When it is the other way the sad mother pardons her child for a wandering imagination; but the sad child, jealous and miserable, does not forgive the mother, who has so much to fall back upon. Reine had never been able to forgive her mother's marriage. She never named her by her new name without a thrill of irritation. Her stepfather seemed a standing shame to her, and every new brother and sister who came into the world was a new offence against Reine's delicacy. She had been glad, very glad, of Madame de Mirfleur's aid in transporting Herbert hither, and at first her mother's society, apart from the new family, had been very sweet to the girl, who loved her, notwithstanding the fantastic sense of shame which possessed her, and her jealousy of all her new connections. But when Reine, quick-sighted with the sharpened vision of jealousy and wounded love, saw, or thought she saw, that her mother began to weary of the long vigil, that she began to wonder what her little ones were doing, and to talk of all the troubles of a long absence, her heart rose impatient in an agony of anger and shame and deep mortification. Weary of waiting for her son's death—her eldest son, who ought to have been her only son—weary of those lingering moments which were now all that remained to Herbert! Reine, in the anguish of her own deep grief and pity and longing hold upon him, felt herself sometimes almost wild against her mother. She did so now, when Madame de Mirfleur, with a certain calm, though she was crying, shook her head and lamented that such gleams of betterness were often the precursors of the end. Reine did not weep when her mother buried her face in her delicate perfumed handkerchief. She said to herself fiercely, "Mamma likes to think so; she wants to get rid of us, and get back to those others," and looked at her with eyes which shone hot and dry, with a flushed cheek and clenched hands. It was all she could do to restrain herself, to keep from saying something which good sense and good taste, and a lingering natural affection, alike made her feel that she must not say. Reine was one of those curious creatures in whom two races mingle. She had the Austin blue eyes, but with a light in them such as no Austin had before; but she had the dark-brown hair, smooth and silky, of her French mother, and something of the piquancy of feature, the little petulant nose, the mobile countenance of the more vivacious blood. Her figure was like a fairy's, little and slight; her movements, both of mind and body, rapid as the stirrings of a bird; she went from one mood to another instantaneously, which was not the habit of her father's deliberate race. Miss Susan thought her all French—Madame de Mirfleur all English; and indeed both with some reason—for when in England this perverse girl was full of enthusiasm for everything that belonged to her mother's country, and when in France was the most prejudiced and narrow-minded of English women. Youth is always perverse, more or less, and there was a double share of its fanciful self-will and changeableness in Reine, whose circumstances were so peculiar and her temptations so many. She was so rent asunder by love and grief, by a kind of adoration for her dying brother, the only being in the world who belonged exclusively to herself, and jealous suspicion that he did not get his due from others, that her petulance was very comprehensible. She waited till Madame de Mirfleur came out of her handkerchief, still with hot and dry and glittering eyes.

"You think it would be well if it were over," said Reine; "that is what I have heard people say. It would be well—yes, in order to release his nurses and attendants, it would be well if it should come to an end. Ah, mamma, you think so too—you, his mother! You would not harm him nor shorten his life, but yet you think, as it is hopeless, it might be well: you want to go to your husband and your children!"

"If I do, that is simple enough," said Madame de Mirfleur. "Ciel! how unjust you are, Reine! because I tell you the result of a little rally like Herbert's is often not happy. I want to go to my husband, and to your brothers and sisters, yes—I should be unnatural if I did not—but that my duty, which I will never neglect, calls upon me here."

"Oh, do not stay!" cried Reine vehemently—"do not stay! I can do all the duty. If it is only duty that keeps you, go, mamma, go! I would not have you, for that reason, stay another day."

"Child! how foolish you are!" said the mother. "Reine, you should not show at least your repugnance to everything I am fond of. It is wicked—and more, it is foolish. What can any one think of you? I will stay while I am necessary to my poor boy; you may be sure of that."

"Not necessary," said Reine—"oh, not necessary! I can do all for him that is necessary. He is all I have in the world. There are neither husband nor children that can come between Herbert and me. Go, mamma,—for Heaven's sake, go! When your heart is gone already, why should you remain? I can do all he requires. Oh, please, go!"

"You are very wicked, Reine," said her mother, "and unkind! You do not reflect that I stay for you. What are you to do when you are left all alone?—you, who are so unjust to your mother? I stay for that. What would you do?"

"Me!" said Reine. She grew pale suddenly to her very lips, struck by this sudden suggestion in the sharpest way. She gave a sob of tearless passion. She knew very well that her brother was dying; but thus to be compelled to admit and realize it, was more than she could bear. "I will do the best I can," she said, closing her eyes in the giddy faintness that came over her. "What does it matter about me?"

"The very thought makes you ill," said Madame de Mirfleur. "Reine, you know what is coming, but you will never allow yourself to think of it. Pause now, and reflect; when my poor Herbert is gone, what will become of you, unless I am here to look after you? You will have to do everything yourself. Why should we refuse to consider things which we know must happen? There will be the funeral—all the arrangements—"

"Mamma! mamma! have you a heart of stone?" cried Reine. She was shocked and wounded, and stung to the very soul. To speak of his funeral, almost in his presence, seemed nothing less than brutal to the excited girl; and all these matter-of-fact indications of what was coming jarred bitterly upon the heart, in which, I suppose, hope will still live while life lasts. Reine felt her whole being thrill with the shock of this terrible, practical touch, which to her mother seemed merely a simple putting into words of the most evident and unavoidable thought.

"I hope I have a heart like all the rest of the world," said Madame de Mirfleur. "And you are excited and beside yourself, or I could not pass over your unkindness as I do. Yes, Reine, it is my duty to stay for poor Herbert, but still more for you. What would you do?"

"What would it matter?" cried Reine, bitterly—"not drop into his grave with him—ah, no; one is not permitted that happiness. One has to stay behind and live on, when there is nothing to live for more!"

"You are impious, my child," said her mother. "And, again, you are foolish; you do not reflect how young you are, and that life has many interests yet in store for you—new connections, new duties—"

"Husbands and children!" cried Reine with scornful bitterness, turning her blue eyes, agleam with that feverish fire which tells at once of the necessity and impossibility of tears, upon her mother. Then her countenance changed all in a moment. A little bell tinkled faintly from the next room. "I am coming," she cried, in a tone as soft as the Summer air that caressed the flowers in the balcony. The expression of her face was changed and softened; she became another creature in a moment. Without a word or a look more, she opened the door of the inner room and disappeared.

Madame de Mirfleur looked after her, not without irritation; but she was not so fiery as Reine, and she made allowances for the girl's folly, and calmed down her own displeasure. She listened for a moment to make out whether the invalid's wants were anything more than usual, whether her help was required; and then drawing toward her a blotting-book which lay on the table, she resumed her letter to her husband. She was not so much excited as Reine by this interview, and, indeed, she felt she had only done her duty in indicating to the girl very plainly that life must go on and be provided for, even after Herbert had gone out of it. "My poor boy!" she said to herself, drying some tears; but she could not think of dying with him, or feel any despair from that one loss; she had many to live for, many to think of, even though she might have him no longer. "Reine is excited and unreasonable, as usual," she wrote to her husband; "always jealous of you, mon ami, and of our children. This arises chiefly from her English ideas, I am disposed to believe. Perhaps when the sad event which we are awaiting is over, she will see more clearly that I have done the best for her as well as for myself. We must pardon her in the meantime, poor child. It is in her blood. The English are always more or less fantastic. We others, French, have true reason. Reassure yourself, mon cher ami, that I will not remain a day longer than I can help away from you and our children. My poor Herbert sinks daily. Think of our misery!—you cannot imagine how sad it is. Probably in a week, at the furthest, all will be over. Ah, mon Dieu! what it is to have a mother's heart! and how many martyrdoms we have to bear!" Madame de Mirfleur wrote this sentence with a very deep sigh, and once more wiped from her eyes a fresh gush of tears. She was perfectly correct in every way as a mother. She felt as she ought to feel, and expressed her sorrow as it was becoming to express it, only she was not absorbed by it—a thing which is against all true rules of piety and submission. She could not rave like Reine, as if there was nothing else worth caring for, except her poor Herbert, her dear boy. She had a great many other things to care for; and she recognized all that must happen, and accepted it as necessary. Soon it would be over; and all recovery being hopeless, and the patient having nothing to look forward to but suffering, could it be doubted that it was best for him to have his suffering over? though Reine, in her rebellion against God and man, could not see this, and clung to every lingering moment which could lengthen out her brother's life.

Reine herself cleared like a Summer sky as she passed across the threshold into her brother's room. The change was instantaneous. Her blue eyes, which had a doubtful light in them, and looked sometimes fierce and sometimes impassioned, were now as soft as the sky. The lines of irritation were all smoothed from her brow and from under her eyes. Limpid eyes, soft looks, an unruffled, gentle face, with nothing in it but love and tenderness, was what she showed always to her sick brother. Herbert knew her only under this aspect, though, with the clear-sightedness of an invalid, he had divined that Reine was not always so sweet to others as to himself.

"You called me," she said, coming up to his bed-side with something caressing, soothing, in the very sound of her step and voice; "you want me, Herbert?"

"Yes; but I don't want you to do anything. Sit down by me, Reine; I am tired of my own company, that is all."

"And so am I—of everybody's company but yours," she said, sitting down by the bed-side and stooping her pretty, shining head to kiss his thin hand.

"Thanks, dear, for saying such pretty things to me. But, Reine, I heard voices; you were talking—was it with mamma?—not so softly as you do to me."

"Oh, it was nothing," said Reine, with a flush. "Did you hear us, poor boy? Oh, that was wicked! Yes, you know there are things that make me—I do not mean angry—I suppose I have no right to be angry with mamma—"

"Why should you be angry with any one?" he said, softly. "If you had to lie here, like me, you would think nothing was worth being angry about. My poor Reine! you do not even know what I mean."

"Oh, no; there is so much that is wrong," said Reine; "so many things that people do—so many that they think—their very ways of doing even what is right enough. No, no; it is worth while to be angry about many, many things. I do not want to learn to be indifferent; besides, that would be impossible to me—it is not my nature."

The invalid smiled and shook his head softly at her. "Your excuse goes against yourself," he said. "If you are ruled by your nature, must not others be moved by theirs? You active-minded people, Reine, you would like every one to think like you; but if you could accomplish it, what a monotonous world you would make! I should not like the Kanderthal if all the mountain-tops were shaped the same; and I should not perhaps love you so much if you were less yourself. Why not let other people, my Reine, be themselves, too?"

The brother and sister spoke French, which, more than English, had been the language of their childhood.

"Herbert, don't say such things!" cried the girl. "You do not love me for this or for that, as strangers might, but because I am I, Reine, and you are you, Herbert. That is all we want. Ah, yes, perhaps if I were very good I should like to be loved for being good. I don't know; I don't think it even then. When they used to promise to love me if I was good at Whiteladies, I was always naughty—on purpose?—yes, I am afraid. Herbert, should not you like to be at Whiteladies, lying on the warm, warm grass in the orchard, underneath the great apple-tree, with the bees humming all about, and the dear white English clouds floating and floating, and the sky so deep, deep, that you could not fathom it? Ah!" cried Reine, drawing a deep breath, "I have not thought of it for a long time; but I wish we were there."

The sick youth did not say anything for a moment; his eyes followed her look, which she turned instinctively to the open window. Then he sighed; then raising himself a little, said, with a gleam of energy, "I am certainly better, Reine. I should like to get up and set out across the Gemmi, down the side of the lake that must be shining so in the sun. That's the brightest way home." Then he laughed, with a laugh which, though feeble, had not lost the pleasant ring of youthfulness. "What wild ideas you put into my head!" he said. "No, I am not up to that yet; but, Reine, I am certainly better. I have such a desire to get up: and I thought I should never get up again."

"I will call François!" cried the girl, eagerly. He had been made to get up for days together without any will of his own, and now that he should wish it seemed to her a step toward that recovery which Reine could never believe impossible. She rushed out to call his servant, and waited, with her heart beating, till he should be dressed, her thoughts already dancing forward to brighter and brighter possibilities.

"He has never had the good of the mountain air," said Reine to herself, "and the scent of the pine-woods. He shall sit on the balcony to-day, and to-morrow go out in the chair, and next week, perhaps—who knows?—he may be able to walk up to the waterfall, and—O God! O Dieu tout-puissant! O doux Jesu!" cried the girl, putting her hands together, "I will be good! I will be good! I will endure anything; if only he may live!—if only he may live!"

CHAPTER X

This little scene took place in the village of Kandersteg, at the foot of the hills, exactly on the day when Miss Susan executed her errand in the room behind the shop, in low-lying Bruges, among the flat canals and fat Flemish fields. The tumult in poor Reine's heart would have been almost as strange to Miss Susan as it was to Reine's mother; for it was long now since Herbert had been given up by everybody, and since the doctors had all said, that "nothing short of a miracle" could save him. Neither Miss Susan nor Madame de Mirfleur believed in miracles. But Reine, who was young, had no such limitation of mind, and never could or would acknowledge that anything was impossible. "What does impossible mean?" Reine cried in her vehemence, on this very evening, after Herbert had accomplished her hopes, had stayed for an hour or more on the balcony and felt himself better for it, and ordered François to prepare his wheeled chair for to-morrow. Reine had much ado not to throw her arms around François's neck, when he pronounced solemnly that "Monsieur est mieux, décidément mieux." "Même," added François, "il a un petit air de je ne sais quoi—quelque chose—un rien—un regard—"

"N'est ce pas, mon ami!" cried Reine transported. Yes, there was a something, a nothing, a changed look which thrilled her with the wildest hopes,—and it was after this talk that she confronted Madame de Mirfleur with the question, "What does impossible mean? It means only, I suppose, that God does not interfere—that He lets nature go on in the common way. Then nothing is impossible; because at any moment, God may interfere if He pleases. Ah! He has His reasons, I suppose. If He were never to interfere at all, but leave nature to do her will, it is not for us to blame Him," cried Reine, with tears, "but yet always He may: so there is always hope, and nothing is impossible in this world."

"Reine, you speak like a child," said her mother. "Have I not prayed and hoped too for my boy's life? But when all say it is impossible—"

"Mamma," said Reine, "when my piano jars, it is impossible for me to set it right—if I let it alone, it goes worse and worse; if I meddle with it in my ignorance, it goes worse and worse. If you, even, who know more than I do, touch it, you cannot mend it. But the man comes who knows, et voilà! c'est tout simple," cried Reine. "He touches something we never observed, he makes something rise or fall, and all is harmonious again. That is like God. He does not do it always, I know. Ah! how can I tell why? If it was me," cried the girl, with tears streaming from her eyes, "I would save every one—but He is not like me."

"Reine, you are impious—you are wicked; how dare you speak so?"

"Oh, no, no! I am not impious," she cried, dropping upon her knees—all the English part in her, all her reason and self-restraint broken down by extreme emotion. "The bon Dieu knows I am not! I know, I know He does, and sees me, the good Father, and is sorry, and considers with Himself in His great heart if He will do it even yet. Oh, I know, I know!" cried the weeping girl, "some must die, and He considers long; but tell me He does not see me, does not hear me, is not sorry for me—how is He then my Father? No!" she said softly, rising from her knees and drying the tears from her face, "what I feel is that He is thinking it over again."

Madame de Mirfleur was half afraid of her daughter, thinking she was going out of her mind. She laid her hand on Reine's shoulder with a soothing touch. "Chérie!" she said, "don't you know it was all decided and settled before you were born, from the beginning of the world?"

"Hush!" said Reine, in her excitement. "I can feel it even in the air. If our eyes were clear enough, we should see the angels waiting to know. I dare not pray any more, only to wait like the angels. He is considering. Oh! pray, pray!" the poor child cried, feverish and impassioned. She went out into the balcony and knelt down there, leaning her forehead against the wooden railing. The sky shone above with a thousand stars, the moon, which was late that night, had begun to throw upward from behind the pinnacles of snow, a rising whiteness, which made them gleam; the waterfall murmured softly in the silence; the pines joined in their continual cadence, and sent their aromatic odors like a breath of healing, in soft waves toward the sick man's chamber. There was a stillness all about, as if, as poor Reine said, God himself was considering, weighing the balance of death or life. She did not look at the wonderful landscape around, or see or even feel its beauty. Her mind was too much absorbed—not praying, as she said, but fixed in one wonderful voiceless aspiration. This fervor and height of feeling died away after a time, and poor little Reine came back to common life, trembling with a thrill in all her nerves, and chilled with over-emotion, but yet calm, having got some strange gleam of encouragement, as she thought, from the soft air and the starry skies.

"He is fast asleep," she said to her mother when they parted for the night, with such a smile on her face as only comes after many tears, and the excitement of great suffering, "quite fast asleep, breathing like a child. He has not slept so before, almost for years."

"Poor child," said Madame de Mirfleur, kissing her. She was not moved by Reine's visionary hopes. She believed much more in the doctors, who had described to her often enough—for she was curious on such subjects—how Herbert's disease had worked, and of the "perforations" that had taken place, and the "tissue that was destroyed." She preferred to know the worst, she had always said, and she had a strange inquisitive relish for these details. She shook her head and cried a little, and said her prayers too with much more fervor than usual, after she parted from Reine. Poor Herbert, if he could live after all, how pleasant it would be! how sweet to take M. de Mirfleur and the children to her son's château in England, and to get the good of his wealth. Ah! what would not she give for his life, her poor boy, her eldest, poor Austin's child, whom indeed she had half forgotten, but who had always been so good to her! Madame de Mirfleur cried over the thought, and said her prayers fervently, with a warmer petition for Herbert than usual; but even as she prayed she shook her head; she had no faith in her own prayers. She was a French Protestant, and knew a great deal about theology, and perhaps had been shaken by the many controversies which she had heard. And accordingly she shook her head; to be sure, she said to herself, there was no doubt that God could do everything—but, as a matter of fact, it was evident that this was not an age of miracles; and how could we suppose that all the economy of heaven and earth could be stopped and turned aside, because one insignificant creature wished it! She shook her head; and I think whatever theory of prayer we may adopt, the warmest believer in its efficacy would scarcely expect any very distinct answer to such prayers as those of Madame de Mirfleur.

Herbert and Reine Austin had been brought up almost entirely together from their earliest years. Partly from his delicate health and partly from their semi-French training, the boy and girl had not been separated as boys and girls generally are by the processes of education. Herbert had never been strong, and consequently had never been sent to school or college. He had had tutors from time to time, but as nobody near him was much concerned about his mental progress, and his life was always precarious, the boy was allowed to grow up, as girls sometimes are, with no formal education at all, but a great deal of reading; his only superiority in this point was, he knew after a fashion Latin and Greek, which Madame de Mirfleur and even Miss Susan Austin would have thought it improper to teach a girl; while she knew certain arts of the needle which it was beneath man's dignity to teach a boy. Otherwise they had gone through the selfsame studies, read the same books, and mutually communicated to each other all they found therein. The affection between them, and their union, was thus of a quite special and peculiar character. Each was the other's family concentrated in one. Their frequent separations from their mother and isolation by themselves at Whiteladies, where at first the two little brown French mice, as Miss Susan had called them, were but little appreciated, had thrown Reine and Herbert more and more upon each other for sympathy and companionship. To be sure, as they grew older they became by natural process of events the cherished darlings of Whiteladies, to which at first they were a trouble and oppression; but the aunts were old and they were young, and except Everard Austin, had no companions but each other. Then their mother's marriage, which occurred when Herbert was about fourteen and his sister two years younger, gave an additional closeness, as of orphans altogether forsaken, to their union. Herbert was the one who took this marriage most easily. "If mamma likes it, it is no one else's business," he said with unusual animation when Miss Susan began to discuss the subject; it was not his fault, and Herbert had no intention of being brought to account for it. He took it very quietly, and had always been quite friendly to his stepfather, and heard of the birth of the children with equanimity. His feelings were not so intense as those of Reine; he was calm by nature, and illness had hushed and stilled him. Reine, on the other hand, was more shocked and indignant at this step on her mother's part, than words can say. It forced her into precocious womanhood, so much did it go to her heart. To say that she hated the new husband and the new name which her mother had chosen, was little. She felt herself insulted by them, young as she was. The blood came hot to her face at the thought of the marriage, as if it had been something wrong—and her girlish fantastic delicacy never recovered the shock. It turned her heart from her mother who was no longer hers, and fixed it more and more upon Herbert, the only being in the world who was hers, and in whom she could trust fully. "But if I were to marry, too!" he said to her once, in some moment of gayer spirits. "It is natural that you should marry, not unnatural," cried Reine; "it would be right, not wretched. I might not like it; probably I should not like it—but it would not change my ideal." This serious result had happened in respect to her mother, who could no longer be Reine's ideal, whatever might happen. The girl was so confused in consequence, and broken away from all landmarks, that she, and those who had charge of her, had anything but easy work in the days before Herbert's malady declared itself. This had been the saving of Reine; she had devoted herself to her sick brother heart and soul, and the jar in her mind had ceased to communicate false notes to everything around.

It was now two years since the malady which had hung over him all his life, had taken a distinct form; though even now, the doctors allowed, there were special points which made Herbert unlike other consumptive patients, and sometimes inclined a physician who saw him for the first time, to entertain doubts as to what the real cause of his sufferings was, and to begin hopefully some new treatment, which ended like all the rest in disappointment. He had been sent about from one place to another, to sea air, to mountain air, to soft Italian villas, to rough homes among the hills, and wherever he went Reine had gone with him. One Winter they had passed in the south of France, another on the shores of the Mediterranean just across the Italian border. Sometimes the two went together where English ladies were seldom seen, and where the girl half afraid, clinging to Herbert's arm as long as he was able to keep up a pretence of protecting her, and protecting him when that pretence was over, had to live the homeliest life, with almost hardship in it, in order to secure good air or tending for him.

This life had drawn them yet closer and closer together. They had read and talked together, and exchanged with each other all the eager, irrestrainable opinions of youth. Sometimes they would differ on a point and discuss it with that lively fulness of youthful talk which so often looks like eloquence; but more often the current of their thoughts ran in the same channel, as was natural with two so nearly allied. During all this time Reine had been subject to a sudden vertigo, by times, when looking at him suddenly, or recalled to it by something that was said or done, there would come to her, all at once, the terrible recollection that Herbert was doomed. But except for this and the miserable moments when a sudden conviction would seize her that he was growing worse, the time of Herbert's illness was the most happy in Reine's life. She had no one to find fault with her, no one to cross her in her ideas of right and wrong. She had no one to think of but Herbert, and to think of him and be with him had been her delight all her life. Except in the melancholy moments I have indicated, when she suddenly realized that he was going from her, Reine was happy; it is so easy to believe that the harm which is expected will not come, when it comes softly au petit pas—and so easy to feel that good is more probable than evil. She had even enjoyed their wandering, practising upon herself an easy deception; until the time came when Herbert's strength had failed altogether, and Madame de Mirfleur had been sent for, and every melancholy preparation was made which noted that it was expected of him that now he should die. Poor Reine woke up suddenly out of the thoughtless happiness she had permitted herself to fall into; might she perhaps have done better for him had she always been dwelling upon his approaching end, and instead of snatching so many flowers of innocent pleasure on the road, had thought of nothing but the conclusion which now seemed to approach so rapidly? She asked herself this question sometimes, sitting in her little chamber behind her brother's, and gazing at the snow-peaks where they stood out against the sky—but she did not know how to answer it. And in the meantime Herbert had grown more and more to be all in all to her, and she did not know how to give him up. Even now, at what everybody thought was his last stage, Reine was still ready to be assailed by those floods of hope which are terrible when they fail, as rapidly as they rose. Was this to be so? Was she to lose him, who was all in all to her? She said to herself, that to nurse him all her life long would be nothing—to give up all personal prospects and anticipations such as most girls indulge in would be nothing—nor that he should be ill always, spending his life in the dreary vicissitudes of sickness. Nothing, nothing! so long as he lived. She could bear all, be patient with everything, never grumble, never repine; indeed, these words seemed as idle words to the girl, who could think of nothing better or brighter than to nurse Herbert forever and be his perpetual companion.

Without him her life shrank into a miserable confusion and nothingness. With him, however ill he might be, however weak, she had her certain and visible place in the world, her duties which were dear to her, and was to herself a recognizable existence; but without Herbert, Reine could not realize herself. To think, as her mother had suggested, of what would happen to her when he died, of the funeral, and the dismal desolation after, was impossible to her. Her soul sickened and refused to look at such depths of misery; but yet when, more vaguely, the idea of being left alone had presented itself to her, Reine had felt with a gasp of breathless anguish, that nothing of her except the very husk and rind of herself could survive Herbert. How could she live without him? To be the least thought of in her mother's house, the last in it, yet not of it, disposed of by a man who was not her father, and whose very existence was an insult to her, and pushed aside by the children whom she never called brothers and sisters; it would not be she who should bear this, but some poor shell of her, some ghost who might bear her name.

On the special night which we have just described, when the possibility of recovery for her brother again burst upon her, she sat up late with her window open, looking out upon the moonlight as it lighted up the snow-peaks. They stood round in a close circle, peak upon peak, noiseless as ghosts and as pale, abstracted, yet somehow looking to her excited imagination as if they put their great heads together in the silence, and murmured to each other something about Herbert. It seemed to Reine that the pines too were saying something, but that was sadder, and chilled her. Earth and heaven were full of Herbert, everything was occupied about him; which indeed suited well enough with that other fantastic frenzy of hers, that God was thinking it over again, and that there was a pause in all the elements of waiting, to know how it was to be. François, Herbert's faithful servant, always sat up with him at night or slept in his room when the vigil was unnecessary, so that Reine was never called upon thus to exhaust her strength. She stole into her brother's room again in the middle of the night before she went to bed. He was still asleep, sleeping calmly without any hardness of breathing, without any feverish flush on his cheek or exhausting moisture on his forehead. He was still and in perfect rest, so happy and comfortable that François had coiled himself upon his truckle-bed and slept as soundly as the invalid he was watching. Reine laid her hand upon Herbert's forehead lightly, to feel how cool it was; he stirred a little, but no more than a child would, and by the light of the faint night-lamp, she saw that a smile came over his face like a ray of sunshine. After this she stole away back to her own room like a ghost, and dropped by the side of her little bed, unable to pray any longer, being exhausted—able to do nothing but weep, which she did in utter exhaustion of joy. God had considered, and He had found it could be done, and had pity upon her. So she concluded, poor child! and dropped asleep in her turn a little while after, helpless and feeble with happiness. Poor child! on so small a foundation can hope found itself and comfort come.

On the same night Miss Susan went back again from Antwerp to London. She had a calm passage, which was well for her, for Miss Susan was not so sure that night of God's protection as Reine was, nor could she appeal to Him for shelter against the wind and waves with the same confidence of being heard and taken care of as when she went from London to Antwerp. But happily the night was still, and the moon shining as bright and clear upon that great wayward strait, the Channel, as she did upon the noiseless whiteness of the Dolden-horn; and about the same hour when Reine fell asleep, her relation did also, lying somewhat nervous in her berth, and thinking that there was but a plank between her and eternity. She did not know of the happy change which Reine believed had taken place in the Alpine valley, any more than Reine knew in what darker transactions Miss Susan had become involved; and thus they met the future, one happy in wild hopes in what God had done for her, the other with a sombre confidence in what (she thought) she had managed for herself.

CHAPTER XI

"Reine, is it long since you heard from Aunt Susan? Look here, I don't want her tender little notes to the invalid. I am tired of always recollecting that I am an invalid. When one is dying one has enough of it, without always being reminded in one's correspondence. Is there no news? I want news. What does she say?"

"She speaks only of the Farrel-Austins,—who had gone to see her," said Reine, almost under her breath.

"Ah!" Herbert too showed a little change of sentiment at this name. Then he laughed faintly. "I don't know why I should mind," he said; "every man has a next-of-kin, I suppose, an heir-at-law, though every man does not die before his time, like me. That's what makes it unpleasant, I suppose. Well, what about Farrel-Austin, Reine? There is no harm in him that I know."

"There is great harm in him," said Reine, indignantly; "why did he go there to insult them, to make them think? And I know there was something long ago that makes Aunt Susan hate him. She says Everard was there too—I think, with Kate and Sophy—"

"And you do not like that either?" said Herbert, putting his hand upon hers and looking at her with a smile.

"I do not mind," said Reine sedately. "Why should I mind? I do not think they are very good companions for Everard," she added, with that impressive look of mature wisdom which the most youthful countenance is fond of putting on by times; "but that is my only reason. He is not very settled in his mind."

"Are you settled in your mind, Reine?"

"I? I have nothing to unsettle me," she said with genuine surprise. "I am a girl; it is different. I can stop myself whenever I feel that I am going too far. You boys cannot stop yourselves," Reine added, with the least little shake of her pretty head; "that makes frivolous companions so bad for Everard. He will go on and on without thinking."

"He is a next-of-kin, too," said Herbert with a smile. "How strange a light it throws upon them all when one is dying! I wonder what they think about me, Reine? I wonder if they are always waiting, expecting every day to bring them the news? I daresay Farrel-Austin has settled exactly what he is to do, and the changes he will make in the old house. He will be sure to make changes, if only to show that he is the master. The first great change of all will be when the White ladies themselves have to go away. Can you believe in the house without Aunt Susan, Reine? I think, for my part, it will drop to pieces, and Augustine praying against the window like a saint in painted glass. Do you know where they mean to go?"

"Herbert! you kill me when you ask me such questions."

"Because they all imply my own dying?" said Herbert. "Yes, my queen, I know. But just for the fun of the thing, tell me what do you think Farrel means to do? Will he meddle with the old almshouses, and show them all that he is Lord of the Manor and nobody else? or will he grudge the money and let Augustine keep possession of the family charities? That is what I think; he is fond of his money, and of making a good show with it, not feeding useless poor people. But then if he leaves the almshouses to her undisturbed, where will Augustine go? By Jove!" said Herbert, striking his feeble hand against his couch with the energy of a new idea, "I should not be in the least surprised if she went and lived at the almshouses herself, like one of her own poor people; she would think, poor soul, that that would please God. I am more sorry for Aunt Susan," he added after a pause, "for she is not so simple; and she has been the Squire so long, how will she ever bear to abdicate? It will be hard upon her, Reine."

Reine had turned away her head to conceal the bitter tears of disappointment that had rushed to her eyes. She had been so sure that he was better—and to be thus thrown back all at once upon this talk about his death was more than she could bear.

"Don't cry, dear," he said, "I am only discussing it for the fun of the thing; and to tell you the truth, Reine, I am keeping the chief point of the joke to myself all this time. I don't know what you will think when I tell you—"

"What, Bertie, what?"

"Don't be so anxious; I daresay it is utter nonsense. Lean down your ear that I may whisper; I am half-ashamed to say it aloud. Reine, hush! listen! Somehow I have got a strange feeling, just for a day or two, that I am not going to die at all, but to live."

"I am sure of it," cried the girl, falling on her knees and throwing her arms round him. "I know it! It was last night. God did not make up His mind till last night. I felt it in the air. I felt it everywhere. Some angel put it into my head. For all this time I have been making up my mind, and giving you up, Bertie, till yesterday; something put it into my head—the thought was not mine, or I would not have any faith in it. Something said to me, God is thinking it all over again. Oh, I know! He would not let them tell you and me both unless it was true."

"Do you think so, Reine? do you really think so?" said the sick boy—for he was but a boy—with a sudden dew in his large liquid exhausted eyes. "I thought you would laugh at me—no, of course, I don't mean laugh—but think it a piece of folly. I thought it must be nonsense myself; but do you really, really think so too?"

The only answer she could make was to kiss him, dashing off her tears that they might not come upon his face; and the two kept silent for a moment, two young faces, close together, pale, one with emotion, the other with weakness, half-angelic in their pathetic youthfulness and the inspiration of this sudden hope, smiles upon their lips, tears in their eyes, and the trembling of a confidence too ethereal for common mortality in the two hearts that beat so close together. There was something even in the utter unreasonableness of their hope which made it more touching, more pathetic still. The boy was less moved than the girl in his weakness, and in the patience which that long apprenticeship to dying had taught him. It was not so much to him who was going as to her who must remain.

"If it should be so," he said after awhile, almost in a whisper, "oh, how good we ought to be, Reine! If I failed of my duty, if I did not do what God meant me to do in everything, if I took to thinking of myself— then it would be better that things had gone on—as they are going."

"As they were going, Bertie!"

"You think so, really; you think so? Don't just say it for my feelings, for I don't mind. I was quite willing, you know, Reine."

Poor boy! already he had put his willingness in the past, unawares.

"Bertie," she said solemnly, "I don't know if you believe in the angels like me. Then tell me how this is; sometimes I have a thought in the morning which was not there at night; sometimes when I have been puzzling and wondering what to do—about you, perhaps, about mamma, about one of the many, many things," said Reine, with a celestial face of grave simplicity, "which perplex us in life,—and all at once I have had a thought which made everything clear. One moment quite in the dark, not seeing what to do; and the next, with a thought that made everything clear. Now, how did that come, Bertie? tell me. Not from me—it was put into my head, just as you pull my dress, or touch my arm, and whisper something to me in the dark. I always believe in things that are like this, put into my head."

Was it wonderful that the boy was easy to convince by this fanciful argument, and took Reine's theory very seriously? He was in a state of weakened life and impassioned hope, when the mind is very open to such theories. When the mother came in to hear that Herbert was much better, and that he meant to go out in his wheeled-chair in the afternoon, even she could scarcely guard herself against a gleam of hope. He was certainly better. "For the moment, chérie," she said to Reine, who followed her out anxiously to have her opinion; "for the moment, yes, he is better; but we cannot look for anything permanent. Do not deceive yourself, ma Reine. It is not to be so."

"Why is it not to be so? when I am sure it is to be so; it shall be so!" cried Reine.

Madame de Mirfleur shook her head. "These rallyings are often very deceitful," she said. "Often, as I told you, they mean only that the end is very near. Almost all those who die of lingering chronic illness, like our poor dear, have a last blaze-up in the socket, as it were, before the end. Do not trust to it; do not build any hopes upon it, Reine."

"But I do; but I will!" the girl said under her breath, with a shudder. When her mother went into those medical details, which she was fond of, Reine shrank always, as if from a blow.

"Yet it is possible that it might be more than a momentary rally," said Madame de Mirfleur. "I am disposed almost to hope so. The perforation may be arrested for the time by this beautiful air and the scent of the pines. God grant it! The doctors have always said it was possible. We must take the greatest care, especially of his nourishment, Reine; and if I leave you for a little while alone with him—" "Are you going away, mamma?" said Reine, with a guilty thrill of pleasure which she rebuked and heartily tried to cast out from her mind; for had she not pledged herself to be good, to bear everything, never to suffer a thought that was unkind to enter her mind, if only Herbert might recover? She dared not risk that healing by permitting within her any movement of feeling that was less than tender and kind. She stopped accordingly and changed her tone, and repeated with eagerness, "Mamma, do you think of going away?" Madame de Mirfleur felt that there was a difference in the tone with which these two identical sentences were spoken; but she was not nearly enough in sympathy with her daughter to divine what that difference meant.

"If Herbert continues to get better—and if the doctor thinks well of him when he comes to-morrow, I think I will venture to return home for a little while, to see how everything is going on." Madame de Mirfleur was half apologetic in her tone. "I am not like you, Reine," she said, kissing her daughter's cheek, "I have so many things to think of; I am torn in so many pieces; dear Herbert here; the little ones lá-bas; and my husband. What a benediction of God is this relief in the midst of our anxiety, if it will but last! Chérie, if the doctor thinks as we do, I will leave you with François to take care of my darling boy, while I go and see that all is going well in Normandy. See! I was afraid to hope; and now your hope, ma Reine, has overcome me and stolen into my heart."

Yesterday this speech would have roused one of the devils who tempted her in Reine's thoughts—and even now the evil impulse swelled upward and struggled for the mastery, whispering that Madame de Mirfleur was thinking more of the home "lá-bas," than of poor Herbert; that she was glad to seize the opportunity to get away, and a hundred other evil things. Reine grew crimson, her mother could not tell why. It was with her a struggle, poor child, to overcome this wicked thought and to cast from her mind all interpretations of her mother's conduct except the kindest one. The girl grew red with the effort she made to hold fast by her pledge and resist all temptation. It was better to let her mind be a blank without thought at all, than to allow evil thoughts to come in after she had promised to God to abandon them.

I do not think Reine had any idea that she was paying a price for Herbert's amendment by "being good," as she had vowed in her simplicity to be. It was gratitude, profound and trembling, that the innocent soul within her longed to express by this means; but still I think all unawares she had a feeling—which made her determination to be good still more pathetically strong—that perhaps if God saw her gratitude and her purpose fail, He might be less disposed to continue His great blessings to one so forgetful of them. Thus, as constantly happens in human affairs, the generous sense of gratitude longing to express itself, mingled with that secret fear of being found wanting, which lies at the bottom of every heart. Reine could not disentangle them any more than I can, or any son of Adam; but fortunately, she was less aware of the mixture than we are who look on.

"Yes mamma," she answered at length, with a meekness quite unusual to her, "I am sure you must want to see the little ones; it is only natural." This was all that Reine could manage to stammer forth.

"N'est ce pas?" said the mother pleased, though she could not read her daughter's thoughts, with this acknowledgment of the rights and claims of her other children. Madame de Mirfleur loved to ménager, and was fond of feeling herself to be a woman disturbed with many diverse cares, and generally sacrificing herself to some one of them; but she had a great deal of natural affection, and was glad to have something like a willing assent on the part of her troublesome girl to the "other ties," which she was herself too much disposed to bring in on all occasions. She kissed Reine very affectionately; and went off again to write to her husband a description of the change.

"He is better, unquestionably better," she said. "At first I feared it was the last gleam before the end; but I almost hope now it may be something more lasting. Ah, if my poor Herbert be but spared, what a benediction for all of us, and his little brothers and sisters! I know you will not be jealous, mon cher ami, of my love for my boy. If the doctor thinks well I shall leave this frightful village to-morrow, and be with thee as quickly as I can travel. What happiness, bon Dieu, to see our own house again!" She added in a P.S., "Reine is very amiable to me; hope and happiness, mon ami, are better for some natures than sorrow. She is so much softer and humbler since her brother was better." Poor Reine! Thus it will be perceived that Madame de Mirfleur, like most of her nation, was something of a philosopher too.

When Reine was left alone she did not even then make any remark to herself upon mamma's eagerness to get away to her children, whose very names on ordinary occasions the girl disliked to hear. To punish and to school herself now she recalled them deliberately; Jeannot and Camille and little Babette, all French to their finger-tips, spoilt children, whose ears the English sister, herself trained in nursery proprieties under Miss Susan's rule, had longed to box many times. She resolved now to buy some of the carved wood which haunts the traveller at every corner in Switzerland, for them, and be very good to them when she saw them again. Oh, how good Reine meant to be! Tender visions of an ideal purity arose in her mind. Herbert and she—the one raised from the brink of the grave, the other still more blessed in receiving him from that shadow of death—how could they ever be good enough, gentle enough, kind enough, to show their gratitude? Reine's young soul seemed to float in a very heaven of gentler meanings, of peace with all men, of charity and tenderness. Never, she vowed to herself, should poor man cross her path without being the better for it; never a tear fall that she could dry. Herbert, when she went to him, was much of the same mind. He had begun to believe in himself and in life, with all those unknown blessings which the boy had sweetly relinquished, scarcely knowing them, but which now seemed to come back fluttering about his head on sunny wings, like the swallows returning with the Summer.

Herbert was younger even than his years, in heart, at least—in consequence of his long ill health and seclusion, and the entire retirement from a boy's ordinary pursuits which that had made necessary; and I do not think that he had ever ventured to realize warmly, as in his feebleness he was now doing, through that visionary tender light which is the prerogative of youth, all the beauty and brightness and splendor of life. Heretofore he had turned his eyes from it, knowing that his doom had gone forth, and with a gentle philosophy avoided the sight of that which he could never enjoy. But lo! now, an accidental improvement, or what might prove an accidental improvement, acting upon a fantastic notion of Reine's, had placed him all at once, to his own consciousness, in the position of a rescued man. He was not much like a man rescued, but rather one trembling already at the gates of death, as he crept downstairs on François's arm to his chair. The other travellers in the place stood by respectfully to let him pass, and lingered after he had passed, looking after him with pity and low comments to each other. "Not long for this world," said one and another, shaking their heads; while Herbert, poor fellow, feeling his wheel-chair to be something like a victor's car, held his sister's hand as they went slowly along the road toward the waterfall, and talked to her of what they should do when they got home. It might have been heaven they were going to instead of Whiteladies, so bright were their beautiful young resolutions, their innocent plans. They meant, you may be sure, to make a heaven on earth of their Berkshire parish, to turn Whiteladies into a celestial palace and House Beautiful, and to be good as two children, as good as angels. How beautiful to them was the village road, the mountain stream running strong under the bridge, the waves washing on the pebbly edge, the heather and herbage that encroached upon the smoothness of the way! "We must not go to the waterfall; it is too far and the road is rough; but we will rest here a little, where the air comes through the pines. It is as pretty here as anywhere," said Reine. "Pretty! you mean it is beautiful; everything is beautiful," said Herbert, who had not been out of doors before since his arrival, lying back in his chair and looking at the sky, across which some flimsy cloudlets were floating. It chilled Reine somehow in the midst of her joy, to see how naturally his eyes turned to the sky.

"Never mind the clouds, Bertie dear," she said hastily, "look down the valley, how beautiful it is; or let François turn the chair round, and then you can see the mountains."

"Must I give up the sky then as if I had nothing more to do with it?" said Herbert with a boyish, pleasant laugh. Even this speech made Reine tremble; for might not God perhaps think that they were taking Him too quickly at His word and making too sure?

"The great thing," she said, eluding the question, "is to be near the pines; everybody says the pines are so good. Let them breathe upon you, Bertie, and make you strong."

"At their pleasure," said Herbert, smiling and turning his pale head toward the strong trees, murmuring with odorous breath overhead. The sunshine glowed and burned upon their great red trunks, and the dark foliage which stood close and gave forth no reflection. The bees filled the air with a continuous hum, which seemed the very voice of the warm afternoon, of the sunshine which brought forth every flimsy insect and grateful flower among the grass. Herbert sat listening in silence for some time, in that beatitude of gentle emotion which after danger is over is so sweet to the sufferer. "Sing me something, Reine," he said at last, in the caprice of that delightful mood.

Reine was seated on a stone by the side of the road, with a broad hat shading her eyes, and a white parasol over her head. She did not wait to be asked a second time. What would not she have done at Herbert's wish? She looked at him tenderly where he sat in his chair under the shadow of a kindly pine which seemed to have stepped out of the wood on purpose—and without more ado began to sing. Many a time had she sang to him when her heart was sick to death, and it took all her strength to form the notes; but to-day Reine's soul was easy and at home, and she could put all her heart into it. She sang the little air that Everard Austin had whistled as he came through the green lanes toward Whiteladies, making Miss Susan's heart glad:

"Ce que je désire, et que j'aime,
C'est toujours toi,
De mon âme le bien suprême
C'est encore toi, c'est encore toi."

Some village children came and made a little group around them listening, and the tourists in the village, much surprised, gathered about the bridge to listen too, wondering. Reine did not mind; she was singing to Herbert, no one else; and what did it matter who might be near?

CHAPTER XI

Herbert continued much better next day. It had done him good to be out, and already François, with that confidence in all simple natural remedies which the French, and indeed all continental nations, have so much more strongly than we, asserted boldly that it was the pines which had already done so much for his young master. I do not think that Reine and Herbert, being half English, had much faith in the pines. They referred the improvement at once, and directly, to a higher hand, and were glad, poor children, to think that no means had been necessary, but that God had done it simply by willing it, in that miraculous simple way which seems so natural to the primitive soul. The doctor, when he came next day upon his weekly visit from Thun or Interlaken, was entirely taken by surprise. I believe that from week to week he had scarcely expected to see his patient living; and now he was up, and out, coming back to something like appetite and ease, and as full of hope as youth could be. The doctor shook his head, but was soon infected, like the others, by this atmosphere of hopefulness. He allowed that a wonderful progress had been made; that there always were special circumstances in this case which made it unlike other cases, and left a margin for unexpected results. And when Madame de Mirfleur took him aside to ask about the state of the tissue, and whether the perforations were arrested, he still said, though with hesitation and shakings of the head, that he could not say that it might not be the beginning of a permanent favorable turn in the disease, or that healing processes might not have set in. "Such cases are very unlikely," he said. "They are of the nature of miracles, and we are very reluctant to believe in them; but still at M. Austin's age, it is impossible to deny that results utterly unexpected happen sometimes. Sometimes, at rare intervals; and no one can calculate upon them. It might be that it was really the commencement of a permanent improvement; and nothing can be better for him than the hopeful state of mind in which he is."

"Then, M. le docteur," said Madame de Mirfleur, anxiously, "you think I may leave him? You think I may go and visit my husband and my little ones, for a little time—a very little time—without fear?"

"Nothing is impossible," said the doctor, "nor can I guarantee anything till we see how M. Austin goes on. If the improvement continues for a week or two—"

"But I shall be back in a week or two," said the woman, whose heart was torn asunder, in a tone of dismay; and at length she managed to extort from the doctor something which she took for a permission. It was not that she loved Herbert less—but perhaps it was natural that she should love the babies, and the husband whose name she bore, and who had separated her from the life to which the other family belonged—more. Madame de Mirfleur did not enter into any analysis of her feelings, as she hurried in a flutter of pleasant excitement to pack her necessaries for the home journey. Reine, always dominated by that tremulous determination to do good at any cost, carefully refrained also, but with more difficulty, from any questioning with herself about her mother's sentiments. She made the best of it to Herbert, who was somewhat surprised that his mother should leave him, having acquired that confidence of the sick in the fact of their own importance, to which everything must give way. He was not wounded, being too certain, poor boy, of being the first object in his little circle, but he was surprised.

"Reflect, Herbert, mamma has other people to think of. There are the little ones; little children are constantly having measles, and colds, and indigestions; and then, M. de Mirfleur—"

"I thought you disliked to think of M. de Mirfleur, Reine?"

"Ah! so I do; but, Bertie, I have been very unkind, I have hated him, and been angry with mamma, without reason. It seems to be natural to some people to marry," said the girl, after a pause, "and we ought not to judge them; it is not wrong to wish that one's mother belonged to one, that she did not belong to other people, is it? But that is all. Mamma thought otherwise. Bertie, we were little, and we were so much away in England. Six months in the year, fancy, and then she must have been lonely. We do not take these things into account when we are children," said Reine; "but after, when we can think, many things become clear."

It was thus with a certain grandeur of indulgence and benevolence that the two young people saw their mother go away. That she should have a husband and children at all was a terrible infringement of the ideal, and brought her down unquestionably to a lower level in their primitive world; but granting the husband and the children, as it was necessary to do, no doubt she had, upon that secondary level, a certain duty to them. They bade her good-bye tenderly, their innate disapproval changing, with their altered moral view, from irritation and disappointment into a condescending sweetness. "Poor mamma! I do not see that it was possible for her to avoid going," Reine said; and perhaps, after all, it was this disapproved of, and by no means ideal mother, who felt the separation most keenly when the moment came. When a woman takes a second life upon her, no doubt she must resign herself to give up something of the sweetness of the first; and it would be demanding too much of human nature to expect that the girl and boy, who were fanciful and even fantastic in their poetical and visionary youth, could be as reverent of mother as if she had altogether belonged to them. Men and women, I fear, will never be equal in this world, were all conventional and outside bonds removed to-morrow. The widower-father does not descend from any pedestal when he forms what Madame de Mirfleur called "new ties," as does the widow-mother; and it will be a strange world, when, if ever, we come to expect no more from women than we do from men; it being granted, sure enough, that in other ways more is to be expected from men than from women. Herbert sat in his chair on the balcony to see her go away, smiling and waving his thin hand to his mother; and Reine, at the carriage-door, kissed her blandly, and watched her drive off with a tender, patronizing sense that was quite natural. But the mother, poor woman, though she was eager to get away, and had "other ties" awaiting her, looked at them through eyes half blinded with tears, and felt a pang of inferiority of which she had never before been sensible. She was not an ideal personage, but she felt, without knowing how, the loss of her position, and that descent from the highest, by which she had purchased her happiness.

These momentary sensations would be a great deal more hard upon us if we could define them to ourselves, as you and I, dear reader, can define them when we see them thus going on before us; but fortunately few people have the gift to do this in their own case. So that Madame de Mirfleur only knew that her heart was wrung with pain to leave her boy, who might be dying still, notwithstanding his apparent improvement. And, by-and-by, as her home became nearer, and Herbert farther off, the balance turned involuntarily, and she felt only how deep must be her own maternal tenderness when the pang of leaving Herbert could thus overshadow her pleasure in the thought of meeting all the rest.

Reine came closer to her brother when she went back to him, with a sense that if she had not been trying with all her might to be good, she would have felt injured and angry at her mother's desertion. "I don't know so much as mamma, but I know how to take care of you, Bertie," she said, smoothing back the hair from his forehead with that low caressing coo of tenderness which mothers use to their children.

"You have always been my nurse, Reine," he said gratefully,—then after a pause—"and by-and-by I mean to require no nursing, but to take care of you."

And thus they went out again, feeling half happy, half forsaken, but gradually grew happier and happier, as once more the air from the pines blew about Herbert's head; and he got out of his chair on François's arm and walked into the wood, trembling a little in his feebleness, but glad beyond words, and full of infinite hope. It was the first walk he had taken, and Reine magnified it, till it came to look, as Bertie said, as if he had crossed the pass without a guide, and was the greatest pedestrian in all the Kanderthal. He sat up to dinner, after a rest; and how they laughed over it, and talked, projecting expeditions of every possible and impossible kind, to which the Gemmi was nothing, and feeling their freedom from all comment, and happy privilege of being as foolish as they pleased! Grave François even smiled at them as he served their simple meal; "Enfants!" he said, as they burst into soft peals of laughter—unusual and delicious laughter, which had sounded so sick and faint in the chamber to which death seemed always approaching. They had the heart to laugh now, these two young creatures, alone in the world. But François did not object to their laughter, or think it indecorous, by reason of the strong faith he had in the pines, which seemed to him, after so many things that had been tried in vain, at last the real cure.

Thus they went on for a week or more, after Madame de Mirfleur left them, as happy as two babies, doing (with close regard to Herbert's weakness and necessities) what seemed good in their own eyes—going out daily, sitting in the balcony, watching the parties of pilgrims who came and went, amusing themselves (now that the French mother was absent, before whom neither boy nor girl would betray that their English country-folks were less than perfect) over the British tourists with their alpenstocks. Such of these same tourists as lingered in the valley grew very tender of the invalid and his sister, happily unaware that Reine laughed at them. They said to each other, "He is looking much better," and, "What a change in a few days!" and, "Please God, the poor young fellow will come round after all." The ladies would have liked to go and kiss Reine, and God bless her for a good girl devoted to her sick brother; and the men would have been fain to pat Herbert on the shoulder, and bid him keep a good heart, and get well, to reward his pretty sister, if for nothing else; while all the time the boy and girl,

Heaven help them, made fun of the British tourists from their balcony, and felt themselves as happy as the day was long, fear and the shadow of death having melted quite away.

I am loath to break upon this gentle time, or show how their hopes came to nothing; or at least sank for the time in deeper darkness than ever. One sultry afternoon the pair sallied forth with the intention of staying in the pine-wood a little longer than usual, as Herbert daily grew stronger. It was very hot, not a leaf astir, and insupportable in the little rooms, where all the walls were baked, and the sun blazing upon the closed shutters. Once under the pines, there would be nature and air, and there they could stay till the sun was setting; for no harm could come to the tenderest invalid on such a day. But as the afternoon drew on, ominous clouds appeared over the snow of the hills, and before preparations could be made to meet it, one of the sudden storms of mountainous countries broke upon the Kanderthal. Deluges of rain swept down from the sky, an hour ago so blue, rain, and hail in great solid drops like stones beating against the wayfarer. When it was discovered that the brother and sister were out of doors, the little inn was in an immediate commotion. One sturdy British tourist, most laughable of all, who had just returned with a red face, peeled and smarting, from a long walk in the sun, rushed at the only mule that was to be had, and harnessed it himself, wildly swearing (may it be forgiven him!) unintelligible oaths, into the only covered vehicle in the place, and lashed the brute into a reluctant gallop, jolting on the shaft or running by the side in such a state of redness and moisture as is possible only to an Englishman of sixteen-stone weight. They huddled Herbert, faintly smiling his thanks, and Reine, trembling and drenched, and deadly pale, into the rude carriage, and jolted them back over the stony road, the British tourist rushing on in advance to order brandy and water enough to have drowned Herbert. But, alas! the harm was done. It is a long way to Thun from the Kanderthal, but the doctor was sent for, and the poor lad had every attention that in such a place it was possible to give him. Reine went back to her seat by the bedside with a change as from life to death in her face. She would not believe it when the doctor spoke to her, gravely shaking his head once more, and advised that her mother should be sent for. "You must not be alone," he said, looking at her pitifully, and in his heart wondering what kind of stuff the mother was made of who could leave such a pair of children in such circumstances. He had taken Reine out of the room to say this to her, and to add that he would himself telegraph, as soon as he got back to Thun, for Madame de Mirfleur. "One cannot tell what may happen within the next twenty-four hours," said the doctor, "and you must not be alone." Then poor Reine's pent-up soul burst forth. What was the use of being good, of trying so hard, so hard! as she had done, to make the best of everything, to blame no one, to be tender, and kind, and charitable? She had tried, O Heaven, with all her heart and might; and this was what it had come back to again!

"Oh, don't! don't!" she cried, in sharp anguish. "No; let me have him all to myself. I love him. No one else does. Oh, let her alone! She has her husband and her children. She was glad when my Bertie was better, that she might go to them. Why should she come back now? What is he to her? the last, the farthest off, less dear than the baby, not half so much to her as her house and her husband, and all the new things she cares for. But he is everything to me, all I have, and all I want. Oh, let us alone! let us alone!"

"Dear young lady," said the compassionate doctor, "your grief is too much for you; you don't know what you say."

"Oh, I know! I know!" cried Reine. "She was glad he was better, that she might go; that was all she thought of. Don't send for her; I could not bear to see her. She will say she knew it all the time, and blame you for letting her go—though you know she longed to go. Oh, let me have him to myself! I care for nothing else—nothing—now—nothing in the world!"

"You must not say so; you will kill yourself," said the doctor.

"Oh, I wish, I wish I could; that would be the best. If you would only kill me with Bertie! but you have not the courage—you dare not. Then, doctor, leave us together—leave us alone, brother and sister. I have no one but him, and he has no one but me. Mamma is married; she has others to think of; leave my Bertie to me. I know how to nurse him, doctor," said Reine, clasping her hands. "I have always done it, since I was so high; he is used to me, and he likes me best. Oh, let me have him all to myself!"

These words went to the hearts of those who heard them; and, indeed, there were on the landing several persons waiting who heard them—some English ladies, who had stopped in their journey out of pity to "be of use to the poor young creature," they said; and the landlady of the inn, who was waiting outside to hear how Herbert was. The doctor, who was a compassionate man, as doctors usually are, gave them what satisfaction he could; but that was very small. He said he would send for the mother, of course; but, in the meantime, recommended that no one should interfere with Reine unless "something should happen." "Do you think it likely anything should happen before you come back?" asked one of the awe-stricken women. But the doctor only shook his head, and said he could answer for nothing; but that in case anything happened, one of them should take charge of Reine. More than one kind-hearted stranger in the little inn kept awake that night, thinking of the poor forlorn girl and dying boy, whose touching union had been noted by all the village. The big Englishman who had brought them home out of the storm, cried like a baby in the coffee-room as he told to some new-comers how Reine had sat singing songs to her brother, and how the poor boy had mended, and began to look like life again. "If it had not been for this accursed storm!" cried the good man, upon which one of the new arrivals rebuked him. There was little thought of in the village that night but the two young Englanders, without their mother, or a friend near them. But when the morning came, Herbert still lived; he lived through that dreary day upon the little strength he had acquired during his temporary improvement. During this terrible time Reine would not leave him except by moments now and then, when she would go out on the balcony and look up blank and tearless to the skies, which were so bright again. Ah! why were they bright, after all the harm was done? Had they covered themselves with clouds, it would have been more befitting, after all they had brought about. I cannot describe the misery in Reine's heart. It was something more, something harder and more bitter than grief. She had a bewildered sense that God Himself had wronged her, making her believe something which He did not mean to come true. How could she pray? She had prayed once, and had been answered, she thought, and then cast aside, and all her happiness turned into woe. If He had said No at first it would have been hard enough, but she could have borne it; but He had seemed to grant, and then had withdrawn the blessing; He had mocked her with a delusive reply. Poor Reine felt giddy in the world, having lost the centre of it, the soul of it, the God to whom she could appeal. She had cast herself rashly upon this ordeal by fire, staked her faith of every day, her child's confidence, upon a miracle, and, holding out her hand for it, had found it turn to nothing. She stood dimly looking out from the balcony on the third night after Herbert's relapse. The stars were coming out in the dark sky, and to anybody but Reine, who observed nothing external, the wind was cold. She stood in a kind of trance, saying nothing, feeling the wind blow upon her with the scent of the pines, which made her sick; and the stars looked coldly at her, friends no longer, but alien inquisitive lights peering out of an unfriendly heaven. Herbert lay in an uneasy sleep, weary and restless as are the dying, asking in his dreams to be raised up, to have the window opened, to get more air. Restless, too, with the excitement upon her of what was coming, she had wandered out, blank to all external sounds and sights, not for the sake of the air, but only to relieve the misery which nothing relieved. She did not even notice the carriage coming along the darkening road, which the people at the inn were watching eagerly, hoping that it brought the mother. Reine was too much exhausted by this time to think even of her mother. She was still standing in the same attitude, neither hearing nor noticing, when the carriage drew up at the door. The excitement of the inn people had subsided, for it had been apparent for some time that the inmate of the carriage was a man. He jumped lightly down at the door, a young man light of step and of heart, but paused, and looked up at the figure in the balcony, which stood so motionless, seeming to watch him. "Ah, Reine! is it you? I came off at once to congratulate you," he said, in his cheery English voice. It was Everard Austin, who had heard of Herbert's wonderful amendment, and had come on at once, impulsive and sanguine, to take part in their joy. That was more in his way than consoling suffering, though he had a kind heart.

CHAPTER XIII

Miss Susan's absence from home had been a very short one—she left and returned within the week; and during this time matters went on very quietly at Whiteladies. The servants had their own way in most things—they gave Miss Augustine her spare meals when they pleased, though Martha, left in charge, stood over her to see that she ate something. But Stevens stood upon no ceremony—he took off his coat and went into the garden, which was his weakness, and there enjoyed a carnival of digging and dibbling, until the gardener grumbled, who was not disposed to have his plants meddled with.

"He has been a touching of my geraniums," said this functionary; "what do he know about a garden? Do you ever see me a poking of myself into the pantry a cleaning of his spoons?"

"No, bless you," said the cook; "nobody don't see you a putting of your hand to work as you ain't forced to. You know better, Mr. Smithers."

"That ain't it, that ain't it," said Smithers, somewhat discomfited; and he went out forthwith, and made an end of the amateur. "Either it's my garden, or it ain't," said the man of the spade; "if it is, you'll get out o' that in ten minutes' time. I can't be bothered with fellers here as don't know the difference between a petuniar and a nasty choking rubbish of a bindweed."

"You might speak a little more civil to them as helps you," said Stevens, humbled by an unfortunate mistake he had made; but still not without some attempt at self-assertion.

"Help! you wait till I asks you for your help," said the gardener. And thus Stevens was driven back to his coat, his pantry, and the proprieties of life, before Miss Susan's return.

As for Augustine, she gathered her poor people round her in the almshouse chapel every morning, and said her prayers among the pensioners, whom she took so much pains to guide in their devotion, for the benefit of her family and the expiation of their sins. The poor people in the almshouses were not perhaps more pious than any other equal number of people in the village; but they all hobbled to their seats in the chapel, and said their Amens, led by Josiah Tolladay—who had been parish clerk in his day, and pleased himself in this shadow of his ancient office—with a certain fervor. Some of them grumbled, as who does not grumble at a set duty, whatever it may be? but I think the routine of the daily service was rather a blessing to most of them, giving them a motive for exerting themselves, for putting on clean caps, and brushing their old coats. The almshouses lay near the entrance of the village of St. Austin's, a square of old red-brick houses, built two hundred years ago, with high dormer windows, and red walls, mellowed into softness by age. They had been suffered to fall into decay by several generations of Austins, but had been restored to thorough repair and to their original use by Miss Augustine, who had added a great many conveniences and advantages, unthought of in former days, to the little cottages, and had done everything that could be done to make the lives of her beadsmen and beadswomen agreeable. She was great herself on the duty of self-denial, fasted much, and liked to punish her delicate and fragile outer woman, which, poor soul, had little strength to spare; but she petted her pensioners, and made a great deal of their little ailments, and kept the cook at Whiteladies constantly occupied for them, making dainty dishes to tempt the appetites of old humbugs of both sexes, who could eat their own plain food very heartily when this kind and foolish lady was out of the way. She was so ready to indulge them, that old Mrs. Tolladay was quite right in calling the gentle foundress, the abstract, self-absorbed, devotional creature, whose life was dedicated to prayer for her family, a great temptation to her neighbors. Miss Augustine was so anxious to make up for all her grandfathers and grandmothers had done, and to earn a pardon for their misdeeds, that she could deny nothing to her poor.

The almshouses formed a square of tiny cottages, with a large garden in the midst, which absorbed more plants, the gardener said, than all the gardens at Whiteladies. The entrance from the road was through a gateway, over which was a clock-tower; and in this part of the building were situated the pretty, quaint little rooms occupied by the chaplain. Right opposite, at the other end of the garden, was the chapel; and all the houses opened upon the garden which was pretty and bright with flowers, with a large grassplot in the midst, and a fine old mulberry tree, under which the old people would sit and bask in the sunshine. There were about thirty of them, seven or eight houses on each side of the square—a large number to be maintained by one family; but I suppose that the first Austins had entertained a due sense of their own wickedness, and felt that no small price was required to buy them off. Half of these people at least, however, were now at Miss Augustine's charges. The endowment, being in land, and in a situation where land rises comparatively little in value, had ceased to be sufficient for so large a number of pensioners—and at least half of the houses had been left vacant, and falling into decay in the time of the late Squire and his father. It had been the enterprise of Miss Augustine's life to set this family charity fully forth again, according to the ordinance of the first founder—and almost all her fortune was dedicated to that and to the new freak of the chantry. She had chosen her poor people herself from the village and neighborhood, and perhaps on the whole they were not badly chosen. She had selected the chaplain herself, a quaint, prim little old man, with a wife not unlike himself, who fitted into the rooms in the tower, and whose object in life for their first two years had been to smooth down Miss Augustine, and keep her within the limits of good sense. Happily they had given that over before the time at which this story commences, and now contented themselves with their particular mission to the old almspeople themselves. These were enough to give them full occupation. They were partly old couples, husband and wife, and partly widows and single people; and they were as various in their characteristics as every group of human persons are, "a sad handful," as old Mrs. Tolladay said. Dr. Richard and his wife had enough to do, to keep them in order, what with Miss Augustine's vagaries, and what with the peculiarities of the Austin pensioners themselves.

The two principal sides of the square, facing each other—the gate side and the chapel side—had each a faction of its own. The chapel side was led by old Mrs. Matthews, who was the most prayerful woman in the community, or at least had the credit among her own set of being so—the gate side, by Sarah Storton, once the laundress at Whiteladies, who was, I fear, a very mundane personage, and did not hesitate to speak her mind to Miss Augustine herself. Old Mrs. Tolladay lived on the south side, and was the critic and historian, or bard, of both the factions. She was the wife of the old clerk, who rang the chapel bell, and led with infinite self-importance the irregular fire of Amens, which was so trying to Dr. Richard; but many of the old folks were deaf, and not a few stupid, and how could they be expected to keep time in the responses? Old Mrs. Matthews, who had been a Methodist once upon a time, and still was suspected of proclivities toward chapel, would groan now and then, without any warning, in the middle of the service, making Dr. Richard, whose nerves were sensitive, jump; and on Summer days, when the weather was hot, and the chapel close and drowsy, one of the old men would indulge in an occasional snore, quickly strangled by his helpmate—which had a still stronger effect on the Doctor's nerves. John Simmons, who had no wife to wake him, was the worst offender on such occasions. He lived on the north side, in the darkest and coldest of all the cottages, and would drop his head upon his old breast, and doze contentedly, filling the little chapel with audible indications of his beatific repose. Once Miss Augustine herself had risen from her place, and walking solemnly down the chapel, in the midst of the awe-stricken people, had awakened John, taking her slim white hand out of her long sleeves, and making him start with a cold touch upon his shoulder. "It will be best to stay away out of God's house if you cannot join in our prayers," Miss Augustine had said, words which in his fright and compunction the old man did not understand. He thought he was to be turned out of his poor little cold cottage, which was a palace to him, and awaited the next Monday, on which he received his weekly pittance from the chaplain, with terrified expectation. "Be I to go, sir?" said old John, trembling in all his old limbs; for he had but "the House" before him as an alternative, and the reader knows what a horror that alternative is to most poor folks.

"Miss Augustine has said nothing about it," said Dr. Richard; "but John, you must not snore in church; if you will sleep, which is very reprehensible, why should you snore, John?"

"It's my misfortune, sir," said the old man. "I was always a snoring sleeper, God forgive me; there's many a one, as you say, sir, as can take his nap quiet, and no one know nothing about it; but, Doctor, I don't mean no harm, and it ain't my fault."

"You must take care not to sleep, John," said Dr. Richard, shaking his head, "that is the great thing. You'll not snore if you don't sleep."

"I donnow that," said John doubtfully, taking up his shillings. The old soul was hazy, and did not quite know what he was blamed for. Of all the few enjoyments he had, that Summer doze in the warm atmosphere was perhaps the sweetest. Sleep that knits up the ravelled sleeve of care—John felt it to be one of the best things in this world, though he did not know what any idle book had said.

At nine o'clock every morning James Tolladay sallied out of his cottage, with the key of the chapel, opened the door, and began to tug at the rope, which dangled so temptingly just out of the reach of the children, when they came to see their grandfathers and grandmothers at the almshouses. The chapel was not a very good specimen of architecture, having been built in the seventeenth century; and the bell which James Tolladay rung was not much of a bell; but still it marked nine o'clock to the village, the clergyman of the parish being a quiet and somewhat indolent person, who had, up to this time, resisted the movement in favor of daily services. Tolladay kept on ringing while the old people stumbled past him into their benches, and the Doctor, in his surplice, and little Mrs. Richard in her little trim bonnet—till Miss Augustine came along the path from the gate like a figure in a procession, with her veil on her head in Summer, and her hood in Winter, and with her hands folded into her long, hanging sleeves. Miss Augustine always came alone, a solitary figure in the sunshine, and walked abstracted and solemn across the garden, and up the length of the chapel to the seat which was left for her on one side of the altar rails. Mrs. Richard had a place on the other side, but Miss Augustine occupied a sort of stall, slightly raised, and very visible to all the congregation. The Austin arms were on this stall, a sign of proprietorship not perhaps quite in keeping with the humble meaning of the chapel; and Miss Augustine had blazoned it with a legend in very ecclesiastical red and blue—"Pray for us," translated with laudable intentions, out of the Latin, in order to be understood by the congregation, but sent back into obscurity by the church decorator, whose letters were far too good art to be comprehensible. The old women, blinking under their old dingy bonnets, which some of them still insisted upon wearing "in the fashion," with here and there a tumbled red and yellow rose, notwithstanding all that Mrs. Richard could say; and the old men with their heads sunk into the shabby collars of their old coats, sitting tremulous upon the benches, over which Miss Augustine could look from her high seat, immediately finding out any defaulter—were a pitiful assemblage enough, in that unloveliness of age and weakness which the very poor have so little means of making beautiful; but they were not without interest, nor their own quaint humor had any one there been of the mind to discover it. Of this view of the assemblage I need not say Miss Augustine was quite unconscious; her ear caught Mrs. Matthews's groan of unction with a sense of happiness, and she was pleased by the fervor of the dropping Amen, which made poor Dr. Richard so nervous. She did not mind the painful fact that at least a minute elapsed between John Tolladay's clerkly solemnity of response and the fitful gust with which John Simmons in the background added his assisting voice.

Miss Augustine was too much absorbed in her own special interests to be a Ritualist or not a Ritualist, or to think at all of Church politics. She was confused in her theology, and determined to have her family prayed for, and their sins expiated, without asking herself whether it was release from purgatory which she anticipated as the answer to her prayers, or simply a turning aside of the curse for the future. I think the idea in her mind was quite confused, and she neither knew nor was at any trouble to ascertain exactly what she meant. Accordingly, though many people, and the rector himself among them, thought Miss Augustine to be of the highest sect of the High Church, verging upon Popery itself, Miss Augustine in reality found more comfort in the Dissenting fervor of the old woman who was a "Methody," than in the most correct Church worship. What she wanted, poor soul, was that semi-commercial, semi-visionary traffic, in which not herself but her family were to be the gainers. She was a merchant organizing this bargain with heaven, the nature of which she left vague even to herself; and those who aided her with most apparent warmth of supplications, were the people whom she most appreciated, with but little regard to the fashion of their exertions. John Simmons, when he snored, was like a workman shirking work to Miss Augustine. But even Dr. Richard and his wife had not fathomed this downright straightforward business temper which existed without her own knowledge, or any one else's, in the strange visionary being with whom they had to do. She, indeed, put her meaning simply into so many words, but it was impossible for those good people to take her at her own word, and to believe that she expressed all she meant, and nothing less or more.

There was a little prayer used in the almshouse chapel for the family of the founder, which Dr. Richard had consented, with some difficulty, to add after the collects at Morning and Evening Service, and which he had a strong impression was uncanonical, and against the rubrics, employing it, so to speak, under protest, and explaining to every chance stranger that it was "a tradition of the place from time immemorial."

"I suppose we are not at liberty to change lightly any ancient use," said the chaplain, "at least such was the advice of my excellent friend the Bishop of the Leeward Islands, in whose judgment I have great confidence. I have not yet had an opportunity of laying the matter before the Bishop of my own diocese, but I have little doubt his lordship will be of the same opinion."

With this protestation of faith, which I think was much stronger than Dr. Richard felt, the chaplain used the prayer; but he maintained a constant struggle against Miss Augustine, who would have had him add sentences to it from time to time, as various family exigencies arose. On one of the days of Miss Susan's absence a thought of this kind came into her sister's head. Augustine felt that Miss Susan being absent, and travelling, and occupied with her business, whatever it was, might, perhaps, omit to read the Lessons for the day, as was usual, or would be less particular in her personal devotions. She thought this over all evening, and dreamed of it at night; and in the morning she sent a letter to the chaplain as soon as she woke, begging him to add to his prayer for the founder's family the words, "and for such among them as may be specially exposed to temptation this day." Dr. Richard took a very strong step on this occasion—he refused to do it. It was a great thing for a man to do, the comfort of whose remnant of life hung upon the pleasure of his patroness; but he knew it was an illegal liberty to take with his service, and he would not do it.

Miss Augustine was very self-absorbed, and very much accustomed (though she thought otherwise) to have everything her own way, and when she perceived that this new petition of hers was not added to the prayer for her family, she disregarded James Tolladay's clerkly leading of the responses even more than John Simmons did. She made a little pause, and repeated it herself, in an audible voice, and then said her Amen, keeping everybody waiting for her, and Dr. Richard standing mute and red on the chancel steps, with the words, as it might be, taken out of his very lips. When they all came out of chapel, Mrs. Matthews had a private interview with Miss Augustine, which detained her, and it was not till after the old people had dispersed to their cottages that she made her way over to the clock-tower in which the chaplain's rooms were situated. "You did not pray for my people, as I asked you," said Augustine, looking at him with her pale blue eyes. She was not angry or irritable, but asked the question softly. Dr. Richard had been waiting for her in his dining-room, which was a quaint room over the archway, with one window looking to the road, another to the garden. He was seated by the table, his wife beside him, who had not yet taken off her bonnet, and who held her smelling-salts in her hand.

"Miss Augustine," said the chaplain, with a little flush on his innocent aged face. He was a plump, neat little old man, with the red and white of a girl in his gentle countenance. He had risen up when she entered, but being somewhat nervous sat down again, though she never sat down. "Miss Augustine," he said, solemnly, "I have told you before, I cannot do anything, even to oblige you, which is against Church law and every sound principle. Whatever happens to me, I must be guided by law."

"Does law forbid you to pray for your fellow-creatures who are in temptation?" said Miss Augustine, without any change of her serious abstracted countenance.

"Miss Augustine, this is a question in which I cannot be dictated to," said the old gentleman, growing redder. "I will ask the prayers of the congregation for any special person who may be in trouble, sorrow, or distress, before the Litany, or the collect for all conditions of men, making a pause at the appropriate petition, as is my duty; but I cannot go beyond the rubrics, whatever it may cost me," said Dr. Richard, with a look of determined resolution, as though he looked for nothing better than to be led immediately to the stake. And his wife fixed her eyes upon him admiringly, backing him up; and put, with a little pressure of his fingers, her smelling-salts into his hand.

"In that case," said Miss Augustine, in her abstract way, "in that case—I will not ask you; but it is a pity the rubrics should say it is your duty not to pray for any one in temptation; it was Susan," she added, softly, with a sigh.

"Miss Susan!" said the chaplain, growing hotter than ever at the thought that he had nearly been betrayed into the impertinence of praying for a person whom he so much respected. He was horrified at the risk he had run. "Miss Augustine," he said, severely, "if my conscience had permitted me to do this, which I am glad it did not, what would your sister have said? I could never have looked her in the face again, after taking such a liberty with her."

"We could never have looked her in the face again," echoed Mrs. Richard; "but, thank God, my dear, you stood fast!"

"Yes. I hope true Church principles and a strong resolution will always save me," said the Doctor, with gentle humility, "and that I may always have the resolution to stand fast."

Miss Augustine made no reply to this for the moment. Then she said, without any change of tone, "Say, to-morrow, please, that prayers are requested for Susan Austin, on a voyage, and in temptation abroad."

"My dear Miss Augustine!" said the unhappy clergyman, taking a sniff at the salts, which now were truly needed.

"Yes, that will come to the same thing," said Miss Augustine quietly to herself.

She stood opposite to the agitated pair, with her hands folded into her great sleeves, her hood hanging back on her shoulders, her black veil falling softly about her pale head. There was no emotion in her countenance. Her mind was not alarmed about her sister. The prayer was a precautionary measure, to keep Susan out of temptation—not anything strenuously called for by necessity. She sighed softly as she made the reflection, that to name her sister before the Litany was said would answer her purpose equally well; and thus with a faint smile, and slight wave of her hand toward the chaplain and his wife, she turned and went away. The ordinary politenesses were lost upon Miss Augustine, and the door stood open behind her, so that there was no need for Dr. Richard to get up and open it; and, indeed, they were so used to her ways, her comings and her goings, that he did not think of it. So the old gentleman sat with his wife by his side, backing him up, gazing with consternation, and without a word, at the gray retreating figure. Mrs. Richard, who saw her husband's perturbed condition, comforted him as best she could, patting his arm with her soft little hand, and whispering words of consolation. When Miss Augustine was fairly out of the house, the distressed clergyman at last permitted his feelings to burst forth.

"Pray for Susan Austin publicly by name!" he said, rising and walking about the room. "My dear, it will ruin us! This comes of women having power in the Church! I don't mean to say anything, my dear, injurious to your sex, which you know I respect deeply—in its own place; but a woman's interference in the Church is enough to send the wisest man out of his wits."

"Dear Henery," said Mrs. Richard, for it was thus she pronounced her husband's name, "why should you be so much disturbed about it, when you know she is mad?"

"It is only her enemies who say she is mad," said Dr. Richard; "and even if she is mad, what does that matter? There is nothing against the rubrics in what she asks of me now. I shall be forced to do it; and what will Miss Susan say? And consider that all our comfort, everything depends upon it. Ellen, you are very sensible; but you don't grasp the full bearing of the subject as I do."

"No, my dear, I do not pretend to have your mind," said the good wife; "but things never turn out so bad as we fear," she said a moment after, with homely philosophy—"nor so good, either," she added, with a sigh.

CHAPTER XIV

Miss Susan came home on the Saturday night. She was very tired, and saw no one that evening; but Martha, her old maid, who returned into attendance upon her natural mistress at once, thought and reported to the others that "something had come over Miss Susan." Whether it was tiredness or crossness, or bad news, or that her business had not turned out so well as she expected, no one could tell; but "something had come, over her." Next morning she did not go to church—a thing which had not happened in the Austin family for ages.

"I had an intuition that you were yielding to temptation," Miss Augustine said, with some solemnity, as she went out to prayers at the almshouses; after which she meant to go to Morning Service in the church, as always.

"I am only tired, my dear," said Miss Susan, with a little shiver.

The remarks in the kitchen were more stringent than Miss Augustine's.

"Foreign parts apparently is bad for the soul," said Martha, when it was ascertained that Jane, too, following her mistress's example, did not mean to go to Church.

"They're demoralizin', that's what they are," said Stevens, who liked a long word.

"I've always said as I'd never set foot out o' my own country, not for any money," said Cook, with the liberal mind natural to her craft.

Poor Jane, who had been very ill on the crossing, though the sea was calm, sat silent at the chimney corner with a bad headache, and very devout intentions to the same effect.

"If you knew what it was to go a sea-voyage, like I do," she protested with forlorn pride, "you'd have a deal more charity in you." But even Jane's little presents, brought from "abroad," did not quite conciliate the others, to whom this chit of a girl had been preferred. Jane, on the whole, however, was better off, even amid the criticisms of the kitchen, than Miss Susan was, seated by herself in the drawing-room, to which the sun did not come round till the afternoon, with the same picture hanging before her eyes which she had used to tempt the Austins at Bruges, with a shawl about her shoulders, and a sombre consciousness in her heart that had never before been known there. It was one of those dull days which so often interpose their unwelcome presence into an English Summer. The sky and the world were gray with east wind, the sun hidden, the color all gone out. The trees stood about and shivered, striking the clouds with their hapless heads; the flowers looked pitiful and appealing, as if they would have liked to be brought indoors and kept in shelter; and the dreariness of the fire-place, done up in white paper ornaments, as is the orthodox Summer fashion of England, was unspeakable. Miss Susan, drawing her shawl round her, sat in her easy-chair near the fire by habit; and a more dismal centre of the room could not have been than that chilly whiteness. How she would have liked a fire! but in the beginning of July, what Englishwoman, with the proper fear of her housemaid before her eyes, would dare to ask for that indulgence? So Miss Susan sat and shivered, and watched the cold trees looking in at the window, and the gray sky above, and drew her shawl closer with a shiver that went through her very heart. The vibration of the Church bells was in the still, rural air, and not a sound in the house.

Miss Susan felt as if she were isolated by some stern power; set apart from the world because of "what had happened;" which was the way she described her own very active agency during the past week to herself. But this did not make her repent, or change her mind in any respect; the excitement of her evil inspiration was still strong upon her; and then there was yet no wrong done, only intended, and of course, at any moment, the wrong which was only in intention might be departed from, and all be well. She had that morning received a letter from Reine, full of joyous thanksgiving over Herbert's improvement. Augustine, who believed in miracles, had gone off to church in great excitement, to put up Herbert's name as giving thanks, and to tell the poor people that their prayers had been so far heard; but Miss Susan, who was more of this world, and did not believe in miracles, and to whom the fact that any human event was very desirable made it at once less likely, put very little faith in Reine's letter. "Poor child! poor boy!" she said to herself, shaking her head and drying her eyes; then put it aside, and thought little more of it. Her own wickedness that she planned was more exciting to her. She sat and brooded over that, while all the parish said their prayers in church, where she, too, ought to have been. For she was not, after all, so very tired; her mind was as full and lively as if there had been no such a thing as fatigue in the world; and I do not think she had anything like an adequate excuse for staying at home.

On the Sunday afternoon Miss Susan received a visit which roused her a little from the self-absorption which this new era in her existence had brought about, though it was only Dr. and Mrs. Richard, who walked across the field to see her after her journey, and to take a cup of tea. They were a pleasant little couple to see, jogging across the fields arm in arm—he the prettiest fresh-colored little old gentleman, in glossy black and ivory white, a model of a neat, little elderly clergyman; she not quite so pretty, but very trim and neat too, in a nice black silk gown, and a bonnet with a rose in it. Mrs. Richard was rather hard upon the old women at the almshouses for their battered flowers, and thought a little plain uniform bonnet of the cottage shape, with a simple brown ribbon, would have been desirable; but for her own part she clung to the rose, which nodded on the summit of her head. Both of them, however, had a conscious look upon their innocent old faces. They had come to "discharge a duty," and the solemnity of this duty, which was, as they said to each other, a very painful one, overwhelmed and slightly excited them. "What if she should be there herself?" said Mrs. Richard, clasping a little closer her husband's arm, to give emphasis to her question. "It does not matter who is there; I must do my duty," said the Doctor, in heroic tones; "besides," he added, dropping his voice, "she never notices anything that is not said to her, poor soul!"

But happily Miss Augustine was not present when they were shown into the drawing-room where Miss Susan sat writing letters. A good deal was said, of course, which was altogether foreign to the object of the visit: How she enjoyed her journey, whether it was not very fatiguing, whether it had not been very delightful, and a charming change, etc. Miss Susan answered all their questions benignly enough, though she was very anxious to get back to the letter she was writing to Farrel-Austin, and rang the bell for tea and poured it out, and was very gracious, secretly asking herself, what in the name of wonder had brought them here to-day to torment her? But it was not till he had been strengthened by these potations that Dr. Richard spoke.

"My dear Miss Susan," he said at length, "my coming to-day was not purely accidental, or merely to ask for you after your journey. I wanted to—if you will permit me—put you on your guard."

"In what respect?" said Miss Susan, quickly, feeling her heart begin to beat. Dr. Richard was the last person in the world whom she could suppose likely to know about the object of her rapid journey, or what she had done; but guilt is very suspicious, and she felt herself immediately put upon her defence.

"I trust that you will not take it amiss that I should speak to you on such a subject," said the old clergyman, clearing his throat; his pretty, old pink cheek growing quite red with agitation. "I take the very greatest interest in both you and your sister, Miss Susan. You are both of you considerably younger than I am, and I have been here now more than a dozen years, and one cannot help taking an interest in anything connected with the family—"

"No, indeed; one cannot help it; it would be quite unnatural if one did not take an interest," said Mrs. Richard, backing him up.

"But nobody objects to your taking an interest," said Miss Susan. "I think it, as you say, the most natural thing in the world."

"Thanks, thanks, for saying so!" said Dr. Richard with enthusiasm; and then he looked at his wife, and his wife at him, and there was an awful pause.

"My dear, good, excellent people," said Miss Susan, hurriedly, "for Heaven's sake, if there is any bad news coming, out with it at once!"

"No, no; no bad news!" said Dr. Richard; and then he cleared his throat. "The fact is, I came to speak to you—about Miss Augustine. I am afraid her eccentricity is increasing. It is painful, very painful to me to say so, for but for her kindness my wife and I should not have been half so comfortable these dozen years past; but I think it a friend's duty, not to say a clergyman's. Miss Susan, you are aware that people say that she is—not quite right in her mind!"

"I am aware that people talk a great deal of nonsense," said Miss Susan, half-relieved, half-aggravated. "I should not wonder if they said I was mad myself."

"If they knew!" she added mentally, with a curious thrill of self-arraignment, judging her own cause, and in the twinkling of an eye running over the past and the future, and wondering, if she should ever be found out, whether people would say she was mad too.

"No, no," said the Doctor; "you are well known for one of the most sensible women in the county."

"Quite one of the most influential and well-known people in the county," said Mrs. Richard, with an echo in which there was always an individual tone.

"Well, well; let that be as it may," said Miss Susan, not dissatisfied with this appreciation; "and what has my sister done—while I have been absent, I suppose?"

"It is a matter of great gravity, and closely concerning myself," said Dr. Richard, with some dignity. "You are aware, Miss Susan, that my office as Warden of the Almshouses is in some respects an anomalous one, making me, in some degree, subordinate, or apparently so, in my ecclesiastical position to—in fact, to a lady. It is quite a strange, almost unprecedented, combination of circumstances."

"Very strange indeed," said Mrs. Richard. "My husband, in his ecclesiastical position, as it were subordinate—to a lady."

"Pardon me," said Miss Susan; "I never interfere with Augustine. You knew how it would be when you came."

"But there are some things one was not prepared for," said the Doctor, with irrestrainable pathos. "It might set me wrong with the persons I respect most, Miss Susan. Your sister not only attempted to add a petition to the prayers of the Church, which nobody is at liberty to do except the Archbishops themselves, acting under the authority of Government; but finding me inexorable in that—for I hope nothing will ever lead me astray from the laws of the Church—she directed me to request the prayers of the congregation for you, the most respectable person in the neighborhood—for you, as exposed to temptation!"

A strange change passed over Miss Susan's face. She had been ready to laugh, impatient of the long explanation, and scarcely able to conceal her desire to get rid of her visitors. She sat poising the pen in her hand with which she had been writing, turning over her papers, with a smile on her lip; but when Dr. Richard came to those last words, her face changed all at once. She dropped the pen out of her hand, her face grew gray, the smile disappeared in a moment, and Miss Susan sat looking at them, with a curious consciousness about her, which the excellent couple could not understand.

"What day was that?" she said quickly, almost under her breath.

"It was on Thursday."

"Thursday morning," added Mrs. Richard. "If you remember, Henery, you got a note about it quite early; and after chapel she spoke—"

"Yes, it was quite early; probably the note," said the chaplain, "was written on Wednesday night."

Miss Susan was ashy gray; all the blood seemed to have gone out of her. She made them no answer at first, but sat brooding, like a woman struck into stone. Then she rose to her feet suddenly as the door opened, and Augustine, gray and silent, came in, gliding like a mediæval saint.

"My sister is always right," said Miss Susan, almost passionately, going suddenly up to her and kissing her pale cheek with a fervor no one understood, and Augustine least of all. "I always approve what she does;" and having made this little demonstration, she returned to her seat, and took up her pen again with more show of preoccupation than before.

What could the old couple do after this but make their bow and their courtesy, and go off again bewildered? "I think Miss Susan is the maddest of the two," said Mrs. Richard, when they had two long fields between them and Whiteladies; and I am not surprised, I confess, that they should have thought so, on that occasion, at least.

Miss Susan was deeply struck with this curious little incident. She had always entertained a half visionary respect for her sister, something of the reverential feeling with which some nations regard those who are imperfectly developed in intelligence; and this curious revelation deepened the sentiment into something half-adoring, half-afraid. Nobody knew what she had done, but Augustine knew somehow that she had been in temptation. I cannot describe the impression this made upon her mind and her heart, which was guilty, but quite unaccustomed to guilt. It thrilled her through and through; but it did not make her give up her purpose, which was perhaps the strangest thing of all.

"My dear," she said, assuming with some difficulty an ordinary smile, "what made you think I was going wrong when I was away?"

"What made me think it? nothing; something that came into my mind. You do not understand how I am moved and led," said Augustine, looking at her sister seriously.

"No, dear, no—I don't understand; that is true. God bless you, my dear!" said the woman who was guilty, turning away with a tremor which Augustine understood as little—her whole being tremulous and softened with love and reverence, and almost awe, of the spotless creature by her; but I suspect, though Miss Susan felt so deeply the wonderful fact that her sister had divined her moral danger, she was not in the least moved thereby to turn away from that moral danger, or give up her wicked plan; which is as curious a problem as I remember to have met with. Having all the habits of truth and virtue, she was touched to the heart to think that Augustine should have had a mysterious consciousness of the moment when she was brought to abandon the right path, and felt the whole situation sentimentally, as if she had read of it in a story; but it had not the slightest effect otherwise. With this tremor of feeling upon her, she went back to her writing-table, and finished her letter to Farrel-Austin, which was as follows:

"DEAR COUSIN: Having had some business which called me abroad last week, my interest in the facts you told me, the last time I had the pleasure of seeing you, led me to pass by Bruges, where I saw our common relations, the Austins. They seem very nice, homely people, and I enjoyed making their acquaintance, though it was curious to realize relations of ours occupying such a position. I heard from them, however, that a discovery had been made in the meantime which seriously interferes with the bargain which they made with you; indeed, is likely to invalidate it altogether. I took in hand to inform you of the facts, though they are rather delicate to be discussed between a lady and a gentleman; but it would have been absurd of a woman of my age to make any difficulty on such a matter. If you will call on me, or appoint a time at which I can see you at your own house, I will let you know exactly what are the facts of the case; though I have no doubt you will at once divine them, if you were informed at the time you saw the Bruges Austins, that their son who died had left a young widow.

With compliments to Mrs. Farrel-Austin and your girls,

Believe me, truly yours,

SUSAN AUSTIN."

I do not know that Miss Susan had ever written to Farrel-Austin in so friendly a spirit before. She felt almost cordial toward him as she put her letter into the envelope. If this improvement in friendly feeling was the first product of an intention to do the man wrong, then wrong-doing, she felt, must be rather an amiable influence than otherwise; and she went to rest that night with a sense of satisfaction in her mind. In the late Professor Aytoun's quaint poem of "Firmilian," it is recorded that the hero of that drama committed many murders and other crimes in a vain attempt to study the sensation usually called remorse, but was entirely unsuccessful, even when his crimes were on the grandest scale, and attended by many aggravating circumstances. Miss Susan knew nothing about Firmilian, but I think her mind was in a very similar state. She was not at all affected in sentiment by her conspiracy. She felt the same as usual, nay, almost better than usual, more kindly toward her enemy whom she was going to injure, and more reverential and admiring to her saintly sister, who had divined something of her evil intentions—or at least had divined her danger, though without the slightest notion what the kind of evil was to which she was tempted. Miss Susan was indeed half frightened at herself when she found how very little impression her own wickedness had made upon her. The first night she had been a little alarmed when she said her prayers, but this had all worn off, and she went to bed without a tremor, and slept the sleep of innocence—the sleep of the just. She was so entirely herself that she was able to reflect how strange it was, and how little the people who write sermons know the state of the real mind. She was astonished herself at the perfect calm with which she regarded her own contemplated crime, for crime it was.

CHAPTER XV

Mr. Farrel-Austin lived in a house which was called the Hatch, though I cannot tell what is the meaning of the name. It was a modern house, like hundreds of others, solid and ugly, and comfortable enough, with a small park round it, and—which it could scarcely help having in Berkshire—some fine trees about it. Farrel-Austin had a good deal of property; his house stood upon his own land, though his estate was not very extensive, and he had a considerable amount of money in good investments, and some house-property in London, in the City, which was very valuable. Altogether, therefore, he was very well off, and lived in a comfortable way with everything handsome about him. All his family at present consisted of the two daughters who came with him to visit Whiteladies, as we have seen; but he had married a second time, and had an ailing wife who was continually, as people say, having "expectations," which, however, never came to anything. He had been married for about ten years, and during this long period Mrs. Farrel-Austin's expectations had been a joke among her neighbors; but they were no joke to her husband, nor to the two young ladies, her step-daughters, who, as they could not succeed to the Austin lands themselves, were naturally very desirous to have a brother who could do so. They were not very considerate of Mrs. Austin generally, but in respect to her health they were solicitous beyond measure. They took such care of her that the poor woman's life became a burden to her, and especially at the moment when there were expectations did this care and anxiety overflow. The poor soul had broken down, body and mind, under this surveillance. She had been a pretty girl enough when she was married, and entered with a light heart upon her functions, not afraid of what might happen to her; but Mr. Farrel-Austin's unsatisfied longing for an heir, and the supervision of the two sharp girls who grew up so very soon to be young ladies, and evidently considered, as their father did, that the sole use and meaning of their mild young stepmother was to produce that necessary article, soon made an end of all her light-heartedness. Her courage totally failed. She had no very strong emotions any way, but a little affection and kindness were necessary to keep her going, and this she did not get, in the kind that was important, at least. Her husband, I suppose, was fond of her, as (of course) all husbands are of all wives, but she could not pet or make friends with the girls, who, short of her possible use as the mother of an heir, found her very much in their way, and had no inclination to establish affectionate relations with her. Therefore she took to her sofa, poor soul, and to tonics, and the state of an invalid—a condition which, when one has nothing in particular to do in the world, and nothing to amuse or occupy a flat existence, is not a bad expedient in its way for the feeble soul, giving it the support of an innocent, if not very agreeable routine—rules to observe and physic to take. This was how poor Mrs. Farrel-Austin endeavored to dédommager herself for the failure of her life. She preserved a pale sort of faded prettiness even on her sofa; and among the society which the girls collected round them, there was now and then one who would seek refuge with the mild invalid, when the fun of the younger party grew too fast and furious. Even, I believe, the stepmother might have set up a flirtation or two of her own had she cared for that amusement; but fortunately she had her tonics to take, which was a more innocent gratification, and suited all parties better; for a man must be a very robust flirt indeed, whose attentions can support the frequent interpositions of a maid with a medicine-bottle and a spoon.

The society of the Farrel-Austins was of a kind which might be considered very fine, or the reverse, according to the taste of the critic, though that, indeed, may be said of almost all society. They knew, of course, and visited, all the surrounding gentry, among whom there were a great many worthy people, though nothing so remarkable as to stand out from the general level; but what was more important to the young ladies, at least, they had the officers of the regiment which was posted near, and in which there were a great many very noble young personages, ornaments to any society, who accepted Mr. Farrel-Austin's invitations freely, and derived a great deal of amusement from his household, without perhaps paying that natural tribute of respect and civility to their entertainers behind their backs, which is becoming in the circumstances. Indeed, the Farrel-Austins were not quite on the same social level as the Marquis of Dropmore, or Lord Ffarington, who were constantly at the Hatch when their regiment was stationed near, nor even of Lord Alf Groombridge, though he was as poor as a church-mouse; and the same thing might be said of a great many other honorable and distinguished young gentlemen who kept a continual riot at the house, and made great havoc with the cellar, and on Sundays, especially, would keep this establishment, which ought to have been almost pious in its good order, in a state of hurry and flurry, and noise and laughter, as if it had been a hotel. The Austins, it is true, boasted themselves of good family, though nothing definite was known of them before Henry VIII.—and they were rich enough to entertain their distinguished visitors at very considerable cost; but they had neither that rank which introduces the possessor into all circles, nor that amount of money which makes up every deficiency. Had one of the Miss Farrel-Austins married the Marquis or the Earl, or even Lord Alf in his impecuniosity, she would have been said to have "succeeded in catching" poor Dropmore, or poor Ffarington, and would have been stormed or wept over by the gentleman's relations as if she had been a ragged girl off the streets—King Cophetua's beggar-maid herself; notwithstanding that these poor innocents, Ffarington and Dropmore, had taken advantage of the father's hospitalities for months or years before. I am bound to add that the Farrel-Austins were not only fully aware of this, but would have used exactly the same phraseology themselves in respect to any other young lady of their own standing whose fascinations had been equally exercised upon the well-fortified bosoms of Dropmore and Company. Nevertheless they adapted themselves to the amusements which suited their visitors, and in Summer lived in a lively succession of outdoor parties, spending half of their time in drags, in boats, on race courses, at cricket-matches, and other energetic diversions. Sometimes their father was their chaperon, sometimes a young married lady belonging to the same society, and with the same tastes.

The very highest and the very lowest classes of society have a great affinity to each other. There was always something planned for Sunday in this lively "set"—they were as eager to put the day to use as if they had been working hard all the week and had this day only to amuse themselves in. I suppose they, or perhaps their father, began to do this because there was in it the delightful piquancy of sensation which the blasé appetite feels when it is able to shock somebody else by its gratifications; and though they have long ago ceased to shock anybody, the flavor of the sensation lasted. All the servants at the Hatch, indeed, were shocked vastly, which preserved a little of this delightful sense of naughtiness. The quieter neighbors round, especially those houses in which there were no young people, disapproved, also, in a general way, and called the Miss Austins fast; and Miss Susan disapproved most strenuously, I need not say, and expressed her contempt in terms which she took no trouble to modify. But I cannot deny that there was a general hankering among the younger members of society for a share in these bruyant amusements; and Everard Austin could not see what harm it did that the girls should enjoy themselves, and had no objection to join them, and liked Kate and Sophy so much that sometimes he was moved to think that he liked one of them more. His house, indeed, which was on the river, was a favorite centre for their expeditions, and I think even that though he was not rich, neither of his cousins would have rejected Everard off-hand without deliberation—for, to be sure, he was the heir, at present, after their father, and every year made it less likely that Mrs. Austin would produce the much-wished-for successor. Neither of them would have quite liked to risk accepting him yet, in face of all the possibilities which existed in the way of Dropmore, Ffarington, and Company; but yet they would not have refused him off-hand.

Now I may as well tell the reader at once that Kate and Sophy Farrel-Austin were not what either I or he (she) would call nice girls. I am fond of girls, for my own part. I don't like to speak ill of them, or give an unfavorable impression, and as it is very probable that my prejudice in favor of the species may betray me into some relentings in respect to these particular examples, some softening of their after proceedings, or explanation of their devices, I think it best to say at once that they were not nice girls. They had not very sweet natures to begin with; for the fact is—and it is a very terrible one—that a great many people do come into the world with natures which are not sweet, and enter upon the race of life handicapped (if I may be permitted an irregular but useful expression) in the most frightful way. I do not pretend to explain this mystery, which, among all the mysteries of earth, is one of the most cruel, but I am forced to believe it. Kate and Sophy had never been very nice. Their father before them was not nice, but an extremely selfish and self-regarding person, often cross, and with no generosity or elevation of mind to set them a better example. They had no mother, and no restraint, except that of school, which is very seldom more than external and temporary. The young stepmother had begun by petting them, but neither could nor wished to attempt to rule the girls, who soon acquired a contempt for her; and as her invalidism grew, they took the control of the house, as well as themselves, altogether out of her hands. From sixteen they had been in that state of rampant independence and determination to have their own way, which has now, I fear, become as common among girls as it used to be among boys, when education was more neglected than it is nowadays. Boys who are at school—and even when they are young men at the university—must be in some degree of subordination; but girls who do not respect their parents are absolutely beyond this useful power, and can be described as nothing but rampant—the unloveliest as well as the unwholesomest of all mental and moral attitudes. Kate had come out at sixteen, and since that time had been constantly in this rampant state; by sheer force and power of will she had kept Sophy back until she also attained that mature age, but her power ended at that point, and Sophy had then become rampant too. They turned everything upside down in the house, planned their life according to their pleasure, over-rode the stepmother, coaxed the father, who was fond and proud of them—the best part of his character—and set out thus in the Dropmore and Ffarington kind of business. At sixteen girls do not plan to be married—they plan to enjoy themselves; and these noble young gentlemen seemed best adapted to second their intentions. But it is inconceivable how old a young woman is at twenty-one who has begun life at sixteen in this tremendous way. Kate, who had been for five long years thus about the world—at all the balls, at all the pleasure-parties, at all the races, regattas, cricket-matches, flower-shows, every kind of country entertainment—and at everything she could attain to in town in the short season which her father could afford to give them—felt herself about a hundred when she attained her majority. She had done absolutely everything that can be done in the way of amusement—at least in England—and the last Winter and Spring had been devoted to doing the same sort of thing "abroad." There was nothing new under the sun to this unfortunate young woman—unless, perhaps, it might be getting married, which had for some time begun to appear a worthy object in her eyes. To make a good match and gain a legitimate footing in the society to which Dropmore, etc., belonged; to be able to give "a good setting down" to the unapproachable women who ignored her from its heights—and to snatch the delights of a title by sheer strength and skill from among her hurly-burly of Guardsmen, this had begun to seem to Kate the thing most worth thinking of in the world. It was "full time" she should take some such step, for she was old, blasée, beginning to fear that she must be passée too,—at one and twenty! Nineteen at the outside is the age at which the rampant girl ought to marry in order to carry out her career without a cloud—the marriage, of course, bien entendu, being of an appropriate kind.

The Sunday which I have just described, on which Miss Susan did not go to church, had been spent by the young ladies in their usual way. There had been a river party, preceded by a luncheon at Everard's house, which, having been planned when the weather was hot, had of course to be carried out, though the day was cold with that chill of July which is more penetrating than December. The girls in their white dresses had paid for their pleasure, and the somewhat riotous late dinner which awaited the party at the Hatch had scarcely sufficed to warm their feet and restore their comfort. It was only next morning, pretty late, over the breakfast which they shared in Kate's room, the largest of the two inhabited by the sisters, that they could talk over their previous day's pleasure. And even then their attention was disturbed by a curious piece of news which had been brought to them along with their tray, and which was to the effect that Herbert Austin had suddenly and miraculously recovered his health, thanks having been given for him in the parish church at St. Austin's on the previous morning. The gardener had gone to church there, with the intention of negotiating with the gardener at Whiteladies about certain seedlings, and he had brought back the information. His wife had told it to the housekeeper, and the housekeeper to the butler, and the butler to the young ladies' maid, so that the report had grown in magnitude as it rolled onward. Sarah reported with a courtesy that Mr. Herbert was quite well, and was expected home directly—indeed, she was not quite sure whether he was not at home already, and in church when the clergyman read out his name as returning thanks—that would be the most natural way; and as she thought it over, Sarah concluded, and said, that this must have been what she heard.

"Herbert better! what a bore!" said Sophy, not heeding the presence of the maid. "What right has he to get better, I should like to know, and cut papa out?"

"Everybody has a right to do the best for themselves, when they can," said Kate, whose rôle it was to be sensible; "but I don't believe it can be true."

"I assure you, miss," said Sarah, who was a pert maid, such as should naturally belong to such young ladies, "as gardener heard it with his own ears, and there could be no doubt on the subject. I said, 'My young ladies won't never believe it;' and Mr. Beaver, he said, 'They'll find as it's too true!'"

"It was very impudent of Beaver to say anything of the sort," said Kate, "and you may tell him so. Now go; you don't require to wait any longer. I'll ring when I'm ready to have my hair done. Hold your tongue, Soph, for two minutes, till that girl's gone. They tell everything, and they remember everything."

"What do I care?" said Sophy; "if twenty people were here I'd just say the same. What an awful bore, when papa had quite made up his mind to have Whiteladies! I should like to do something to that Herbert, if it's true; and it's sure to be true."

"I don't believe it," said Kate reflectively. "One often hears of these cases rallying just for a week or two—but there's no cure for consumption. It would be too teasing if—but you may be sure it isn't and can't be—"

"Everything that is unpleasant comes true," said Sophy. This was one of the sayings with which she amused her monde, and made Dropmore and the rest declare that "By Jove! that girl was not so soft as she looked." "I think it is an awful bore for poor papa."

After they had exhausted this gloomy view of the subject, they began to look at its brighter side, if it had one.

"After all," said Sophy, "having Whiteladies won't do very much for papa. It is clear he is not going to have an heir, and he can't leave it to us; and what good would it do him, poor old thing, for the time he has to live?"

"Papa is not so very old," said Kate, "nor so very fond of us, either, Sophy. He wants it for himself; and so should I, if I were in his place."

"He wants it for the coming man," said Sophy, "who won't come. I wonder, for my part, that poor mamma don't steal a child; I should in her place. Where would be the harm? and then everybody would be pleased."

"Except Everard, and whoever marries Everard."

"So long as that is neither you nor me," said Sophy, laughing, "I don't mind; I should rather like to spite Everard's wife, if she's somebody else. Why should men ever marry? I am sure they are a great deal better as they are."

"Speaking of marrying," said Kate seriously, "far the best thing for you to do, if it is true about Herbert, is to marry him, Sophy. You are the one that is the most suitable in age. He is just a simple innocent, and knows nothing of the world, so you could easily have him, if you liked to take the trouble; and then Whiteladies would be secured, one way or another, and papa pleased."

"But me having it would not be like him having it," said Sophy. "Would he be pleased? You said not just now."

"It would be the best that could be done," said Kate; and then she began to recount to her sister certain things that Dropmore had said, and to ask whether Sophy thought they meant anything? which Sophy, wise in her sister's concerns, however foolish in her own, did not think they did, though she herself had certain words laid up from "Alf," in which she had more faith, but which Kate scouted. "They are only amusing themselves," said the elder sister. "If Herbert does get better, marry him, Sophy, with my blessing, and be content."

"And you could have Everard, and we should neither of us change our names, but make one charming family party—"

"Oh, bosh! I hate your family parties; besides, Everard would have nothing in that case," said Kate, ringing the bell for the maid, before whom they did not exactly continue their discussion, but launched forth about Dropmore and Alf.

"There's been some one over here from the barracks this morning," said Sarah, "with a note for master. I think it was the Markis's own man, miss."

"Whatever could it be?" cried both the sisters together, for they were very slipshod in their language, as the reader will perceive.

"And Miss Kate did go all of a tremble, and her cheeks like strawberries," Sarah reported in the servants' hall, where, indeed, the Markis's man had already learned that nothing but a wedding could excuse such goings on.

"We ain't such fools as we look," that functionary had answered with a wink, witty as his master himself.

I do not think that Kate, who knew the world, had any idea, after the first momentary thrill of curiosity, that Dropmore's note to her father could contain anything of supreme importance, but it might be, and probably was, a proposal for some new expedition, at any one of which matters might come to a crisis; and she sallied forth from her room accordingly, in her fresh morning dress, looking a great deal fresher than she felt, and with a little subdued excitement in her mind. She went to the library, where her father generally spent his mornings, and gave him her cheek to kiss, and asked affectionately after his health.

"I do hope you have no rheumatism, papa, after last night. Oh, how cold it was! I don't think I shall ever let myself be persuaded to go on the water in an east wind again."

"Not till the next time Dropmore asks," said her father, in his surliest voice.

"Dropmore, oh!" Kate shrugged her shoulders. "A great deal I care for what he asks. By-the-bye, I believe this is his cipher. Have you been hearing from Dropmore this morning, papa? and what does his most noble lordship please to want?"

"Bah! what does it matter what he wants?" said Mr. Farrel-Austin, savagely. "Do you suppose I have nothing to do but act as secretary for your amusements? Not when I have news of my own like what I have this morning," and his eye reverted to a large letter which lay before him with "Whiteladies" in a flowery heading above the date.

"Is it true, then, that Herbert is better?" said Kate.

"Herbert better! rubbish! Herbert will never be better; but that old witch has undermined me!" cried the disappointed heir, with flashing eyes.

CHAPTER XVI

"Papa has just heard that Herbert Austin, who has Whiteladies, you know—our place that is to be—is much better; and he is low about it," said Sophy. "Of course, if Herbert were to get better it would be a great disappointment for us."

This speech elicited a shout of laughter from Dropmore and the rest, with running exclamations of "Frank, by Jove," and "I like people who speak their minds."

"Well," said Sophy, "if I were to say we were all delighted, who would believe me? It is the most enchanting old house in the world, and a good property, and we have always been led to believe that he was in a consumption. I declare I don't know what is bad enough for him, if he is going to swindle us out of it, and live."

"Sophy, you should not talk so wildly," said mild Mrs. Austin from her sofa. "People will think you mean what you say."

"And I do," said the girl. "I hate a cheat. Papa is quite low about it, and so is cousin Everard. They are down upon their luck."

"Am I?" said Everard, who was a little out of temper, it must be allowed, but chiefly because in the presence of the Guardsmen he was very much thrown into the shade. "I don't know about being down on my luck; but it's not a sweet expression for a young lady to use."

"Oh, I don't mind about expressions that young ladies ought to use!" said Sophy. A tinge of color came on her face at the reproof, but she tossed her pretty head, and went on all the more: "Why shouldn't girls use the same words as other people do? You men want to keep the best of everything to yourselves—nice strong expressions and all the rest."

"By Jove!" said Lord Alf; "mind you, I don't like a girl to swear—it ain't the thing somehow; but for a phrase like 'down on his luck,' or 'awful fun,' or anything like that—"

"And pray why shouldn't you like a girl to swear?" said Kate. "'By Jove,' for instance? I like it. It gives a great deal of point to your conversation, Lord Alf."

"Oh, bless you, that ain't swearing. But it don't do. I am not very great at reasons; but, by Jove, you must draw the line somewhere. I don't think now that a girl ought to swear."

"Except 'her pretty oath of yea and nay,'" said Everard, who had a little, a very little, literature.

The company in general stared at him, not having an idea what he meant; and as it is more humbling somehow to fail in a shot of this description, which goes over the head of your audience, than it is to show actual inferiority, Everard felt himself grow very red and hot, and feel very angry.

The scene was the drawing-room at the Hatch, where a party of callers were spending the afternoon, eating bread-and-butter and drinking tea, and planning new delights. After this breakdown, for so he felt it, Everard withdrew hastily to Mrs. Austin's sofa, and began to talk to her, though he did not quite know what it was about. Mild Mrs. Austin, though she did not understand the attempts which one or two of the visitors of the house had made to flirt with her, was pleased to be talked to, and approved of

Everard, who was never noisy, though often "led away," like all the others, by the foolishness of the girls.

"I am glad you said that about this slang they talk," said Mrs. Austin. "Perhaps coming from you it may have some weight with them. They do not mind what I say. And have you heard any more about poor Herbert? You must not think Mr. Austin is low about it, as they said. They only say such things to make people laugh."

This charitable interpretation arose from the poor lady's desire to do the best for her step children, whom it was one of the regrets of her faded life, now and then breathed into the ear of a confidential friend, that she did not love as she ought.

"I have only heard he is better," said Everard; "and it is no particular virtue on my part to be heartily glad of it. I am not poor Herbert's heir."

He spoke louder than he had any need to speak; for Mrs. Austin, though an invalid, was not at all deaf. But I fear that he had a hankering to be heard and replied to, and called back into the chattering circle which had formed round the girls. Neither Kate nor Sophy, however, had any time at the moment to attend to Everard, whom they felt sure they could wheedle back at any time. He gave a glance toward them with the corner of his eye, and saw Kate seriously inclining her pretty pink ear to some barrack joke which the most noble Marquis of Dropmore was recounting with many interruptions of laughter; while Sophy carried on with Lord Alf and an applauding auditory that discussion where the line should be drawn, and what girls might and might not do. "I hunt whenever I can," Sophy was saying; "and wish there was a ladies' club at Hurlingham or somewhere; I should go in for all the prizes. And I'm sure I could drive your team every bit as well as you do. Oh, what I would give just to have the ribbons in my hand! You should see then how a drag could go."

Everard listened, deeply disgusted. He had not been in the least disgusted when the same sort of thing had been said to himself, but had laughed and applauded with the rest, feeling something quite irresistible in the notion of pretty Sophy's manly longings. Her little delicate hands, her slim person, no weightier than a bird, the toss of her charming head, with its wavy, fair locks, like a flower, all soft color and movement, had put ineffable humor into the suggestion of those exploits in which she longed to emulate the heroes of the household brigade. But now, when Everard was outside the circle, he felt a totally different sentiment move him. Clouds and darkness came over his face, and I do not know what further severity might have come from his lips had not Mr. Farrel-Austin, looking still blacker than himself, come into the room, in a way which added very little to the harmony, though something to the amusement, of the party. He nodded to the visitors, snarled at the girls, and said something disagreeable to his wife, all in two minutes by the clock.

"How can you expect to be well, if you go on drinking tea for ever and ever?" he said to the only harmless member of the party. "Afternoon tea must have been invented by the devil himself to destroy women's nerves and their constitutions." He said this as loudly and with the same intention as had moved Everard; and he had more success, for Dropmore, Alf, and the rest turned round with their teacups in their hands, and showed their excellent teeth under their moustachios in a roar of laughter. "I had not the least idea I was so amusing," said Mr. Farrel, sourer than ever. "Here, Everard, let me have a word with you."

"By Jove! he is down on his luck," said Lord Alf to Sophy in an audible aside.

"Didn't I tell you so?" said the elegant young lady; "and when he's low he's always as cross as two sticks."

"Everard," said Mr. Farrel-Austin, "I am going over to Whiteladies on business. That old witch, Susan Austin, has outwitted us both. As it is your interest as well as mine, you had better drive over with me—unless you prefer the idiocy here to all the interests of life, as some of these fools seem to do."

"Not I," said Everard with much stateliness, "as you may perceive, for I am taking no part in it. I am quite at your service. But if it's about poor Herbert, I don't see what Miss Susan can have to do with it," he added, casting a longing look behind.

"Bah! Herbert is neither here nor there," said the heir-presumptive. "You don't suppose I put any faith in that. She has spread the rumor, perhaps, to confuse us and put us off the scent. These old women," said Mr. Farrel with deliberate virulence, "are the very devil when they put their minds to it. And you are as much interested as I am, Everard, as I have no son—and what with the absurdity and perverseness of women," he added, setting his teeth with deliberate virulence, "don't seem likely to have."

I don't know whether the company in the drawing-room heard this speech. Indeed, I do not think they could have heard it, being fully occupied by their own witty and graceful conversation. But there came in at this moment a burst of laughter which drove the two gentlemen furious in quite different ways, as they strode with all the dignity of ill-temper down stairs. Farrel-Austin did not care for the Guardsmen's laughter in itself, nor was he critical of the manners of his daughters, but he was in a state of irritation which any trifle would have made to boil over. And Everard was in that condition of black disapproval which every word and tone increases, and to which the gayety of a laugh is the direst of offences. He would have laughed as gayly as any of them had he been seated where Lord Alf was; but being "out of it," to use their own elegant language, he could see nothing but what was objectionable, insolent, nay, disgusting, in the sound.

What influenced Farrel-Austin to take the young man with him, however, I am unable to say. Probably it was the mere suggestion of the moment, the congenial sight of a countenance as cloudy as his own, and perhaps a feeling that as (owing to the perverseness of women) their interests were the same, Everard might help him to unravel Miss Susan's meaning, and to ascertain what foundation in reality there was for her letter which had disturbed him so greatly; and then Everard was the friend and pet of the ladies, and Farrel felt that to convey him over as his own second and backer up, would inflict a pang upon his antagonist; which, failing victory for yourself, is always a good thing to do. As for Everard, he went in pure despite, a most comprehensible reason, hoping to punish by his dignified withdrawal the little company whose offence was that it did not appreciate his presence. Foolish yet natural motive—which will continue to influence boys and girls, and even men and women, as long as there are two sets of us in the world; and that will be as long as the world lasts, I suppose.

The two gentlemen got into the dog-cart which stood at the door, and dashed away across the Summer country in the lazy, drowsy afternoon, to Whiteladies. The wind had changed and was breathing softly from the west, and Summer had reconquered its power. Nothing was moving that could help it through all the warm and leafy country. The kine lay drowsy in the pastures, not caring even to graze, or stood about, the white ones dazzling in the sunshine, contemplating the world around in a meditative calm. The heat had stilled every sound, except that of the insects whose existence it is; and the warm grass basked, and the big white daisies on the roadside trembled with a still pleasure, drinking in the golden light into their golden hearts.

But the roads were dusty, which was the chief thing the two men thought of except their business. Everard heard for the first time of the bargain Farrel had made with the Austins of Bruges, and did not quite know what to think of it, or which side to take in the matter. A sensation of annoyance that his companion had succeeded in finding people for whom he had himself made so many vain searches, was the first feeling that moved him. But whether he liked or did not like Farrel's bargain, he could not tell. He did not like it, because he had no desire to see Farrel-Austin reigning at Whiteladies; and he did not dislike it because, on the whole, Farrel would probably make a better Squire than an old shopkeeper from the Netherlands; and thus his mind was so divided that he could not tell what he thought. But he was very curious about Miss Susan's prompt action in the matter, and looked forward with some amusement and interest to hear what she had done, and how she had outwitted the expectant heir.

This idea even beguiled his mind out of the dispositions of general misanthropy with which he had started. He grew eager to know all about it, and anticipated with positive enjoyment the encounter between the old lady who was the actual Squire, and his companion who was the prospective one. As they neared Whiteladies, too, another change took place in Everard. He had almost been Farrel's partisan when they started, feeling in the mutual gloom, which his companion shared so completely, a bond of union which was very close for the moment. But Everard's gloom dispersed in the excitement of this new object; in short, I believe the rapid movement and change of the air would of themselves have been enough to dispel it—whereas the gloom of the other deepened. And as they flew along the familiar roads, Everard felt the force of all the old ties which attached him to the old house and its inmates, and began to feel reluctant to appear before Miss Susan by the side of her enemy. "If you will go in first I'll see to putting up the horse," he said when they reached the house.

"There is no occasion for putting up the horse," said Farrel, and though Everard invented various other excuses for lingering behind, they were all ineffectual. Farrel, I suppose, had the stronger will of the two, and he would not relinquish the pleasure of giving a sting to Miss Susan by exhibiting her favorite as his backer. So the young man was forced to follow him whether he would or not; but it was with a total revolution of sentiment. "I only hope she will outwit the fellow; and make an end of him clean," Everard said to himself.

They were shown into the hall, where Miss Susan chose, for some reason of her own, to give them audience. She appeared in a minute or two in her gray gown, and with a certain air of importance, and shook hands with them.

"What, you here, Everard?" she said with a smile and a cordial greeting. "I did not look for this pleasure. But of course the business is yours as well as Mr. Farrel's." It was very seldom that Miss Susan condescended to add Austin to that less distinguished name.

"I happened—to be—at the Hatch," said Everard, faltering.

"Yes, he was with my daughters; and as he was there I made him come with me, because of course he may have the greatest interest," said Mr. Farrel, "as much interest almost as myself—"

"Just the same," said Miss Susan briskly; "more indeed, because he is young and you are old, cousin Farrel. Sit down there, Everard, and listen; though having a second gentleman to hear what I have to say is alarming, and will make it all the harder upon me."

Saying this, she indicated a seat to Farrel and one to Everard (he did not know if it was with intention that she placed him opposite to the gallery with which he had so many tender associations) and seated herself in the most imposing chair in the room, as in a seat of judgment. There was a considerable tremor about her as she thus, for the first time, personally announced what she had done; but this did not appear to the men who watched her, one with affectionate interest and a mixture of eagerness and amusement, the other with resolute opposition, dislike, and fear. They thought her as stately and strong as a rock, informing her adversary thus, almost with a proud indifference, of the way in which her will had vanquished his, and were not the least aware of the flutter of consciousness which sometimes seemed almost to take away her breath.

"I was much surprised, I need not say, by your letter," said Farrel, "surprised to hear you had been at Bruges, as I know you are not given to travelling; and I do not know how to understand the intimation you send me that my arrangement with our old relative is not to stand. Pardon me, cousin Susan, but I cannot imagine why you should have interfered in the matter, or why you should prefer him to me."

"What has my interference to do with it?" she said, speaking slowly to preserve her composure; though this very expedient of her agitation made her appear more composed. "I had business abroad," she went on with elaborate calm, "and I have always taken a great interest in these Austins. They are excellent people—in their way; but it can scarcely be supposed that I should prefer people in their way to any other. They are not the kind of persons to step into my father's house."

"Ah, you feel that!" said Farrel, with an expression of relief.

"Of course I must feel that," said Miss Susan, with that fervor of truth which is the most able and successful means of giving credence to a lie; "but what has my preference to do with it? I don't know if they told you, poor old people, that the son they were mourning had left a young widow?—a very important fact."

"Yes, I know it. But what of that?"

"What of that? You ask me so, you a married man with children of your own! It is very unpleasant for a lady to speak of such matters, especially before a young man like Everard; but of course I cannot shrink from performing my promise. This young widow, who is quite overwhelmed by her loss, is—in short, there is a baby expected. There now, you know the whole."

It was honestly unpleasant to Miss Susan, though she was a very mature, and indeed, old woman, to speak to the men of this, so much had the bloom of maidenhood, that indefinable fragrance of youthfulness which some unwedded people carry to the utmost extremity of old age, lingered in her. Her cheek colored, her eyes fell; nature came in again to lend an appearance of perfect verity to all she said, and, so complicated are our human emotions, that, at the moment, it was in reality this shy hesitation, so natural yet so absurd at her years, and not any consciousness of her guilt, which was uppermost in her mind. She cast down her eyes for the moment, and a sudden color came to her face; then she looked up again, facing Farrel, who in the trouble of his mind, repeating the words after her, had risen from his seat.

"Yes," she said, "of course you will perceive that in these circumstances they cannot compromise themselves, but must wait the event. It may be a girl, of course," Miss Susan added, steadily, "as likely as not; and in that case I suppose your bargain stands. We must all"—and here her feelings got the better of her, and she drew along shivering breath of excitement—"await the event."

With this she turned to Everard, making a hasty movement of her hands and head as if glad to throw off an unpleasing subject. "It is some time since I have seen you," she said. "I am surprised that you should have taken so much interest in this news as to come expressly to hear it: when you had no other motive—"

How glad she was to get rid of a little of her pent-up feelings by this assault.

"I had another motive," said the young man, taken by surprise, and somewhat aggrieved as well; "I heard Herbert was better—getting well. I heartily hope it is true."

"You heartily hope it is true? Yes, yes, I believe you do, Everard, I believe you do!" said Miss Susan, melting all of a sudden. She put up her handkerchief to her eyes to dry the tears which belonged to her excitement as much as the irritation. "As for getting well, there are no miracles nowadays, and I don't hope it, though Augustine does, and my poor little Reine does, God help her. No, no, I cannot hope for that; but better he certainly is—for the moment. They have been able to get him out again, and the doctor says—Stop, I have Reine's letter in my pocket; I will read you what the doctor says."

All this time Farrel-Austin, now bolt upright on the chair which he had resumed after receiving the thunderbolt, sat glooming with his eyes fixed on air, and his mind transfixed with this tremendous arrow. He gnawed his under lip, out of which the blood had gone, and clenched his hands furtively, with a secret wish to attack some one, but a consciousness that he could do nothing, which was terrible to him. He never for a moment doubted the truth of the intimation he had just received, but took it as gospel, doubting Miss Susan no more than he doubted the law, or any other absolutely certain thing. A righteous person has thus an immense advantage over all false and frivolous people in doing wrong as well as in other things. The man never doubted her. He did not care much for a lie himself, and would perhaps have shrunk from few deceits to secure Whiteladies for himself; but he no more suspected her than he suspected Heaven itself. He sat like one stunned, and gnawed his lip and devoured his heart in sharp disappointment, mortification, and pain. He did not know what to say or do in this sudden downfall from the security in which he had boasted himself, but sat hearing dully what the other two said, without caring to make out what it was. As for Miss Susan, she watched him narrowly, holding her breath, though she did nothing to betray her scrutiny. She had expected doubt, questioning, cross-examination; and he said nothing. In her guilty consciousness she could not realize that this man whom she despised and disliked could have faith in her, and watched him stealthily, wondering when he would break out into accusations and blasphemies. She was almost as wretched as he was, sitting there so calmly opposite to him, making conversation for Everard, and wondering, Was it possible he could believe her? Would he go off at once to find out? Would her accomplices stand fast? Her heart beat wildly in her sober bosom, when, feeling herself for the first time in the power of another, she sat and asked herself what was going to happen, and what Farrel-Austin could mean?

CHAPTER XVII

After affairs had come to the point described in our last chapter, when Miss Susan had committed herself openly to her scheme for the discomfiture of Farrel-Austin, and that personage had accepted, with a bitterness I cannot describe, the curious contretemps (as he thought) which thus thrust him aside from the heirship, of which he had been so certain, and made everything more indefinite than ever—there occurred a lull in the family story. All that could be done was to await the event which should determine whether a new boy was to spring of the old Austin stock, or the conspiracy to come to nothing in the person of a girl. All depended upon Providence, as Miss Susan said, with the strange mixture of truth and falsehood which distinguished this extraordinary episode in her life. She said this without a change of countenance, and it was absolutely true. If Providence chose to defeat her fraud, and bring all her wicked plans to nothing, it was still within the power of Heaven to do so in the most natural and simple way. In short, it thus depended upon Providence—she said to herself, in the extraordinary train of casuistical reasoning which went through her mind on this point—whether she really should be guilty of this wrong or not. It was a kind of Sortes into which she had thrown herself—much as a man might do who put it upon the hazard of a "toss-up" whether he should kill another man or not. The problematical murderer might thus hold that some power outside of himself had to do with his decision between crime and innocence; and so did Miss Susan. It was, she said to herself, within the arbitration of Providence—Providence alone could decide; and the guilty flutter with which her heart sometimes woke in her, in the uncertainty of the chances before her, was thus calmed down by an almost pious sense (as she felt it) of dependence upon "a higher hand." I do not attempt to explain this curious mixture of the habits of an innocent and honorable and even religious mind, with the one novel and extraordinary impulse to a great wrong which had seized upon Miss Susan once in her life, without, so to speak, impairing her character, or indeed having any immediate effect upon its general strain. She would catch herself even saying a little prayer for the success of her crime sometimes, and would stop short with a hard-drawn breath, and such a quickening of all her pulses as nothing in her life had ever brought before; but generally her mind was calmed by the thought that as yet nothing was certain, but all in the hands of Providence; and that her final guilt, if she was doomed to be guilty, would be in some way sanctioned and justified by the deliberate decision of Heaven.

This uncertainty it was, no doubt, which kept up an excitement in her, not painful except by moments, a strange quickening of life, which made the period of her temptation feel like a new era in her existence. She was not unhappy, neither did she feel guilty, but only excited, possessed by a secret spring of eagerness and intentness which made all life more energetic and vital. This, as I have said, was almost more pleasurable than painful, but in one way she paid the penalty. The new thing became her master-thought; she could not get rid of it for a moment. Whatever she was doing, whatever thinking of, this came constantly uppermost. It looked her in the face, so to speak, the first thing in the morning, and never left her but reluctantly when she went to sleep at the close of the day, mingling broken visions of itself even with her dreams, and often waking her up with a start in the dead of night. It haunted her like a ghost; and though it was not accompanied by any sense of remorse, her constant consciousness of its presence gradually had an effect upon her life. Her face grew anxious; she moved less steadily than of old; she almost gave up her knitting and such meditative occupations, and took to reading desperately when she was not immersed in business—all to escape from the thing by her side, though it was not in itself painful. Thus gradually, insidiously, subtly, the evil took possession of her life.

As for Farrel-Austin, his temper and general sensibility were impaired by Miss Susan's intimation to an incalculable degree. There was no living with him, all his family said. He too awaited the decision of Providence, yet in anything but a pious way; and poor Mrs. Farrel-Austin had much to bear which no one heard of.

"Feel poorly. What is the good of your feeling poorly," he would say to her with whimsical brutality. "Any other woman but you would have seen what was required of her. Why, even that creature at Bruges—that widow! It is what women were made for; and there isn't a laborer's wife in the parish but is up to as much as that."

"Oh, Farrel, how can you be so unkind?" the poor woman would say. "But if I had a little girl you would be quite as angry, and that could not be my fault."

"Have a girl if you dare!" said the furious heir-presumptive. And thus he awaited the decision of Providence—more innocently, but in a much less becoming way, than Miss Susan did. It was not a thing that was publicly spoken of, neither was the world in general aware what was the new question which had arisen between the two houses, but its effects were infinitely less felt in Whiteladies than in the internal comfort of the Hatch.

In the midst of this sourd and suppressed excitement, however, the new possibility about Herbert, which poor Augustine had given solemn thanks for, but which all the experienced people had treated as folly, began to grow and acquire something like reality. A dying life may rally and flicker in the socket for a day or two, but when the improvement lasts for a whole month, and goes on increasing, even the greatest sceptic must pause and consider. It was not till Reine's letter arrived, telling the doctor's last opinion that there had always been something peculiar in the case, and that he could no longer say that recovery was impossible, that Miss Susan's mind first really opened to the idea. She was by herself when this letter came, and read it, shaking her head and saying, "Poor child!" as usual; but when she had got to the end, Miss Susan made a pause and drew a long breath, and began at the beginning again, with a curiously awakened look in her face. In the middle of this second reading, she suddenly sprang up from her seat, said out loud (being all alone), "There will be no need for it then!" and burst into a sudden flood of tears. It was as if some fountain had opened in her breast; she could not stop crying, or saying things to herself, in the strange rapture that came upon her. "No need, no need; it will not matter!" she said again and again, not knowing that she was speaking.

"What will not matter?" said Augustine, who had come in softly and stood by, looking on with grave surprise.

Augustine knew nothing about Bruges—not even of the existence of the Austins there, and less (I need not say) of the decision of Providence for which her sister waited. Miss Susan started to her feet and ran to her, and put the letter into her hand.

"I do begin to believe the boy will get well," she cried, her eyes once more overflowing.

Her sister could not understand her excitement; she herself had made up her simple mind to Herbert's certain recovery long before, when the first letter came.

"Yes, he will recover," she said; "I do not go by the doctor, but by my feelings. For some time I have been quite sure that an answer was coming, and Mary Matthews has said the same thing to me. We did not know, of course, when it would come. Yes, he will get better. Though it was so very discouraging, we have never ceased, never for a day—"

"Oh, my dear!" said Miss Susan, her heart penetrated and melting, "you have a right to put confidence in your prayers, for you are as good as a child. Pray for us all, that our sins may be forgiven us. You don't know, you could not think, what evil things come into some people's minds."

"I knew you were in temptation," said Augustine gently; and she went away, asking no questions, for it was the time for her almshouses' service, which nothing ever was permitted to disturb.

And the whole parish, which had shaken its head and doubted, yet was very ready to believe news that had a half-miraculous air, now accepted Herbert's recovery as certain. "See what it is to be rich," some of the people said; "if it had been one o' our poor lads, he'd been dead years ago." The people at the almshouses regarded it in a different way. Even the profane ones among them, like old John, who was conscious of doing very little to swell the prayers of the community, felt a certain pride in the news, as if they had something to do with the event. "We've prayed him back to life," said old Mrs. Matthews, who was very anxious that some one should send an account of it to the Methodist Magazine, and had the courage to propose this step to Dr. Richard, who nearly fainted at the proposition. Almost all the old people felt a curious thrill of innocent vanity at having thus been instrumental in so important an event; but the village generally resented this view, and said it was like their impudence to believe that God Almighty would take so much notice of folks in an alms-house. Dr. Richard himself did not quite know what to say on the subject. He was not sure that it was "in good taste" to speak of it so, and he did not think the Church approved of any such practical identification of the benefit of her prayers. In a more general way, yes; but to say that Herbert's recovery and the prayers of the almshouses were cause and effect was rather startling to him. He said to his wife that it was "Dissenterish"—a decision in which she fully agreed. "Very dissenterish, my dear, and not at all in good taste," Mrs. Richard said.

But while the public in general, and the older persons involved, were thus affected by the news, it had its effect too, in conjunction with other circumstances, upon the young people, who were less immediately under its influence. Everard Austin, who was not the heir-presumptive, and indeed now knew himself to be another degree off from that desirable position, felt nothing but joy at his cousin's amendment; and the girls at the Hatch were little affected by the failure of their father's immediate hopes. But other things came in to give it a certain power over their future lives. Kate took it so seriously upon herself to advise Sophy as to her future conduct in respect to the recovered invalid, that Sophy was inspired to double efforts for the enjoyment of the present moment, which might, if she accepted her sister's suggestion, be all that was left to her of the pleasure she enjoyed most.

"Do it myself? No; I could not do it myself," said Kate, when they discussed the subject, "for he is younger than I am; you are just the right age for him. You will have to spend the Winters abroad," she added, being of a prudent and forecasting mind, "so you need not say you will get no fun out of your life. Rome and those sorts of places, where he would be sure to be sent to, are great fun, when you get into a good set. You had far better make up your mind to it; for, as for Alf, he is no good, my dear; he is only amusing himself; you may take my word for that."

"And so am I amusing myself," Sophy said, her cheeks blazing with indignation at this uncalled-for stroke; "and, what's more, I mean to, like you and Dropmore are doing. I can see as far into a milestone as any of you," cried the young lady, who cared as little for grammar as for any other colloquial delicacies.

And thus it was that the fun grew faster and more furious than ever; and these two fair sisters flew about both town and country, wherever gayety was going, and were seen on the top of more drags, and had more dancing, more flirting, and more pleasuring than two girls of unblemished character are often permitted to indulge in. Poor Everard was dreadfully "out of it" in that bruyant Summer. He had no drag, nor any particular way of being useful, except by boats; and, as Kate truly said, a couple of girls cannot drag about a man with them, even though he is their cousin. I do not think he would have found much fault with their gayety had he shared in it; and though he did find fault with their slang, there is a piquancy in acting as mentor to two girls so pretty which seems to carry its own reward with it. But Everard disapproved very much when he found himself left out, and easily convinced himself that they were going a great deal too far, and that he was grieved, annoyed, and even disgusted by their total departure from womanly tranquillity. He did not know what to do with himself in his desolate and délaissé condition, hankering after them and their society, and yet disapproving of it, and despising their friends and their pleasures, as he said to himself he did. He felt dreadfully, dolefully superior, after a few days, in his water-side cottage, and as if he could never again condescend to the vulgar amusements which were popular at the Hatch; and an impulse moved him, half from a generous and friendly motive, half on his own behalf, to go to Switzerland, where there was always variety to be had, and to join his young cousins there, and help to nurse Herbert back into strength and health.

It was a very sensible reaction, though I do not think he was sensible of it, which made his mind turn with a sudden rebound to Reine, after Kate and Sophy had been unkind to him. Reine was hasty and high-spirited, and had made him feel now and then that she did not quite approve of him; but she never would have left him in the lurch, as the other girls had done; and he was very fond of Herbert, and very glad of his recovery; and he wanted change: so that all these causes together worked him to a sudden resolution, and this was how it happened that he appeared all at once, without preface or announcement, in the Kanderthal, before the little inn, like an angel sent to help her in her extremity, at Reine's moment of greatest need.

And whether it was the general helpfulness, hopefulness, and freshness of the stranger, like a wholesome air from home, or whether it was a turning-point in the malady, I cannot tell, but Herbert began to mend from that very night. Everard infused a certain courage into them all. He relieved Reine, whose terrible disappointment had stupefied her, and who for the first time had utterly broken down under the strain which overtasked her young faculties. He roused up François, who though he went on steadily with his duty, was out of heart too, and had resigned himself to his young master's death. "He has been as bad before, and got better," Everard said, though he did not believe what he was saying; but he made both Reine and François believe it, and, what was still better, Herbert himself, who rallied and made a last desperate effort to get hold again of the thread of life, which was so fast slipping out of his languid fingers. "It is a relapse," said Everard, "an accidental relapse, from the wetting; he has not really lost ground." And to his own wonder he gradually saw this pious falsehood grow into a truth.

To the great wonder of the valley too, which took so much interest in the poor young Englishman, and which had already settled where to bury him, and held itself ready at any moment to weep over the news which everybody expected, the next bulletin was that Herbert was better; and from that moment he gradually, slowly mended again, toiling back by languid degrees to the hopeful though invalid state from which he had fallen. Madame de Mirfleur arrived two days after, when the improvement had thoroughly set in, and she never quite realized how near death her son had been. He was still ill enough, however, to justify her in blaming herself much for having left him, and in driving poor Reine frantic with the inference that only in his mother's absence could he have been exposed to such a danger. She did not mean to blame Reine, whose devotion to her brother and admirable care for him she always boasted of, but I think she sincerely believed that under her own guardianship, in this point at least, her son would have been more safe. But the sweet bells of Reine's nature had all been jangled out of tune by these events. The ordinary fate of those who look for miracles had befallen her: her miracle, in which she believed so firmly, had failed, and all heaven and earth had swung out of balance. Her head swam, and the world with it, swaying under her feet at every step she took. Everything was out of joint to Reine. She had tried to be angelically good, subduing every rising of temper and unkind feeling, quenching not only every word on her lips, but every thought in her heart, which was not kind and forbearing.

But what did it matter? God had not accepted the offering of her goodness nor the entreaties of her prayers; He had changed His mind again; He had stopped short and interrupted His own work. Reine allowed all the old bitterness which she had tried so hard to subdue to pour back into her heart. When Madame de Mirfleur, going into her son's room, made that speech at the door about her deep regret at having left her boy, the girl could not restrain herself. She burst out to Everard, who was standing by, the moment her mother was out of the room.

"Oh, it is cruel, cruel!" she cried. "Is it likely that I would risk Herbert's life—I that have only Herbert in all the world? We are nothing to her—nothing! in comparison with that—that gentleman she has married, and those babies she has," cried poor Reine.

It seemed somewhat absurd to Everard that she should speak with such bitterness of her mother's husband; but he was kind, and consoled her.

"Dear Reine, she did not blame you," he said; "she only meant that she was sorry to have been away from you; and of course it is natural that she should care—a little, for her husband and her other children."

"Oh! you don't, you cannot understand!" said Reine. "What did she want with a husband?—and other children? That is the whole matter. Your mother belongs to you, doesn't she? or else she is not your mother."

When she had given forth this piece of triumphant logic with all the fervor and satisfaction of her French blood, Reine suddenly felt the shame of having betrayed herself and blamed her mother. Her flushed face grew pale, her voice faltered. "Everard, don't mind what I say. I am angry and unhappy and cross, and I don't know what is the matter with me," cried the poor child.

"You are worn out; that is what is the matter with you," said Everard, strong in English common-sense. "There is nothing that affects the nerves and the temper like an overstrain of your strength. You must be quite quiet, and let yourself be taken care of, now Herbert is better, and you will get all right again. Don't cry; you are worn out, my poor little queen."

"Don't call me that," said the girl, weeping; "it makes me think of the happy times before he was ill, and of Aunt Susan and home."

"And what could you think of better?" said Everard. "By-and-by—don't cry, Queeny!—the happy days will come back, and you and I will take Herbert home."

And he took her hand and held it fast, and as she went on crying, kissed it and said many a soft word of consolation. He was her cousin, and had been brought up with her; so it was natural. But I do not know what Everard meant, neither did he know himself: "You and I will take Herbert home." The words had a curious effect upon both the young people—upon her who listened and he who spoke. They seemed to imply a great deal more than they really meant.

Madame de Mirfleur did not see this little scene, which probably would have startled and alarmed her; but quite independently there rose up in her mind an idea which pleased her, and originated a new interest in her thoughts. It came to her as she sat watching Herbert, who was sleeping softly after the first airing of his renewed convalescence. He was so quiet and doing so well that her mind was at ease about him, and free to proceed to other matters; and from these thoughts of hers arose a little comedy in the midst of the almost tragedy which kept the little party so long prisoners in the soft seclusion of the Kanderthal.

CHAPTER XVIII

Madame de Mirfleur had more anxieties connected with her first family than merely the illness of her son; she had also the fate of her daughter to think of, and I am not sure that the latter disquietude did not give her the most concern. Herbert, poor boy, could but die, which would be a great grief, but an end of all anxiety, whereas Reine was likely to live, and cause much anxiety, unless her future was properly cared for. Reine's establishment in life had been a very serious thought to Madame de Mirfleur since the girl was about ten years old, and though she was only eighteen as yet, her mother knew how negligent English relatives are in this particular, leaving a girl's marriage to chance, or what they are pleased to call Providence, or more likely her own silly fancy, without taking any trouble to establish her suitably in life. She had thought much, very much of this, and of the great unlikelihood, on the other hand, of Reine, with her English ways, submitting to her mother's guidance in so important a matter, or accepting the husband whom she might choose; and if the girl was obstinate and threw herself back, as was most probable, on the absurd laisser-aller of the English, the chances were that she would never find a proper settlement at all. These thoughts, temporarily suspended when Herbert was at his worst, had come up again with double force as she ceased to be completely occupied by him; and when she found Everard with his cousins, a new impulse was given to her imagination. Madame de Mirfleur had known Everard more or less since his boyhood; she liked him, for his manners were always pleasant to women. He was of suitable age, birth, and disposition; and though she did not quite know the amount of his means, which was the most important preliminary of all, he could not be poor, as he was of no profession, and free to wander about the world as only rich young men can do. Madame de Mirfleur felt that it would be simply criminal on her part to let such an occasion slip. In the intervals of their nursing, accordingly, she sought Everard's company, and had long talks with him when no one else was by. She was a pretty woman still, though she was Reine's mother, and had all the graces of her nation, and that conversational skill which is so thoroughly French; and Everard, who liked the society of women, had not the least objection on his side to her companionship. In this way she managed to find out from him what his position was, and to form a very good guess at his income, and to ascertain many details of his life, with infinite skill, tact, and patience, and without in the least alarming the object of her study. She found out that he had a house of his own, and money enough to sound very well, indeed, if put into francs, which she immediately did by means of mental calculations, which cost her some time and a considerable effort. This, with so much more added to it, in the shape of Reine's dot, would make altogether, she thought, a very pretty fortune; and evidently the two were made for each other. They had similar tastes and habits in many points; one was twenty-five, the other eighteen; one dark, the other fair; one impulsive and high-spirited, with quick French blood in her veins, the other tranquil, with all the English ballast necessary. Altogether, it was such a marriage as might have been made in heaven;

and if heaven had not seen fit to do it, Madame de Mirfleur felt herself strong enough to remedy this inadvertence. It seemed to her that she would be neglecting her chief duty as Reine's mother if she allowed this opportunity to slip through her hands. To be sure, it would have been more according to les convenances, had there been a third party at hand, a mutual friend to undertake the negotiation; but, failing any one else, Madame de Mirfleur felt that, rather than lose such an "occasion," she must, for once, neglect the convenances, and put herself into the breach.

"I do not understand how it is that your friends do not marry you," she said one day when they were walking together. "Ah, you laugh, Monsieur Everard. I know that is not your English way; but believe me, it is the duty of the friends of every young person. It is a dangerous thing to choose for yourself; for how should you know what is in a young girl? You can judge by nothing but looks and outside manners, which are very deceitful, while a mother or a judicious friend would sound her character. You condemn our French system, you others, but that is because you don't know. For example, when I married my present husband, M. de Mirfleur, it was an affair of great deliberation. I did not think at first that his property was so good as I had a right to expect, and there was some scandal about his grandparents, which did not quite please me. But all that was smoothed away in process of time, and a personal interview convinced me that I should find in him everything that a reasonable woman desires. And so I do; we are as happy as the day. With poor Herbert's father the affair was very different. There was no deliberation—no time for thought. With my present experience, had I known that daughters do not inherit in England, I should have drawn back, even at the last moment. But I was young, and my friends were not so prudent as they ought to have been, and we did what you call fall in love. Ah! it is a mistake! a mistake! In France things are a great deal better managed. I wish I could convert you to my views."

"It would be very easy for Madame de Mirfleur to convert me to anything," said Everard, with a skill which he must have caught from her, and which, to tell the truth, occasioned himself some surprise.

"Ah, you flatter!" said the lady; "but seriously, if you will think of it, there are a thousand advantages on our side. For example, now, if I were to propose to you a charming young person whom I know—not one whom I have seen on the surface, but whom I know au fond, you understand—with a dot that would be suitable, good health, and good temper, and everything that is desirable in a wife? I should be sure of my facts, you could know nothing but the surface. Would it not then be much better for you to put yourself into my hands, and take my advice?"

"I have no doubt of it," said Everard, once more gallantly; "if I wished to marry, I could not do better than put myself in such skilful hands."

"If you wished to marry—ah, bah! if you come to that, perhaps there are not many who wish to marry, for that sole reason," said Madame de Mirfleur.

"Pardon me; but why then should they do it?" said Everard.

"Ah, fie, fie! you are not so innocent as you appear," she said.

"Need I tell to you the many reasons? Besides, it is your duty. No man can be really a trustworthy member of society till he has married and ranged himself. It is clearly your duty to range yourself at a certain time of life, and accept the responsibilities that nature imposes. Besides, what would become of us if young men did not marry? There would be a mob of mauvais sujets, and no society at all. No, mon ami, it is your duty; and when I tell you I have a very charming young person in my eye—"

"I should like to see her very much. I have no doubt your taste is excellent, and that we should agree in most points," said Everard, with a laugh.

"Perhaps," said Madame de Mirfleur, humoring him, "a very charming young person," she added, seriously, "with, let us say, a hundred and fifty thousand francs. What would you say to that for the dot?"

"Exactly the right sum, I have no doubt—if I had the least notion how much it was," said Everard, entering into the joke, as he thought; "but, pardon my impatience, the young person herself—"

"Extremely comme il faut," said the lady, very gravely. "You may be sure I should not think of proposing any one who was not of good family; noble, of course; that is what you call gentlefolks—you English. Young—at the most charming age indeed—not too young to be a companion, nor too old to adapt herself to your wishes. A delightful disposition, lively—a little impetuous, perhaps."

"Why this is a paragon!" said Everard, beginning to feel a slight uneasiness. He had not yet a notion whom she meant; but a suspicion that this was no joke, but earnest, began to steal over his mind: he was infinitely amused; but notwithstanding his curiosity and relish of the fun, was too honorable and delicate not to be a little afraid of letting it go too far. "She must be ugly to make up for so many virtues; otherwise how could I hope that such a bundle of excellence would even look at me?"

"On the contrary, there are many people who think her pretty," said Madame de Mirfleur; "perhaps I am not quite qualified to judge. She has charming bright eyes, good hair, good teeth, a good figure, and, I think I may say, a very favorable disposition, Monsieur Everard, toward you."

"Good heavens!" cried the young man; and he blushed hotly, and made an endeavor to change the subject. "I wonder if this Kanderthal is quite the place for Herbert," he said hastily; "don't you think there is a want of air? My own opinion is that he would be better on higher ground."

"Yes, probably," said Madame de Mirfleur, smiling. "Ah, Monsieur Everard, you are afraid; but do not shrink so, I will not harm you. You are very droll, you English—what you call prude. I will not frighten you any more; but I have a regard for you, and I should like to marry you all the same."

"You do me too much honor," said Everard, taking off his hat and making his best bow. Thus he tried to carry off his embarrassment; and Madame de Mirfleur did not want any further indication that she had gone far enough, but stopped instantly, and began to talk to him with all the ease of her nation about a hundred other subjects, so that he half forgot this assault upon him, or thought he had mistaken, and that it was merely her French way. She was so lively and amusing, indeed, that she completely reassured him, and brought him back to the inn in the best of humors with her and with himself. Reine was standing on the balcony as they came up, and her face brightened as he looked up and waved his hand to her. "It works," Madame de Mirfleur said to herself; but even she felt that for a beginning she had said quite enough.

In a few days after, to her great delight, a compatriot—a gentleman whom she knew, and who was acquainted with her family and antecedents—appeared in the Kanderthal, on his way, by the Gemmi pass, to the French side of Switzerland. She hailed his arrival with the sincerest pleasure, for, indeed, it was much more proper that a third party should manage the matter. M. de Bonneville was a gray-haired, middle-aged Frenchman, very straight and very grave, with a grizzled moustache and a military air. He understood her at a word, as was natural, and when she took him aside and explained to him all her fears and difficulties about Reine, and the fearful neglect of English relations, in this, the most important point in a girl's life, his heart was touched with admiration of the true motherly solicitude thus confided to him.

"It is not, perhaps, the moment I would have chosen," said Madame de Mirfleur, putting her handkerchief to her eyes, "while my Herbert is still so ill; but what would you, cher Baron? My other child is equally dear to me; and when she gets among her English relations, I shall never be able to do anything for my Reine."

"I understand, I understand," said M. de Bonneville; "believe me, dear lady, I am not unworthy of so touching a confidence. I will take occasion to make myself acquainted with this charming young man, and I will seize the first opportunity of presenting the subject to him in such a light as you would wish."

"I must make you aware of all the details," said the lady, and she disclosed to him the amount of Reine's dot, which pleased M. de Bonneville much, and made him think, if this negotiation came to nothing, of a son of his own, who would find it a very agreeable addition to his biens. "Decidedly, Mademoiselle Reine is not a partie to be neglected," he said, and made a note of all the chief points. He even put off his journey for three or four days, in order to be of use to his friend, and to see how the affair would end.

From this time Everard found his company sought by the new-comer with a persistency which was very flattering. M. de Bonneville praised his French, and though he was conscious he did not deserve the praise, he was immensely flattered by it; and his new friend sought information upon English subjects with a serious desire to know, which pleased Everard still more. "I hope you are coming to England, as you want to know so much about it," he said, in an Englishman's cordial yet unmannerly way.

"I propose to myself to go some time," said the cautious Baron, thinking that probably if he arranged this marriage, the grateful young people might give him an invitation to their château in England; but he was very cautious, and did not begin his attack till he had known Everard for three days at least, which, in Switzerland, is as good as a friendship of years.

"Do you stay with your cousins?" he said one day when they were walking up the hillside on the skirts of the Gemmi. M. de Bonneville was a little short of breath, and would pause frequently, not caring to confess this weakness, to admire the view. The valley lay stretched out before them like a map, the snowy hills retiring at their right hand, the long line of heathery broken land disappearing into the distance on the other, and the village, with its little bridge and wooden houses straggling across its river. Herbert's wheeled chair was visible on the road like a child's toy, Reine walking by her brother's side. "It is beautiful, the devotion of that charming young person to her brother," M. de Bonneville said, with a sudden burst of sentiment; "pardon me, it is too much for my feelings! Do you mean to remain with this so touching group, Monsieur Austin, or do you proceed to Italy, like myself?"

"I have not made up my mind," said Everard. "So long as I can be of any use to Herbert, I will stay."

"Poor young man! it is to be hoped he will get better, though I fear it is not very probable. How sad it is, not only for himself, but for his charming sister! One can understand Madame de Mirfleur's anxiety to see her daughter established in life."

"Is she anxious on that subject?" said Everard, half laughing. "I think she may spare herself the trouble. Reine is very young, and there is time enough."

"That is one of the points, I believe, on which our two peoples take different views," said M. de Bonneville, good-humoredly. "In France it is considered a duty with parents to marry their children well and suitably—which is reasonable, you will allow, at least."

"I do not see, I confess," said Everard, with a little British indignation, "how, in such a matter, any one man can choose for another. It is the thing of all others in which people must please themselves."

"You think so? Well," said M. de Bonneville, shrugging his shoulders, "the one does not hinder the other. You may still please yourself, if your parents are judicious and place before you a proper choice."

Everard said nothing. He cut down the thistles on the side of the road with his cane to give vent to his feelings, and mentally shrugged his shoulders too. What was the use of discussing such a subject with a Frenchman? As if they could be fit to judge, with their views!

"In no other important matter of life," said M. de Bonneville, insinuatingly, "do we allow young persons at an early age to decide for themselves; and this, pardon me for saying so, is the most impossible of all. How can a young girl of eighteen come to any wise conclusion in a matter so important? What can her grounds be for forming a judgment? She knows neither men nor life; it is not to be desired that she should. How then is she to judge what is best for her? Pardon me, the English are a very sensible people, but this is a bêtise: I can use no other word."

"Well, sir," said Everard, hotly, with a youthful blush, "among us we still believe in such a thing as love."

"Mon jeune ami," said his companion, "I also believe in it; but tell me, what is a girl to love who knows nothing? Black eyes or blue, light hair or dark, him who valses best, or him who sings? What does she know more? what do we wish the white creature to know more? But when her parents say to her— 'Chérie, here is some one whom with great care we have chosen, whom we know to be worthy of your innocence, whose sentiments and principles are such as do him honor, and whose birth and means are suitable. Love him if you can; he is worthy'—once more pardon me," said M. de Bonneville, "it seems to me that this is more accordant with reason than to let a child decide her fate upon the experience of a soirée du bal. We think so in France."

Everard could not say much in reply to this. There rose up before him a recollection of Kate and Sophy mounted high on Dropmore's drag, and careering over the country with that hero and his companions under the nominal guardianship of a young matron as rampant as themselves. They were perfectly able to form a judgment upon the relative merits of the Guardsmen; perfectly able to set himself aside coolly as nobody; which was, I fear, the head and front of their offending. Perhaps there were cases in which the Frenchman might be right.

"The case is almost, but I do not say quite, as strong with a young man," said M. de Bonneville. "Again, it is the experience of the soirée du bal which you would trust to in place of the anxious selection of friends and parents. A young girl is not a statue to be measured at a glance. Her excellences are modest," said the mutual friend, growing enthusiastic. "She is something cachée, sacred; it is but her features, her least profound attractions, which can be learned in a valse or a party of pleasure. Mademoiselle Reine is a very charming young person," he continued in a more business-like tone. "Her mother has confided to me her anxieties about her. I have a strong inclination to propose to Madame de Mirfleur my second son, Oscar, who, though I say it who should not, is as fine a young fellow as it is possible to see."

Everard stopped short in his walk, and looked at him menacingly, clenching his fist unawares. It was all he could do to subdue his fury and keep himself from pitching the old match-maker headlong down the hill. So that was what the specious old humbug was thinking of? His son, indeed; some miserable, puny Frenchman—for Reine! Everard's blood boiled in his veins, and he could not help looking fiercely in his companion's face; he was speechless with consternation and wrath. Reine! that they should discuss her like a bale of goods, and marry her perhaps, poor little darling!—if there was no one to interfere.

"Yes," said M. de Bonneville, meditatively. "The dot is small, smaller than Oscar has a right to expect; but in other ways the partie is very suitable. It would seal an old friendship, and it would secure the happiness of two families. Unfortunately the post has gone to-day, but to-morrow I will write to Oscar and suggest it to him. I do not wish for a more sweet daughter-in-law than Mademoiselle Reine."

"But can you really for a moment suppose that Reine—!" thundered forth the Englishman. "Good heavens! what an extraordinary way you have of ordering affairs! Reine, poor girl, with her brother ill, her heart bursting, all her mind absorbed, to be roused up in order to have some fine young gentleman presented to her! It is incredible—it is absurd—it is cruel!" said the young man, flushed with anger and indignation. His companion while he stormed did nothing but smile.

"Cher Monsieur Everard," he said, "I think I comprehend your feelings. Believe me, Oscar shall stand in no one's way. If you desire to secure this pearl for yourself, trust to me; I will propose it to Madame de Mirfleur. You are about my son's age; probably rich, as all you English are rich. To be sure, there is a degree of relationship between you; but then you are Protestants both, and it does not matter. If you will favor me with your confidence about preliminaries, I understand all your delicacy of feeling. As an old friend of the family I will venture to propose it to Madame de Mirfleur."

"You will do nothing of the kind," said Everard furious. "I—address myself to any girl by a go-between! I—insult poor Reine at such a moment! You may understand French delicacy of feeling, M. de Bonneville, but when we use such words we English mean something different. If any man should venture to interfere so in my private affairs—or in my cousin's either for that matter—"

"Monsieur Everard, I think you forgot yourself," said the Frenchman with dignity.

"Yes; perhaps I forget myself. I don't mean to say anything disagreeable to you, for I suppose you mean no harm; but if a countryman of my own had presumed—had ventured—. Of course I don't mean to use these words to you," said Everard, conscious that a quarrel on such a subject with a man of double his age would be little desirable; "it is our different ways of thinking. But pray be good enough, M. de Bonneville, to say nothing to Madame de Mirfleur about me."

"Certainly not," said the Frenchman with a smile, "if you do not wish it. Here is the excellence of our system, which by means of leaving the matter in the hands of a third party, avoids all offence or misunderstanding. Since you do not wish it, I will write to Oscar to-night."

Everard gave him a look, which if looks were explosive might have blown him across the Gemmi. "You mistake me," he said, not knowing what he said; "I will not have my cousin interfered with, any more than myself—"

"Ah, forgive me! that is going too far," said the Frenchman; "that is what you call dog in the manger. You will not eat yourself, and you would prevent others from eating. I have her mother's sanction, which is all that is important, and my son will be here in three days. Ah! the sun is beginning to sink behind the hills. How beautiful is that rose-flush on the snow! With your permission I will turn back and make the descent again. The hour of sunset is never wholesome. Pardon, we shall meet at the table d'hôte."

Everard made him the very slightest possible salutation, and pursued his walk in a state of excitement and rage which I cannot describe. He went miles up the hill in his fervor of feeling, not knowing where he went. What! traffic in Reine—sell Reine to the best bidder; expose her to a cold-blooded little beast of a Frenchman, who would come and look at the girl to judge whether he liked her as an appendage to her dot! Everard's rage and dismay carried him almost to the top of the pass before he discovered where he was.

CHAPTER XIX

Everard was too late, as might have been expected, for the table d'hôte. When he reached the village, very tired after his long walk, he met the diners there, strolling about in the soft evening—the men with their cigars, the ladies in little groups in their evening toilettes, which were of an unexciting character. On the road, at a short distance from the hotel, he encountered Madame de Mirfleur and M. de Bonneville, no doubt planning the advent of M. Oscar, he thought to himself, with renewed fury; but, indeed, they were only talking over the failure of their project in respect to himself. Reine was seated in the balcony above, alone, looking out upon the soft night and the distant mountains, and soothed, I think, by the hum of voices close at hand, which mingled with the sound of the waterfall, and gave a sense of fellowship and society. Everard looked up at her and waved his hand, and begged her to wait till he should come. There was a new moon making her way upward in the pale sky, not yet quite visible behind the hills. Reine's face was turned toward it with a certain wistful stillness which went to Everard's heart. She was in this little world, but not of it. She had no part in the whisperings and laughter of those groups below. Her young life had been plucked out of the midst of life, as it were, and wrapped in the shadows of a sick-chamber, when others like her were in the full tide of youthful enjoyment. As Everard dived into the dining-room of the inn to snatch a hasty meal, the perpetual contrast which he felt himself to make in spite of himself, came back to his mind. I think he continued to have an unconscious feeling, of which he would have been ashamed had it been forced upon his notice or put into words, that he had himself a choice to make between his cousins—though how he could have chosen both Kate and Sophy, I am at a loss to know, and he never separated the two in his thoughts. When he looked, as it were, from Reine to them, he felt himself to descend ever so far in the scale. Those pretty gay creatures "enjoyed themselves" a great deal more than poor Reine had ever had it in her power to do. But it was no choice of Reine's which thus separated her from the enjoyments of her kind—was it the mere force of circumstances? Everard could remember Reine as gay as a bird, as bright as a flower; though he could not connect any idea of her with drags or race-courses. He had himself rowed her on the river many a day, and heard her pretty French songs rising like a fresh spontaneous breeze of melody over the water. Now she looked to him like something above the common course of life—with so much in her eyes that he could not fathom, and such an air of thought and of emotion about her as half attracted, half repelled him. The emotions of Sophy and Kate were all on the surface—thrown off into the air in careless floods of words and laughter. Their sentiments were all boldly expressed; all the more boldly when they were sentiments of an equivocal character. He seemed to hear them, loud, noisy, laughing, moving about in their bright dresses, lawless, scorning all restraint; and then his mind recurred to the light figure seated overhead in the evening darkness, shadowy, dusky, silent, with only a soft whiteness where her face was, and not a sound to betray her presence. Perhaps she was weeping silently in her solitude; perhaps thinking unutterable thoughts; perhaps anxiously planning what she could do for her invalid to make him better or happier, perhaps praying for him. These ideas brought a moisture to Everard's eyes. It was all a peradventure, but there was no peradventure, no mystery about Kate and Sophy; no need to wonder what they were thinking of. Their souls moved in so limited an orbit, and the life which they flattered themselves they knew so thoroughly ran in such a narrow channel, that no one who knew them could go far astray in calculation of what they were about; but Reine was unfathomable in her silence, a little world of individual thought and feeling, into which Everard did not know if he was worthy to enter, and could not divine.

While the young man thus mused—and dined, very uncomfortably—Madame de Mirfleur listened to the report of her agent. She had a lace shawl thrown over her head, over the hair which was still as brown and plentiful as ever, and needed no matronly covering. They walked along among the other groups, straying a little further than the rest, who stopped her from moment to moment as she went on, to ask for her son.

"Better, much better; a thousand thanks," she kept saying. "Really better; on the way to get well, I hope;" and then she would turn an anxious ear to M. de Bonneville. "On such matters sense is not to be expected from the English," she said, with a cloud on her face; "they understand nothing. I could not for a moment doubt your discretion, cher Monsieur Bonneville; but perhaps you were a little too open with him, explained yourself too clearly; not that I should think for a moment of blaming you. They are all the same, all the same!—insensate, unable to comprehend."

"I do not think my discretion was at fault," said the Frenchman. "It is, as you say, an inherent inability to understand. If he had not seen the folly of irritating himself, I have no doubt that your young friend would have resorted to the brutal weapons of the English in return for the interest I showed him; in which case," said M. de Bonneville, calmly, "I should have been under a painful necessity in respect to him. For your sake, Madame, I am glad that he was able to apologize and restrain himself."

"Juste ciel! that I should have brought this upon you!" cried Madame de Mirfleur; and it was after the little sensation caused in her mind by this that he ventured to suggest that other suitor for Reine.

"My son is already sous-préfet," he said. "He has a great career before him. It is a position that would suit Mademoiselle your charming daughter. In his official position, I need not say, a wife of Mademoiselle Reine's distinction would be everything for him; and though we might look for more money, yet I shall willingly waive that question in consideration of the desirable connections my son would thus acquire; a mother-in-law like Madame de Mirfleur is not to be secured every day," said the negotiant, bowing to his knees.

Madame de Mirfleur, on her part, made such a curtsey as the Kanderthal, overrun by English tourists, had never seen before; and she smiled upon the idea of M. Oscar and his career, and felt that could she but see Reine the wife of a sous-préfet, the girl would be well and safely disposed of. But after her first exultation, a cold shiver came over Reine's mother. She drew her shawl more closely round her.

"Alas!" she said, "so far as I am concerned everything would be easy; but, pity me, cher Baron, pity me! Though I trust I know my duty, I cannot undertake for Reine. What suffering it is to have a child with other rules of action than those one approves of! It should be an example to every one not to marry out of their own country. My child is English to the nail-tips. I cannot help it; it is my desolation. If it is her fancy to find M. Oscar pleasing, all will go well; but if it is not, then our project will be ended; and with such uncertainty can I venture to bring Monsieur your son here, to this little village at the end of the world?"

Thus the elder spirits communed not without serious anxiety; for Reine herself, and her dot and her relationships, seemed so desirable that M. de Bonneville did not readily give up the idea.

"She will surely accept your recommendation," he said, discouraged and surprised.

"Alas! my dear friend, you do not understand the English," said the mother. "The recommendation would be the thing which would spoil all."

"But then the parti you had yourself chosen—Monsieur Everard?" said the Frenchman, puzzled.

"Ah, cher Baron, he would have managed it all in the English way," said Madame de Mirfleur, almost weeping. "I should have had no need to recommend. You do not know, as I do, the English way."

And they turned back and walked on together under the stars to the hotel door, where all the other groups were clustering, talking of expeditions past and to come. The warm evening air softened the voices and gave to the flitting figures, the half-visible colors, the shadowy groups, a refinement unknown to them in broad daylight. Reine on her balcony saw her mother coming back, and felt in her heart a wondering bitterness. Reine did not care for the tourist society in which, as in every other, Madame de Mirfleur made herself acquaintances and got a little amusement; yet she could not help feeling (as what girl could in the circumstances?) a secret sense that it was she who had a right to the amusement, and that her own deep and grave anxiety, the wild trembling of her own heart, the sadness of the future, and the burden which she was bearing and had to bear every day, would have been more appropriate to her mother, at her mother's age, than to herself. This thought—it was Reine's weakness to feel this painful antagonism toward her mother—had just come into a mind which had been full of better thoughts, when Everard came upstairs and joined her in the balcony. He too had met Madame de Mirfleur as he came from the hotel, and he thought he had heard the name "Oscar" as he passed her; so that his mind had received a fresh impulse, and was full of belligerent and indignant thoughts. He came quite softly, however, to the edge of the balcony where Reine was seated, and stood over her, leaning against the window, a dark figure, scarcely distinguishable. Reine's heart stirred softly at his coming; she did not know why; she did not ask herself why; but took it for granted that she liked him to come, because of his kindness and his kinship, and because they had been brought up together, and because of his brotherly goodness to Herbert, and through Herbert to herself.

"I have got an idea, Reine," Everard said, in the quick, sharp tones of suppressed emotion. "I think the Kanderthal is too close; there is not air enough for Herbert. Let us take him up higher—that is, of course, if the doctor approves."

"I thought you liked the Kanderthal," said Reine, raising her eyes to him, and touched with a visionary disappointment. It hurt her a little to think that he was not pleased with the place in which he had lingered so long for their sakes.

"I like it well enough," said Everard; "but it suddenly occurred to me to-day that, buried down here in a hole, beneath the hills, there is too little air for Bertie. He wants air. It seems to me that is the chief thing he wants. What did the doctor say?"

"He said—what you have always said, Everard—that Bertie had regained his lost ground, and that this last illness was an accident, like the thunderstorm. It might have killed him; but as it has not killed him, it does him no particular harm. That sounds nonsense," said Reine, "but it is what he told me. He is doing well, the doctor says—doing well; and I can't be half glad—not as I ought."

"Why not, Reine?"

"I can't tell, my heart is so heavy," she cried, putting her hand to her wet eyes. "Before this—accident, as you call it—I felt, oh, so different! There was one night that I seemed to see and hear God deciding for us. I felt quite sure; there was something in the air, something coming down from the sky. You may laugh, Everard; but to feel that you are quite, quite sure that God is on your side, listening to you, and considering and doing what you ask—oh, you can't tell what a thing it is."

"I don't laugh, Reine; very, very far from it, dear."

"And then to be disappointed!" she cried; "to feel a blank come over everything, as if there was no one to care, as if God had forgotten or was thinking of something else! I am not quite so bad as that now," she added, with a weary gesture; "but I feel as if it was not God, but only nature or chance or something, that does it. An accident, you all say—going out when we had better have stayed in; a chance cloud blowing this way, when it might have blown some other way. Oh!" cried Reine, "if that is all, what is the good of living? All accident, chance; Nature turning this way or the other; no one to sustain you if you are stumbling; no one to say what is to be—and it is! I do not care to live, I do not want to live, if this is all there is to be in the world."

She put her head down in her lap, hidden by her hands. Everard stood over her, deeply touched and wondering, but without a word to say. What could he say? It had never in his life occurred to him to think on such subjects. No great trouble or joy, nothing which stirs the soul to its depths, had ever happened to the young man in his easy existence. He had sailed over the sunny surface of things, and had been content. He could not answer anything to Reine in her first great conflict with the undiscovered universe—the first painful, terrible shadow that had ever come across her childish faith. He did not even understand the pain it gave her, nor how so entirely speculative a matter could give pain. But though he was thus prevented from feeling the higher sympathy, he was very sorry for his little cousin, and reverent of her in this strange affliction. He put his hand softly, tenderly upon her hidden head, and stroked it in his ignorance, as he might have consoled a child.

"Reine, I am not good enough to say anything to you, even if I knew," he said, "and I don't know. I suppose God must always be at the bottom of it, whatever happens. We cannot tell or judge, can we? for, you know, we cannot see any more than one side. That's all I know," he added, humbly stroking once more with a tender touch the bowed head which he could scarcely see. How different this was from the life he had come from—from Madame de Mirfleur conspiring about Oscar and how to settle her daughter in life! Reine, he felt, was as far away from it all as heaven is from earth; and somehow he changed as he stood there, and felt a different man; though, indeed, he was not, I fear, at all different, and would have fallen away again in ten minutes, had the call of the gayer voices to which he was accustomed come upon his ear. His piety was of the good, honest, unthinking kind—a sort of placid, stubborn dependence upon unseen power and goodness, which is not to be shaken by any argument, and which outlasts all philosophy—thank heaven for it!—a good sound magnet in its way, keeping the compass right, though it may not possess the higher attributes of spiritual insight or faith.

Reine was silent for a time, in the stillness that always follows an outburst of feeling; but in spite of herself she was consoled—consoled by the voice and touch which were so soft and kind, and by the steady, unelevated, but in its way certain, reality of his assurance. God must be at the bottom of it all—Everard, without thinking much on the subject, or feeling very much, had always a sort of dull, practical conviction of that; and this, like some firm strong wooden prop to lean against, comforted the visionary soul of Reine. She felt the solid strength of it a kind of support to her, though there might be, indeed, more faith in her aching, miserable doubt than there was in half-a-dozen such souls as Everard's; yet the commonplace was a support to the visionary in this as in so many other things.

"You want a change, too," said Everard. "You are worn out. Let us go to some of the simple places high up among the hills. I have a selfish reason. I have just heard of some one coming who would—bore you very much. At least, he would bore me very much," said the young man, with forced candor. "Let us get away before he comes."

"Is it some one from England?" said Reine.

"I don't know where he is from—last. You don't know him. Never mind the fellow; of course that's nothing to the purpose. But I do wish Herbert would try a less confined air."

"It is strange that the doctor and you should agree so well," said Reine, with a smile. "You are sure you did not put it into his head. He wants us to go up to Appenzell, or some such place; and Herbert is to take the cure des sapins and the cure de petit lait. It is a quiet place, where no tourists go. But, Everard, I don't think you must come with us; it will be so dull for you."

"So what? It is evident you want me to pay you compliments. I am determined to go. If I must not accompany you, I will hire a private mule of my own with a side-saddle. Why should not I do the cure de petit lait too?"

"Ah, because you don't want it."

"Is that a reason to be given seriously to a British tourist? It is the very thing to make me go."

"Everard, you laugh; I wish I could laugh too," said Reine. "Probably Herbert would get better the sooner. I feel so heavy—so serious—not like other girls."

"You were neither heavy nor serious in the old times," said Everard, looking down upon her with a stirring of fondness which was not love, in his heart, "when you used to be scolded for being so French. Did you ever dine solemnly in the old hall since you grew up, Reine? It is very odd. I could not help looking up to the gallery, and hearing the old scuffle in the corner, and wondering what you thought to see me sitting splendid with the aunts at table. It was very bewildering. I felt like two people, one sitting grown-up down below, the other whispering up in the corner with Reine and Bertie, looking on and thinking it something grand and awful. I shall go there and look at you when we are all at home again. You have never been at Whiteladies since you were grown up, Reine?"

"No," she said, turning her face to him with a soft ghost of a laugh. It was nothing to call a laugh; yet Everard felt proud of himself for having so far succeeded in turning her mood. The moon was up now, and shining upon her, making a whiteness all about her, and throwing shadows of the rails of the balcony, so that Reine's head rose as out of a cage; but the look she turned to him was wistful, half-beseeching, though Reine was not aware of it. She half put out her hand to him. He was helping her out of that prison of grief and anxiety and wasted youth. "How wonderful," she said, "to think we were all children once, not afraid of anything! I can't make it out."

"Speak for yourself, my queen," said Everard. "I was always mortally afraid of the ghost in the great staircase. I don't like to go up or down now by myself. Reine, I looked into the old playroom the last time I was there. It was when poor Bertie was so ill. There were all our tops and our bats and your music, and I don't know what rubbish besides. It went to my heart. I had to rush off and do something, or I should have broken down and made a baby of myself."

A soft sob came from Reine's throat and relieved her; a rush of tears came to her eyes. She looked up at him, the moon shining so whitely on her face, and glistening in those drops of moisture, and took his hand in her impulsive way and kissed it, not able to speak. The touch of those velvet lips on his brown hand made Everard jump. Women the least experienced take such a salutation sedately, like Maud in the poem; it comes natural. But to a man the effect is different. He grew suddenly red and hot, and tingling to his very hair. He took her hand in both his with a kind of tender rage, and knelt down and kissed it over and over, as if to make up by forced exaggeration for that desecration of her maiden lips.

"You must not do that," he said, quick and sharply, in tones that sounded almost angry; "you must never do that, Reine;" and could not get over it, but repeated the words, half-scolding her, half-weeping over her hand, till poor Reine, confused and bewildered, felt that something new had come to pass between them, and blushed overwhelmingly too, so that the moon had hard ado to keep the upper hand. She had to rise from her seat on the balcony before she could get her hand from him, and felt, as it were, another, happier, more trivial life come rushing back upon her in a strange maze of pleasure and apprehension, and wonder and shamefacedness.

"I think I hear Bertie calling," she said, out of the flutter and confusion of her heart, and went away like a ghost out of the moonlight, leaving Everard, come to himself, leaning against the window, and looking out blankly upon the night.

Had he made a dreadful fool of himself? he asked, when he was thus left alone; then held up his hand, which she had kissed, and looked at it in his strange new thrill of emotion with a half-imbecile smile. He felt himself wondering that the place did not show in the moonlight, and at last put it up to his face, half-ashamed, though nobody saw him. What had happened to Everard? He himself could not tell.

CHAPTER XX

I do not know that English doctors have the gift of recommending those pleasant simple fictions of treatment which bring their patient face to face with nature, and give that greatest nurse full opportunity to try her powers, as Continental doctors do, in cases where medicine has already tried its powers and failed—the grape cure, the whey cure, the fir-tree cure—turning their patient as it were into the fresh air, among the trees, on the hillsides, and leaving the rest to the mother of us all. François was already strong in the opinion that his master's improvement arose from the sapins that perfumed the air in the Kanderthal, and made a solemn music in the wind; and the cure de petit lait in the primitive valleys of Appenzell commended itself to the young fanciful party, and to Herbert himself, whose mind was extremely taken up by the idea. He had no sooner heard of it than he began to find the Kanderthal close and airless, as Everard suggested to him, and in his progressing convalescence the idea of a little change and novelty was delightful to the lad thus creeping back across the threshold of life. Already he felt himself no invalid, but a young man, with all a young man's hopes before him. When he returned from his daily expedition in his chair he would get out and saunter about for ten minutes, assuming an easy and, as far as he could, a robust air, in front of the hotel, and would answer to the inquiries of the visitors that he was getting strong fast, and hoped soon to be all right. That interruption, however, to his first half-miraculous recovery had affected Herbert something in the same way as it affected Reine. He too had fallen out of the profound sense of an actual interposition of Providence in his favor, out of the saintliness of that resolution to be henceforward "good" beyond measure, by way of proving their gratitude, which had affected them both in so childlike a way. The whole matter had slid back to the lower level of ordinary agencies, nature, accident, what the doctor did and the careful nurses, what the patient swallowed, the equality of the temperature kept up in his room, and so forth.

This shed a strange blank over it all to Herbert as well as to his sister. He did not seem to have the same tender and awestruck longing to be good. His recovery was not the same thing as it had been. He got better in a common way, as other men get better. He had come down from the soft eminence on which he had felt himself, and the change had a vulgarizing effect, lowering the level somehow of all his thoughts. But Herbert's mind was not sufficiently visionary to feel this as a definite pain, as Reine did. He accepted it, sufficiently content, and perhaps easier on the lower level, and then to feel the springs of health stirring and bubbling after the long languor of deadly sickness is delight enough to dismiss all secondary emotions from the heart. Herbert was anxious to make another move, to appear before a new population, who would not be so sympathetic, so conscious that he had just escaped the jaws of death.

"They are all a little disappointed that I did not die," he said. "The village people don't like it—they have been cheated out of their sensation. I should like to come back in a year or so, when I am quite strong, and show myself; but in the meantime let's move on. If Everard stays, we shall be quite jolly enough by ourselves, we three. We shan't want any other society. I am ready whenever you please."

As for Madame de Mirfleur, however, she was quite indisposed for this move. She protested on Herbert's behalf, but was silenced by the physician; she protested on her own account that it was quite impossible she could go further off into those wilds further and further from her home, but was stopped by Reine, who begged her mamma not to think of that, since François and she had so often had the charge of Herbert.

"I am sure you will be glad to get back to M. de Mirfleur and the children," Reine said with an ironical cordiality which she might have spared, as her mother never divined what she meant.

"Yes," Madame de Mirfleur answered quite seriously, "that is true, chérie. Of course I shall be glad to get home where they all want me so much; though M. de Mirfleur, to whom I am sorry to see you never do justice, has been very good and has not complained. Still the children are very young, and it is natural I should be anxious to get home. But see what happened last time when I went away," said the mother, not displeased perhaps, much as she lamented its consequences, to have this proof of her own importance handy. "I should never forgive myself if it occurred again."

Reine grew pale and then red, moved beyond bearing, but she dared not say anything, and could only clench her little hands and go out to the balcony to keep herself from replying. Was it her fault that the thunder-storm came down so suddenly out of a clear sky? She was not the only one who had been deceived. Were there not ever so many parties on the mountains who came home drenched and frightened, though they had experienced guides with them who ought to have known the changes of the sky better than little Reine? Still she could not say that this might not have been averted had the mother been there, and thus she was driven frantic and escaped into the balcony and shut her lips close that she might not reply.

"But I shall go with them and see them safe, for the journey, at least; you may confide in my discretion," said Everard.

Madame de Mirfleur gave him a look, and then looked at Reine upon the balcony. It was a significant glance, and filled Everard with very disagreeable emotions. What did the woman mean? He fell back upon the consciousness that she was French, which of course explained a great deal. French observers always have nonsensical and disagreeable thoughts in their mind. They never can be satisfied with what is, but must always carry out every line of action to its logical end—an intolerable mode of proceeding. Why should she look from him to Reine? Everard did not consider that Madame de Mirfleur had a dilemma of her own in respect to the two which ought to regulate her movements, and which in the meantime embarrassed her exceedingly. She took Reine aside, not knowing what else to say.

"Chérie," she said, for she was always kind and indulgent, and less moved than an English mother might have been by her child's petulance, "I am not happy about this new fancy my poor Herbert and you have in the head—the cousin, this Everard; he is very comme il faut, what you call nice, and sufficiently good-looking and young. What will any one say to me if I let my Reine go away wandering in lonely places with this young man?"

"It is with Herbert I am going," said Reine, hastily. "Mamma, do not press me too far; there are some things I could not bear. Everard is nothing to me," she added, feeling her cheeks flush and a great desire to cry come over her. She could not laugh and take this suggestion lightly, easily, as she wished to do, but grew serious, and flushed, and angry in spite of herself.

"My dearest, I did not suppose so," said the mother, always kind, but studying the girl's face closely with her suspicions aroused. "I must think of what is right for you, chérie," she said. "It is not merely what one feels; Herbert is still ill; he will require to retire himself early, to take many precautions, to avoid the chill of evening and of morning, to rest at midday; and what will my Reine do then? You will be left with the cousin. I have every confidence in the cousin, my child; he is good and honorable, and will take no advantage."

"Mamma, do you think what you are saying?" said Reine, almost with violence; "have not you confidence in me? What have I ever done that you should speak like this?"

"You have done nothing, chérie, nothing," said Madame de Mirfleur. "Of course in you I have every confidence—that goes without saying; but it is the man who has to be thought of in such circumstances, not the young girl who is ignorant of the world, and who is never to blame. And then we must consider what people will say. You will have to pass hours alone with the cousin. People will say, 'What is Madame de Mirfleur thinking of to leave her daughter thus unprotected?' It will be terrible; I shall not know how to excuse myself."

"Then it is of yourself, not of me, you are thinking," said Reine with fierce calm.

"You are unkind, my child," said Madame de Mirfleur. "I do indeed think what will be said of me—that I have neglected my duty. The world will not blame you; they will say, 'What could the mother be thinking of?' But it is on you, chérie, that the penalty would fall."

"You could tell the world that your daughter was English, used to protect herself, or rather, not needing any protection," said Reine; "and that you had your husband and children to think of, and could not give your attention to me," she added bitterly.

"That is true, that is true," said Madame de Mirfleur. The irony was lost upon her. Of course the husband and children were the strongest of all arguments in favor of leaving Reine to her own guidance; but as she was a conscientious woman, anxious to do justice to all her belongings, it may be believed that she did not make up her mind easily. Poor soul! not to speak of M. de Mirfleur, the babble of Jeanot and Babette, who never contradicted nor crossed her, in whose little lives there were no problems, who, so long as they were kept from having too much fruit and allowed to have everything else they wanted, were always pleased and satisfactory, naturally had a charm to their mother which these English children of hers, who were only half hers, and who set up so many independent opinions and caused her so much anxiety, were destitute of. Poor Madame de Mirfleur felt very deeply how different it was to have grown-up young people to look after, and how much easier as well as sweeter to have babies to pet and spoil. She sighed a very heavy sigh. "I must take time to think it over again," she said. "Do not press me for an answer, chérie; I must think it over; though how I can go away so much further, or how I can let you go alone, I know not. I will take to-day to think of it; do not say any more to-day."

Now I will not say that after the scene on the balcony which I have recorded, there had not been a little thrill and tremor in Reine's bosom, half pleasure, half fright, at the notion of going to the mountains in Everard's close company; and that the idea her mother had suggested, that Herbert's invalid habits must infallibly throw the other two much together, had not already passed through Reine's mind with very considerable doubts as to the expediency of the proceeding; but as she was eighteen, and not a paragon of patience or any other perfection, the moment that Madame de Mirfleur took up this view of the question, Reine grew angry and felt insulted, and anxious to prove that she could walk through all the world by Everard's side, or that of any other, without once stooping from her high maidenly indifference to all men, or committing herself to any foolish sentiment.

Everard, too, had his private cogitations on the same subject. He was old enough to know a little, though only a very little, about himself, and he did ask himself in a vague, indolent sort of way, whether he was ready to accept the possible consequences of being shut in a mountain solitude like that of Appenzell, not even with Reine, dear reader, for he knew his own weakness, but with any pretty and pleasant girl. Half whimsically, he admitted to himself, carefully and with natural delicacy endeavoring to put away Reine personally from the question, that it was more than likely that he would put himself at the feet, in much less than six weeks, of any girl in these exceptional circumstances. And he tried conscientiously to ask himself whether he was prepared to accept the consequences, to settle down with a wife in his waterside cottage, on his very moderate income, or to put himself into unwelcome and unaccustomed harness of work in order to make that income more. Everard quaked and trembled, and acknowledged within himself that it would be much better policy to go away, and even to run the risk of being slighted by Kate and Sophy, who would lead him into no such danger. He felt that this was the thing to do; and almost made up his mind to do it. But in the course of the afternoon, he went out to walk by Herbert's wheeled chair to the fir-trees, and instantly, without more ado or any hesitation, plunged into all sorts of plans for what they were to do at Appenzell.

"My dear fellow," said Herbert, laughing, "you don't think I shall be up to all those climbings and raids upon the mountains? You and Reine must do them, while I lie under the fir-trees and drink whey. I shall watch you with a telescope," said the invalid.

"To be sure," said Everard, cheerily; "Reine and I will have to do the climbing," and this was his way of settling the question and escaping out of temptation. He looked at Reine, who did not venture to look at him, and felt his heart thrill with the prospect. How could he leave Herbert, who wanted him so much? he asked himself. Cheerful company was half the battle, and variety, and some one to laugh him out of his invalid fancies; and how was it to be expected that Reine could laugh and be cheery all by herself? It would be injurious to both brother and sister, he felt sure, if he left them, for Reine was already exhausted with the long, unassisted strain; and what would kind Aunt Susan, the kindest friend of his youth, say to him if he deserted the young head of the house?

Thus the question was decided with a considerable divergence, as will be perceived, between the two different lines of argument, and between the practical and the logical result.

Madame de Mirfleur, though she was more exact in her reasonings, by right of her nation, than these two unphilosophical young persons, followed in some respect their fashion of argument, being swayed aside, as they were, by personal feelings. She did not at all require to think on the disadvantages of the projected expedition, which were as clear as noonday. Reine ought not, she knew, to be left alone, as she would constantly be, by her brother's sickness, with Everard, whom she herself had selected as a most desirable parti for her daughter. To throw the young people thus together was against all les convenances; it was actually tempting them to commit some folly or other, putting the means into their hands, encouraging them to forget themselves. But then, on the other hand, Madame de Mirfleur said to herself, if the worst came to the worst, and they did fall absurdly in love with each other, and make an exhibition of themselves, there would be no great harm done, and she would have the ready answer to all objectors, that she had already chosen the young man for her daughter, and considered him as Reine's fiancé. This she knew would stop all mouths. "Comme nous devons nous marier!" says the charming ingenue in Alfred de Musset's pretty play, when her lover, half awed, half emboldened by her simplicity, wonders she should see no harm in the secret interview he asks. Madame de Mirfleur felt that if anything came of it she could silence all cavillers by "C'est son fiancé," just as at present she could make an end of all critics by "C'est son cousin." As for Oscar de Bonneville, all hopes of him were over if the party made this sudden move, and she must resign herself to that misfortune.

Thus Madame de Mirfleur succeeded like the others in persuading herself that what she wanted to do, i. e., return to her husband and children, and leave the young people to their own devices, was in reality the best and kindest thing she could do for them, and that she was securing their best interests at a sacrifice of her own feelings.

It was Herbert whose office it was to extort this consent from her; but to him in his weakness she skimmed lightly over the difficulties of the situation. He could talk of nothing else, having got the excitement of change, like wine, into his head.

"Mamma, you are not going to set yourself against it. Reine says you do not like it; but when you think what the doctor said—"

He was lying down for his rest after his airing, and very bright-eyed he looked in his excitement, and fragile, like a creature whom the wind might blow away.

"I will set myself against nothing you wish, my dearest," said his mother; "but you know, mon 'Erbert, how I am torn in pieces. I cannot go further from home. M. de Mirfleur is very good; but now that he knows you are better, how can I expect him to consent that I should go still further away?"

"Reine will take very good care of me, petite mère," said Herbert coaxingly, "and that kind fellow, Everard—"

"Yes, yes, chéri, I know they will take care of you; though your mother does not like to trust you altogether even to your sister," she said with a sigh; "but I must think of my Reine too," she added. "Your kind Everard is a young man and Reine a young girl, a fille à marier, and if I leave them together with only you for a chaperon, what will everybody say?"

Upon which Herbert burst into an unsteady boyish laugh. "Why, old Everard!" he cried; "he is Reine's brother as much as I am. We were all brought up together; we were like one family."

"I have already told mamma so," said Reine rising, and going to the window with a severe air of youthful offence, though with her heart beating and plunging in her breast. She had not told her mother so, and this Madame de Mirfleur knew, though perhaps the girl herself was not aware of it; but the mother was far too wise to take any advantage of this slip.

"Yes, my darlings," she said, "I know it is so; I have always heard him spoken of so, and he is very kind to you, my Herbert, so kind that he makes me love him," she said with natural tears coming to her eyes. "I have been thinking about it till my head aches. Even if you were to stay here, I could not remain much longer now you are better, and as we could not send him away, it would come to the same thing here. I will tell you what I have thought of doing. I will leave my maid, my good Julie, who is fond of you both, to take care of Reine."

Reine turned round abruptly, with a burning blush on her face, and a wild impulse of resistance in her heart. Was Julie to be left as a policeman to watch and pry, as if she, Reine, could not take care of herself? But the girl met her mother's eye, which was quite serene and always kind, and her heart smote her for the unnecessary rebellion. She could not yield or restrain herself all at once, but she turned round again and stared out of the window, which was uncivil, but better, the reader will allow, than flying out in unfilial wrath.

"Well," said Herbert, approvingly, on whom the intimation had a very soothing effect, "that will be a good thing, mamma, for Reine certainly does not take care of herself. She would wear herself to death, if I and Everard and François would let her. Par example!" cried the young man, laughing, "who is to be

Julie's chaperon? If you are afraid of Reine flirting with Everard, which is not her way, who is to prevent Julie flirting with François? And I assure you he is not all rangé, he, but a terrible fellow. Must I be her chaperon too?"

"Ah, mon bien-aimé, how it does me good to hear you laugh!" cried Madame de Mirfleur, with tears in her eyes; and this joke united the little family more than tons of wisdom could have done; for Reine, too, mollified in a moment, came in from the window half-crying, half-laughing, to kiss her brother out of sheer gratitude to him for having recovered that blessed faculty. And the invalid was pleased with himself for the effect he had produced, and relished his own wit and repeated it to Everard, when he made his appearance, with fresh peals of laughter, which made them all the best of friends.

The removal was accomplished two days after, Everard in the meantime making an expedition to that metropolitan place, Thun, which they all felt to be a greater emporium of luxury than London or Paris, and from which he brought a carriage full of comforts of every description to make up what might be wanting to Herbert's ease, and to their table among the higher and more primitive hills. I cannot tell you how they travelled, dear reader, because I do not quite know which is the way—but they started from the Kanderthal in the big carriage Everard had brought from Thun, with all the people in the hotel out on the steps to watch them, and wave kindly farewells, and call out to them friendly hopes for the invalid. Madame de Mirfleur cried and sobbed and smiled, and waved her handkerchief from her own carriage, which accompanied theirs a little bit of the way, when the moment of parting came. Her mind was satisfied when she saw Julie safe on the banquette by François's side. Julie was a kind Frenchwoman of five-and-thirty, very indulgent to the young people, who were still children to her, and whom she had spoilt in her day. She had wept to think she was not going back to Babette, but had dried her eyes on contemplating Reine. And the young party themselves were not alarmed by Julie. They made great capital of Herbert's joke, which was not perhaps quite so witty as they all thought; and thus went off with more youthful tumult, smiles, and excitement than the brother and sister had known for years, to the valleys of the High Alps and all the unknown things—life or death, happiness or misery—that might be awaiting them in those unknown regions. It would perhaps be wrong to say that they went without fear of one kind or another; but the fear had a thrill in it which was almost as good as joy.

CHAPTER XXI

The news of Herbert's second rally, and the hopeful state in which he was, did not create so great a sensation among his relations as the first had done. The people who were not so deeply interested as Reine, and to whom his life or death was of secondary importance, nevertheless shared something of her feeling. He was no longer a creature brought up from the edge of the grave, miraculously or semi-miraculously restored to life and hope, but a sick man fallen back again into the common conditions of nature, varying as others vary, now better, now worse, and probably as all had made up their mind to the worst, merely showing, with perhaps more force than usual, the well-known uncertainty of consumptive patients, blazing up in the socket with an effort which, though repeated, was still a last effort, and had no real hopefulness in it. This they all thought, from Miss Susan, who wished for his recovery, to Mr. Farrel-Austin, whose wishes were exactly the reverse. They wished, and they did not wish that he might get better; but they no longer believed it as possible. Even Augustine paused in her absolute faith, and allowed a faint wonder to cross her mind as to what was meant by this strange dispensation. She asked to have some sign given her whether or not to go on praying for Herbert's restoration.

"It might be that this was a token to ask no more," she said to Dr. Richard, who was somewhat scandalized by the suggestion. "If it is not intended to save him, this may be a sign that his name should be mentioned no longer." Dr. Richard, though he was not half so truly confident as Augustine was in the acceptability of her bedesmen's and bedeswomen's prayers, was yet deeply shocked by this idea. "So long as I am chaplain at the alms-houses, so long shall the poor boy be commended to God in every litany I say!" he declared with energy, firm as ever in his duty and the Church's laws. It was dreadful to him, Dr. Richard said, to be thus, as it were, subordinate to a lady, liable to her suggestions, which were contrary to every rubric, though, indeed, he never took them. "I suffer much from having these suggestions made to me, though I thank God I have never given in—never! and never will!" said the old chaplain, with tremulous heroism. He bemoaned himself to his wife, who believed in him heartily, and comforted him, and to Miss Susan, who gave him a short answer, and to the rector, who chuckled and was delighted. "I always said it was an odd position," he said, "but of course you knew when you entered upon it how you would be." This was all the consolation he got, except from his wife, who always entered into his feelings, and stood by him on every occasion with her smelling-salts. And the more Miss Augustine thought that it was unnecessary to pray further for her nephew, the more clearly Dr. Richard enunciated his name every time that the Litany was said. The almshouses sided with the doctor, I am bound to add, in this, if not in the majority of subjects; and old Mrs. Matthews was one of the chief of his partisans, "for while there is life there is hope," she justly said.

But while they were thus thrown back from their first hopes about Herbert, Miss Susan was surprised one night by another piece of information, to her as exciting as anything about him could be. She had gone to her room one August night rather earlier than usual, though the hours kept by the household at Whiteladies were always early. Martha had gone to bed in the anteroom, where she slept within call of her mistress, and all the house, except Miss Susan herself, was stilled in slumber. Miss Susan sat wrapped in her dressing-gown, reading before she went to bed, as it had always been her habit to do. She had a choice of excellent books for this purpose on a little shelf at the side of her bed, each with markers in it to keep the place. They were not all religious literature, but good "sound reading" books, of the kind of which a little goes a long way. She was seated with one of these excellent volumes on her knee, perhaps because she was thinking over what she had just read, perhaps because her attention had flagged. Her attention, it must be allowed, had lately flagged a good deal, since she had an absorbing subject of thought, and she had taken to novels and other light reading, to her considerable disgust, finding that these trifling productions had more power of distracting her from her own contemplations than works more worth studying. She was seated thus, as I have said, in the big easy chair, with her feet on a foot-stool, her dressing-gown wrapping her in its large and loose folds, and her lamp burning clearly on the little table—with her book on her lap, not reading, but thinking—when all at once her ear was caught by the sound of a horse galloping heavily along the somewhat heavy road. It was not later than half-past ten when this happened, but half-past ten was a very late hour in the parish of St. Augustine. Miss Susan knew at once, by intuition, the moment she heard the sound, that this laborious messenger, floundering along upon his heavy steed, was coming to her. Her heart began to beat. Whiteladies was at some distance from a telegraph station, and she had before now received news in this way. She opened her window softly and looked out. It was a dark night, raining hard, cold and comfortless. She listened to the hoofs coming steadily, noisily along, and waited till the messenger appeared, as she felt sure he would, at the door. Then she went downstairs quickly, and undid the bolts and bars, and received the telegram. "Thank you; good night," she said to him, mechanically, not knowing what she was about, and stumbling again up the dark, oaken staircase, which creaked under her foot, and where a ghost was said to "walk." Miss Susan herself, though she was not superstitious, did not like to turn her head toward the door of the glazed passage, which led to the old playroom and the musicians' gallery. Her heart felt sick and faint within her: she believed that she held the news of Herbert's death in her hand, though she had no light to read it, and if Herbert himself had appeared to her, standing wan and terrible at that door, she would not have felt surprised. Her own room was in a disorder which she could not account for when she reached it again and shut the door, for it did not at first occur to her that she had left the window wide open, letting in the wind, which had scattered her little paraphernalia about, and the rain which had made a great wet stain upon the old oak floor. She tore the envelope open, feeling more and more sick and faint, the chill of the night going through and through her, and a deeper chill in her heart. So deeply had one thought taken possession of her, that when she read the words in this startling missive, she could not at first make out what they meant. For it was not an intimation of death, but of birth. Miss Susan stared at it first, and then sat down in a chair and tried to understand what it meant. And this was what she read:

"Dieu soit loué, un garçon. Né à deux heures et demi de l'après-midi ce 16 Août. Loué soit le bon Dieu."

Miss Susan could not move; her whole being seemed seized with cruel pain. "Praised be God. God be praised!" She gave a low cry, and fell on her knees by her bedside. Was it to echo that ascription of praise? The night wind blew in and blew about the flame of the lamp and of the dim night-light in the other corner of the room, and the rain rained in, making a larger and larger circle, like a pool of blood upon the floor. A huge shadow of Miss Susan flickered upon the opposite wall, cast by the waving lamp which was behind her. She lay motionless, now and then uttering a low, painful cry, with her face hid against the bed.

But this could not last. She got up after awhile, and shut the window, and drew the curtains as before, and picked up the handkerchief, the letters, the little Prayer Book, which the wind had tossed about, and put back her book on its shelf. She had no one to speak to, and she did not, you may suppose, speak to herself, though a strong impulse moved her to go and wake Martha; not that she could have confided in Martha, but only to have the comfort of a human face to look at, and a voice to say something to her, different from that "Dieu soit loué—loué soit le bon Dieu," which seemed to ring in her ears. But Miss Susan knew that Martha would be cross if she were roused, and that no one in the peaceful house would do more than stare at this information she had received; no one would take the least interest in it for itself, and no one, no one! could tell what it was to her. She was very cold, but she could not go to bed; the hoofs of the horse receding into the distance seemed to keep echoing into her ears long after they must have got out of hearing; every creak of the oaken boards, as she walked up and down, seemed to be some voice calling to her. And how the old boards creaked! like so many spectators, ancestors, old honorable people of the house, crowding round to look at the one who had brought dishonor into it. Miss Susan had met with no punishment for her wicked plan up to this time. It had given her excitement, nothing more, but now the deferred penalty had come. She walked about on the creaking boards afraid of them, and terrified at the sound, in such a restless anguish as I cannot describe. Up to this time kind chance, or gracious Providence, might have made her conspiracy null; but neither God nor accident (how does a woman who has done wrong know which word to use?) had stepped in to help her. And now it was irremediable, past her power or any one's to annul the evil. And the worst of all was those words which the old man in Bruges, who was her dupe and not her accomplice, had repeated in his innocence, that the name of the new-born might have God's name on either side to protect it. "Dieu soit loué!" she repeated to herself, shuddering. She seemed to hear it repeated to all round, not piously, but mockingly, shouted at her by eldrich voices. "Praised be God! God be praised!" for what? for the accomplishment of a lie, a cheat, a conspiracy! Miss Susan's limbs trembled under her. She could not tell how it was that the vengeance of heaven did not fall and crush the old house which had never before sheltered such a crime. But Augustine was asleep, praying in her sleep like an angel, under the same old roof, offering up continual adorations, innocent worship for the expiation of some visionary sins which nobody knew anything of; would they answer for the wiping away of her sister's sin which was so real? Miss Susan walked up and down all the long night. She lay down on her bed toward morning, chiefly that no one might see how deeply agitated she had been, and when Martha got up at the usual hour asked for a cup of tea to restore her a little. "I have not been feeling quite well," said Miss Susan, to anticipate any remarks as to her wan looks.

"So I was afraid, miss," said Martha, "but I thought as you'd call me if you wanted anything." This lukewarm devotion made Miss Susan smile.

Notwithstanding all her sufferings, however, she wrote a letter to Mr. Farrel-Austin that morning, and sent it by a private messenger, enclosing her telegram, so undeniably genuine, with a few accompanying words. "I am afraid you will not be exhilarated by this intelligence," she wrote, "though I confess for my part it gives me pleasure, as continuing the family in the old stock. But anyhow, I feel it is my duty to forward it to you. It is curious to think," she added, "that but for your kind researches, I might never have found out these Austins of Bruges." This letter Miss Susan sealed with her big Whiteladies seal, and enclosed the telegram in a large envelope. And she went about all her ordinary occupations that day, and looked and even felt very much as usual. "I had rather a disturbed night, and could not sleep," she said by way of explanation of the look of exhaustion she was conscious of. And she wrote to old Guillaume Austin of Bruges a very kind and friendly letter, congratulating him, and hoping that, if she had the misfortune to lose her nephew (who, however, she was very happy to tell him, was much better), his little grandson might long and worthily fill the place of master of Whiteladies. It was a letter which old Guillaume translated with infinite care and some use of the dictionary, not only to his family, but also to his principal customers, astonishing them by the news of his good fortune. To be sure his poor Gertrude, his daughter, was mourning the loss of her baby, born on the same day as his daughter-in-law's fine boy, but which had not survived its birth. She was very sad about it, poor child; but still that was a sorrow which would glide imperceptibly away, while this great joy and pride and honor would remain.

I need not tell how Mr. Farrel-Austin tore his hair. He received his cousin Susan's intimation of the fact that it was he who had discovered the Austins of Bruges for her with an indescribable dismay and rage, and showed the telegram to his wife, grinding his teeth at her. "Every poor wretch in the world—except you!" he cried, till poor Mrs. Farrel-Austin shrank and wept. There was nothing he would not have done to show his rage and despite, but he could do nothing except bully his wife and his servants. His daughters were quite matches for him, and would not be bullied. They were scarcely interested in the news of a new heir. "Herbert being better, what does it matter?" said Kate and Sophy. "I could understand your being in a state of mind about him. It is hard, after calculating upon the property, to have him get better in spite of you," said one of these young ladies, with the frankness natural to her kind; "but what does it matter now if there were a whole regiment of babies in the way? Isn't a miss as good as a mile?" This philosophy did not affect the wrathful and dissatisfied man, who had no faith in Herbert's recovery—but it satisfied the girls, who thought papa was getting really too bad; yet, as they managed to get most things they wanted, were not particularly impressed even by the loss of Whiteladies. "What with Herbert getting better and this new baby, whoever it is, I suppose old Susan will be in great fig," the one sister said. "I wish them joy of their old tumbledown hole of a place," said the other; and so their lament was made for their vanished hope.

Thus life passed on with all the personages involved in this history. The only other incident that happened just then was one which concerned the little party in Switzerland. Everard was summoned home in haste, when he had scarcely done more than escort his cousins to their new quarters, and so that little romance, if it had ever been likely to come to a romance, was nipped in the bud. He had to come back about business, which, with the unoccupied and moderately rich, means almost invariably bad fortune. His money, not too much to start with, had been invested in doubtful hands; and when he reached England he found that he had lost half of it by the delinquency of a manager who had run away with his money, and that of a great many people besides. Everard, deprived at a blow of half his income, was fain to take the first employment that offered, which was a mission to the West Indies, to look after property there, partly his own, partly belonging to his fellow-sufferers, which had been allowed to drop into that specially hopeless Slough of Despond which seems natural to West Indian affairs. He went away, poor fellow, feeling that life had changed totally for him, and leaving behind both the dreams and the reality of existence. His careless days were all over. What he had to think of now was how to save the little that remained to him, and do his duty by the others who, on no good grounds, only because he had been energetic and ready, had intrusted their interests to him. Why they should have trusted him, who knew nothing of business, and whose only qualification was that gentlemanly vagabondage which is always ready to go off to the end of the world at a moment's notice, Everard could not tell; but he meant to do his best, if only to secure some other occupation for himself when this job was done.

This was rather a sad interruption, in many ways, to the young man's careless life; and they all felt it as a shock. He left Herbert under the pine-trees, weak but hopeful, looking as if any breeze might make an end of him, so fragile was he, the soul shining through him almost visibly, yet an air of recovery about him which gave all lookers-on a tremulous confidence; and Reine, with moisture in her eyes which she did not try to conceal, and an ache in her heart which she did conceal, but poorly. Everard had taken his cousin's privilege, and kissed her on the forehead when he went away, trying not to think of the deep blush which surged up to the roots of her hair. But poor Reine saw him go with a pang which she could disclose to nobody, and which at first seemed to fill her heart too full of pain to be kept down. She had not realized, till he was gone, how great a place he had taken in her little world; and the surprise was as great as the pain. How dreary the valley looked, how lonely her life when his carriage drove away down the hill to the world! How the Alpine heights seemed to close in, and the very sky to contract! Only a few days before, when they arrived, everything had looked so different. Now even the friendly tourists of the Kanderthal would have been some relief to the dead blank of solitude which closed over Reine. She had her brother, as always, to nurse and care for, and watch daily and hourly on his passage back to life, and many were the forlorn moments when she asked herself what did she want more? what had she ever desired more? Many and many a day had Reine prayed, and pledged herself in her prayers, to be contented with anything, if Herbert was but spared to her; and now Herbert was spared and getting better—yet lo! she was miserable. The poor girl had a tough battle to fight with herself in that lonely Swiss valley, but she stood to her arms, even when capable of little more, and kept up her courage so heroically, that when, for the first time, Herbert wrote a little note to Everard as he had promised, he assured the traveller that he had scarcely missed him, Reine had been so bright and so kind. When Reine read this little letter, she felt a pang of mingled pain and pleasure. She had not betrayed herself. "But it is a little unkind to Everard to say I have been so bright since his going," she said, feeling her voice thick with tears. "Oh, he will not mind," said Herbert, lightly, "and you know it is true. After all, though he was a delightful companion, there is nothing so sweet as being by ourselves," the sick boy added, with undoubting confidence. "Oh, what a trickster I am!" poor Reine said to herself; and she kissed him, and told him that she hoped he would think so always, always! which Herbert promised in sheer lightness of heart.

And thus we leave this helpless pair, like the rest, to themselves for a year; Herbert to get better as he could, Reine to fight her battle out, and win it so far, and recover the calm of use and wont. Eventually the sky widened to her, and the hills drew farther off, and the oppression loosened from her heart. She took Herbert to Italy in October, still mending; and wrote long and frequent letters about him to Whiteladies, boasting of his walks and increasing strength, and promising that next Summer he should go home. I don't want the reader to think that Reine had altogether lost her heart during this brief episode. It came back to her after awhile, having been only vagrant, errant, as young hearts will be by times. She had but learned to know, for the first time in her life, what a difference happens in this world according to the presence or absence of one being; how such a one can fill up the space and pervade the atmosphere; and how, suddenly going, he seems to carry everything away with him. Her battle and struggle and pain were half owing to the shame and distress with which she found out that a man could do this, and had done it, though only for a few days, to herself; leaving her in a kind of blank despair when he was gone. But she got rid of this feeling (or thought she did), and the world settled back into its right proportions, and she said to herself that she was again her own mistress. Yet there were moments when the stars were shining, when the twilight was falling, when the moon was up—or sometimes in the very heat of the day, when a sensible young woman has no right to give way to folly—when Reine all at once would feel not her own mistress, and the world again would all melt away to make room for one shadow. As the Winter passed, however, she got the better of this sensation daily, she was glad to think. To be sure there was no reason why she should not think of Everard if she liked; but her main duty was to take care of Herbert, and to feel, once more, if she could, as she had once felt, and as she still professed to feel, poor child, in her prayers, that if Herbert only lived she would ask for nothing more.

CHAPTER XXII

About two years after the events I have just described, in the Autumn, when life was low and dreary at Whiteladies, a new and unexpected visitor arrived at the old house. Herbert and his sister had not come home that Summer, as they had hoped—nor even the next. He was better, almost out of the doctor's hands, having taken, it was evident, a new lease of life. But he was not strong, nor could ever be; his life, though renewed, and though it might now last for years, could never be anything but that of an invalid. So much all his advisers had granted. He might last as long as any of the vigorous persons round him, by dint of care and constant watchfulness; but it was not likely that he could ever be a strong man like others, or that he could live without taking care of himself, or being taken care of. This, which they would all have hailed with gratitude while he was very ill, seemed but a pale kind of blessedness now when it was assured, and when it became certain his existence must be spent in thinking about his health, in moving from one place to another as the season went on, according as this place or the other "agreed with him," seeking the cool in Summer and the warmth in Winter, with no likelihood of ever being delivered from this bondage. He had scarcely found this out himself, poor fellow, but still entertained hopes of getting strong, at some future moment always indefinitely postponed. He had not been quite strong enough to venture upon England during the Summer, much as he had looked forward to it; and though in the meantime he had come of age, and nominally assumed the control of his own affairs, the celebration of this coming of age had been a dreary business enough. Farrel-Austin, looking black as night, and feeling himself a man swindled and cheated out of his rights, had been present at the dinner of the tenantry, in spite of himself, and with sentiments toward Herbert which may be divined; and with only such dismal pretence at delight as could be shown by the family solicitor, whose head was full of other things, the rejoicings had passed over. There had been a great field-day, indeed, at the almshouse chapel, where the old people, with their cracked voices, tried to chant Psalms xx. and xxi., and were much bewildered in their old souls as to whom "the king" might be whose desire of his heart they thus prayed God to grant. Mrs. Matthews alone, who was more learned, theologically, than her neighbors, having been brought up a Methody, professed to some understanding of it; but even she was wonderfully confused between King David and a greater than he, and poor young Herbert, whose birthday it was. "He may be the squire, if you please, and if so be as he lives," said old Sarah, who was Mrs. Matthews's rival, "many's the time I've nursed him, and carried him about in my arms, and who should know if I don't? But there ain't no power in this world as can make young Mr. Herbert king o' England, so long as the Prince o' Wales is to the fore, and the rest o' them. If Miss Augustine was to swear to it, I knows better; and you can tell her that from me."

"He can't be King o' England," said Mrs. Matthews, "neither me nor Miss Augustine thinks of anything of the kind. It's awful to see such ignorance o' spiritual meanings. What's the Bible but spiritual meanings? You don't take the blessed Word right off according to what it says."

"That's the difference between you and me," said old Sarah, boldly. "I does; and I hope I practise my Bible, instead of turning of it off into any kind of meanings. I've always heard as that was one of the differences atween Methodies and good steady Church folks."

"Husht, husht, here's the doctor a-coming," said old Mrs. Tolladay, who kept the peace between the parties, but liked to tell the story of their conflicts afterward to any understanding ear. "I dunno much about how Mr. Herbert, poor lad, could be the King myself," she said to the vicar, who was one of her frequent auditors, and who dearly liked a joke about the almshouses, which were a kind of imperium in imperio, a separate principality within his natural dominions; "but Miss Augustine warn't meaning that. If she's queer, she ain't a rebel nor nothing o' that sort, but says her prayers for the Queen regular, like the rest of us. As for meanings, Tolladay says to me, we've no call to go searching for meanings like them two, but just to do what we're told, as is the whole duty of man, me and Tolladay says. As for them two, they're as good as a play. 'King David was 'im as had all his desires granted 'im, and long life and help out o' Zion,' said Mrs. Matthews. 'And a nice person he was to have all his wants,' says old Sarah. 'I'd ha' shut my door pretty fast in the man's face, if he'd come here asking help, I can tell you. Call him a king if you please, but I calls him no better nor the rest—a peepin' and a spyin'—'"

"What did she mean by that?" asked the vicar, amused, but wondering.

"'Cause of the woman as was a-washing of herself, sir," said Mrs. Tolladay, modestly looking down. "Sarah can't abide him for that; but I says as maybe it was a strange sight so long agone. Folks wasn't so thoughtful of washings and so forth in old times. When I was in service myself, which is a good bit since, there wasn't near the fuss about baths as there is nowadays, not even among the gentlefolks. Says Mrs. Matthews, 'He was a man after God's own heart, he was.' 'I ain't a-goin' to find fault with my Maker, it ain't my place,' says Sarah; 'but I don't approve o' his taste.' And that's as true as I stand here. She's a bold woman, is old Sarah. There's many as might think it, but few as would say it. Anyhow, I can't get it out o' my mind as it was somehow Mr. Herbert as we was a chanting of, and never King David. Poor man, he's dead this years and years," said Mrs. Tolladay, "and you know, as well as me, sir, that there are no devices nor labors found, nor wisdom, as the hymn says, underneath the ground."

"Well, Mrs. Tolladay," said the vicar, who had laughed his laugh out, and bethought himself of what was due to his profession, "let us hope that young Mr. Austin's desires will all be good ones, and that so we may pray God to give them to him, without anything amiss coming of it."

"That's just what I say, sir," said Mrs. Tolladay, "it's for all the world like the toasts as used to be the fashion in my young days, when folks drank not to your health, as they do now, but to your wishes, if so be as they were vartuous. Many a time that's been done to me, when I was a young girl; and I am sure," she added with a curtsey, taking the glass of wine with which the vicar usually rewarded the amusement her gossip gave him, "as I may say that to you and not be afraid; I drink to your wishes, sir."

"As long as they are virtuous," said the vicar, laughing; and for a long time after he was very fond of retailing old Sarah's difference of opinion with her Maker, which perhaps the gentle reader may have heard attributed to a much more important person.

Miss Susan gave the almshouse people a gorgeous supper in the evening, at which I am grieved to say old John Simmons had more beer than was good for him, and volunteered a song, to the great horror of the chaplain and the chaplain's wife, and many spectators from the village who had come to see the poor old souls enjoying this unusual festivity. "Let him sing if he likes," old Sarah cried, who was herself a little jovial. "It's something for you to tell, you as comes a-finding fault and a-prying at poor old folks enjoying themselves once in a way." "Let them stare," said Mrs. Matthews, for once backing up her rival; "it'll do 'em good to see that we ain't wild beasts a-feeding, but poor folks as well off as rich folks, which ain't common." "No it ain't, misses; you're right there," said the table by general consent; and after this the spectators slunk away. But I am obliged to admit that John Simmons was irrepressible, and groaned out a verse of song which ran into a deplorable chorus, in which several of the old men joined in the elation of their hearts—but by means of their wives and other authorities suffered for it next day.

Thus Herbert's birthday passed without Herbert, who was up among the pines again, breathing in their odors and getting strong, as they all said, though not strong enough to come home. Herbert enjoyed this lazy and languid existence well enough, poor fellow; but Reine since that prick of fuller and warmer life came momentarily to her, had not enjoyed it. She had lost her pretty color, except at moments when she was excited, and her eyes had grown bigger, and had that wistful look in them which comes when a girl has begun to look out into the world from her little circle of individuality, and to wonder what real life is like, with longing to try its dangers. In a boy, this longing is the best thing that can be, inspiriting him to exertion; but in a girl, what shape can it take but a longing for some one who will open the door of living to her, and lead her out into the big world, of which girls too, like boys, form such exaggerated hopes? Reine was not thinking of any one in particular, she said to herself often; but her life had grown just a little weary to her, and felt small and limited and poor, and as if it must go on in the same monotony forever and ever. There came a nameless, restless sense upon her of looking for something that might happen at any moment, which is the greatest mental trouble young woman have to encounter, who are obliged to be passive, not active, in settling their own fate. I remember hearing a high-spirited and fanciful girl, who had been dreadfully sobered by her plunge into marriage, declare the chief advantage of that condition to be—that you had no longer any restlessness of expectation, but had come down to reality, and knew all that was ever to come of you, and at length could fathom at once the necessity and the philosophy of content. This is, perhaps, rather a dreary view to take of the subject; but, however, Reine was in the troublous state of expectation, which this young woman declared to be thus put an end to. She was as a young man often is, whose friends keep him back from active occupation, wondering whether this flat round was to go on forever, or whether next moment, round the next corner, there might not be something waiting which would change her whole life.

As for Miss Susan and her sister, they went on living at Whiteladies as of old. The management of the estate had been, to some extent, taken out of Miss Susan's hands at Herbert's majority, but as she had done everything for it for years, and knew more about it than anybody else, she was still so much consulted and referred to that the difference was scarcely more than in name. Herbert had written "a beautiful letter" to his aunts when he came of age, begging them not so much as to think of any change, and declaring that even were he able to come home, Whiteladies would not be itself to him unless the dear White ladies of his childhood were in it as of old. "That is all very well," said Miss Susan, "but if he gets well enough to marry, poor boy, which pray God he may, he will want his house to himself." Augustine took no notice at all of the matter. To her it was of no importance where she lived; a room in the Almshouses would have pleased her as well as the most sumptuous chamber, so long as she was kept free from all domestic business, and could go and come, and muse and pray as she would. She gave the letter back to her sister without a word on its chief subject. "His wife should be warned of the curse that is on the house," she said with a soft sigh; and that was all.

"The curse, Austine?" said Miss Susan with a little shiver. "You have turned it away, dear, if it ever existed. How can you speak of a curse when this poor boy is spared, and is going to live?"

"It is not turned away, it is only suspended," said Augustine. "I feel it still hanging like a sword over us. If we relax in our prayers, in our efforts to make up, as much as we can, for the evil done, any day it may fall."

Miss Susan shivered once more; a tremulous chill ran over her. She was much stronger, much more sensible of the two; but what has that to do with such a question? especially with the consciousness she had in her heart. This consciousness, however, had been getting lighter and lighter, as Herbert grew stronger and stronger. She had sinned, but God was so good to her that He was making her sin of no effect, following her wickedness, to her great joy, not by shame or exposure, as He might so well have done, but by His blessing which neutralized it altogether. Thinking over it for all these many days, now that it seemed likely to do no practical harm to any one, perhaps it was not, after all, so great a sin. Three people only were involved in the guilt of it; and the guilt, after all, was but a deception. Deceptions are practised everywhere, often even by good people, Miss Susan argued with herself, and this was one which, at present, could scarcely be said to harm anybody, and which, even in the worst of circumstances, was not an actual turning away of justice, but rather a lawless righting, by means of a falsehood, of a legal wrong which was false to nature. Casuistry is a science which it is easy to learn. The most simple minds become adepts in it; the most virtuous persons find a refuge there when necessity moves them. Talk of Jesuitry! as if this art was not far more universal than that maligned body, spreading where they were never heard of, and lying close to every one of us! As time went on Miss Susan might have taken a degree in it—mistress of the art—though there was nobody who knew her in all the country round, who would not have sworn by her straightforwardness and downright truth and honor. And what with this useful philosophy, and what with Herbert's recovery, the burden had gone off her soul gradually; and by this time she had so put her visit to Bruges, and the telegrams and subsequent letters she had received on the same subject out of her mind, that it seemed to her, when she thought of it, like an uneasy dream, which she was glad to forget, but which had no more weight than a dream upon her living and the course of events. She had been able to deal Farrel-Austin a good downright blow by means of it: and though Miss Susan was a good woman, she was not sorry for that. And all the rest had come to nothing—it had done no harm to any one, at least, no harm to speak of— nothing that had not been got over long ago. Old Austin's daughter, Gertrude, the fair young matron whom Miss Susan had seen at Bruges, had already had another baby, and no doubt had forgotten the little one she lost; and the little boy, who was Herbert's heir presumptive, was the delight and pride of his grandfather and of all the house. So what harm was done? The burden grew lighter and lighter, as she asked herself this question, at Miss Susan's heart.

One day in this Autumn there came, however, as I have said, a change and interruption to these thoughts. It was October, and though there is no finer month sometimes in our changeable English climate, October can be chill enough when it pleases, as all the world knows. It was not a time of the year favorable, at least when the season was wet, to the country about Whiteladies. To be sure, the wealth of trees took on lovely tints of Autumn colors when you could see them; but when it rained day after day, as it did that season, every wood and byway was choked up with fallen leaves; the gardens were all strewn with them; the heaviness of decaying vegetation was in the air; and everything looked dismal, ragged, and worn out. The very world seemed going to pieces, rending off its garments piecemeal, and letting them rot at its melancholy feet. The rain poured down out of the heavy skies as if it would never end. The night fell soon on the ashamed and pallid day. The gardener at Whiteladies swept his lawn all day long, but never got clear of those rags and scraps of foliage which every wind loosened. Berks was like a dissipated old-young man, worn out before his time. On one of those dismal evenings, Augustine was coming from the Evening Service at the almshouses in the dark, just before nightfall. With her gray hood over her head, and her hands folded into her great gray sleeves, she looked like a ghost gliding through the perturbed and ragged world; but she was a comfortable ghost, her peculiar dress suiting the season. As she came along the road, for the byway through the fields was impassable, she saw before her another shrouded figure, not gray as she was, but black, wrapped in a great hooded cloak, and stumbling forward against the rain and wind. I will not undertake to say that Augustine's visionary eyes noticed her closely; but any unfamiliar figure makes itself remarked on a country road, where generally every figure is most familiar. This woman was unusually tall, and she was evidently a stranger. She carried a child in her arms, and stopped at every house and at every turning to look eagerly about her, as if looking for something or some one, in a strange place. She went along more and more slowly, till Augustine, walking on in her uninterrupted, steady way, turning neither to the right nor to the left hand, came up to her. The stranger had seen her coming, and, I suppose, Augustine's dress had awakened hopes of succor in her mind, bearing some resemblance to the religious garb which was well known to her. At length, when the leafy road which led to the side door of Whiteladies struck off from the highway, bewildering her utterly, she stood still at the corner and waited for the approach of the other wayfarer, the only one visible in all this silent, rural place. "Ma sœur!" she said softly, to attract her attention. Then touching Augustine's long gray sleeve, stammered in English, "I lost my way. Ma sœur, aidez-moi pour l'amour de Dieu!"

"You are a stranger," said Augustine; "you want to find some one? I will help you if I can. Where is it you want to go?"

The woman looked at her searchingly, which was but a trick of her imperfect English, to make out by study of her face and lips, as well as by hearing, what she said. Her child began to cry, and she hushed it impatiently, speaking roughly to the curiously-dressed creature, which had a little cap of black stuff closely tied down under its chin. Then she said once more, employing the name evidently as a talisman to secure attention, "Ma sœur! I want Viteladies; can you tell me where it is?"

"Whiteladies!"

"That is the name. I am very fatigued, and a stranger, ma sœur."

"If you are very fatigued and a stranger, you shall come to Whiteladies, whatever you want there," said Augustine. "I am going to the house now; come with me—by this way."

She turned into Priory Lane, the old avenue, where they were soon ankle-deep in fallen leaves. The child wailed on the woman's shoulder, and she shook it, lightly indeed, but harshly. "Tais-toi donc, petit sot!" she said sharply; then turning with the ingratiating tone she had used before. "We are very fatigued, ma sœur. We have come over the sea. I know little English. What I have learn, I learn all by myself, that no one know. I come to London, and then to Viteladies. It is a long way."

"And why do you want to come to Whiteladies?" said Augustine. "It was a strange place to think of— though I will never send a stranger and a tired person away without food and rest, at least. But what has brought you here?"

"Ah! I must not tell it, my story; it is a strange story. I come to see one old lady, who other times did come to see me. She will not know me, perhaps; but she will know my name. My name is like her own. It is Austin, ma sœur."

"Osteng?" said Augustine, struck with surprise; "that is not my name. Ah, you are French, to be sure. You mean Austin? You have the same name as we have; who are you, then? I have never seen you before."

"You, ma sœur! but it was not you. It was a lady more stout, more large, not religious. Ah, no, not you; but another. There are, perhaps, many lady in the house?"

"It may be my sister you mean," said Augustine; and she opened the gate and led up to the porch, where on this wet and chilly day there was no token of the warm inhabited look it bore in Summer. There was scarcely any curiosity roused in her mind, but a certain pity for the tired creature whom she took in, opening the door, as Christabel took in the mysterious lady. "There is a step, take care," said Augustine holding out her hand to the stranger, who grasped at it to keep herself from stumbling. It was almost dark, and the glimmer from the casement of the long, many-cornered passage, with its red floor, scarcely gave light enough to make the way visible. "Ah, merci, ma sœur!" said the stranger, "I shall not forget that you have brought me in, when I was fatigued and nearly dead."

"Do not thank me," said Augustine; "if you know my sister you have a right to come in; but I always help the weary; do not thank me. I do it to take away the curse from the house."

The stranger did not know what she meant, but stood by her in the dark, drawing a long, hard breath, and staring at her with dark, mysterious, almost menacing, eyes.

CHAPTER XXIII

"Here is some one, Susan, who knows you," said Augustine, introducing the newcomer into the drawing-room where her sister sat. It was a wainscoted room, very handsome and warm in its brown panelling, in which the firelight shone reflected. There was a bright fire, and the room doubled itself by means of a large mirror over the mantelpiece, antique like the house, shining out of black wood and burnished brass. Miss Susan sat by the fire with her knitting, framing one of those elaborate meshes of casuistry which I have already referred to. The table close by her was heaped with books, drawings for the chantry, and for the improvement of an old house in the neighborhood which she had bought in order to be independent, whatever accidents might happen. She was more tranquil than usual in the quiet of her thoughts, having made an effort to dismiss the more painful subject altogether, and to think only of the immediate future as it appeared now in the light of Herbert's recovery. She was thinking how to improve the house she had bought, which at present bore the unmeaning title of St. Augustine's Grange, and which she mirthfully announced her intention of calling Gray-womans, as a variation upon Whiteladies. Miss Susan was sixty, and pretended to no lingering of youthfulness; but she was so strong and full of life that nobody thought of her as an old woman, and though she professed, as persons of her age do, to have but a small amount of life left, she had no real feeling to this effect (as few have), and was thinking of her future house and planning conveniences for it as carefully as if she expected to live in it for a hundred years. If she had been doing this with the immediate prospect of leaving Whiteladies before her, probably she might have felt a certain pain; but as she had no idea of leaving Whiteladies, there was nothing to disturb the pleasure with which almost every mind plans and plots the arrangement of a house. It is one of the things which everybody likes to attempt, each of us having a confidence that we shall succeed in it. By the fire which felt so warmly pleasant in contrast with the grayness without, having just decided with satisfaction that it was late enough to have the lamp lighted, the curtains drawn, and the grayness shut out altogether; and with the moral consolation about her of having got rid of her spectre, and of having been happily saved from all consequences of her wickedness, Miss Susan sat pondering her new house, and knitting her shawl, mind and hands alike occupied, and as near being happy as most women of sixty ever succeed in being. She turned round with a smile as Augustine spoke.

I cannot describe the curious shock and sense as of a stunning blow that came all at once upon her. She did not recognize the woman, whom she had scarcely seen, nor did she realize at all what was to follow. The stranger stood in the full light, throwing back the hood of her cloak which had been drawn over her bonnet. She was very tall, slight, and dark. Who was she? It was easier to tell what she was. No one so remarkable in appearance had entered the old house for years. She was not pretty or handsome only, but beautiful, with fine features and great dark, flashing, mysterious eyes; not a creature to be overlooked or passed with slighting notice. Unconsciously as she looked at her, Miss Susan rose to her feet in instinctive homage to her beauty, which was like that of a princess. Who was she? The startled woman could not tell, yet felt somehow, not only that she knew her, but that she had known of her arrival all her life, and was prepared for it, although she could not tell what it meant. She stood up and faced her faltering, and said, "This lady—knows me? but, pardon me, I don't know you."

"Yes; it is this one," said the stranger. "You not know me, Madame? You see me at my beau-père's house at Bruges. Ah! you remember now. And this is your child," she said suddenly, with a significant smile, putting down the baby by Miss Susan's feet. "I have brought him to you."

"Ah!" Miss Susan said with a suppressed cry. She looked helplessly from one to the other for a moment, holding up her hands as if in appeal to all the world against this sudden and extraordinary visitor. "You are—Madame Austin," she said still faltering, "their son's wife? Yes. Forgive me for not knowing you," she said, "I hope—you are better now?"

"Yes, I am well," said the young woman, sitting down abruptly. The child, which was about two years old, gave a crow of delight at sight of the fire, and crept toward it instantly on his hands and knees. Both the baby and the mother seemed to take possession at once of the place. She began to undo and throw back on Miss Susan's pretty velvet-covered chairs her wet cloak, and taking off her bonnet laid it on the table, on the plans of the new house. The boy, for his part, dragged himself over the great soft rug to the fender, where he sat down triumphant, holding his baby hands to the fire. His cap, which was made like a little night-cap of black stuff, with a border of coarse white lace very full round his face, such as French and Flemish children wear, was a headdress worn in-doors, and out-of-doors and not to be taken off— but he kicked himself free of the shawl in which he had been enveloped on his way to the fender. Augustine stood in her abstract way behind, not noticing much and waiting only to see if anything was wanted of her; while Miss Susan, deeply agitated, and not knowing what to say or do, stood also, dispossessed, looking from the child to the woman, and from the woman to the child.

"You have come from Bruges?" she said, rousing herself to talk a little, yet in such a confusion of mind that she did not know what she said. "You have had bad weather, unfortunately. You speak English? My French is so bad that I am glad of that."

"I know ver' little," said the stranger. "I have learn all alone, that nobody might know. I have planned it for long time to get a little change. Enfant, tais-toi; he is bad; he is disagreeable; but it is to you he owes his existence, and I have brought him to you."

"You do not mean to give him a bad character, poor little thing," Miss Susan said with a forced smile. "Take care, take care, baby!"

"He will not take care. He likes to play with fire, and he does not understand you," said the woman, with almost a look of pleasure. Miss Susan seized the child and, drawing him away from the fender, placed him on the rug; and then the house echoed with a lusty cry, that startling cry of childhood which is so appalling to the solitary. Miss Susan, desperate and dismayed, tried what she could to amend her mistake. She took the handsomest book on the table in her agitation and thrust its pictures at him; she essayed to take him on her lap; she rushed to a cabinet and got out some curiosities to amuse him. "Dear, dear! cannot you pacify him?" she said at last. Augustine had turned away and gone out of the room, which was a relief.

"He does not care for me," said the woman with a smile, leaning back in her chair and stretching out her feet to the fire. "Sometimes he will scream only when he catches sight of me. I brought him to you;—his aunt," she added meaningly, "Madame knows—Gertrude, who lost her baby—can manage him, but not me. He is your child, Madame of the Viteladies. I bring him to you."

"Oh, heaven help me! heaven help me!" cried Miss Susan wringing her hands.

However, after awhile the baby fell into a state of quiet, pondering something, and at last, overcome by the warmth, fell fast asleep, a deliverance for which Miss Susan was more thankful than I can say. "But he will catch cold in his wet clothes," she said bending over him, not able to shut out from her heart a thrill of natural kindness as she looked at the little flushed face surrounded by its closely-tied cap, and the little sturdy fat legs thrust out from under his petticoats.

"Oh, nothing will harm him," said the mother, and with again a laugh that rang harshly. She pushed the child a little aside with her foot, not for his convenience, but her own. "It is warm here," she added, "he likes it, and so do I."

Then there was a pause. The stranger eyed Miss Susan with a half-mocking, defiant look, and Miss Susan, disturbed and unhappy, looked at her, wondering what had brought her, what her object was, and oh! when it would be possible to get her away!

"You have come to England—to see it?" she asked, "for pleasure? to visit your friends? or perhaps on business? I am surprised that you should have found an out-of-the-way place like this."

"I sought it," said the new-comer. "I found the name on a letter and then in a book, and so got here. I have come to see you."

"It is very kind of you, I am sure," said Miss Susan, more and more troubled. "Do you know many people in England? We shall, of course, be very glad to have you for a little while, but Whiteladies is not—amusing—at this time of the year."

"I know nobody—but you," said the stranger again. She sat with her great eyes fixed upon Miss Susan, who faltered and trembled under their steady gaze, leaning back in her chair, stretching out her feet to the fire with the air of one entirely at home, and determined to be comfortable. She never took her eyes from Miss Susan's face, and there was a slight smile on her lip.

"Listen," she said. "It was not possible any longer there. They always hated me. Whatever I said or did, it was wrong. They could not put me out, for others would have cried shame. They quarreled with me and scolded me, sometimes ten times in a day. Ah, yes. I was not a log of wood. I scolded, too; and we all hated each other. But they love the child. So I thought to come away, and bring the child to you. It is you that have done it, and you should have it; and it is I, madame knows, that have the only right to dispose of it. It is I—you acknowledge that?"

Heaven and earth! was it possible that the woman meant anything like what she said? "You have had a quarrel with them," said Miss Susan, pretending to take it lightly, falling at every word into a tremor she could not restrain. "Ah! that happens sometimes, but fortunately it does not last. If I can be of any use to make it up, I will do anything I can."

As she spoke she tried to return, and to overcome, if possible, the steady gaze of the other; but this was not an effort of which Miss Susan was capable. The strange, beautiful creature, who looked like some being of a new species treading this unaccustomed soil, looked calmly at her and smiled again.

"No," she said, "you will keep me here; that will be change, what I lofe. I will know your friends. I will be as your daughter. You will not send me back to that place where they hate me. I like this better. I will stay here, and be a daughter to you."

Miss Susan grew pale to her very lips; her sin had found her out. "You say so because you are angry," she said, trembling; "but they are your friends; they have been kind to you. This is not really my house, but my nephew's, and I cannot pretend to have—any right to you; though what you say is very kind," she added, with a shiver. "I will write to M. Austin, and you will pay us a short visit, for we are dull here—and then you will go back to your home. I know you would not like the life here."

"I shall try," said the stranger composedly. "I like a room like this, and a warm, beautiful house; and you have many servants and are rich. Ah, madame must not be too modest. She has a right to me—and the child. She will be my second mother, I know it. I shall be very happy here."

Miss Susan trembled more and more. "Indeed you are deceiving yourself," she said. "Indeed, I could not set myself against Mousheer Austin, your father-in-law. Indeed, indeed—"

"And indeed, indeed!" said her visitor. "Yes; you have best right to the child. The child is yours—and I cannot be separated from him. Am not I his mother?" she said, with a mocking light on her face, and laughed—a laugh which was in reality very musical and pleasant, but which sounded to Miss Susan like the laugh of a fiend.

And then there came a pause; for Miss Susan, at her wits' end, did not know what to say. The child lay with one little foot kicked out at full length, the other dimpled knee bent, his little face flushed in the firelight, fast asleep at their feet; the wet shawl in which he had been wrapped steaming and smoking in the heat; and the tall, fine figure of the young woman, slim and graceful, thrown back in the easy-chair in absolute repose and comfort. Though Miss Susan stood on her own hearth, and these two were intruders, aliens, it was she who hesitated and trembled, and the other who was calm and full of easy good-humor. She lay back in her chair as if she had lived there all her life; she stretched herself out before the welcome fire; she smiled upon the mistress of the house with benign indifference. "You would not separate the mother and the child," she repeated. "That would be worse than to separate husband and wife."

Miss Susan wrung her hands in despair. "For a little while I shall be—glad to have you," she said, putting force on herself; "for a—week or two—a fortnight. But for a longer time I cannot promise. I am going to leave this house."

"One house is like another to me," said the stranger. "I will go with you where you go. You will be good to me and the child."

Poor Miss Susan! This second Ruth looked at her dismay unmoved, nay, with a certain air of half humorous amusement. She was not afraid of her, nor of being turned away. She held possession with the bold security of one who, she knows, cannot be rejected. "I shall not be dull or fatigued of you, for you will be kind; and where you go I will go," she repeated, in Ruth's very words; while Miss Susan's heart sank, sank into the very depths of despair. What could she do or say? Should she give up her resistance for the moment, and wait to see what time would bring forth? or should she, however difficult it was, stand out now at the beginning, and turn away the unwelcome visitor? At that moment, however, while she tried to make up her mind to the severest measures, a blast of rain came against the window, and moaned and groaned in the chimneys of the old house. To turn a woman and a child out into such a night was impossible; they must stay at least till morning, whatever they did more.

"And I should like something to eat," said the stranger, stretching her arms above her head with natural but not elegant freedom, and distorting her beautiful face with a great yawn. "I am very fatigued; and then I should like to wash myself and rest."

"Perhaps it is too late to do anything else to-night," said Miss Susan, with a troubled countenance; "to-morrow we must talk further; and I think you will see that it will be better to go back where you are known—among your friends—"

"No, no; never go back!" she cried. "I will go where you go; that is, I will not change any more. I will stay with you—and the child."

Miss Susan rang the bell with an agitated hand, which conveyed strange tremors even to the sound of the bell, and let the kitchen, if not into her secret, at least into the knowledge that there was a secret, and something mysterious going on. Martha ran to answer the summons, pushing old Stevens out of the way. "If it's anything particular, it's me as my lady wants," Martha said, moved to double zeal by curiosity; and a more curious scene had never been seen by wondering eyes of domestic at Whiteladies than that which Martha saw. The stranger lying back in her chair, yawning and stretching her arms; Miss Susan standing opposite, with black care upon her brow; and at their feet between them, roasting, as Martha said, in front of the fire, the rosy baby with its odd dress, thrown down like a bundle on the rug. Martha gave a scream at sight of the child. "Lord! it's a baby! and summun will tread on't!" she cried, with her eyes starting out of her head.

"Hold your tongue, you foolish woman," cried Miss Susan; "do you think I will tread on the child? It is sleeping, poor little thing. Go at once, and make ready the East room; light a fire, and make everything comfortable. This—lady—is going to stay all night."

"Yes—every night," interposed the visitor, with a smile.

"You hear what I say to you, Martha," said Miss Susan, seeing that her maid turned gaping to the other speaker. "The East room, directly; and there is a child's bed, isn't there, somewhere in the house?"

"Yes, sure, Miss Susan; Master Herbert's, as he had when he come first, and Miss Reine's, but that's bigger, as it's the one she slept in at ten years old, afore you give her the little dressing-room; and then there's an old cradle—"

"I don't want a list of all the old furniture in the house," cried Miss Susan, cutting Martha short, "and get a bath ready and some food for the child. Everything is to be done to make—this lady—comfortable—for the night."

"Ah! I knew Madame would be a mother to me," cried the stranger, suddenly rising up, and folding her unwilling hostess in an unexpected and unwelcome embrace. Miss Susan, half-resisting, felt her cheek touch the new-comer's damp and somewhat rough black woollen gown with sensations which I cannot describe. Utter dismay took possession of her soul. The punishment of her sin had taken form and shape; it was no longer to be escaped from. What should she do, what could she do? She withdrew herself almost roughly from the hold of her captor, which was powerful enough to require an effort to get free, and shook her collar straight, and her hair, which had been deranged by this unexpected sign of affection. "Let everything be got ready at once," she said, turning with peremptory tones to Martha, who had witnessed, with much dismay and surprise, her mistress's discomfiture. The wind sighed and groaned in the great chimney, as if it sympathized with her trouble, and blew noisy blasts of rain against the windows. Miss Susan suppressed the thrill of hot impatience and longing to turn this new-comer to the door which moved her. It could not be done to-night. Nothing could warrant her in turning out her worst enemy to the mercy of the elements to-night.

That was the strangest night that had been passed in Whiteladies for years. The stranger dined with the ladies in the old hall, which astonished her, but which she thought ugly and cold. "It is a church; it is not a room," she said, with a shiver. "I do not like to eat in a church." Afterward, however, when she saw Augustine sit down, whom she watched wonderingly, she sat down also. "If ma sœur does it, I may do it," she said. But she did a great many things at table which disgusted Miss Susan, who could think of nothing else but this strange intruder. She ate up her gravy with a piece of bread, pursuing the savory liquid round her plate. She declined to allow her knife and fork to be changed, to the great horror of Stevens. She addressed that correct and high-class servant familiarly as "my friend"—translating faithfully from her natural tongue—and drawing him into the conversation; a liberty which Stevens on his own account was not indisposed to take, but which he scorned to be led into by a stranger. Miss Susan breathed at last when her visitor was taken upstairs to bed. She went with her solemnly, and ushered her into the bright, luxurious English room, with its blazing fire, and warm curtains and soft carpet. The young woman's eyes opened wide with wonder. "I lofe this," she said, basking before the fire, and kissed Miss Susan again, notwithstanding her resistance. There was no one in the house so tall, not even Stevens, and to resist her effectually was not in anybody's power at Whiteladies. The child had been carried upstairs, and lay, still dressed, fast asleep upon the bed.

"Shall I stay, ma'am, and help the—lady—with the chyild?" said Martha, in a whisper.

"No, no; she will know how to manage it herself," said Miss Susan, not caring that any of the household should see too much of the stranger.

A curious, foreign-looking box, with many iron clamps and bands, had been brought from the railway in the interval. The candles were lighted, the fire burning, the kettle boiling on the hob, and a plentiful supply of bread and milk for the baby when it woke. What more could be required? Miss Susan left her undesired guests with a sense of relief, which, alas, was very short-lived. She had escaped, indeed, for the moment; but the prospect before her was so terrible, that her very heart sickened at it. What was she to do? She was in this woman's power; in the power of a reckless creature, who could by a word hold her up to shame and bitter disgrace; who could take away from her all the honor she had earned in her long, honorable life, and leave a stigma upon her very grave. What could she do to get rid of her, to send her back again to her relations, to get her out of the desecrated house? Miss Susan's state of mind, on this dreadful night, was one chaos of fear, doubt, misery, remorse, and pain. Her sin had found her out. Was she to be condemned to live hereafter all her life in presence of this constant reminder of it? If she had suffered but little before, she suffered enough to make up for it now.

CHAPTER XXIV

The night was terrible for this peaceful household in a more extended sense than that deep misery which the arrival of the stranger cost Miss Susan. Those quiet people, mistresses and servants, had but just gone to bed when the yells of the child rang through the silence, waking and disturbing every one, from Jane, who slept with the intense sleep of youth, unwakable by all ordinary commotions, to Augustine, who spent the early night in prayer, and Miss Susan, who neither prayed nor slept, and felt as if she should be, henceforth, incapable of either. These yells continued for about an hour, during which time the household, driven distracted, made repeated visits in all manner of costumes to the door of the East room, which was locked, and from which the stranger shrilly repelled them.

"Je dois le dompter!" she cried through the thick oaken door, and in the midst of those screams, which, to the unaccustomed ear, seem so much more terrible than they really are.

"It'll bust itself, that's what it'll do," said the old cook: "particular as it's a boy. Boys should never be let scream like that; it's far more dangerous for them than it is for a gell."

Cook was a widow, and therefore an authority on all such subjects. After an hour or so the child was heard to sink into subdued sobbings, and Whiteladies, relieved, went to bed, thanking its stars that this terrible experience was over. But long before daylight the conflict recommenced, and once more the inmates, in their night-dresses, and Miss Susan in her dressing-gown, assembled round the door of the East room.

"For heaven's sake, let some one come in and help you," said Miss Susan through the door.

"Je dois le dompter," answered the other fiercely. "Go away, away! Je dois le dompter!"

"What's she a-going to do, ma'am?" said Cook. "Dump 'um? Good Lord, she don't mean to beat the child, I 'ope—particular as it's a boy."

Three times in the night the dreadful experience was repeated, and I leave the reader to imagine with what feelings the family regarded its new inmate. They were all downstairs very early, with that exhausted and dissipated feeling which the want of sleep gives. The maids found some comfort in the tea, which Cook made instantly to restore their nerves, but even this brought little comfort to Miss Susan, who lay awake and miserable in her bed, fearing every moment a repetition of the cries, and feeling herself helpless and enslaved in the hands of some diabolical creature, who, having no mercy on the child, would, she felt sure, have none on her, and whom she had no means of subduing or getting rid of. All the strength had gone out of her, mind and body. She shrank even from the sight of the stranger, from getting up to meet her again, from coming into personal contact and conflict with her. She became a weak old woman, and cried hopelessly on her pillow, not knowing where to turn, after the exhaustion of that terrible night. This, however, was but a passing mood like another, and she got up at her usual time, and faced the world and her evil fortune, as she must have done had an earthquake swept all she cared for out of the world—as we must all do, whatever may have happened to us, even the loss of all that makes life sweet. She got up and dressed herself as usual, with the same care as always, and went downstairs and called the family together for prayers, and did everything as she was used to do it— watching the door every moment, however, and trembling lest that tall black figure should come through it. It was a great relief, however, when, by way of accounting for Cook's absence at morning prayers, Martha pointed out that buxom personage in the garden, walking about with the child in her arms.

"The—lady's—a-having her breakfast in bed," said Martha. "What did the child do, ma'am, but stretches out its little arms when me and Cook went in first thing, after she unlocked the door."

"Why did two of you go?" said Miss Susan. "Did she ring the bell?"

"Well, ma'am," said Martha, "you'll say it's one o' my silly nervish ways. But I was frightened—I don't deny. What with Cook saying as the child would bust itself, and what with them cries—but, Lord bless you, it's all right," said Martha; "and a-laughing and crowing to Cook, and all of us, as soon as it got down to the kitchen, and taking its sop as natural! I can't think what could come over the child to be that wicked with its ma."

"Some people never get on with children," said Miss Susan, feeling some apology necessary; "and no doubt it misses the nurse it was used to. And it was tired with the journey—"

"That's exactly what Cook says," said Martha. "Some folks has no way with children—even when it's the ma—and Cook says—"

"I hope you have taken the lady's breakfast up to her comfortably," said Miss Susan; "tell her, with my compliments, that I hope she will not hurry to get up; as she must have had a very bad night."

"Who is she?" said Augustine, quietly.

Miss Susan knew that this question awaited her; and it was very comforting to her mind to know that Augustine would accept the facts of the story calmly without thinking of any meaning that might lie below them, or asking any explanations. She told her these facts quite simply.

"She is the daughter-in-law of the Austins of Bruges—their son's widow—her child is Herbert's next of kin and heir presumptive. Since dear Bertie has got better, his chances, of course, have become very much smaller; and, as I trust," said Miss Susan fervently, with tears of pain coming to her eyes, "that my dear boy will live to have heirs of his own, this baby, poor thing, has no chance at all to speak of; but, you see, as they do not know that, and heard that Herbert was never likely to recover, and are people quite different from ourselves, and don't understand things, they still look upon him as the heir."

"Yes," said Augustine, "I understand; and they think he has a right to live here."

"It is not that, dear. The young woman has quarrelled with her husband's parents, or she did not feel happy with them. Such things happen often, you know; perhaps there were faults on both sides. So she took it into her head to come here. She is an orphan, with no friends, and a young widow, poor thing, but I am most anxious to get her sent away."

"Why should she be sent away?" said Augustine. "It is our duty to keep her, if she wishes to stay. An orphan—a widow! Susan, you do not see our duties as I wish you could. We who are eating the bread which ought to be the property of the widow and the orphan—how dare we cast one of them from our doors! No, if she wishes it, she must stay."

"Augustine!" cried her sister, with tears, "I will do anything you tell me, dear; but don't ask me to do this! I do not like her—I am afraid of her. Think how she must have used the child last night! I cannot let her stay."

Augustine put down the cup of milk which was her habitual breakfast, and looked across the table at her sister. "It is not by what we like we should be ruled," she said. "Alas, most people are; but we have a duty. If she is not good, she has the more need of help; but I would not leave the child with her," she added, for she, too, had felt what it was to be disturbed. "I would give the child to some one else who can manage it. Otherwise you cannot refuse her, an orphan and widow, if she wishes to stay."

"Austine, you mistake, you mistake!" cried Miss Susan, driven to her wits' end.

"No, I do not mistake; from our door no widow and no orphan should ever be driven away. When it is Herbert's house, he must do as he thinks fit," said Augustine; "at least I know he will not be guided by me. But for us, who live to expatiate—No, she must not be sent away. But I would give the charge of the child to some one else," she added with less solemnity of tone; "certainly I would have some one else for the child."

With this Augustine rose and went away, her hands in her sleeves, her pace as measured as ever. She gave forth her solemn decision on general principles, knowing no other, with an abstract superiority which offended no one, because of its very abstraction, and curious imperfection in all practical human knowledge. Miss Susan was too wise to be led by her sister in ordinary affairs; but she listened to this judgment, her heart wrung by pangs which she could not avow to any one. It was not the motive which weighed so largely with Augustine, and was, indeed, the only one she took account of, which affected her sister. It was neither Christian pity for the helpless, nor a wish to expatiate the sins of the past, that moved Miss Susan. The emotion which was battling in her heart was fear. How could she bear it to be known what she had done? How could she endure to let Augustine know, or Herbert, or Reine?—or even Farrel-Austin, who would rejoice over her, and take delight in her shame! She dared not turn her visitor out of the house, for this reason. She sat by herself when Augustine had gone, with her hands clasped tight, and a bitter, helpless beating and fluttering of her heart. Never before had she felt herself in the position of a coward, afraid to face the exigency before her. She had always dared to meet all things, looking danger and trouble in the face; but then she had never done anything in her life to be ashamed of before. She shrank now from meeting the unknown woman who had taken possession of her house. If she had remained there in her room shut up, Miss Susan felt as if she would gladly have compounded to let her remain, supplying her with as many luxuries as she cared for. But to face her, to talk to her, to have to put up with her, and her companionship, this was more than she could bear.

She had not been able to look at her letters in her preoccupied and excited state; but when she turned them over now, in the pause that ensued after Augustine's departure, she found a letter from old Guillaume Austin, full of trouble, narrating to her how his daughter-in-law had fled from the house in consequence of some quarrel, carrying the child with her, who was the joy of their hearts. So far as she was concerned, the old man said, they were indifferent to the loss, for since Giovanna's child was born she had changed her character entirely, and was no longer the heart-broken widow who had obtained all their sympathies. "She had always a peculiar temper," the father wrote. "My poor son did not live happy with her, though we were ready to forget everything in our grief. She is not one of our people, but by origin an Italian, fond of pleasure, and very hot-tempered, like all of that race. But recently she has been almost beyond our patience. Madame will remember how good my old wife was to her—though she cannot bear the idle—letting her do nothing, as is her nature. Since the baby was born, however, she has been most ungrateful to my poor wife, looking her in the face as if to frighten her, and with insolent smiles; and I have heard her even threaten to betray the wife of my bosom to me for something unknown—some dress, I suppose, or other trifle my Marie has given her without telling me. This is insufferable; but we have borne it all for the child, who is the darling of our old age. Madame will feel for me, for it is your loss, too, as well as ours. The child, the heir, is gone! who charmed us and made us feel young again. My wife thinks she may have gone to you, and therefore I write; but I have no hopes of this myself, and only fear that she may have married some one, and taken our darling from us forever—for who would separate a mother from her child?—though the boy does not love her, not at all, not so much as he loves us and his aunt Gertrude, who thinks she sees in him the boy whom she lost. Write to me in pity, dear and honored madame, and if by any chance the unhappy Giovanna has gone to you, I will come and fetch her away."

The letter was balm to Miss Susan's wounds. She wrote an answer to M. Austin at once, then bethought herself of a still quicker mode of conveying information, and wrote a telegram, which she at once dispatched by the gardener, mounted on the best horse in the stable, to the railway. "She is here with the child, quite well. I shall be glad to see you," Miss Susan wrote; then sat down again, tremulous, but resolute to think of what was before her. But for the prospect of old Guillaume's visit, what a prospect it was that lay before her! She could understand how that beautiful face would look, with its mocking defiance at the helpless old woman who was in her power, and could not escape from her. Poor old Madame Austin! Her sin was the greatest of all, Miss Susan felt, with a sense of relief, for was it not her good husband whom she was deceiving, and had not all the execution of the complot been left in her hands? Miss Susan knew she herself had lied; but how much oftener Madame Austin must have lied, practically, and by word and speech! Everything she had done for weeks and months must have been a lie, and thus she had put herself in this woman's power, who cruelly had taken advantage of it. Miss Susan realized, with a shudder, how the poor old Flemish woman, who was her confederate, must have been put to the agony! how she must have been held over the precipice, pushed almost to the verge, obliged perhaps to lie and lie again, in order to save herself. She trembled at the terrible picture; and now all that had been done to Madame Austin was about to be done to herself—for was not she, too, in this pitiless woman's power?

A tap at the door. She thought it was the invader of her peace, and said "Come in" faintly. Then the door was pushed open, and a tottering little figure, so low down that Miss Susan, unprepared for this pygmy, did not see it at first, came in with a feeble rush, as babies do, too much afraid of its capabilities of progress to have any confidence of holding out. "Did you ever see such a darling, ma'am?" said Cook. "We couldn't keep him not to ourselves a moment longer. I whips him up, and I says, 'Miss Susan must see him.' Now, did you ever set your two eyes on a sweeter boy?"

Miss Susan, relieved, did as she was told; she fixed her eyes upon the boy, who, after his rush, subsided on to the floor, and gazed at her in silence. He was as fair as any English child, a flaxen-headed, blue-eyed Flemish baby, with innocent, wide-open eyes.

"He ain't a bit like his ma, bless him, and he takes to strangers quite natural. Look at him a-cooing and a-laughing at you, ma'am, as he never set eyes on before! But human nature is unaccountable," said Cook, with awe-stricken gravity, "for he can't abide his ma."

"Did you ever know such a case before?" said Miss Susan, who, upon the ground that Cook was a widow, looked up to her judgment on such matters as all the rest of the household did. Cook was in very high feather at this moment, having at last proved beyond doubt the superiority of her knowledge and experience as having once had a child of her own.

"Well, ma'am," said Cook, "that depends. There's some folk as never have no way with children, married or single, it don't matter. Now that child, if you let him set at your feet, and give him a reel out of your work-box to play with, will be as good as gold; for you've got a way with children, you have; but he can't abide his ma."

"Leave him there, if you think he will be good," said Miss Susan. She did more than give the baby a reel out of her work-box, for she took out the scissors, pins, needles, all sharp and pointed things, and put down the work-box itself on the carpet. And then she sat watching the child with the most curious, exquisite mixture of anguish and a kind of pleasure in her heart. Poor old Guillaume Austin's grandchild, a true scion of the old stock! but not as was supposed. She watched the little tremulous dabs the baby made at the various articles that pleased him. How he grasped them in the round fat fingers that were just long enough to close on a reel; how he threw them away to snatch at others; the pitiful look of mingled suffering, injured feeling, and indignation which came over his face in a moment when the lid of the box dropped on his fingers; his unconscious little song to himself, cooing and gurgling in a baby monologue. What was the child thinking? No clue had he to the disadvantages under which he was entering life, or the advantages which had been planned for him before he was born, and which, by the will of Providence, were falling into nothing. Poor little unconscious baby! The work-box and its reels were at this moment quite world enough for him.

It was an hour or two later before the stranger came downstairs. She had put on a black silk dress, and done up her hair carefully, and made her appearance as imposing as possible; and, indeed, so far as this went, she required few external helps. The child took no notice of her, sheltered as he was under Miss Susan's wing, until she took him up roughly, disturbing his toys and play. Then he pushed her away with a repetition of last night's screams, beating with his little angry hands against her face, and shrieking, "No, no!" his only intelligible word, at the top of his lungs. The young woman grew exasperated, too, and repaid the blows he gave with one or two hearty slaps and a shake, by means of which the cries became tremulous and wavering, though they were as loud as ever. By the time the conflict had come to this point, however, Cook and Martha, flushed with indignation, were both at the door.

"Il ne faut pas frapper l'enfang!" Miss Susan called out loudly in her peculiar French. "Vous ne restez pas un moment ici vous no donnez pas cet enfang au cook; vous écoutez? Donnez, donnez, touto de suite!" Her voice was so imperative that the woman was cowed. She turned and tossed the child to Cook, who, red as her own fire, stood holding out her arms to receive the screaming and struggling boy.

"What do I care?" said the stranger. "Petit sot! cochon! va! I slept not all night," she added. "You heard? Figure to yourself whether I wish to keep him now. Ah, petit fripon, petit vaurient! Va!"

"Madame Austin," said Miss Susan solemnly, as the women went away, carrying the child, who clung to Cook's broad bosom and sobbed on her shoulder, "you do not stay here another hour, unless you promise to give up the child to those who can take care of him. You cannot, that is clear."

"And yet he is my child," said the young woman, with a malicious smile. "Madame knows he is my child! He is always sage with his aunt Gertrude, and likes her red and white face. Madame remembers Gertrude, who lost her baby? But mine belongs to me."

"He may belong to you," said Miss Susan, with almost a savage tone, "but he is not to remain with you another hour, unless you wish to take him away; in which case," said Miss Susan, going to the door and throwing it open, "you are perfectly at liberty to depart, him and you."

The stranger sat for a moment looking at her, then went and looked out into the red-floored passage, with a kind of insolent scrutiny. Then she made Miss Susan a mock curtsey, and sat down.

"They are welcome to have him," she said, calmly. "What should I want him for? Even a child, a baby, should know better than to hate one; I do not like it; it is a nasty little thing—very like Gertrude, and with her ways exactly. It is hard to see your child resemble another woman; should not madame think so, if she had been like me, and had a child?"

"Look here," Miss Susan said, going up to her, and shaking her by the shoulders, with a whiteness and force of passion about her which cowered Giovanna in spite of herself—"look here! This is how you treated your poor mother-in-law, no doubt, and drove her wild. I will not put up with it—do you hear me? I will drive you out of the house this very day, and let you do what you will and say what you will, rather than bear this. You hear me? and I mean what I say."

Giovanna stared, blank with surprise, at the resolute old woman, who, driven beyond all patience, made this speech to her. She was astounded. She answered quite humbly, sinking her voice, "I will do what you tell me. Madame is not a fool, like my belle mère."

"She is not a fool, either!" cried Miss Susan. "Ah, I wish now she had been! I wish I had seen your face that day! Oh, yes, you are pretty—pretty enough! but I never should have put anything in your power if I had seen your face that day."

Giovanna gazed at her for a moment, still bewildered. Then she rose and looked at herself in the old glass, which distorted that beautiful face a little. "I am glad you find me pretty," she said. "My face! it is not a white and red moon, like Gertrude's, who is always praised and spoiled; but I hope it may do more for me than hers has done yet. That is what I intend. My poor pretty face—that it may win fortune yet! my face or my boy."

Miss Susan, her passion dying out, stood and looked at this unknown creature with dismay. Her face or her boy!—what did she mean? or was there any meaning at all in these wild words—words that might be mere folly and vanity, and indeed resembled that more than anything else. Perhaps, after all, she was but a fool who required a little firmness of treatment—nothing more.

CHAPTER XXV

Miss Susan Austin was not altogether devoid in ordinary circumstances of one very common feminine weakness to which independent women are especially liable. She had the old-fashioned prejudice that it was a good thing to "consult a man" upon points of difficulty which occurred in her life. The process of consulting, indeed, was apt to be a peculiar one. If he distinctly disagreed with herself, Miss Susan set the man whom she consulted down as a fool, or next to a fool, and took her own way, and said nothing about the consultation. But when by chance he happened to agree with her, then she made great capital of his opinion, and announced it everywhere as the cause of her own action, whatever that might be. Everard, before his departure, had been the depositary of her confidence on most occasions, and as he was very amenable to her influence, and readily saw things in the light which she wished him to see them in, he had been very useful to her, or so at least she said; and the idea of sending for Everard, who had just returned from the West Indies, occurred to her almost in spite of herself, when this new crisis happened at Whiteladies. The idea came into her mind, but next moment she shivered at the thought, and turned from it mentally as though it had stung her. What could she say to Everard to account for the effect Giovanna produced upon her—the half terror, half hatred, which filled her mind toward the new-comer, and the curious mixture of fright and repugnance with which even the child seemed to regard its mother? How could she explain all this to him? She had so long given him credit for understanding everything, that she had come to believe in this marvellous power and discrimination with which she had herself endowed him; and now she shrank from permitting Everard even to see the infliction to which she had exposed herself, and the terrible burden she had brought upon the house. He could not understand—and yet who could tell that he might not understand? see through her trouble, and perceive that some reason must exist for such a thraldom? If he, or any one else, ever suspected the real reason, Miss Susan felt that she must die. Her character, her position in the family, the place she held in the world, would be gone. Had things been as they were when she had gone upon her mission to the Austins at Bruges, I have no doubt the real necessities of the case, and the important issues depending upon the step she had taken, would have supported Miss Susan in the hard part she had now to play; but to continue to have this part to play after the necessity was over, and when it was no longer, to all appearance, of any immediate importance at all who Herbert's heir should be, gave a bitterness to this unhappy rôle which it is impossible to describe. The strange woman who had taken possession of the house without any real claim to its shelter, had it in her power to ruin and destroy Miss Susan, though nothing she could do could now affect Whiteladies; and for this poor personal reason Miss Susan felt, with a pang, she must bear all Giovanna's impertinences, and the trouble of her presence, and all the remarks upon her—her manners, her appearance, her want of breeding, and her behavior in the house, which no doubt everybody would notice. Everard, should he appear, would be infinitely annoyed to find such an inmate in the house. Herbert, should he come home, would with equal certainty wish to get rid of so singular a visitor.

Miss Susan saw a hundred difficulties and complications in her way. She hoped a little from the intervention of Monsieur Guillaume Austin, to whom she had written, after sending off her telegram, in full detail, begging him to come to Whiteladies, to recover his grandchild, if that was possible; but Giovanna's looks were not very favorable to this hope. Thus the punishment of her sin, for which she had felt so little remorse when she did it, found her out at last. I wonder if successful sin ever does fill the sinner with remorse, or whether human nature, always so ready in self-defence, does not set to work, in every case, to invent reasons which seem to justify, or almost more than justify, the wickedness which serves its purpose? This is too profound an inquiry for these pages; but certainly Miss Susan, for one, felt the biting of remorse in her heart when sin proved useless, and when it became nothing but a menace and a terror to her, as she had never felt it before. Oh, how could she have charged her conscience and sullied her life (she said to herself) for a thing so useless, so foolish, so little likely to benefit any one? Why had she done it? To disappoint Farrel-Austin! that had been her miserable motive—nothing more; and this was how it had all ended. Had she left the action of Providence alone, and refrained from interfering, Farrel-Austin would have been discomfited all the same, but her conscience would have been clear. I do not think that Miss Susan had as yet any feeling in her mind that the discomfiture of Farrel-Austin was not a most righteous object, and one which justified entirely the interference of heaven.

But, in the meantime, what a difference was made in her peaceable domestic life! No doubt she ought to have been suffering as much for a long time past, for the offence was not new, though the punishment was; but if it came late, it came bitterly. Her pain was like fire in her heart. This seemed to herself as she thought of it—and she did little but think of it—to be the best comparison. Like fire—burning and consuming her, yet never completing its horrible work—gnawing continually with a red-hot glow, and quivering as of lambent flame. She seemed to herself now and then to have the power, as it were, of taking her heart out of these glowing ashes, and looking at it, but always to let it drop back piteously into the torment. Oh, how she wished and longed, with an eager hopelessness which seemed to give fresh force to her suffering, that the sin could be undone, that these two last years could be wiped out of time, that she could go back to the moment before she set out for Bruges! She longed for this with an intensity which was equalled only by its impossibility. If only she had not done it! Once it occurred to her with a thrill of fright, that the sensations of her mind were exactly those which are described in many a sermon and sensational religious book. Was it hell that she had within her? She shuddered, and burst forth into a low moaning when the question shaped itself in her mind. But notwithstanding all these horrors, she had to conduct herself as became a person in good society—to manage all her affairs, and talk to the servants, and smile upon chance visitors, as if everything were well—which added a refinement of pain to these tortures. And thus the days passed on till Monsieur Guillaume Austin arrived from Bruges—the one event which still inspired her with something like hope.

Giovanna, meanwhile, settled down in Whiteladies with every appearance of intending to make it her settled habitation. After the first excitement of the arrival was over, she fell back into a state of indolent comfort, which, for the time, until she became tired of it, seemed more congenial to her than the artificial activity of her commencement, and which was more agreeable, or at least much less disagreeable to the other members of the household. She gave up the child to Cook, who managed it sufficiently well to keep it quiet and happy, to the great envy of the rest of the family. Every one envied Cook her experience and success, except the mother of the child, who shrugged her shoulders, and, with evident satisfaction in getting free from the trouble, fell back upon a stock of books she had found, which made the weary days pass more pleasantly to her than they would otherwise have done. These were French novels, which once had belonged, before her second marriage, to Madame de Mirfleur, and which she, too, had found a great resource. Let not the reader be alarmed for the morality of the house. They were French novels which had passed under Miss Susan's censorship, and been allowed by her, therefore they were harmless of their kind—too harmless, I fear, for Giovanna's taste, who would have liked something more exciting; but in her transplantation to so very foreign a soil as Whiteladies, and the absolute blank which existence appeared to her there, she was more glad than can be described of the poor little unbound books, green and yellow, over which the mother of Herbert and Reine had yawned through many a long and weary day. It was Miss Susan herself who had produced them out of pity for her visitor, unwelcome as that visitor was—and, indeed, for her own relief. For, however objectionable a woman may be who sits opposite to you all day poring over a novel, whether green or yellow, she is less objectionable than the same woman when doing nothing, and following you about, whenever you move, with a pair of great black eyes. Not being able to get rid of the stranger more completely, Miss Susan was very thankful to be so far rid of her as this, and her heart stirred with a faint hope that perhaps the good linen-draper who was coming might be able to exercise some authority over his daughter-in-law, and carry her away with him. She tried to persuade herself that she did not hope for this, but the hope grew involuntarily stronger and stronger as the moment approached, and she sat waiting in the warm and tranquil quiet of the afternoon for the old man's arrival. She had sent the carriage to the station for him, and sat expecting him with her heart beating, as much excited, almost, as if she had been a girl looking for a very different kind of visitor. Miss Susan, however, did not tell Giovanna, who sat opposite to her, with her feet on the fender, holding her book between her face and the fire, who it was whom she expected. She would not diminish the effect of the arrival by giving any time for preparation, but hoped as much from the suddenness of the old man's appearance as from his authority. Giovanna was chilly, like most indolent people, and fond of the fire. She had drawn her chair as close to it as possible, and though she shielded her face with all the care she could, yet there was still a hot color on the cheeks, which were exposed now and then for a moment to the blaze. Miss Susan sat behind, in the background, with her knitting, waiting for the return of the carriage which had been sent to the station for Monsieur Guillaume, and now and then casting a glance over her knitting-needles at the disturber of her domestic peace. What a strange figure to have established itself in this tranquil English house! There came up before Miss Susan's imagination a picture of the room behind the shop at Bruges, so bare of every grace and prettiness, with the cooking going on, and the young woman seated in the corner, to whom no one paid any attention. There, too, probably, she had been self-indulgent and self-absorbed, but what a difference there was in her surroundings! The English lady, I have no doubt, exaggerated the advantages of her own comfortable, softly-cushioned drawing-room, and probably the back-room at Bruges, if less pretty and less luxurious, was also much less dull to Giovanna than this curtained, carpeted place, with no society but that of a quiet Englishwoman, who disapproved of her. At Bruges there had been opportunities to talk with various people, more entertaining than even the novels; and though Giovanna had been disapproved of there, as now, she had been able to give as well as take—at least since power had been put into her hands. At present she yawned sadly as she turned the leaves. It was horribly dull, and horribly long, this vacant, uneventful afternoon. If some one would come, if something would happen, what a relief it would be! She yawned as she turned the page.

At last there came a sound of carriage-wheels on the gravel. Miss Susan did not suppose that her visitor took any notice, but I need not say that Giovanna, to whom something new would have been so great a piece of good fortune, gave instant attention, though she still kept the book before her, a shield not only from the fire, but from her companion's observation. Giovanna saw that Miss Susan was secretly excited and anxious, and I think the younger woman anticipated some amusement at the expense of her companion—expecting an elderly lover, perhaps, or something of a kind which might have stirred herself. But when the figure of her father-in-law appeared at the door, very ingratiating and slightly timid, in two greatcoats which increased his bulk without increasing his dignity, and with a great cache-nez about his neck, Giovanna perceived at once the conspiracy against her, and in a moment collected her forces to meet it. M. Guillaume represented to her a laborious life, frugal fare, plain dress, and domestic authority, such as that was—the things from which she had fled. Here (though it was dull) she had ease, luxury, the consciousness of power, and a future in which she could better herself—in which, indeed, she might look forward to being mistress of the luxurious house, and ordering it so that it should cease to be dull. To allow herself to be taken back to Bruges, to the back-shop, was as far as anything could be from her intentions. How could they be so foolish as to think of it? She let her book drop on her lap, and looked at the plotters with a glow of laughter at their simplicity, lifting up the great eyes.

As for Monsieur Guillaume, he was in a state of considerable excitement, pleasure, and pain. He was pleased to come to the wealthy house in which he felt a sense of proprietorship, much quickened by the comfort of the luxurious English carriage in which he had driven from the station. This was a sign of grandeur and good-fortune comprehensible to everybody; and the old shopkeeper felt at once the difference involved. On the other hand, he was anxious about his little grandchild, whom he adored, and a little afraid of the task of subduing its mother, which had been put into his hands; and he was anxious to make a good appearance, and to impress favorably his new relations, on whose good will, somehow or other, depended his future inheritance. He made a very elaborate bow when he came in, and touched respectfully the tips of the fingers which Miss Susan extended to him. She was a great lady, and he was a shopkeeper; she was an Englishwoman, reserved and stately, and he a homely old Fleming. Neither of them knew very well how to treat the other, and Miss Susan, who felt that all the comfort of her future life depended on how she managed this old man, and upon the success of his mission, was still more anxious and elaborate than he was. She drew forward the easiest chair for him, and asked for his family with a flutter of effusive politeness, quite unlike her usual demeanor.

"And Madame Jean is quite safe with me," she said, when their first salutations were over.

Here was the tug of war. The old man turned to his daughter-in-law eagerly, yet somewhat tremulous. She had pushed away her chair from the fire, and with her book still in her hand, sat looking at him with shining eyes.

"Ah, Giovanna," he said, shaking his head, "how thou hast made all our hearts sore! how could you do it? We should not have crossed you, if you had told us you were weary of home. The house is miserable without you; how could you go away?"

"Mon beau-père," said Giovanna, taking the kiss he bestowed on her forehead with indifference, "say you have missed the child, if you please, that may be true enough; but as for me, no one pretended to care for me."

"Mon enfant—"

"Assez, assez! Let us speak the truth. Madame knows well enough," said Giovanna, "it is the baby you love. If you could have him without me, I do not doubt it would make you very happy. Only that it is impossible to separate the child from the mother—every one knows as much as that."

She said this with a malicious look toward Miss Susan, who shrank involuntarily. But Monsieur Guillaume, who accepted the statement as a simple fact, did not shrink, but assented, shaking his head.

"Assuredly, assuredly," he said, "nor did anyone wish it. The child is our delight; but you, too, Giovanna, you too—"

She laughed.

"I do not think the others would say so—my mother-in-law, for example, or Gertrude; nor, indeed, you either, mon beau-père, if you had not a motive. I was always the lazy one—the useless one. It was I who had the bad temper. You never cared for me, or made me comfortable. Now ces dames are kind, and this will be the boy's home."

"If he succeeds," said Miss Susan, interposing from the background, where she stood watchful, growing more and more anxious. "You are aware that now this is much less certain. My nephew is better; he is getting well and strong."

They both turned to look at her; Giovanna with startled, wide-open eyes, and the old man with an evident thrill of surprise. Then he seemed to divine a secret motive in this speech, and gave Miss Susan a glance of intelligence, and smiled and nodded his head.

"To be sure, to be sure," he said. "Monsieur, the present propriétaire, may live. It is to be hoped that he will continue to live—at least, until the child is older. Yes, yes, Giovanna, what you say is true. I appreciate your maternal care, ma fille. It is right that the boy should visit his future home; that he should learn the manners of the people, and all that is needful to a proprietor. But he is very young—a few years hence will be soon enough. And why should you have left us so hastily, so secretly? We have all been unhappy," he added, with a sigh.

I cannot describe how Miss Susan listened to all this, with an impatience which reached the verge of the intolerable. To hear them taking it all calmly for granted—calculating on Herbert's death as an essential preliminary of which they were quite sure. But she kept silence with a painful effort, and kept in the background, trembling with the struggle to restrain herself. It was best that she should take no part, say nothing, but leave the issue as far as she could to Providence. To Providence! the familiar word came to her unawares; but what right had she to appeal to Providence—to trust in Providence in such a matter. She quaked, and withdrew a little further still, leaving the ground clear. Surely old Austin would exercise his authority—and could overcome this young rebel without her aid!

The old man waited for an answer, but got none. He was a good man in his way, but he had been accustomed all his life to have his utterances respected, and he did not understand the profane audacity which declined even to reply to him. After a moment's interval he resumed, eager, but yet damped in his confidence:

"Le petit! where is he? I may see him, may not I?"

Miss Susan rose at once to ring the bell for the child, but to her amazement she was stopped by Giovanna.

"Wait a little," she said, "I am the mother. I have the best right. That is acknowledged? No one has any right over him but me."

Miss Susan quailed before the glance of those eyes, which were so full of meaning. There was something more in the words than mere self-assertion. There was once more a gleam of malicious enjoyment, almost revengeful. What wrong had Giovanna to revenge upon Miss Susan, who had given her the means of asserting herself—who had changed her position in the world altogether, and given her a standing-ground which she never before possessed? The mistress of Whiteladies, so long foremost and regnant, sat down again behind their backs with a sense of humiliation not to be described. She left the two strangers to fight out their quarrel without any interference on her part. As for Giovanna, she had no revengeful meaning whatever; but she loved to feel and show her power.

"Assuredly, ma fille," said the old man, who was in her power too, and felt it with not much less dismay than Miss Susan.

"Then understand," said the young woman, rising from her chair with sudden energy, and throwing down the book which she had up to this moment kept in her hands, "I will have no one interfere. The child is to me—he is mine, and I will have no one interfere. It shall not be said that he is more gentil, more sage, with another than with his mother. He shall not be taught any more to love others more than me. To others he is nothing; but he is mine, mine, and mine only!" she said, putting her hands together with a sudden clap, the color mounting to her cheeks, and the light flashing in her eyes.

Miss Susan, who in other circumstances would have been roused by this self-assertion, was quite cowed by it now, and sat with a pang in her heart which I cannot describe, listening and—submitting. What could she say or do?

"Assurement, ma fille; assurement, ma fille," murmured poor old M. Guillaume, looking at this rampant symbol of natural power with something like terror. He was quite unprepared for it. Giovanna had been to him but the feeblest creature in the house, the dependent, generally disapproved of, and always powerless. To be sure, since her child was born, he had heard more complaints of her, and had even perceived that she was not as submissive as formerly; but then it is always so easy for the head of the house to believe that it is his womankind who are to blame, and that when matters are in his own hands all will go well. He was totally discomfited, dismayed, and taken by surprise. He could not understand that this was the creature who had sat in the corner, and been made of no account. He did not know what to do in the emergency. He longed for his wife, to ask counsel of, to direct him; and then he remembered that his wife, too, had seemed a little afraid of Giovanna, a sentiment at which he had loftily smiled, saying to himself, good man, that the girl, poor thing, was a good girl enough, and as soon as he lifted up a finger, would no doubt submit as became her. In this curious reversal of positions and change of circumstances, he could but look at her bewildered, and had not an idea what to say or do.

CHAPTER XXVI

The evening which followed was most uncomfortable. Good M. Guillaume—divided between curiosity and the sense of novelty with which he found himself in a place so unlike his ideas; a desire to please the ladies of the house, and an equally strong desire to settle the question which had brought him to Whiteladies—was altogether shaken out of his use and wont. He had been allowed a little interview with the child, which clung to him, and could only be separated from him at the cost of much squalling and commotion, in which even the blandishments of Cook were but partially availing. The old man, who had been accustomed to carry the baby about with him, to keep it on his knee at meals, and give it all those illegitimate indulgences which are common where nurseries and nursery laws do not exist, did not understand, and was much afflicted by the compulsory separation.

"It is time for the baby to go to bed, and we are going in to dinner," Miss Susan said; as if this was any reason (thought poor M. Guillaume) why the baby should not come to dinner too, or why inexorably it should go to bed! How often had he kept it on his knee, and fed it with indigestible morsels till its countenance shone with gravy and happiness! He had to submit, however, Giovanna looking at him while he did so (he thought) with a curious, malicious satisfaction. M. Guillaume had never been in England before, and the dinner was as odd to him as the first foreign dinner is to an Englishman. He did not understand the succession of dishes, the heavy substantial soup, the solid roast mutton; neither did he understand the old hall, which looked to him like a chapel, or the noiseless Stevens behind his chair, or the low-toned conversation, of which indeed there was very little. Augustine, in her gray robes, was to him simply a nun, whom he also addressed, as Giovanna had done, as "Ma sœur." Why she should be thus in a private house at an ordinary table, he could not tell, but supposed it to be merely one of those wonderful ways of the English which he had so often heard of. Giovanna, who sat opposite to him, and who was by this time familiarized with the routine of Whiteladies, scarcely talked at all; and though Miss Susan, by way of setting him "at his ease," asked a civil question from time to time about his journey, what kind of crossing he had experienced, and other such commonplace matters; yet the old linendraper was abashed by the quiet, the dimness of the great room around him, the strangeness of the mansion and of the meal. The back room behind the shop at Bruges, where the family dined, and for the most part lived, seemed to him infinitely more comfortable and pleasant than this solemn place, which, on the other hand, was not in the least like a room in one of the great châteaux of his own rich country, which was the only thing to which he could have compared it. He was glad to accept the suggestion that he was tired, and retire to his room, which, in its multiplicity of comforts, its baths, its carpets, and its curtains, was almost equally bewildering. When, however, rising by skreigh of day, he went out in the soft, mellow brightness of the Autumn morning, M. Guillaume's reverential feelings sensibly decreased. The house of Whiteladies did not please him at all; its oldness disgusted him; and those lovely antique carved gables, which were the pride of all the Austins, filled him with contempt. Had they been in stone, indeed, he might have understood that they were unobjectionable; but brick and wood were so far below the dignity of a château that he felt a sensible downfall. After all, what was a place like this to tempt a man from the comforts of Bruges, from his own country, and everything he loved.

He had formed a very different idea of Whiteladies. Windsor Castle might have come up better to his sublime conception; but this poor little place, with its homely latticed windows, and irregular outlines, appeared to the good old shopkeeper a mere magnified cottage, nothing more. He was disturbed, poor man, in a great many ways. It had appeared to him, before he came, that he had nothing to do but to exert his authority, and bring his daughter-in-law home, and the child, who was of much more importance than she, and without whom he scarcely ventured to face his wife and Gertrude. Giovanna had never counted for much in the house, and to suppose that he should have difficulty in overcoming her will had never occurred to him. But there was something in her look which made him very much more doubtful of his own power than up to this time he had ever been; and this was a humbling and discouraging sensation. Visions, too, of another little business which this visit gave him a most desirable opportunity to conclude, were in his mind; and he had anticipated a few days overflowing with occupation, in which, having only women to encounter, he could not fail to be triumphantly successful. He had entertained these agreeable thoughts of triumph up to the very moment of arriving at Whiteladies; but somehow the aspect of things was not propitious. Neither Giovanna nor Miss Susan looked as if she were ready to give in to his masculine authority, or to yield to his persuasive influence. The one was defiant, the other roused and on her guard. M. Guillaume had been well managed throughout his life. He had been allowed to suppose that he had everything his own way; his solemn utterances had been listened to with awe, his jokes had been laughed at, his verdict acknowledged as final. A man who was thus treated at home is apt to be easily mortified abroad, where nobody cares to ménager his feelings, or to receive his sayings, whether wise or witty, with sentiments properly apportioned to the requirements of the moment. Nothing takes the spirit so completely out of such a man as the first suspicion that he is among people to whom he is not authority, and who really care no more for his opinion than for that of any other man. M. Guillaume was in this uncomfortable position now. Here were two women, neither of them in the least impressed by his superiority, whom, by sheer force of reason, it was necessary for him to get the better of. "And women, as is well known, are inaccessible to reason," he said to himself scornfully. This was somewhat consolatory to his pride, but I am far from sure whether a lingering doubt of his own powers of reasoning, when unassisted by prestige and natural authority, had not a great deal to do with it; and the good man felt somewhat small and much discouraged, which it is painful for the father of a family to do.

After breakfast, Miss Susan brought him out to see the place. He had done his very best to be civil, to drink tea which he did not like, and eat the bacon and eggs, and do justice to the cold partridge on the sideboard, and now he professed himself delighted to make an inspection of Whiteladies. The leaves had been torn by the recent storm from the trees, so that the foliage was much thinned, and though it was a beautiful Autumn morning, with a brilliant blue sky, and the sunshine full of that regretful brightness which Autumn sunshine so often seems to show, yellow leaves still came floating, moment by moment, through the soft atmosphere, dropping noiselessly on the grass, detached by the light air, which could not even be called a breeze. The gables of Whiteladies stood out against the blue, with a serene superiority to the waning season, yet a certain sympathetic consciousness in their gray age, of the generations that had fallen about the old place like the leaves. Miss Susan, whose heart was full, looked at the house of her fathers with eyes touched to poetry by emotion.

"The old house has seen many a change," she said, "and not a few sad ones. I am not superstitious about it, like my sister, but you must know, M. Guillaume, that our property was originally Church lands, and that is supposed to bring with it—well, the reverse of a blessing."

"Ah!" said M. Guillaume, "that is then the chapel, as I supposed, in which you dine?"

"The chapel!" cried Miss Susan in dismay. "Oh, dear, no—the house is not monastic, as is evident. It is, I believe, the best example, or almost the best example, extant of an English manor-house."

M. Guillaume saw that he had committed himself, and said no more. He listened with respectful attention while the chief architectural features of the house were pointed out to him. No doubt it was fine, since his informer said so—he would not hurt her feelings by uttering any doubts on the subject—only, if it ever came into his hands—he murmured to himself.

"And now about your business," cried Miss Susan, who had done her best to throw off her prevailing anxiety. "Giovanna? you mean to take her back with you—and the child? Your poor good wife must miss the child."

M. Guillaume took off his hat in his perplexity, and rubbed his bald head. "Ah!" he said, "here is my great trouble. Giovanna is more changed than I can say. I have been told of her wilfulness, but Madame knows that women are apt to exaggerate—not but that I have the greatest respect for the sex—." He paused, and made her a reverence, which so exasperated Miss Susan that she could with pleasure have boxed his ears as he bowed. But this was one of the many impulses which it is best for "the sex," as well as other human creatures, to restrain.

"But I find it is true," said M. Guillaume. "She does not show any readiness to obey. I do not understand it. I have always been accustomed to be obeyed, and I do not understand it," he added, with plaintive iteration. "Since she has the child she has power, I suppose that is the explanation. Ladies—with every respect—are rarely able to support the temptation of having power. Madame will pardon me for saying so, I am sure."

"But you have power also," said Miss Susan. "She is dependent upon you, is she not? and I don't see how she can resist what you say. She has nothing of her own, I suppose?" she continued, pausing upon this point in her inquiries. "She told me so. If she is dependent upon you, she must do as you say."

"That is very true," said the old shopkeeper, with a certain embarrassment; "but I must speak frankly to Madame, who is sensible, and will not be offended with what I say. Perhaps it is for this she has come here. It has occurred to my good wife, who has a very good head, that le petit has already rights which should not be forgotten. I do not hesitate to say that women are very quick; these things come into their heads sooner than with us, sometimes. My wife thought that there should be a demand for an allowance, a something, for the heir. My wife, Madame knows, is very careful of her children. She loves to lay up for them, to make a little money for them. Le petit had never been thought of, and there was no provision made. She has said for a long time that a little rente, a—what you call allowance, should be claimed for the child. Giovanna has heard it, and that has put another idea into her foolish head; but Madame will easily perceive that the claim is very just, of a something—a little revenue—for the heir."

"From whom is this little revenue to come?" said Miss Susan, looking at him with a calm which she did not feel.

M. Guillaume was embarrassed for the moment; but a man who is accustomed to look at his fellow-creatures from the other side of a counter, and to take money from them, however delicate his feelings may be, has seldom much hesitation in making pecuniary claims. From whom? He had not carefully considered the question. Whiteladies in general had been represented to him by that metaphorical pronoun which is used for so many vague things. They ought to give the heir this income; but who they were, he was unable on the spur of the moment to say.

"Madame asks from whom?" he said. "I am a stranger. I know little more than the name. From Vite-ladies—from Madame herself—from the estates of which le petit is the heir."

"I have nothing to do with the estates," said Miss Susan. She was so thankful to be able to speak to him without any one by to make her afraid, that she explained herself with double precision and clearness, and took pains to put a final end to his hopes.

"My sister and I are happily independent; and you are aware that the proprietor of Whiteladies is a young man of twenty-one, not at all anxious about an heir, and indeed likely to marry and have children of his own."

"To marry?—to have children?" said M. Guillaume in unaffected dismay. "But, pardon me, M. Herbert is dying. It is an affair of a few weeks, perhaps a few days. This is what you said."

"I said so eighteen months ago, M. Guillaume. Since then there has been a most happy change. Herbert is better. He will soon, I hope, be well and strong."

"But he is poitrinaire," said the old man, eagerly. "He is beyond hope. There are rallyings and temporary recoveries, but these maladies are never cured—never cured. Is it not so? You said this yesterday, to help me with Giovanna, and I thanked you. But it cannot be, it is not possible. I will not believe it!—such maladies are never cured. And if so, why then—why then!—no, Madame deceives herself. If this were the case, it would be all in vain, all that has been done; and le petit—"

"I am not to blame, I hope, for le petit," said Miss Susan, trying to smile, but with a horrible constriction at her heart.

"But why then?" said M. Guillaume, bewildered and indignant, "why then? I had settled all with M. Farrel-Austin. Madame has misled me altogether; Madame has turned my house upside down. We were quiet, we had no agitations; our daughter-in-law, if she was not much use to us, was yet submissive, and gave no trouble. But Madame comes, and in a moment all is changed. Giovanna, whom no one thought of, has a baby, and it is put into our heads that he is the heir to a great château in England. Bah! this is your château—this maison de campagne, this construction partly of wood—and now you tell me that le petit is not the heir!"

Miss Susan stood still and looked at the audacious speaker. She was stupefied. To insult herself was nothing, but Whiteladies! It appeared to her that the earth must certainly open and swallow him up.

"Not that I regret your château!" said the linendraper, wild with wrath. "If it were mine, I would pull it down, and build something which should be comme il faut, which would last, which should not be of brick and wood. The glass would do for the fruit-houses, early fruits for the market; and with the wood I should make a temple in the garden, where ces dames could drink of the tea! It is all it is good for—a maison de campagne, a house of farmers, a nothing—and so old! the floors swell upward, and the roofs bow downward. It is eaten of worms; it is good for rats, not for human beings to live in. And le petit is not the heir! and it is Guillaume Austin of Bruges that you go to make a laughing-stock of, Madame Suzanne! But it shall not be—it shall not be!"

I do not know what Miss Susan would have replied to this outburst, had not Giovanna suddenly met them coming round the corner of the house. Giovanna had many wrongs to avenge, or thought she had many wrongs to avenge, upon the family of her husband generally, and she had either a favorable inclination toward the ladies who had taken her in and used her kindly, or at least as much hope for the future as tempted her to take their part.

"What is it, mon beau-père, that shall not be?" she cried. "Ah, I know! that which the mother wishes so much does not please here? You want money, money, though you are so rich. You say you love le petit, but you want money for him. But he is my child, not yours, and I do not ask for any money. I am not so fond of it as you are. I know what the belle-mère says night and day, night and day. 'They should give us money, these rich English, they should give us money; we have them in our power.' That is what she is always saying. Ces dames are very good to me, and I will not have them robbed. I speak plain, but it is true. Ah! you may look as you please, mon beau-père; we are not in Bruges, and I am not frightened. You cannot do anything to me here."

M. Guillaume stood between the two women, not knowing what to do or say. He was wild with rage and disappointment, but he had that chilling sense of discomfiture which, even while it gives the desire to speak and storm, takes away the power. He turned from Giovanna, who defied him, to Miss Susan, who had not got over her horror. Between the old gentlewoman who was his social superior, and the young creature made superior to him by the advantages of youth and by the stronger passions that moved her, the old linendraper stood transfixed, incapable of any individual action. He took off his hat once more, and took out his handkerchief, and rubbed his bald head with baffled wrath and perplexity. "Sotte!" he said under his breath to his daughter-in-law; and at Miss Susan he cast a look, which was half of curiosity, to see what impression Giovanna's revelations had made upon her, and the other half made up of fear and rage, in equal portions. Miss Susan took the ascendant, as natural to her superior birth and breeding.

"If you will come down this way, through the orchard, I will show you the ruins of the priory," she said blandly, making a half-curtsey by way of closing the discussion, and turning to lead the way. Her politeness, in which there was just that admixture of contempt which keeps an inferior in his proper place, altogether cowed the old shopkeeper. He turned too, and followed her with increased respect, though suppressed resentment. But he cast another look at Giovanna before he followed, and muttered still stronger expressions, "Imbecile! idiote!" between his teeth, as he followed his guide along the leafy way. Giovanna took this abuse with great composure. She laughed as she went back across the lawn, leaving them to survey the ruins with what interest they might. She even snapped her fingers with a significant gesture. "That for thee and thy evil words!" she said.

CHAPTER XXVII

Miss Susan felt that it was beyond doubt the work of Providence to increase her punishment that Everard should arrive as he did quite unexpectedly on the evening of this day. M. Guillaume had calmed down out of the first passion of his disappointment, and as he was really fond of the child, and stood in awe of his wife and daughter, who were still more devoted to it, he was now using all his powers to induce Giovanna to go back with him. Everard met them in the green lane, on the north side of the house, when he arrived. Their appearance struck him with some surprise. The old man carried in his arms the child, which was still dressed in its Flemish costume, with the little close cap concealing its round face. The baby had its arms clasped closely round the old man's neck, and M. Guillaume, in that conjunction, looked more venerable and more amiable than when he was arguing with Miss Susan. Giovanna walked beside him, and a very animated conversation was going on between them. It would be difficult to describe the amazement with which Everard perceived this singularly un-English group so near Whiteladies. They seemed to have come from the little gate which opened on the lane, and they were in eager, almost violent controversy about something. Who were they? and what could they have to do with Whiteladies? he asked himself, wondering. Everard walked in, unannounced, through the long passages, and opened softly the door of the drawing-room. Miss Susan was seated at a small desk near one of the windows. She had her face buried in her hands, most pathetic, and most suggestive of all the attitudes of distress. Her gray hair was pushed back a little by the painful grasp of her fingers. She was giving vent to a low moaning, almost more the breathing of pain than an articulate cry of suffering.

"Aunt Susan! What is the matter?"

She raised herself instantly, with a smile on her face—a smile so completely and unmistakably artificial, and put on for purposes of concealment, that it scared Everard almost more than her trouble did. "What, Everard!" she said, "is it you? This is a pleasure I was not looking for—" and she rose up and held out her hands to him. There was some trace of redness about her eyes; but it looked more like want of rest than tears; and as her manner was manifestly put on, a certain jauntiness, quite unlike Miss Susan, had got into it. The smile which she forced by dint of the strong effort required to produce it, got exaggerated, and ran almost into a laugh; her head had a little nervous toss. A stranger would have said her manner was full of affectation. This was the strange aspect which her emotion took.

"What is the matter?" Everard repeated, taking her hands into his, and looking at her earnestly. "Is there bad news?"

"No, no; nothing of the kind. I had a little attack of—that old pain I used to suffer from—neuralgia, I suppose. As one gets older one dislikes owning to rheumatism. No, no, no bad news; a little physical annoyance—nothing more."

Everard tried hard to recollect what the "old pain" was, but could not succeed in identifying anything of the kind with the always vigorous Miss Susan. She interrupted his reflections by saying with a very jaunty air, which contrasted strangely with her usual manner, "Did you meet our aristocratic visitors?"

"An old Frenchman, with a funny little child clasped round his neck," said Everard, to whose simple English understanding all foreigners were Frenchmen, "and a very handsome young woman. Do they belong here? I did meet them, and could not make them out. The old man looked a genial old soul. I liked to see him with the child. Your visitors! Where did you pick them up?"

"These are very important people to the house and to the race," said Miss Susan, with once more, so to speak, a flutter of her wings. "They are—but come, guess; does nothing whisper to you who they are?"

"How should it?" said Everard, in his dissatisfaction with Miss Susan's strange demeanor growing somewhat angry. "What have such people to do with you? The old fellow is nice-looking enough, and the woman really handsome; but they don't seem the kind of people one would expect to see here."

Miss Susan made a pause, smiling again in that same sickly forced way. "They say it is always good for a race when it comes back to the people, to the wholesome common stock, after a great many generations of useless gentlefolk. These are the Austins of Bruges, Everard, whom you hunted all over the world. They are simple Belgian tradespeople, but at the same time Austins, pur sang."

"The Austins of Bruges?"

"Yes; come over on a visit. It was very kind of them, though we are beginning to tire of each other. The old man, M. Guillaume, he whom Farrel thought he had done away with, and his daughter-in-law, a young widow, and the little child, who is—the heir."

"The heir?—of the shop, you mean, I suppose."

"I do nothing of the kind, Everard, and it is unkind of you not to understand. The next heir to Whiteladies."

"Bah!" said Everard. "Make your mind easy, Aunt Susan. Herbert will marry before he has been six months at home. I know Herbert. He has been helpless and dependent so long, that the moment he has a chance of proving himself a man by the glorious superiority of having a wife, he will do it. Poor fellow! after you have been led about and domineered over all your life, of course you want, in your turn, to domineer over some one. See if my words don't come true."

"So that is your idea of marriage—to domineer over some one? Poor creatures!" said Miss Susan, compassionately; "you will soon find out the difference. I hope he may, Everard—I hope he may. He shall have my blessing, I promise you, and willing consent. To be quit of that child and its heirship, and know there was some one who had a real right to the place—Good heavens, what would I not give!"

"It appears, then, you don't admire those good people from Bruges?"

"Oh, I have nothing to say against them," said Miss Susan, faltering—"nothing! The old man is highly respectable, and Madame Austin le jeune, is—very nice-looking. They are quite a nice sort of people— for their station in life."

"But you are tired of them," said Everard, with a laugh.

"Well, perhaps to say tired is too strong an expression," said Miss Susan, with a panting at the throat which belied her calm speech. "But we have little in common, as you may suppose. We don't know what to say to each other; that is the great drawback at all times between the different classes. Their ideas are different from ours. Besides, they are foreign, which makes more difference still."

"I have come to stay till Monday, if you will have me," said Everard; "so I shall be able to judge for myself. I thought the young woman was very pretty. Is there a Monsieur Austin le jeune? A widow! Oh, then you may expect her, if she stays, to turn a good many heads."

Miss Susan gave him a searching, wondering look. "You are mistaken," she said. "She is not anything so wonderful good-looking, even handsome—but not a beauty to turn men's heads."

"We shall see," said Everard lightly. "And now tell me what news you have of the travellers. They don't write to me now."

"Why?" said Miss Susan, eager to change the subject, and, besides, very ready to take an interest in anything that concerned the intercourse between Everard and Reine.

"Oh, I don't know," he said, shrugging his shoulders. "Somehow we are not so intimate as we were. Reine told me, indeed, the last time she wrote that it was unnecessary to write so often, now that Herbert was well—as if that was all I cared for!" These last words were said low, after a pause, and there was a tone of indignation and complaint in them, subdued yet perceptible, which, even in the midst of her trouble, was balmy to Miss Susan's ear.

"Reine is a capricious child," she said, with a passing gleam of enjoyment. "You saw a great deal of them before you went to Jamaica. But that is nearly two years since," she added, maliciously; "many changes have taken place since then."

"That is true," said Everard. And it was still more true, though he did not say so, that the change had not all been on Reine's part. He, too, had been capricious, and two or three broken and fugitive flirtations had occurred in his life since that day when, deeply émotionné and not knowing how to keep his feelings to himself, he had left Reine in the little Alpine valley. That Alpine valley already looked very far off to him; but he should have preferred, on the whole, to find its memory and influence more fresh with Reine. He framed his lips unconsciously to a whistle as he submitted to Miss Susan's examination, which meant to express that he didn't care, that if Reine chose to be indifferent and forgetful, why, he could be indifferent too. Instantly, however, he remembered, before any sound became audible, that to whistle was indecorous, and forbore.

"And how are your own affairs going on?" said Miss Susan; "we have not had any conversation on the subject since you came back. Well? I am glad to hear it. You have not really been a loser, then, by your fright and your hard work?"

"Rather a gainer on the whole," said Everard; "besides the amusement. Work is not such a bad thing when you are fond of it. If ever I am in great need, or take a panic again, I shall enjoy it. It takes up your thoughts."

"Then why don't you go on, having made a beginning?" said Miss Susan. "You are very well off for a young man, Everard; but suppose you were to marry? And now that you have made a beginning, and got over the worst, I wish you could go on."

"I don't think I shall ever marry," said Everard, with a vague smile creeping about the corners of his lips.

"Very likely! You should have gone on, Everard. A little more money never comes amiss; and as you really like work—"

"When I am forced to it," he said, laughing. "I am not forced now; that makes all the difference. You don't expect a young man of the nineteenth century, brought up as I have been, to go to work in cold blood without a motive. No, no, that is too much."

"If you please, ma'am," said Martha, coming in, "Stevens wishes to know if the foreign lady and gentleman is staying over Sunday. And Cook wishes to say, please—"

A shadow came over Miss Susan's face. She forgot the appearances which she had been keeping up with Everard. The color went out of her cheeks; her eyes grew dull and dead, as if the life had died out of them. She put up her hands to stop this further demand upon her.

"They cannot go on Sunday, of course," she said, "and it is too late to go to-day. Stevens knows that as well as I do, and so do you all. Of course they mean to stay."

"And if you please, ma'am, Cook says the baby—"

"No more, please, no more!" cried Miss Susan, faintly. "I shall come presently and talk to Cook."

"You want to get rid of these people," said Everard, sympathetically, startled by her look. "You don't like them, Aunt Susan, whatever you may say."

"I hate them!" she said, low under her breath, with a tone of feeling so intense that he was alarmed by it. Then she recovered herself suddenly, chased the cloud from her face, and fell back into the jaunty manner which had so much surprised and almost shocked him before. "Of course I don't mean that," she said, with a laugh. "Even I have caught your fashion of exaggeration; but I don't love them, indeed, and I think a Sunday with them in the house is a very dismal affair to look forward to. Go and dress, Everard; there is the bell. I must go and speak to Cook."

While this conversation had been going on in-doors, the two foreigners thus discussed were walking up and down Priory Lane, in close conversation still. They did not hear the dressing-bell, or did not care for it. As for Giovanna, she had never yet troubled herself to ask what the preliminary bell meant. She had no dresses to change, and having no acquaintance with the habit which prescribed this alteration of costume in the evening, made no attempt to comply with it. The child clung about M. Guillaume's neck, and gave power to his arguments, though it nearly strangled him with its close clasp. "My good Giovanna," he said, "why put yourself in opposition to all your friends? We are your friends, though you will not think so. This darling, the light of our eyes, you will not steal him from us. Yes, my own! it is of thee I speak. The blessed infant knows; look how he holds me! You would not deprive me of him, my daughter—my dear child?"

"I should not steal him, anyhow," said the young woman, with an exultation which he thought cruel. "He is mine."

"Yes, I know. I have always respected zight, chérie; you know I have. When thy mother-in-law would have had me take authority over him, I have said 'No; she is his mother; the right is with her'—always, ma fille! I ask thee as a favor—I do not command thee, though some, you know, might think—. Listen, my child. The little one will be nothing but a burden to you in the world. If you should wish to go away, to see new faces, to be independent, though it is so strange for a woman, yet think, my child, the little one would be a burden. You have not the habits of our Gertrude, who understands children. Leave thy little one with us! You will then be free to go where you will."

"And you will be rid of me!" cried the young woman, with passionate scorn. "Ah, I know you! I know what you mean. To get the child without me would be victory. Ma belle-mère would be glad, and Gertrude, who understands children. Understand me, then, mon beau-père. The child is my power. I will never leave hold of him; he is my power. By him I can revenge myself; without him I am nobody, and you do not fear me. Give my baby to me!"

She seized the child, who struggled to keep his hold, and dragged him out of his grandfather's arms. The little fellow had his mouth open to cry, when she deftly filled it with her handkerchief, and, setting him down forcibly on his little legs, shook him into frightened silence. "Cry, and I will beat thee!" she said. Then turning to the grandfather, who was remonstrating and entreating, "He shall walk; he is big enough; he shall not be carried nor spoiled, as you would spoil him. Listen, bon papa. I have not anything else to keep my own part with; but he is mine."

"Giovanna! Giovanna! think less of thyself and more of thy child!"

"When I find you set me a good example," she said. "Is it not your comfort you seek, caring nothing for mine? Get rid of me, and keep the child! Ah, I perceive my belle-mère in that! But it is his interest to be here. Ces dames, though they don't love us, are kind enough. And listen to me; they will never give you the rente you demand for the boy—never; but if he stays here and I stay here, they will not turn us out. Ah, no, Madame Suzanne dares not turn me out! See, then, the reason of what I am doing. You love the child, but you do not wish a burden; and if you take him away, it will be as a burden; they will never give you a sous for him. But leave us here, and they will be forced to nourish us and lodge us. Ah, you perceive! I am not without reason; I know what I do."

M. Guillaume was staggered. Angry as he was to have the child dragged from his arms, and dismayed as he was by Giovanna's indifference to its fright and tears, there was still something in this argument which compelled his attention. It was true that the subject of an allowance for the baby's maintenance and education had been of late very much talked of at Bruges, and the family had unanimously concluded that it was a right and necessary thing, and the letter making the claim had begun to be concocted, when Giovanna, stung by some quarrel, had suddenly taken the matter into her own hands. To take back the child would be sweet; but to take it back pensionless and almost hopeless, with its heirship rendered uncertain, and its immediate claims denied, would not be sweet. M. Guillaume was torn in twain by conflicting sentiments, his paternal feelings struggling against a very strong desire to make what could be honestly made out of Whiteladies, and to have the baby provided for. His wife was eager to have the child, but would she be as eager if she knew that it was totally penniless, and had only visionary expectations. Would not she complain more and more of Giovanna, who did nothing, and even of the child itself, another mouth to be fed? This view of the subject silenced and confounded him. "If I could hope that thou wouldst be kind!" he said, falteringly, eying the poor baby, over whom his heart yearned. His heart yearned over the child; and yet he felt it would be something of a triumph could he exploit Miss Susan, and transfer an undesirable burden from his own shoulders to hers. Surely this was worth doing, after her English coldness and her aristocratic contempt. M. Guillaume did not like to be looked down upon. He had been wounded in his pride and hurt in his tender feelings; and now he would be revenged on her! He put his hand on Giovanna's shoulder, and drew closer to her, and they held a consultation with their heads together, which was only interrupted by the appearance of Stevens, very dark and solemn, who begged to ask if they were aware that the dinner-bell had rung full five minutes before?

CHAPTER XXVIII

The dinner-table in the old hall was surrounded by a very odd party that night. Miss Susan, at the head of the table, in the handsome matronly evening dress which she took to always at the beginning of Winter, did her best to look as usual, though she could not quite keep the panting of her breast from being visible under her black silk and lace. She was breathless, as if she had been running hard; this was the form her agitation took. Miss Augustine, at the other end of the table, sat motionless, absorbed in her own thoughts, and quite unmoved by what was going on around her. Everard had one side to himself, from which he watched with great curiosity the pair opposite him, who came in abruptly— Giovanna, with her black hair slightly ruffled by the wind, and M. Guillaume, rubbing his bald head. This was all the toilet they had made. The meal began almost in silence, with a few remarks only between Miss Susan and Everard. M. Guillaume was pre-occupied. Giovanna was at no time disposed for much conversation. Miss Susan, however, after a little interval, began to talk significantly, so as to attract the strangers.

"You said you had not heard lately from Herbert," she said, addressing her young cousin. "You don't know, then, I suppose, that they have made all their plans for coming home?"

"Not before the Winter, I hope."

"Oh, no, not before the Winter—in May, when we hope it will be quite safe. They are coming home, not for a visit, but to settle. And we must think of looking for a house," said Miss Susan, with a smile and a sigh.

"Do you mean that you—you who have been mistress of Whiteladies for so long—that you will leave Whiteladies? They will never allow that," said Everard.

Miss Susan looked him meaningly in the face, with a gleam of her eye toward the strangers on the other side of the table. How could he tell what meaning she wished to convey to him? Men are not clever at interpreting such communications in the best of circumstances, and, perfectly ignorant as he was of the circumstances, how could Everard make out what she wanted? But the look silenced and left him gaping with his mouth open, feeling that something was expected of him, and not knowing what to say.

"Yes, that is my intention," said Miss Susan, with that jaunty air which had so perplexed and annoyed him before. "When Herbert comes home, he has his sister with him to keep his house. I should be superseded. I should be merely a lodger, a visitor in Whiteladies, and that I could not put up with. I shall go, of course."

"But, Aunt Susan, Reine would never think—Herbert would never permit—"

Another glance, still more full of meaning, but of meaning beyond Everard's grasp, stopped him again. What could she want him to do or say? he asked himself. What could she be thinking of?

"The thing is settled," said Miss Susan; "of course we must go. The house and everything in it belongs to Herbert. He will marry, of course. Did not you say to me this very afternoon that he was sure to marry?"

"Yes," Everard answered faintly; "but—"

"There is no but," she replied, with almost a triumphant air. "It is a matter of course. I shall feel leaving the old house, but I have no right to it, it is not mine, and I do not mean to make any fuss. In six months from this time, if all is well, we shall be out of Whiteladies."

She said this with again a little toss of her head, as if in satisfaction. Giovanna and M. Guillaume exchanged alarmed glances. The words were taking effect.

"Is it settled?" said Augustine, calmly. "I did not know things had gone so far. The question now is, Who will Herbert marry? We once talked of this in respect to you, Everard, and I told you my views—I should say my wishes. Herbert has been restored as by a miracle. He ought to be very thankful—he ought to show his gratitude. But it depends much upon the kind of woman he marries. I thought once in respect to you—"

"Augustine, we need not enter into these questions before strangers," said Miss Susan.

"It does not matter who is present," said Augustine. "Every one knows what my life is, and what is the curse of our house."

"Pardon, ma sœur," said M. Guillaume. "I am of the house, but I do not know."

"Ah!" said Augustine, looking at him. "After Herbert, you represent the elder branch, it is true; but you have not a daughter who is young, under twenty, have you? that is what I want to know."

"I have three daughters, ma sœur," said M. Guillaume, delighted to find a subject on which he could expatiate; "all very good—gentille, kind to every one. There is Madeleine, who is the wife of M. Meeren, the jeweller—François Meeren, the eldest son, very well off; and Marie, who is settled at Courtray, whose husband has a great manufactory; and Gertrude, my youngest, who has married my partner— they will succeed her mother and me when our day is over. Ma sœur knows that my son died. Yes; these are misfortunes that all have to bear. This is my family. They are very good women, though I say it— pious and good mothers and wives, and obedient to their husbands and kind to the poor."

Augustine had continued to look at him, but the animation had faded out of her eyes. "Men's wives are of little interest to me," she said. "What I want is one who is young, and who would understand and do what I say."

Here Giovanna got up from her chair, pushing it back with a force which almost made Stevens drop the dish he was carrying. "Me!" she cried, with a gleam of malice in her eyes, "me, ma sœur! I am younger than Gertrude and the rest. I am no one's wife. Let it be me."

Augustine looked at her with curious scrutiny, measuring her from head to foot, as it were; while Miss Susan, horror-stricken at once by the discussion and the indecorum, looked on breathless. Then Augustine turned away.

"You could not be Herbert's wife," she said, with her usual abstract quiet; and added softly, "I must ask for enlightenment. I shall speak to my people at the almshouses to-morrow. We have done so much. His life has been given to us; why not the family salvation too?"

"These are questions which had better not be discussed at the dinner-table," said Miss Susan; "a place where in England we don't think it right to indulge in expressions of feeling. Madame Jean, I am afraid you are surprised by my sister's ways. In the family we all know what she means exactly; but outside the family—"

"I am one of the family," said Giovanna, leaning back in her chair, on which she had reseated herself. She put up her hands, and clasped them behind her head in an attitude which was of the easiest and freest description. "I eat no more, thank you, take it away; though the cuisine is better than my belle mère's, bon papa; but I cannot eat forever, like you English. Oh, I am one of the family. I understand also, and I think—there are many things that come into my head."

Miss Susan gave her a look which was full of fright and dislike, but not of understanding. Everard only thought he caught for a moment the gleam of sudden malicious meaning in her eyes. She laughed a low laugh, and looked at him across the table, yawning and stretching her arms, which were hidden by her black sleeves, but which Everard divined to be beautiful ones, somewhat large, but fine and shapely. His eyes sought hers half unwillingly, attracted in spite of himself. How full of life and youth and warmth and force she looked among all these old people! Even her careless gestures, her want of breeding, over which Stevens was groaning, seemed to make it more evident; and he thought to himself, with a shudder, that he understood what was in her eye.

But none of the old people thought the rude young woman worth notice. Her father-in-law pulled her skirt sharply under the table, to recall her to "her manners," and she laughed, but did not alter her position. Miss Susan was horrified and angry, but her indignation went no further. She turned to the old linendraper with elaborate politeness.

"I am afraid you will find our English Sunday dull," she said. "You know we have different ideas from those you have abroad; and if you want to go to-morrow, travelling is difficult on Sunday—though to be sure we might make an effort."

"Pardon, I have no intention of going to-morrow," said M. Guillaume. "I have been thinking much—and after dinner I will disclose to Madame what my thoughts have been."

Miss Susan's bosom swelled with suspense and pain. "That will do, Stevens, that will do," she said.

He had been wandering round and round the table for about an hour, she thought, with sweet dishes of which there was an unusual and unnecessary abundance, and which no one tasted. She felt sure, as people always do, when they are aware of something to conceal, that he lingered so long on purpose to spy out what he could of the mystery; and now her heart beat with feverish desire to know what was the nature of M. Guillaume's thoughts. Why did not he say plainly, "We are going on Monday?" That would have been a hundred times better than any thoughts.

"It will be well if you will come to the Almshouses to-morrow," said Miss Augustine, once more taking the conduct of the conversation into her hands. "It will be well for yourself to show at least that you understand what the burden of the family is. Perhaps good thoughts will be put into your heart; perhaps, as you are the next in succession of our family—ah! I must think of that. You are an old man; you cannot be ambitious," she said slowly and calmly; "nor love the world as others do."

"You flatter me, ma sœur," said M. Guillaume. "I should be proud to deserve your commendation; but I am ambitious. Not for myself—for me it is nothing; but if this child were the master here, I should die happy. It is what I wish for most."

"That is," said Miss Susan, with rising color (and oh, how thankful she was for some feasible pretext by which to throw off a little of the rising tide of feeling within her!)—"that is—what M. Guillaume Austin wishes for most is, that Herbert, our boy, whom God has spared, should get worse again, and die."

The old man looked up at her, startled, having, like so many others, thought innocently enough of what was most important to himself, without considering how it told upon the others. Giovanna, however, put herself suddenly in the breach.

"I," she cried, with another quick change of movement—"I am the child's mother, Madame Suzanne, you know; yet I do not wish this. Listen. I drink to the health of M. Herbert!" she cried, lifting up the nearest glass of wine, which happened to be her father-in-law's; "that he comes home well and strong, that he takes a wife, that he lives long! I carry this to his health. Vive M. Herbert!" she cried, and drank the wine, which brought a sudden flush to her cheeks, and lighted up her eyes.

They all gazed at her—I cannot say with what disapproval and secret horror in their elderly calm; except Everard, who, always ready to admire a pretty woman, felt a sudden enthusiasm taking possession of him. He, oddly enough, was the only one to understand her meaning; but how handsome she was! how splendid the glow in her eyes! He looked across the table, and bowed and pledged her. He was the only one who did not look at her with disapproval. Her beauty conciliated the young man, in spite of himself.

"Drinking to him is a vain ceremony," said Augustine; "but if you were to practise self-denial, and get up early, and come to the Almshouses every morning with me—"

"I will," said Giovanna, quickly, "I will! every morning, if ma sœur will permit me—"

"I do not suppose that every morning can mean much in Madame Jean's case," said Miss Susan stiffly, "as no doubt she will be returning home before long."

"Do not check the young woman, Susan, when she shows good dispositions," said Augustine. "It is always good to pray. You are worldly-minded yourself, and do not think as I do; but when I can find one to feel with me, that makes me happy. She may stay longer than you think."

Miss Susan could not restrain a low exclamation of dismay. Everard, looking at her, saw that her face began to wear that terrible look of conscious impotence—helpless and driven into a corner, which is so unendurable to the strong. She was of more personal importance individually than all the tormentors who surrounded her, but she was powerless, and could do nothing against them. Her cheeks flushed hot under her eyes, which seemed scorched, and dazzled too, by this burning of shame. He said something to her in a low tone, to call off her attention, and perceived that the strong woman, generally mistress of the circumstances, was unable to answer him out of sheer emotion. Fortunately, by this time the dessert was on the table, and she rose abruptly. Augustine, slower, rose too. Giovanna, however, sat still composedly by her father-in-law's side.

"The bon papa has not finished his wine," she said, pointing to him.

"Madame Jean," said Miss Susan, "in England you must do as English ladies do. I cannot permit anything else in my house."

It was not this that made her excited, but it was a mode of throwing forth a little of that excitement which, moment by moment, was getting to be more than she could bear. Giovanna, after another look, got up and obeyed her without a word.

"So this is the mode Anglaise!" said the old man when they were gone; "it is not polite; it is to show, I suppose, that we are not welcome; but Madame Suzanne need not give herself the trouble. If she will do her duty to her relations, I do not mean to stay."

"I do not know what it is about," said Everard; "but she always does her duty by everybody, and you need not be afraid."

On this hint M. Guillaume began, and told Everard the whole matter, filling him with perplexity. The story of Miss Susan's visit sounded strangely enough, though the simple narrator knew nothing of its worst consequences; but he told his interested auditor how she had tempted him to throw up his bargain with Farrel-Austin, and raised hopes which now she seemed so little inclined to realize; and the story was not agreeable to Everard's ear. Farrel-Austin, no doubt, had begun this curious oblique dealing; but Farrel-Austin was a man from whom little was expected, and Everard had been used to expect much from Miss Susan. But he did not know, all the time, that he was driving her almost mad, keeping back the old man, who had promised that evening to let her know the issue of his thoughts. She was sitting in a corner, speechless and rigid with agitation, when the two came in from the dining-room to "join the ladies;" and even then Everard, in his ignorance, would have seated himself beside her, to postpone the explanation still longer. "Go away! go away!" she said to him in a wild whisper. What could she mean? for certainly there could be nothing tragical connected with this old man, or so at least Everard thought.

"Madame will excuse me, I hope," said Guillaume blandly; "as it is the mode Anglaise, I endeavored to follow it, though it seems little polite. But it is not for one country to condemn the ways of the other. If Madame wishes it, I will now say the result of my thoughts."

Miss Susan, who was past speaking, nodded her head, and did her best to form her lips into a smile.

"Madame informs me," said M. Guillaume, "that Monsieur Herbert is better, that the chances of le petit are small, and that there is no one to give to the child the rente, the allowance, that is his due?"

"That is true, quite true."

"On the other hand," said M. Guillaume, "Giovanna has told me her ideas—she will not come away with me. What she says is that her boy has a right to be here; and she will not leave Viteladies. What can I say? Madame perceives that it is not easy to change the ideas of Giovanna when she has made up her mind."

"But what has her mind to do with it," cried Miss Susan in despair, "when it is you who have the power?"

"Madame is right, of course," said the old shopkeeper; "it is I who have the power. I am the father, the head of the house. Still, a good father is not a tyrant, Madame Suzanne; a good father hears reason. Giovanna says to me, 'It is well; if le petit has no right, it is for M. le Proprietaire to say so.' She is not without acuteness, Madame will perceive. What she says is, 'If Madame Suzanne cannot provide for le petit—will not make him any allowance—and tells us that she has nothing to do with Viteladies—then it is best to wait until they come who have to do with it. M. Herbert returns in May. Eh, bien! she will remain till then, that M. Herbert, who must know best, may decide."

Miss Susan was thunderstruck. She was driven into silence, paralyzed by this intimation. She looked at the old shopkeeper with a dumb strain of terror and appeal in her face, which moved him, though he did not understand.

"Mon Dieu! Madame," he cried; "can I help it? it is not I; I am without power!"

"But she shall not stay—I cannot have her; I will not have her!" cried Miss Susan, in her dismay.

M. Guillaume said nothing, but he beckoned his step-daughter from the other end of the room.

"Speak for thyself," he said. "Thou art not wanted here, nor thy child either. It would be better to return with me."

Giovanna looked Miss Susan fall in the eyes, with an audacious smile.

"Madame Suzanne will not send me away," she said; "I am sure she will not send me away."

Miss Susan felt herself caught in the toils. She looked from one to another with despairing eyes. She might appeal to the old man, but she knew it was hopeless to appeal to the young woman, who stood over her with determination in every line of her face, and conscious power glancing from her eyes. She subdued herself by an incalculable effort.

"I thought," she said, faltering, "that it would be happier for you to go back to your home—that to be near your friends would please you. It may be comfortable enough here, but you would miss the—society of your friends—"

"My mother-in-law?" said Giovanna, with a laugh. "Madame is too good to think of me. Yes, it is dull, I know; but for the child I overlook that. I will stay till M. Herbert comes. The bon papa is fond of the child, but he loves his rente, and will leave us when we are penniless. I will stay till M. Herbert returns, who must govern everything. Madame Suzanne will not contradict me, otherwise I shall have no choice. I shall be forced to go to M. Herbert to tell him all."

Miss Susan sat still and listened. She had to keep silence, though her heart beat so that it seemed to be escaping out of her sober breast, and the blood filled her veins to bursting.

Heaven help her! here was her punishment. Fiery passion blazed in her, but she durst not betray it; and to keep it down—to keep it silent—was all she was able to do. She answered, faltering,—

"You are mistaken; you are mistaken. Herbert will do nothing. Besides, some one could write and tell you what he says."

"Pardon! but I move not; I leave not," said Giovanna. She enjoyed the triumph. "I am a mother," she said; "Madame Suzanne knows; and mothers sacrifice everything for the good of their children—everything. I am able for the sacrifice," she said, looking down upon Miss Susan with a gleam almost of laughter—of fun, humor, and malicious amusement in her eyes.

To reason with this creature was like dashing one's self against a stone wall. She was impregnable in her resolution. Miss Susan, feeling the blow go to her heart, pushed her chair back into the corner, and hid herself, as it were. It was a dark corner, where her face was in comparative darkness.

"I cannot struggle with you," she said, in a piteous whisper, feeling her lips too parched and dry for another word.

CHAPTER XXIX

"Going to stay till Herbert comes back! but, my dear Aunt Susan, since you don't want her—and of course you don't want her—why don't you say so?" cried Everard. "An unwelcome guest may be endured for a day or two, or a week or two, but for five or six months—"

"My dear," said Miss Susan, who was pale, and in whose vigorous frame a tremble of weakness seemed so out of place, "how can I say so? It would be so—discourteous—so uncivil—"

The young man looked at her with dismay. He would have laughed had she not been so deadly serious. Her face was white and drawn, her lips quivered slightly as she spoke. She looked all at once a weak old woman, tremulous, broken down, and uncertain of herself.

"You must be ill," he said. "I can't believe it is you I am speaking to. You ought to see the doctor, Aunt Susan—you cannot be well."

"Perhaps," she said with a pitiful attempt at a smile, "perhaps. Indeed you must be right, Everard, for I don't feel like myself. I am getting old, you know."

"Nonsense!" he said lightly, "you were as young as any of us last time I was here."

"Ah!" said Miss Susan, with her quivering lips. "I have kept that up too long. I have gone on being young—and now all at once I am old; that is how it is."

"But that does not make any difference in my argument," said Everard; "if you are old—which I don't believe—the less reason is there for having you vexed. You don't like this guest who is going to inflict herself upon you. I shouldn't mind her," he added, with a laugh; "she's very handsome, Aunt Susan; but I don't suppose that affects you in the same way; and she will be quite out of place when Herbert comes, or at least when Reine comes. I advise you to tell her plainly, before the old fellow goes, that it won't do."

"I can't, my dear—I can't!" said Miss Susan; how her lips quivered!—"she is in my house, she is my guest, and I can't say 'Go away.'"

"Why not? She is not a person of very fine feelings, to be hurt by it. She is not even a lady; and till May, till the end of May! you will never be able to endure her."

"Oh, yes I shall," said Miss Susan. "I see you think that I am very weak; but I never was uncivil to any one, Everard, not to any one in my own house. It is Herbert's house, of course," she added quickly, "but yet it has been mine, though I never had any real right to it for so many years."

"And you really mean to leave now?"

"I suppose so," said Miss Susan faltering, "I think, probably—nothing is settled. Don't be too hard upon me, Everard! I said so—for them, to show them that I had no power."

"Then why, for heaven's sake, if you have so strong a feeling—why, for the sake of politeness!—Politeness is absurd, Aunt Susan," said Everard. "Do you mean to say that if any saucy fellow, any cad I may have met, chose to come into my house and take possession, I should not kick him out because it would be uncivil? This is not like your good sense. You must have some other reason. No! do you mean No by that shake of the head? Then if it is so very disagreeable to you, let me speak to her. Let me suggest—"

"Not for the world," cried Miss Susan. "No, for pity's sake, no. You will make me frantic if you speak of such a thing."

"Or to the old fellow," said Everard; "he ought to see the absurdity of it, and the tyranny."

She caught at this evidently with a little hope. "You may speak to Monsieur Guillaume if you feel disposed," she said; "yes, you may speak to him. I blame him very much; he ought not to have listened to her; he ought to have taken her away at once."

"How could he if she wouldn't go? Men no doubt are powerful beings," said Everard laughing, "but suppose the other side refused to be moved? Even a horse at the water, if it declines to drink—you know the proverb."

"Oh, don't worry me with proverbs—as if I had not enough without that!" she said with an impatience which would have been comic had it not been so tragical. "Yes, Everard, yes, if you like you may speak to him—but not to her; not a word to her for the world. My dear boy, my dear boy! You won't go against me in this?"

"Of course I shall do only what you wish me to do," he said more gravely; the sight of her agitation troubled the young man exceedingly. To think of any concealed feeling, any mystery in connection with Susan Austin, seemed not only a blasphemy, but an absurdity. Yet what could she mean, what could her strange terror, her changed looks, her agitated aspect, mean? Everard was more disturbed than he could say.

This was on Sunday afternoon, that hour of all others when clouds hang heaviest, and troubles, where they exist, come most into the foreground. The occupations of ordinary life push them aside, but Sunday, which is devoted to rest, and in which so many people honestly endeavor to put the trifling little cares of every day out of their minds, always lays hold of those bigger disturbers of existence which it is the aim of our lives to forget. Miss Susan would have made a brave fight against the evil which she could not avoid on another day, but this day, with all its many associations of quiet, its outside tranquillity, its peaceful recollections and habits, was too much for her. Everard had found her walking in the Priory Lane by herself, a bitter dew of pain in her eyes, and a tremble in her lips which frightened him. She had come out to collect her thoughts a little, and to escape from her visitors, who sometimes seemed for the moment more than she could bear.

Miss Augustine came up on her way from the afternoon service at the Almshouses, while Everard spoke. She was accompanied by Giovanna, and it was a curious sight to see the tall, slight figure of the Gray sister, type of everything abstract and mystic, with that other by her side, full of strange vitality, watching the absorbed and dreamy creature with those looks of investigation, puzzled to know what her meaning was, but determined somehow to be at the bottom of it. Giovanna's eyes darted a keen telegraphic communication to Everard's as they came up. This glance seemed to convey at once an opinion and an inquiry. "How droll she is! Is she mad? I am finding her out," the eyes said. Everard carefully refrained from making any reply; though, indeed, this was self-denial on his part, for Giovanna certainly made Whiteladies more amusing than it had been when he was last there.

"You have been to church?" said Miss Susan, with her forced and reluctant smile.

"She went with me," said Miss Augustine. "I hope we have a great acquisition in her. Few have understood me so quickly. If anything should happen to Herbert—"

"Nothing will happen to Herbert," cried Miss Susan. "God bless him! It sounds as if you were putting a spell upon our boy."

"I put no spell; I don't even understand such profane words. My heart is set on one thing, and it is of less importance how it is carried out. If anything should happen to Herbert, I believe I have found one who sees the necessity as I do, and who will sacrifice herself for the salvation of the race."

"One who will sacrifice herself!" Miss Susan gasped wildly under her breath.

Giovanna looked at her with defiance, challenging her, as it were, to a mortal struggle; yet there was a glimmer of laughter in her eyes. She looked at Miss Susan from behind the back of the other, and made a slow, solemn courtesy as Augustine spoke. Her eyes were dancing with humorous enjoyment of the situation, with mischief and playfulness, yet with conscious power.

"This—lady?" said Miss Susan, "I think you are mad; Austine, I think you are going mad!"

Miss Augustine shook her head. "Susan, how often do I tell you that you are giving your heart to Mammon and to the world! This is worse than madness. It makes you incapable of seeing spiritual things. Yes! she is capable of it. Heaven has sent her in answer to many prayers."

Saying this, Augustine glided past toward the house with her arms folded in her sleeves, and her abstract eyes fixed on the vacant air. A little flush of displeasure at the opposition had come upon her face as she spoke, but it faded as quickly as it came. As for Giovanna, before she followed her, she stopped, and threw up her hands with an appealing gesture: "Is it then my fault?" she said, as she passed.

Miss Susan stood and looked after them, her eyes dilating; a kind of panic was in her face. "Is it, then, God that has sent her, to support the innocent, to punish the guilty?" she said, under her breath.

"Aunt Susan, take my arm; you are certainly ill."

"Yes, yes," she said, faintly. "Take me in, take me out of sight, and never tell any one, Everard, never tell any one. I think I shall go out of my mind. It must be giving my thoughts to Mammon and the world, as she said."

"Never mind what she says," said Everard, "no one pays any attention to what she says. Your nerves are overwrought somehow or other, and you are ill. But I'll have it out with the old duffer!" cried the young man. They met Monsieur Guillaume immediately after, and I think he must have heard them; but he was happily quite unaware of the nature of a "duffer," or what the word meant, and to tell the truth, so am I.

Miss Susan was not able to come down to dinner, a marvellous and almost unheard of event, so that the party was still less lively than usual. Everard was so concerned about his old friend, and the strange condition in which she was, that he began his attack upon the old shopkeeper almost as soon as they were left alone. "Don't you think, sir," the young man began, in a straightforward, unartificial way, "that it would be better to take your daughter-in-law with you? She will only be uncomfortable among people so different from those you have been accustomed to; I doubt if they will get on."

"Get on?" said Monsieur Guillaume, pleasantly. "Get on what? She does not wish to get on anywhere. She wishes to stay here."

"I mean, they are not likely to be comfortable together, to agree, to be friends."

M. Guillaume shrugged his shoulders. "Mon Dieu," he said, "it will not be my fault. If Madame Suzanne will not grant the little rente, the allowance I demanded for le petit, is it fit that he should be at my charge? He was not thought of till Madame Suzanne came to visit us. There is nothing for him. He was born to be the heir here."

"But Miss Austin could have nothing to do with his being born," cried Everard, laughing. Poor Miss Susan, it seemed the drollest thing to lay to her charge. But M. Guillaume did not see the joke, he went on seriously.

"And I had made my little arrangement with M. Farrel. We were in accord; all was settled; so much to come to me on the spot, and this heritage, this old château—château, mon Dieu, a thing of wood and brick!—to him, eventually. But when Madame Suzanne arrived to tell us of the beauties of this place, and when the women among them made discovery of le petit, that he was about to be born, the contract was broken with M. Farrel. I lost the money—and now I lose the heritage; and it is I who must provide for le petit! Monsieur, such a thing was never heard of. It is incredible; and Madame Suzanne thinks, I am to carry off the child without a word, and take this disappointment tranquilly! But no! I am not a fool, and it cannot be."

"But I thought you were very fond of the child, and were in despair of losing him," said Everard.

"Yes, yes," cried the old shopkeeper, "despair is one thing, and good sense is another. This is contrary to good sense. Giovanna is an obstinate, but she has good sense. They will not give le petit anything, eh bien, let them bear the expense of him! That is what she says."

"Then the allowance is all you want?" said Everard, with British brevity. This seemed to him the easiest of arrangements. With his mind quite relieved, and a few jokes laid up for the amusement of the future, touching Miss Susan's powers and disabilities, he strolled into the drawing-room, M. Guillaume preferring to take himself to bed. The drawing-room of Whiteladies had never looked so thoroughly unlike itself. There seemed to Everard at first to be no one there, but after a minute he perceived a figure stretched out upon a sofa. The lamps were very dim, throwing a sort of twilight glimmer through the room; and the fire was very red, adding a rosy hue, but no more, to this faint illumination. It was the sort of light favorable to talk, or to meditation, or to slumber, but by aid of which neither reading, nor work, nor any active occupation could be pursued. This was of itself sufficient to mark the absence of Miss Susan, for whom a cheerful light full of animation and activity seemed always necessary. The figure on the sofa lay at full length, with an abandon of indolence and comfort which suited the warm atmosphere and subdued light. Everard felt a certain appropriateness in the scene altogether, but it was not Whiteladies. An Italian palace or an Eastern harem would have been more in accordance with the presiding figure. She raised her head, however, as he approached, supporting herself on her elbow, with a vivacity unlike the Eastern calm, and looked at him by the dim light with a look half provoking half inviting, which attracted the foolish young man more perhaps than a more correct demeanor would have done. Why should not he try what he could do, Everard thought, to move the rebel? for he had an internal conviction that even the allowance which would satisfy M. Guillaume would not content Giovanna. He drew a chair to the other side of the table upon which the tall dim lamp was standing, and which was drawn close to the sofa on which the young woman lay.

"Do you really mean to remain at Whiteladies?" he said. "I don't think you can have any idea how dull it is here."

She shrugged her shoulders slightly, and raised her eyebrows. She had let her head drop back upon the sofa cushions, and the faint light threw a kind of dreamy radiance upon her fine features, and great glowing dark eyes.

"Dull! it is almost more than dull," he continued; though even as he spoke he felt that to have this beautiful creature in Whiteladies would be a sensible alleviation of the dulness, and that his effort on Miss Susan's behalf was of the most disinterested kind. "It would kill you, I fear; you can't imagine what it is in Winter, when the days are short; the lamps are lit at half-past four, and nothing happens all the evening, no one comes. You sit before dinner round the fire, and Miss Austin knits, and after dinner you sit round the fire again, and there is not a sound in all the place, unless you have yourself the courage to make an observation; and it seems about a year before it is time to go to bed. You don't know what it is."

What Miss Susan would have said had she heard this account of those Winter evenings, many of which the hypocrite had spent very cosely at Whiteladies, I prefer not to think. The idea occurred to himself with a comic panic. What would she say? He could scarcely keep from laughing as he asked himself the question.

"I have imagination," said Giovanna, stretching her arms. "I can see it all; but I should not endure it, me. I should get up and snap my fingers at them and dance, or sing."

"Ah!" said Everard, entering into the humor of his rôle, "so you think at present; but it would soon take the spirit out of you. I am very sorry for you, Madame Jean. If I were like you, with the power of enjoying myself, and having the world at my feet—"

"Ah! bah!" cried Giovanna, "how can one have the world at one's feet, when one is never seen? And you should see the shop at Bruges, mon Dieu! People do not come and throw themselves at one's feet there. I am not sure even if it is altogether the fault of Gertrude and the belle-mère; but here—"

"You will have no one to see to," said Everard, tickled by the part he was playing, and throwing himself into the spirit of it. "That is worse—for what is the good of being visible when there is no one to see?"

This consideration evidently was not without its effect. Giovanna raised herself lazily on her elbow and looked at him across the table. "You come," said she, "and this 'Erbert."

"Herbert!" said Everard, shading his head, "he is a sickly boy; and as for me—I have to pay my vows at other shrines," he added with a laugh. But he found this conversation immensely entertaining, and went on representing the disadvantages of Whiteladies with more enjoyment than perhaps he had ever experienced in that place on a Sunday evening before. He went on till Giovanna pettishly bade him go. "At the least, it is comfortable," she said. "Ah, go! It is very tranquil, there is no one to call to you with sharp voice like a knife, 'Gi'vanna! tu dors!' Go, I am going to sleep."

I don't suppose she meant him to take her at her word, for Giovanna was amused too, and found the young man's company and his compliments, and that half-mocking, half-real mixture of homage and criticism, to be a pleasant variety. But Everard, partly because he had exhausted all he had got to say, partly lest he should be drawn on to say more, jumped up in a state of amusement and satisfaction with himself and his own cleverness which was very pleasant. "Since you send me away, I must obey," he said; "Dormez, belle enchanteresse!" and with this, which he felt to be a very pretty speech indeed, he left the room more pleased with himself than ever. He had spent a most satisfactory evening, he had ascertained that the old man was to be bought off with money, and he had done his best to disgust the young woman with a dull English country-house; in short, he had done Miss Susan yeoman's service, and amused himself at the same time. Everard was agreeably excited, and felt, after a few moments' reflection over a cigar on the lawn, that he would like to do more. It was still early, for the Sunday dinner at Whiteladies, as in so many other respectable English houses, was an hour earlier than usual; and as he wandered round the house, he saw the light still shining in Miss Susan's window. This decided him; he threw away the end of his cigar, and hastening up the great staircase three steps at once, hurried to Miss Susan's door. "Come in," she said faintly. Everard was as much a child of the house as Herbert and Reine, and had received many an admonition in that well-known chamber. He opened the door without hesitation. But there was something in the very atmosphere which he felt to daunt him as he went in.

Miss Susan was seated in her easy chair by the bedside fully dressed. She was leaning her head back upon the high shoulder of the old-fashioned chair with her eyes shut. She thought it was Martha who had come in, and she was not careful to keep up appearances with Martha, who had found out days before that something was the matter. She was almost ghastly in her paleness, and there was an utter languor of despair about her attitude and her look, which alarmed Everard in the highest degree. But he could not stop the first words that rose upon his lips, or subdue altogether the cheery tone which came naturally from his satisfied feelings. "Aunt Susan," he cried, "come along, come down stairs, now's your time. I have been telling stories of Whiteladies to disgust her, and I believe now you could buy them off with a small annuity. Aunt Susan! forgive my noise, you are ill."

"No, no," she said with a gasp and a forlorn smile. "No, only tired. What did you say, Everard? whom am I to buy off?" This was a last effort at keeping up appearances. Then it seemed to strike her all at once that this was an ungrateful way of treating one who had been taking so much trouble on her account. "Forgive me, Everard," she said; "I have been dozing, and my head is muddled. Buy them off? To be sure, I should have thought of that; for an annuity, after all, though I have no right to give it, is better than having them settled in the house."

"Far better, since you dislike them so much," said Everard; "I don't, for my part. She is not so bad. She is very handsome, and there's some fun in her."

"Fun!" Miss Susan rose up very tremulous and uncertain, and looking ten years older, with her face ashy pale, and a tottering in her steps, all brought about by this unwelcome visitor; and to hear of fun in connection with Giovanna, made her sharply, unreasonably angry for the time. "You should choose your words better at such a moment," she said.

"Never mind my words, come and speak to her," cried Everard. He was very curious and full of wonder, seeing there was something below the surface more than met his eyes, and that the mystery was far more mysterious than his idea of it. Miss Susan hesitated more than ever, and seemed as if she would have gone back before they reached the stairs; but he kept up her courage. "When it's only a little money, and you can afford it," he said. "You don't care so much for a little money."

"No, I don't care much for a little money," she repeated after him mechanically, as she went downstairs.

CHAPTER XXX

Miss Susan entered the drawing-room in the same dim light in which Everard had left it. She was irritable and impatient in her misery. She would have liked to turn up all the lamps, and throw a flood of light upon the stranger whose attitude was indolent and indecorous. Why was she there at all? what right had she to extend herself at full length, to make herself so comfortable? That Giovanna should be comfortable did not do Miss Susan any further harm; but she felt as if it did, and a fountain of hot wrath surged up in her heart. This, however, she felt was not the way in which she could do any good, so she made an effort to restrain herself. She sat down in Everard's seat which he had left. She was not quite sure whether he himself were not lingering in the shadows at the door of the room, and this made her difficulty the greater in what she had to say.

"Do you like this darkness?" she asked. "It is oppressive; we cannot see to do anything."

"Me, I don't want to do anything," said Giovanna. "I sleep and I dream. This is most pleasant to me. Madame Suzanne likes occupation. Me, I do not."

"Yes," said Miss Susan with suppressed impatience, "that is one of the differences between us. But I have something to say to you; you wanted me to make an allowance for the child, and I refused. Indeed, it is not my business, for Whiteladies is not mine. But now that I have thought of it, I will consent. It would be so much better for you to travel with your father-in-law than alone."

Giovanna turned her face toward her companion with again that laughing devil in her eye. "Madame Suzanne mistakes. The bon papa spoke of his rente that he loves, not me. If ces dames will give me money to dress myself, to be more like them, that will be well; but it was the bon-papa, not me."

"Never mind who it was," said Miss Susan, on the verge of losing her temper. "One or the other, I suppose it is all the same. I will give you your allowance."

"To dress myself? thanks, that will be well. Then I can follow the mode Anglaise, and have something to wear in the evening, like Madame Suzanne herself."

"For the child!" cried the suffering woman, in a voice which to Everard, behind backs, sounded like low and muffled thunder. "To support him and you, to keep you independent, to make you comfortable at home among your own people—"

"Merci!" cried Giovanna, shrugging her shoulders. "That is the bon-papa's idea, as I tell madame, not mine. Comfortable! with my belle-mère! Listen, Madame Suzanne—I too, I have been thinking. If you will accept me with bounty, you shall not be sorry. I can make myself good; I can be useful, though it is not what I like best. I stay—I make myself your child—"

"I do not want you," cried Miss Susan, stung beyond her strength of self-control, "I do not want you. I will pay you anything to get you away."

Giovanna's eyes gave forth a gleam. "Très bien," she said, calmly. "Then I shall stay, if madame pleases or not. It is what I have intended from the beginning; and I do not change my mind, me."

"But if I say you shall not stay!" said Miss Susan, wrought to fury, and pushing back her chair from the table.

Giovanna raised herself on her elbow, and leaned across the table, fixing the other with her great eyes.

"Once more, très bien," she said, in a significant tone, too low for Everard to hear, but not a whisper. "Très bien! Madame then wishes me to tell not only M. Herbert, but the bonne sœur, madame's sister, and ce petit monsieur-là?"

Miss Susan sat and listened like a figure of stone. Her color changed out of the flush of anger which had lighted it up, and grew again ashy pale. From her laboring breast there came a great gasp, half groan, half sob. She looked at the remorseless creature opposite with a piteous prayer coming into her eyes. First rage, which was useless; then entreaty, more useless still. "Have pity on me! have pity on me," she said.

"But certainly!" said Giovanna, sinking back upon her cushions with a soft laugh. "Certainly! I am not cruel, me; but I am comfortable, and I stay."

"She will not hear of it," said Miss Susan, meeting Everard's anxious looks as she passed him, hurrying upstairs. "Never mind me. Everard, never mind! we shall do well enough. Do not say any more about it. Never mind! never mind! It is time we were all in bed."

"But, Aunt Susan, tell me—"

"No, no, there is nothing to tell," she said, hurrying from him. "Do not let us say any more about it. It is time we were all in bed."

The next day M. Guillaume left Whiteladies, after a very melancholy parting with his little grandchild. The old man sobbed, and the child sobbed for sympathy. "Thou wilt be good to him, Giovanna!" he said, weeping. Giovanna stood, and looked on with a smile on her face. "Bon papa, it is easy to cry," she said; "but you do not want him without a rente; weep then for the rente, not for the child." "Heartless!" cried the old shopkeeper, turning from her; and her laugh, though it was quite low, did sound heartless to the bystanders; yet there was some truth in what she said. M. Guillaume went away in the morning, and Everard in the afternoon. The young man was deeply perplexed and disturbed. He had been a witness of the conclusive interview on the previous night without hearing all that was said; yet he had heard enough to show him that something lay behind of which he was not cognizant—something which made

Miss Susan unwillingly submit to an encumbrance which she hated, and which made her more deeply, tragically unhappy than a woman of her spotless life and tranquil age had any right to be. To throw such a woman into passionate distress, and make her, so strong in her good sense, so reasonable and thoroughly acquainted with the world, bow her head under an irritating and unnecessary yoke, there must be some cause more potent than anything Everard could divine. He made an attempt to gain her confidence before he went away; but it was still more fruitless than before. The only thing she would say was, that she could speak no more on the subject. "There is nothing to say. She is here now for good or for evil, and we must make the best of it. Probably we shall get on better than we think," said Miss Susan; and that was all he could extract from her. He went away more disturbed than he could tell; his curiosity was excited as well as his sympathy, and though, after awhile, his natural reluctance to dwell on painful subjects made him attempt to turn his mind from this, yet the evident mystery to be found out made that attempt much harder than usual. Everard was altogether in a somewhat uncertain and wavering state of mind at the time. He had returned from his compulsory episode of active life rather better in fortune, and with a perception of his own unoccupied state, which had never disturbed him before. He had not got to love work, which is a thing which requires either genius or training. He honestly believed, indeed, that he hated work, as was natural to a young man of his education; but having been driven to it, and discovered in himself, to his great surprise, some faculty for it, his return to what he thought his natural state had a somewhat strange effect upon him. To do nothing was, no doubt, his natural state. It was freedom; it was happiness (passive); it was the most desirable condition of existence. All this he felt to be true. He was his own master, free to go where he would, do what he would, amuse himself as he liked; and yet the conclusion of the time when he had not been his own master—when he had been obliged to do this and that, to move here and there not by his own will, but as necessity demanded—had left a sense of vacancy in this life. He was dissatisfied with his leisure and his freedom; they were not so good, not so pleasant, as they had once been. He had known storm and tempest, and all the expedients by which men triumph over these commotions, and the calm of his inland existence wearied him, though he had not yet gone so far as to confess it to himself.

This made him think more of the mystery of Whiteladies than perhaps he would have done otherwise, and moved him so far as to indite a letter to Reine, in which perhaps more motives than that of interest in Miss Susan's troubles were involved. He had left them when the sudden storm which he had now surmounted had appeared on the horizon, at a very critical moment of his intercourse with Reine; and then they had been cast altogether apart, driven into totally different channels for two years. Two years is a long time or a short time, according to the constitution of the mind, and the nature of circumstances. It had been about a century to Everard, and he had developed into a different being. And now this different being, brought back to the old life, did not well know what to do with himself. Should he go and join his cousins again, amuse himself, see the world, and perhaps renew some things that were past, and reunite a link half broken, half unmade? Anyhow, he wrote to Reine, setting forth that Aunt Susan was ill and very queer—that there was a visitor at Whiteladies of a very novel and unusual character—that the dear old house threatened to be turned upside down—fourthly, and accidentally, that he had a great mind to spend the next six months on the Continent. Where were they going for the Winter? Only ladies, they say, put their chief subject in a postscript. Everard put his under care of a "By-the-bye" in the last two lines of his letter. The difference between the two modes is not very great.

And thus, while the young man meditated change, which is natural to his age, in which renovation and revolution are always possible, the older people at Whiteladies settled down to make the best of it, which is the philosophy of their age. To say the older people is incorrect, for it was Miss Susan only who had anything novel or heavy to endure. Miss Augustine liked the new guest, who for some time went regularly to the Almshouse services with her, and knelt devoutly, and chanted forth the hymns with a full rich voice, which indeed silenced the quavering tones of the old folks, but filled the chapel with such a flood of melody as had never been heard there before. Giovanna enjoyed singing. She had a fine natural voice, but little instruction, and no opportunity at the moment of getting at anything better in the way of music; so that she was glad of the hymns which gave her pleasure at once in the exercise of her voice, and in the agreeable knowledge that she was making a sensation. As much of a crowd as was possible in St. Austin's began to gather in the Almshouse garden when she was known to be there; and though Mrs. Richard instinctively disapproved of her, the Doctor was somewhat proud of this addition to his service. Giovanna went regularly with her patroness, and gained Augustine's heart, as much as that abstracted heart could be gained, and made herself not unpopular with the poor people, to whom she would speak in her imperfect English with more familiarity than the ladies ever indulged in, and from whom, in lieu of better, she was quite ready to receive compliments about her singing and her beauty. Once, indeed, she sang songs to them in their garden, to the great entertainment of the old Almshouse folks. She was caught in the act by Mrs. Richard, who rushed to the rescue of her gentility with feelings which I will not attempt to describe. The old lady ran out breathless at the termination of a song, with a flush upon her pretty old cheeks, and caught the innovator by the arm.

"The doctor is at home, and I am just going to give him a cup of tea," she said; "won't you come and have some with us?"

Mrs. Richard's tidy little bosom heaved under her black silk gown with consternation and dismay.

Giovanna was not at all willing to give up her al fresco entertainment. "But I will return, I will return," she said.

"Do, madame, do," cried the old people, who were vaguely pleased by her music, and more keenly delighted by having a new event to talk about, and the power of wondering what Miss Augustine (poor thing!) would think; and Mrs. Richard led Giovanna in, with her hand upon her arm, fearful lest her prisoner should escape.

"It is very good of you to sing to them; but it is not a thing that is done in England," said the little old lady.

"I love to sing," said Giovanna, "and I shall come often. They have not any one to amuse them; and neither have I," she added with a sigh.

"My dear, you must speak to the Doctor about it," said Mrs. Richard.

Giovanna was glad of any change, even of little Dr. Richard and the cup of tea, so she was submissive enough for the moment; and to see her between these two excellent and orderly little people was an edifying sight.

"No, it is not usual," said Dr. Richard, "my wife is right; but it is very kind-hearted of madame, my dear, to wish to amuse the poor people. There is nothing to be said against that."

"Very kind-hearted," said Mrs. Richard, though with less enthusiasm. "It is all from those foreigners' love of display," she said in her heart.

"But perhaps it would be wise to consult Miss Augustine, or—any other friend you may have confidence in," said the Doctor. "People are so very censorious, and we must not give any occasion for evil-speaking."

"I think exactly with Dr. Richard, my dear," said the old lady. "I am sure that would be the best."

"But I have nothing done to consult about," cried the culprit surprised. She sipped her tea, and ate a large piece of the good people's cake, however, and let them talk. When she was not crossed, Giovanna was perfectly good-humored. "I will sing for you, if you please," she said when she had finished.

The Doctor and his wife looked at each other, and professed their delight in the proposal. "But we have no piano," they said in chorus with embarrassed looks.

"What does that do to me, when I can sing without it," said Giovanna. And she lifted up her powerful voice, "almost too much for a drawing-room," Mrs. Richard said afterward, and sang them one of those gay peasant songs that abound in Italy, where every village has its own canzone. She sang seated where she had been taking her tea, and without seeming to miss an accompaniment, they remarked to each other, as if she had been a ballad-singer. It was pretty enough, but so very unusual! "Of course foreigners cannot be expected to know what is according to the rules of society in England," Mrs. Richard said with conscious indulgence; but she put on her bonnet and walked with "Madame" part of the way to Whiteladies, that she might not continue her performance in the garden. "Miss Augustine might think, or Miss Susan might think, that we countenanced it; and in the Doctor's position that would never do," said the old lady, breathing her troubles into the ear of a confidential friend whom she met on her way home. And Dr. Richard himself felt the danger not less strongly than she.

Other changes, however, happened to Giovanna, as she settled down at Whiteladies. She was without any fixed principles of morality, and had no code of any kind which interfered with her free action. To give up doing anything she wanted to do because it involved lying, or any kind of spiritual dishonesty, would never have occurred to her, nor was she capable of perceiving that there was anything wrong in securing her own advantage as she had done. But she was by no means all bad, any more than truthful and honorable persons are all good. Her own advantage, or what she thought her own advantage, and her own way, were paramount considerations with her; but having obtained these, Giovanna had no wish to hurt anybody, or to be unkind. She was indolent and loved ease, but still she was capable of taking trouble now and then to do some one else a service. She had had no moral training, and all her faculties were obtuse; and she had seen no prevailing rule but that of selfishness. Selfishness takes different aspects, according to the manner in which you look at it. When you have to maintain hardly, by a constant struggle, your own self against the encroachments and still more rampant selfishness of others, the struggle confers a certain beauty upon the object of it. Giovanna had wanted to have her own way, like the others of the family, but had been usually thrust into a corner, and prevented from having it. What wonder, then, that when she had a chance, she seized it, and emancipated herself, and secured her own comfort with the same total disregard to others which she had been used to see? But now, having got this—having for the moment all she wanted—an entire exemption from work, an existence full of external comfort, and circumstances around her which flattered her with a sense of an elevated position—she began to think a little. Nothing was exacted of her. If Miss Susan was not kind to her, she was not at least unkind, only withdrawing from her as much as possible, a thing which Giovanna felt to be quite natural, and in the quiet and silence the young woman's mind began to work. I do not say her conscience, for that was not in the least awakened, nor was she conscious of any penitential regret in thinking of the past, or religious resolution for the future; it was her mind only that was concerned. She thought it might be as well to make certain changes in her habits. In her new existence, certain modifications of the old use and wont seemed reasonable. And then there gradually developed in her—an invaluable possession which sometimes does more for the character than high principle or good intention—a sense of the ludicrous. This was what Everard meant when he said there was fun in her. She had a sense of humor, a sense of the incongruities which affect some minds so much more powerfully by the fact of being absurd, than by the fact of being wrong. Giovanna, without any actual good motive, thus felt the necessity of amending herself, and making various changes in her life.

This, it may be supposed, took some time to develop; and in the meantime the household in which she had become so very distinct a part, had to make up its mind to her, and resume as best it could its natural habits and use and wont, with the addition of this stranger in the midst. As for the servants, their instinctive repugnance to a foreigner and a new inmate was lessened from the very first by the introduction of the child, who conciliated the maids, and thus made them forgive his mother the extra rooms they had to arrange, and the extra work necessary. The child was fortunately an engaging and merry child, and as he got used to the strange faces round him, became the delight and pride and amusement of the house. Cook was still head nurse, and derived an increased importance and satisfaction from her supremacy. I doubt if she had ever before felt the dignity and happiness of her position as a married woman half so much as now, when that fact alone (as the others felt) gave her a mysterious capacity for the management of the child. The maids overlooked the fact that the child's mother, though equally a married woman, was absolutely destitute of this power; but accuracy of reasoning is not necessary in such an argument, and the entire household bowed to the superior endowments of Cook. The child's pattering, sturdy little feet, and crowings of baby laughter became the music of Whiteladies, the pleasant accompaniment to which the lives at least of the little community in the kitchen were set. Miss Susan, being miserable, resisted the fascination, and Augustine was too abstracted to be sensible of it; but the servants yielded as one woman, and even Stevens succumbed after the feeblest show of resistance. Now and then even, a bell would ring ineffectually in that well-ordered house, and the whole group of attendants be found clustered together worshipping before the baby, who had produced some new word, or made some manifestation of supernatural cleverness; and the sound of the child pervaded all that part of the house in which the servants were supreme. They forgave his mother for being there because she had brought him, and if at the same time they hated her for her neglect of him, the hatred was kept passive by a perception that, but for this insensibility on her part, the child could not have been allowed thus fully and pleasantly to minister to them.

As for Miss Susan, who had felt as though nothing could make her endure the presence of Giovanna, she too was affected unwittingly by the soft effects of time. It was true that no sentiment, no principle in existence was strong enough to make her accept cheerfully this unwelcome guest. Had she been bidden to do it in order to make atonement for her own guilt, or as penance for that guilt, earning its forgiveness, or out of pity or Christian feeling, she would have pronounced the effort impossible; and impossible she had still thought it when she watched with despair the old shopkeeper's departure, and reflected with a sense of suffering intolerable and not to be borne that he had left behind him this terrible witness against her, this instrument of her punishment. Miss Susan had paced about her room in restless anguish, saying to herself under her breath that her punishment was greater than she could bear. She had felt with a sickening sense of helplessness and hopelessness that she could never go downstairs again, never take her place at that table, never eat or drink in the company of this new inmate whom she could not free herself from. And for a few days, indeed, Miss Susan kept on inventing little ailments which kept her in her own room. But this could not last. She had a hundred things to look after which made it necessary for her to be about, to be visible; and gradually there grew upon her a stirring of curiosity to see how things went on, with that woman always there. And then she resumed her ordinary habits, came downstairs, sat down at the familiar table, and by degrees found herself getting accustomed to the new-comer. Strangest effect of those calm, monotonous days! Nothing would have made her do it knowingly; but soft pressure of time made her do it. Things quieted down; the alien was there, and there was no possibility of casting her out; and, most wonderful of all, Miss Susan got used to her, in spite of herself.

And Giovanna, for her part, began to think.

CHAPTER XXXI

Giovanna possessed that quality which is commonly called common-sense, though I doubt if she was herself aware of it. She had never before been in a position in which this good sense could tell much, or in which even it was called forth to any purpose. Her lot had always been determined for her by others. She had never, until the coming of the child, been in a position in which it mattered much one way or another what she thought; and since that eventful moment her thinkings had not been of an edifying description. They had been chiefly bent on the consideration how to circumvent the others who were using her for their own purposes, and to work advantage to herself out of the circumstances which, for the first time in her life, gave her the mastery. Now, she had done this; she had triumphantly overcome all difficulties, and, riding over everybody's objections, had established herself here in comfort. Giovanna had expected a constant conflict with Miss Susan, who was her enemy, and over whom she had got the victory. She had looked for nothing better than a daily fight—rather enlivening, all things considered—with the mistress of the house, to whom, she knew, she was so unwelcome a guest. She had anticipated a long-continued struggle, in which she should have to hold her own, and defend herself, hour by hour. When she found that this was not going to be the case—that poor Miss Susan, in her misery and downfall, gave up and disappeared, and, even when she returned again to her ordinary habits, treated herself, Giovanna, with no harshness, and was only silent and cold, not insulting and disagreeable, a great deal of surprise arose in her mind. There were no little vengeances taken upon her, no jibes directed against her, no tasks attempted to be imposed. Miss Augustine, the bonne sœur, who no doubt (and this Giovanna could understand) acted from religious motives, was as kind to her as it was in her abstract nature to be, talking to her on subjects which the young woman did not understand, but to which she assented easily, to please the other, about the salvation of the race, and how, if anything happened to Herbert, there might be a great work possible to his successor; but even Miss Susan, who was her adversary, was not unkind to her, only cold, and this, Giovanna, accustomed to much rough usage, was not refined enough to take much note of. This gave a strong additional force to her conviction that it would be worth while to put herself more in accord with her position; and I believe that Giovanna, too, felt instinctively the influence of the higher breeding of her present companions.

The first result of her cogitations became evident one Winter day, when all was dreary out of doors, and Miss Susan, after having avoided as long as she could the place in which Giovanna was, felt herself at last compelled to take refuge in the drawing-room. There she found, to her great amazement, the young woman seated on a rug before the fire, playing with the child, who, seated on her lap, seemed as perfectly at home there as on the ample lap of its beloved Cook. Miss Susan started visibly at this unaccustomed sight, but said nothing. It was not her custom, now, to say anything she could help saying. She drew her chair aside to be out of their way, and took up her book. This was another notable change in her habits. She had been used to work, knitting the silent hours away, and read only at set times, set apart for this purpose by the habit of years—and then always what she called "standard books." Now, Miss Susan, though her knitting was always at hand, knitted scarcely at all, but read continually novels, and all the light literature of the circulating library. She was scarcely herself aware of this change. It is a sign of the state of mind in which we have too much to think of, as well as of that in which we have nothing to think of at all.

And I think if any stranger had seen that pretty group, the beautiful young mother cooing over the child, playing with it and caressing it, the child responding by all manner of baby tricks and laughter, and soft clingings and claspings, while the elder woman sat silent and gray, taking no notice of them, he would have set the elder woman down as the severest and sternest of grandmothers—the father's mother, no doubt, emblem of the genus mother-in-law, which so many clever persons have held up to odium. To tell the truth, Miss Susan had some difficulty in going on with her reading, with the sound of those baby babblings in her ear. She was thunderstruck at first by the scene, and then felt unreasonably angry. Was nature nothing then? She had thought the child's dislike of Giovanna—though it was painful to see—was appropriate to the circumstances, and had in it a species of poetic justice. Had it been but a pretence, or what did this sudden fondness mean? She kept silent as long as she could, but after a time the continual babble grew too much for her.

"You have grown very suddenly fond of the child, Madame Jean," she said, abruptly.

"Fond!" said Giovanna, "that is a strange word, that English word of yours; I can make him love me—here."

"You did not love him elsewhere, so far as I have heard," said Miss Susan, "and that is the best way to gain love."

"Madame Suzanne, I wish to speak to you," said Giovanna. "At Bruges I was never of any account; they said the child was more gentil, more sage with Gertrude. Well; it might be he was; they said I knew nothing about children, that I could not learn—that it was not in my nature; things which were pleasant, which were reassuring, don't you think? That was one of the reasons why I came away."

"You did not show much power of managing him, it must be confessed, when you came here."

"No," said Giovanna, "it was harder than I thought. These babies, they have no reason. When you say, 'Be still, I am thy mother, be still!' it does not touch them. What they like is kisses and cakes, and that you should make what in England is called 'a fuss;' that is the hardest, making a fuss; but when it is done, all is done. Voilà! Now, he loves me. If Gertrude approached, he would run to me and cry. Ah, that would make me happy!"

"Then it is to spite Gertrude"—Miss Susan began, in her severest voice.

"No, no; I only contemplate that as a pleasure, a pleasure to come. No; I am not very fond of to read, like you, Madame Suzanne; besides, there is not anything more to read; and so I reflect. I reflect with myself, that not to have love with one's child, or at least amitié, is very strange. It is droll; it gives to think; and people will stare and say, 'Is that her child?' This is what I reflect within myself. To try before would have been without use, for always there was Gertrude, or my belle-mère, or some one. They cried out, 'G'vanna touch it not, thou wilt injure the baby!' 'G'vanna, give it to me, thou knowest nothing of children!' And when I came away it was more hard than I thought. Babies have not sense to know when it is their mother. I said to myself, 'Here is a perverse one, who hates me like the rest;' and I was angry. I beat him—you would have beat him also, Madame Suzanne, if he had screamed when you touched him. And then—petit drôle!—he screamed more."

"Very natural," said Miss Susan. "If you had any heart, you would not beat a baby like that."

Giovanna's eyes flashed. She lifted her hand quickly, as if to give a blow of recollection now; but, changing her mind, she caught the child up in her arms, and laid his little flushed cheek to hers. "A présent, tu m'aimes!" she said. "When I saw how the others did, I knew I could do it too. Also, Madame Suzanne, I recollected that a mother should have de l'amitié for her child."

Miss Susan gave a short contemptuous laugh. "It is a fine thing to have found that out at last," she said.

"And I have reflected further," said Giovanna—"Yes, darling, thou shalt have these jolies choses;" and with this, she took calmly from the table one of a very finely-carved set of chessmen, Indian work, which ornamented it. Miss Susan started, and put out her hand to save the ivory knight, but the little fellow had already grasped it, and a sudden scream arose.

"For shame! Madame Suzanne," cried Giovanna, with fun sparkling in her eyes. "You, too, then, have no heart!"

"This is totally different from kindness, this is spoiling the child," cried Miss Susan. "My ivory chessmen, which were my mother's! Take it away from him at once."

Giovanna wavered a moment between fun and prudence, then coaxing the child, adroitly with something else less valuable, got the knight from him, and replaced it on the table. Then she resumed where she had broken off. "I have reflected further that it is bad to fight in a house. You take me for your enemy, Madame Suzanne?—eh bien, I am not your enemy. I do nothing against you. I seek what is good for me, as all do."

"All don't do it at the cost of other people's comfort—at the cost of everything that is worth caring for in another's life."

This Miss Susan said low, with her eyes bent on the fire, to herself rather than to Giovanna; from whom, indeed, she expected no response.

"Mon Dieu! it is not like that," cried the young woman; "what is it that I do to you? Nothing! I do not trouble, nor tease, nor ask for anything. I am contented with what you give me. I have come here, and I find it well; but you, what is it that I do to you? I do not interfere. It is but to see me one time in a day, two times, perhaps. Listen, it cannot be so bad for you to see me even two times in a day as it would be for me to go back to my belle-mère."

"But you have no right to be here," said Miss Susan, shaking her gray dress free from the baby's grasp, who had rolled softly off the young woman's knee, and now sat on the carpet between them. His little babble went on all through their talk. The plaything Giovanna had given him—a paper-knife of carved ivory—was a delightful weapon to the child; he struck the floor with it, which under no possibility could be supposed capable of motion, and then the legs of the chair, on which Miss Susan sat, which afforded a more likely steed. Miss Susan had hard ado to pull her skirts from the soft round baby fingers, as the child looked up at her with great eyes, which laughed in her angry face. It was all she could do to keep her heart from melting to him; but then, that woman! who looked at her with eyes which were not angry, nor disagreeable, wooing her to smile—which not for the world, and all it contained, would she do.

"Always I have seen that one does what one can for one's self," said Giovanna; "shall I think of you first, instead of myself? But no! is there any in the world who does that? But, no! it is contrary to reason. I do my best for me; and then I reflect, now that I am well off, I will hurt no one. I will be friends if Madame Suzanne will. I wish not to trouble her. I will show de l'amitié for her as well as for le petit. Thus it should be when we live in one house."

Giovanna spoke with a certain earnestness as of honest conviction. She had no sense of irony in her mind; but Miss Susan had a deep sense of irony, and felt herself insulted when she was thus addressed by the intruder who had found her way into her house, and made havoc of her life. She got up hastily to her feet, overturning the child, who had now seated himself on her dress, and for whom this hasty movement had all the effect of an earthquake. She did not even notice this, however, and paid no attention to his cries, but fell to walking about the room in a state of impatience and excitement which would not be kept under.

"You do well to teach me what people should do who live in one house!" cried Miss Susan. "It comes gracefully from you who have forced yourself into my house against my will—who are a burden, and insupportable to me—you and your child. Take him away, or you will drive me mad! I cannot hear myself speak."

"Hush, mon ange," said Giovanna; "hush, here is something else that is pretty for thee—hush! and do not make the bonne maman angry. Ah, pardon, Madame Suzanne, you are not the bonne maman—but you look almost like her when you look like that!"

"You are very impertinent," said Miss Susan, blushing high; for to compare her to Madame Austin of Bruges was more than she could bear.

"That is still more like her!" said Giovanna; "the belle-mère often tells me I am impertinent. Can I help it then? if I say what I think, that cannot be wrong. But you are not really like the bonne maman, Madame Suzanne," she added, subduing the malice in her eyes. "You hate me, but you do not try to make me unhappy. You give me everything I want. You do not grudge; you do not make me work. Ah, what a life she would have made to one who came like me!"

This silenced Miss Susan, in spite of herself; for she herself felt and knew that she was not at all kind to Giovanna, and she was quite unaware that Giovanna was inaccessible to those unkindnesses which more refined natures feel, and having the substantial advantages of her reception at Whiteladies undisturbed by any practical hardship, had no further requirements in a sentimental sort. Miss Susan felt that she was not kind, but Giovanna did not feel it; and as the elder woman could not understand the bluntness of feeling in the younger, which produced this toleration, she was obliged, against her will, to see in it some indication of a higher nature. She thought reluctantly, and for the moment, that the woman whom she loathed was better than herself. She came back to the chair as this thought forced itself upon her, and sat down there and fixed her eyes upon the intruder, who still held her place on the carpet at her feet.

"Why do you not go away?" she said, tempted once more to make a last effort for her own relief. "If you think it good of me to receive you as I do, why will you not listen to my entreaties, and go away? I will give you enough to live on; I will not grudge money; but I cannot bear the sight of you, you know that. It brings my sin, my great sin, to my mind. I repent it; but I cannot undo it," cried Miss Susan. "Oh, God forgive me! But you, Giovanna, listen! You have done wrong, too, as well as I—but it has been for your benefit, not for your punishment. You should not have done it any more than me."

"Madame Suzanne," said Giovanna, "one must think of one's self first; what you call sin does not trouble me. I did not begin it. I did what I was told. If it is wrong, it is for the belle-mère and you; I am safe; and I must think of myself. It pleases me to be here, and I have my plans. But I should like to show de l'amitié for you, Madame Suzanne—when I have thought first of myself."

"But it will be no better for yourself, staying here," cried Miss Susan, subduing herself forcibly. "I will give you money—you shall live where you please—"

"Pardon," said Giovanna, with a smile; "it is to me to know. I have mes idées à moi. You all think of yourselves first. I will be good friends if you will; but, first of all, there is me."

"And the child?" said Miss Susan, with strange forgetfulness, and a bizarre recollection, in her despair, of the conventional self-devotion to be expected from a mother.

"The child, bah! probably what will be for my advantage will be also for his; but you do not think, Madame Suzanne," said Giovanna with a laugh, regarding her closely with a look which, but for its perfect good humor, would have been sarcastic, "that I will sacrifice myself, me, for the child?"

"Then why should you make a pretence of loving him? loving him! if you are capable of love!" cried Miss Susan, in dismay.

Giovanna laughed. She took the little fellow up in her arms, and put his little rosy cheek against the fair oval of her own. "Tu m'aimes à présent," she said; "that is as it ought to be. One cannot have a baby and not have de l'amitié for him; but, naturally, first of all I will think of myself."

"It is all pretence, then, your love," cried Miss Susan, once more starting up wildly, with a sense that the talk, and the sight of her, and the situation altogether, were intolerable. "Oh, it is like you foreigners! You pretend to love the child because it is comme il faut. You want to be friendly with me because it is comme il faut. And you expect me, an honest Englishwoman, to accept this? Oh!" she cried, hiding her face in her hands, with a pang of recollection, "I was that at least before I knew you!"

Curious perversity of nature! For the moment Miss Susan felt bitterly that the loss of her honesty and her innocence was Giovanna's fault. The young woman laughed, in spite of herself, and it was not wonderful that she did so. She got up for the first time from the carpet, raising the child to her shoulder. But she wanted to conciliate, not to offend; and suppressed the inappropriate laughter. She went up to where Miss Susan had placed herself—thrown back in a great chair, with her face covered by her hands—and touched her arm softly, not without a certain respect for her trouble.

"I do not pretend," she said; "because it is comme il faut? but, yes, that is all natural. Yet I do not pretend. I wish to show de l'amitié for Madame Suzanne. I will not give up my ideas, nor do what you will, instead of that which I will; but to be good friends, this is what I desire. Bébé is satisfied—he asks no more—he demands not the sacrifice. Why not Madame Suzanne too?"

"Go away, go away, please," cried Miss Susan, faintly. She was not capable of anything more.

Giovanna shrugged her handsome shoulders, and gave an appealing look round her, as if to some unseen audience. She felt that nothing but native English stupidity could fail to see her good sense and honest meaning. Then, perceiving further argument to be hopeless, she turned away, with the child still on her shoulder, and ere she had reached the end of the passage, began to sing to him with her sweet, rich, untutored voice. The voice receded, carolling through all the echoes of the old house like a bird, floating up the great oaken staircase, and away to the extremity of the long corridor, where her room was. She was perfectly light-hearted and easy-minded in the resolution to do the best for herself; and she was perfectly aware that the further scheme she had concocted for her own benefit would be still more displeasing to the present mistress of the house. She did not care for that the least in the world; but, honestly, she was well-disposed toward Miss Susan, and not only willing, but almost anxious, so far as anxiety was possible to her, to establish a state of affairs in which they might be good friends.

But to Miss Susan it was absolutely impossible to conceive that things so incompatible could yet exist together. Perhaps she was dimly aware of the incongruities in her own mind, the sense of guilt and the sense of innocence which existed there, in opposition, yet, somehow, in that strange concord which welds the contradictions of the human soul into one, despite of all incongruity; but to realize or believe in the strange mixture in Giovanna's mind was quite impossible to her. She sat still with her face covered until she was quite sure the young woman and her child had gone, listening, indeed, to the voice which went so lightly and sweetly through the passages. How could she sing—that woman! whom if she had never seen, Susan Austin would still have been an honest woman, able to look everybody in the face! Miss Susan knew—no one better—how utterly foolish and false it was to say this; she knew that Giovanna was but the instrument, not the originator, of her own guilt; but, notwithstanding the idea having once occurred to her, that had she never seen Giovanna, she would never have been guilty, she hugged it to her bosom with an insane satisfaction, feeling as if, for the moment, it was a relief. Oh, that she had never seen her! How blameless she had been before that unhappy meeting! how free of all weight upon her conscience! and now, how burdened, how miserable, how despotic that conscience was! and her good name dependent upon the discretion of this creature, without discretion, without feeling, this false, bold foreigner, this intruder, who had thrust her way into a quiet house, to destroy its peace! When she was quite sure that Giovanna was out of the way, Miss Susan went to her own room, and looked piteously at her own worn face in the glass. Did that face tell the same secrets to others as it did to herself? she wondered. She had never been a vain woman, even in her youth, though she had been comely enough, if not pretty; but now, a stranger, who did not know Miss Susan, might have thought her vain. She looked at herself so often in the glass, pitifully studying her looks, to see what could be read in them. It had come to be one of the habits of her life.

CHAPTER XXXII

The Winter passed slowly, as Winters do, especially in the silence of the country, where little happens to mark their course. The Autumnal fall of leaves lasted long, but at length cleared off with the fogs and damps of November, leaving the lawn and Priory Lane outside free from the faded garments of the limes and beeches. Slowly, slowly the earth turned to the deepest dark of Winter, and turned back again imperceptibly toward the sun. The rich brown fields turned up their furrows to the darkening damp and whitening frost, and lay still, resting from their labors, waiting for the germs to come. The trees stood out bare against the sky, betraying every knob and twist upon their branches; big lumps of gray mistletoe hung in the apple-trees that bordered Priory Lane; and here and there a branch of Lombardy poplar, still clothed with a few leaves, turning their white lining outward, threw itself up against the blue sky like a flower. The Austin Chantry was getting nearly finished, all the external work having been done some time ago. It was hoped that the ornamentation within would be completed in time for Christmas, when the chaplain, who was likewise to be the curate, and save (though Mr. Gerard mentioned this to no one) sixty pounds a year to the vicar, was to begin the daily service. This chaplain was a nephew of Dr. Richard's, a good young man of very High Church views, who was very ready to pray for the souls of the Austin family without once thinking of the rubrics. Mr. Gerard did not care for a man of such pronounced opinions; and good little Dr. Richard, even after family feeling had led him to recommend his nephew, was seized with many pangs as to the young Ritualist's effect upon the parish.

"He will do what Miss Augustine wants, which is what I never would have done," said the warden of the Almshouses. "He thinks he is a better Churchman than I am, poor fellow! but he is very careless of the Church's directions, my dear; and if you don't attend to the rubrics, where are you to find rest in this world? But he thinks he is a better Churchman than I."

"Yes, my dear, the rubrics have always been your great standard," said the good wife; but as the Rev. Mr. Wrook was related to them by her side, she was reluctant to say anything more.

Thus, however, it was with a careful and somewhat anxious brow that Dr. Richard awaited the young man's arrival. He saved Mr. Gerard the best part of a curate's salary, as I have said. Miss Augustine endowed the Chantry with an income of sixty pounds a year; and with twenty or thirty pounds added to that, who could object to such a salary for a curacy in a country place? The vicar's purse was the better for it, if not himself; and he thought it likely that by careful processes of disapproval any young man in course of time might be put down. The Chantry was to be opened at Christmas; and I think (if it had ever occurred to her) that Miss Augustine might then have been content to sing her Nunc Dimittis; but it never did occur to her, her life being very full, and all her hours occupied. She looked forward, however, to the time when two sets of prayers should be said every day for the Austins with unbounded expectation.

Up to the middle of November, I think, she almost hoped (in an abstract way, meaning no harm to her nephew) that something might still happen to Herbert; for Giovanna, who went with her to the Almshouse service every morning to please her, seemed endowed with heavenly dispositions, and ready to train up her boy—who was a ready-made child, so to speak, and not uncertain, as any baby must be who has to be born to parents not yet so much as acquainted with each other—to make the necessary sacrifice, and restore Whiteladies to the Church. This hope failed a little after November, because then, without rhyme or reason, Giovanna tired of her devotions, and went to the early service no longer; though even then Miss Augustine felt that little Jean (now called Johnny) was within her own power, and could be trained in the way in which he should go; but anyhow, howsoever it was to be accomplished, no doubt the double prayers for the race would accomplish much, and something at the sweetness of an end attained stole into Augustine's heart.

The parish and the neighborhood also took a great interest in the Chantry. Such of the neighbors as thought Miss Augustine mad, awaited, with a mixture of amusement and anxiety, the opening of this new chapel, which was said to be unlike anything seen before—a miracle of ecclesiastical eccentricity;

while those who thought her papistical looked forward with equal interest to a chance of polemics and excitement, deploring the introduction of Ritualism into a quiet corner of the country, hitherto free of that pest, but enjoying unawares the agreeable stimulant of local schism and ecclesiastical strife. The taste for this is so universal that I suppose it must be an instinct of human nature, as strong among the non-fighting portion of the creation as actual combat is to the warlike. I need not say that the foundress of the Chantry had no such thoughts; her object was simple enough; but it was too simple—too onefold (if I may borrow an expressive word from my native tongue: ae-fauld we write it in Scotch) for the apprehension of ordinary persons, who never believe in unity of motive. Most people thought she was artfully bent on introducing the confessional, and all the other bugbears of Protestantism; but she meant nothing of the kind: she only wanted to open another agency in heaven on behalf of the Austins, and nothing else affected her mind so long as this was secured.

The Chantry, however, afforded a very reasonable excuse to Kate and Sophy Farrel-Austin for paying a visit to Whiteladies, concerning which they had heard some curious rumors. Their interest in the place no doubt had considerably died out of late, since Herbert's amendment in health had been proved beyond doubt. Their father had borne that blow without much sympathy from his children, though they had not hesitated, as the reader is aware, to express their own sense that it was "a swindle" and "a sell," and that Herbert had no right to get better. The downfall to Farrel-Austin himself had been a terrible one, and the foolish levity of his children about it had provoked him often, almost past bearing; but time had driven him into silence, and into an appearance at least of forgetting his disappointment. On the whole he had no very deadly reason for disappointment: he was very well off without Whiteladies, and had he got Whiteladies, he had no son to succeed him, and less and less likelihood of ever having one. But I believe it is the man who has much who always feels most deeply when he is hindered from having more.

The charm of adding field to field is, I suppose, a more keen and practical hunger than that of acquiring a little is to him who has nothing. Poverty does not know the sweetness that eludes it altogether, but property is fully aware of the keen delight of possession. The disappointment sank deep into Farrel-Austin's heart. It even made him feel like the victim of retributive justice, as if, had he but kept his word to Augustine, Herbert might have been killed for him, and all been well; whereas now Providence preserved Herbert to spite him, and keep the inheritance from him! It seemed an unwarrantable bolstering up, on the part of Heaven and the doctors, of a miserable life which could be of very little good either to its owner or any other; and Farrel-Austin grew morose and disagreeable at home, by way of avenging himself on some one. Kate and Sophy did not very much care; they were too independent to be under his power, as daughters at home so often are under the power of a morose father. They had emancipated themselves beforehand, and now were strong in the fortresses of habit and established custom, and those natural defences with which they were powerfully provided. Rumors had reached them of a new inmate at Whiteladies, a young woman with a child, said to be the heir, who very much attracted their curiosity; and they had every intention of being kind to Herbert and Reine when they came home, and of making fast friends with their cousins. "For why should families be divided?" Kate said, not without sentiment. "However disappointed we may be, we can't quarrel with Herbert for getting well, can we, and keeping his own property?" The heroes who assembled at afternoon tea grinned under their moustachios, and said "No." These were not the heroes of two years ago; Dropmore was married among his own "set," and Ffarington had sold out and gone down to his estates in Wales, and Lord Alf had been ruined by a succession of misfortunes on the turf, so that there was quite a new party at the Hatch, though the life was very much the same as before. Drags and dinners, and boatings and races and cricket-matches, varied, when Winter came on, and according to the seasons, by hunting, skating, dancing, and every other amusement procurable, went on like clock-work, like treadmill work, or anything else that is useless and monotonous. Kate Farrel-Austin, who was now twenty-three in years, felt a hundred and three in life. She had grown wise, usual (and horrible) conclusion of girls of her sort. She wanted to marry, and change the air and scene of her existence, which began to grow tired of her as she of it. Sophy, on her way to the same state of superannuation, rather wished it too. "One of us ought certainly to do something," she said, assenting to Kate's homilies on the subject. They were not fools, though they were rather objectionable young women; and they felt that such life as theirs comes to be untenable after awhile. To be sure, the young men of their kind, the successors of Dropmore, etc. (I cannot really take the trouble to put down these young gentlemen's names), did carry on for a very long time the same kind of existence; but they went and came, were at London sometimes, and sometimes in the country, and had a certain something which they called duty to give lines, as it were, to their life; while to be always there, awaiting the return of each succeeding set of men, was the fate of the girls. The male creatures here, as in most things, had the advantage of the others; except that perhaps in their consciousness of the tedium of their noisy, monotonous lot, the girls, had they been capable of it, had a better chance of getting weary and turning to better things.

The Austin Chantry furnished the Farrel-Austins with the excuse they wanted to investigate Whiteladies and its mysterious guest. They drove over on a December day, when it was nearly finished, and by right of their relationship obtained entrance and full opportunity of inspection; and not only so, but met Miss Augustine there, with whom they returned to Whiteladies. There was not very much intercourse possible between the recluse and these two lively young ladies, but they accompanied her notwithstanding, plying her with mock questions, and "drawing her out;" for the Farrel-Austins were of those who held the opinion that Miss Augustine was mad, and a fair subject of ridicule. They got her to tell them about her pious purposes, and laid them up, with many a mischievous glance at each other, for the entertainment of their friends. When Stevens showed them in, announcing them with a peculiar loudness of tone intended to show his warm sense of the family hostility, there was no one in the drawing-room but Giovanna, who sat reclining in one of the great chairs, lazily watching the little boy who trotted about her, and who had now assumed the natural demeanor of a child to its mother. She was not a caressing mother even now, and in his heart I do not doubt Johnny still preferred Cook; but they made a pretty group, the rosy little fellow in his velvet frock and snow-white pinafore, and Giovanna in a black dress of the same material, which gave a most appropriate setting to her beauty. Dear reader, let me not deceive you, or give you false ideas of Miss Susan's liberality, or Giovanna's extravagance. The velvet was velveteen, of which we all make our Winter gowns, not the more costly material which lasts you (or lasted your mother, shall we say?) twenty years as a dinner dress, and costs you twice as many pounds as years. The Farrel-Austins were pretty girls both, but they were not of the higher order of beauty, like Giovanna; and they were much impressed by her looks and the indolent grace of her attitude, and the easy at-home air with which she held possession of Miss Susan's drawing-room. She scarcely stirred when they came in, for her breeding, as may be supposed, was still very imperfect, and probably her silence prolonged their respect for her more than conversation would have done; but the child, whom the visitors knew how to make use of as a medium of communication, soon produced a certain acquaintance. "Je suis Johnny," the baby said in answer to their question. In his little language one tongue and another was much the same; but in the drawing-room the mode of communication differed from that in the kitchen, and the child acknowledged the equality of the two languages by mixing them. "But mamma say Yan," he added as an afterthought.

The two girls looked at each other. Here was the mysterious guest evidently before them: to find her out, her ways, her meaning, and how she contemplated her position, could not be difficult. Kate was as usual a reasonable creature, talking as other people talk; while Sophy was the madcap, saying things she ought not to say, whose luck it was not unfrequently to surprise other people into similar indiscretions.

"Then this charming little fellow is yours?" said Kate. "How nice for the old ladies to have a child in the house! Gentlemen don't always care for the trouble, but where there are only ladies it is so cheerful; and how clever he is to speak both English and French."

Giovanna laughed softly. The idea that it was cheerful to have a child in the house amused her, but she kept her own counsel. "They teach him—a few words," she said, making the w more of a v; and rolling the r a great deal more than she did usually, so that this sounded like vorrds, and proved to the girls, who had come to make an examination of her, that she knew very little English, and spoke it very badly, as they afterward said.

"Then you are come from abroad? Pray don't think us impertinent. We are cousins; Farrel-Austins; you may have heard of us."

"Yes, yes, I have heard of you," said Giovanna with a smile. She had never changed her indolent position, and it gave her a certain pleasure to feel herself so far superior to her visitors, though in her heart she was afraid of them, and afraid of being exposed alone to their scrutiny.

Kate looked at her sister, feeling that the stranger had the advantage, but Sophy broke in with an answering laugh.

"It has not been anything very pleasant you have heard; we can see that; but we ain't so bad as the old ladies think us," said Sophy. "We are nice enough; Kate is sensible, though I am silly: we are not so bad as they think us here."

"I heard of you from my beau-père at Bruges," said Giovanna. "Jeanot! 'faut pas gêner la belle dame."

"Oh, I like him," said Kate. "Then you are from abroad? You are one of the Austins of Bruges? we are your cousins too. I hope you like England, and Whiteladies. Is it not a charming old house?"

Giovanna made no reply. She smiled, which might have been assent or contempt; it was difficult to say which. She had no intention of betraying herself. Whatever these young women might be, nothing could put them on her side of the question; this she perceived by instinct, and heroically refrained from all self-committal. The child by this time had gone to Sophy, and stood by her knee, allowing himself to be petted and caressed.

"Oh, what a dear little thing! what a nasty little thing!" said Sophy. "If papa saw him he would like to murder him, and so should I. I suppose he is the heir?"

"But M. Herbert lives, and goes to get well," said Giovanna.

"Yes, what a shame it is! Quel dommage, as you say in French. What right has he to get well, after putting it into everybody's head that he was going to die? I declare, I have no patience with such hypocrisy! People should do one thing or another," said Sophy, "not pretend for years that they are dying, and then live."

"Sophy, don't say such things. She is the silliest rattle, and says whatever comes into her head. To be kept in suspense used to be very trying for poor papa," said Kate. "He does not believe still that Herbert can live; and now that it has gone out of papa's hands, it must be rather trying for you."

"I am not angry with M. Herbert because he gets well," said Giovanna with a smile. She was amused indeed by the idea, and her amusement had done more to dissipate her resentment than reason; for to be sure it was somewhat ludicrous that Herbert should be found fault with for getting well. "When I am sick," she went on, "I try to get better too."

"Well, I think it is a shame," said Sophy. "He ought to think of other people waiting and waiting, and never knowing what is going to happen. Oh! Miss Susan, how do you do? We came to ask for you, and when Herbert and Reine were expected home."

Miss Susan came in prepared for the examination she had to go through. Her aspect was cloudy, as it always was nowadays. She had not the assured air of dignified supremacy and proprietorship which she once had possessed; but the Farrel-Austins were not penetrating enough to perceive more than that she looked dull, which was what they scarcely expected. She gave a glance at Giovanna, still reclining indolently in her easy chair; and curiously enough, quite against her expectation, without warning or reason, Miss Susan felt herself moved by something like a thrill of pleasure! What did it mean? It meant that Farrel's girls, whom she disliked, who were her natural enemies, were not fit to be named in comparison with this young woman who was her torment, her punishment, her bad angel; but at all events hers, on her side pitted with her against them. It was not an elevated sort of satisfaction, but such as it was it surprised her with a strange gleam of pleasure. She sat down near Giovanna, unconsciously ranging herself on that side against the other; and then she relapsed into common life, and gave her visitors a very circumstantial account of Herbert and Reine—how they had wished to come home at Christmas, but the doctors thought it more prudent to wait till May. Kate and Sophy listened eagerly, consulting each other, and comparing notes in frequent looks.

"Yes, poor fellow! of course May will be better," said Kate, "though I should have said June myself. It is sometimes very cold in May. Of course he will always be very delicate; his constitution must be so shattered—"

"His constitution is not shattered at all," said Miss Susan, irritated, as the friends of a convalescent so often are, by doubts of his strength. "Shattered constitutions come from quite different causes, Miss Kate—from what you call 'fast' living and wickedness. Herbert has the constitution of a child; he has no enemy but cold, and I hope we can take care of him here."

"Oh, Kate meant no harm," said Sophy; "we know he could never have been 'fast.' It is easy to keep straight when you haven't health for anything else," said this well-informed young woman.

"Hush!" said her sister in an audible whisper, catching hold of the baby to make a diversion. Then Kate aimed her little broadside too.

"We have been so pleased to make acquaintance with madame," she said, using that title without any name, as badly instructed people are so apt to do. "It must be nice for you to feel yourself provided for, whatever happens. This, I hear, is the little heir?"

"Madame Suzanne," interrupted Giovanna, "I have told ces dames that I am glad M. Herbert goes to get well. I hope he will live long and be happy. Jean, chéri! dis fort 'Vive M. Herbert!' as I taught you, that ces dames may hear."

Johnny was armed with his usual weapon, the paper-knife, which on ordinary occasions Miss Susan could not endure to see in his hand; for I need not say it was her own pet weapon, which Giovanna in her ignorance had appropriated. He made a great flourish in the air with this falchion. "Vive M'sieu 'Erbert!" cried the child, his little round face flushed and shining with natural delight in his achievement. Giovanna snatched him up on her lap to kiss and applaud him, and Miss Susan, with a start of wonder, felt tears of pleasure come to her eyes. It was scarcely credible even to herself.

"Yes, he is the heir," she said quickly, looking her assailants in the face, "that is, if Herbert has no children of his own. I am fortunate, as you say—more fortunate than your papa, Miss Kate."

"Who has only girls," said Sophy, coming to the rescue. "Poor papa! Though if we are not as good as the men, we must be poor creatures," she added with a laugh; and this was a proposition which nobody attempted to deny.

As for Kate, she addressed her sister very seriously when they left Whiteladies. Things were come to a pass in which active measures were necessary, and a thorough comprehension of the situation.

"If you don't make up your mind at once to marry Herbert, that woman will," she said to Sophy. "We shall see before six months are out. You don't mind my advice as you ought, but you had better this time. I'd rather marry him myself than let him drop into the hands of an adventuress like that."

"Do! I shan't interfere," said Sophy lightly; but in her heart she allowed that Kate was right. If one of them was to have Whiteladies, it would be necessary to be alert and vigorous. Giovanna was not an antagonist to be despised. They did not under-value her beauty; women seldom do, whatever fancy-painters on the other side may say.

Miss Susan, for her part, left the drawing-room along with them, with so curious a sensation going through her that she had to retire to her room to get the better of it. She felt a certain thrill of gratefulness, satisfaction, kindness in the midst of her hatred; and yet the hatred was not diminished. This put all her nerves on edge like a jarring chord.

CHAPTER XXXIII

Herbert and Reine had settled at Cannes for the Winter, at the same time when Giovanna settled herself at Whiteladies. They knew very little of this strange inmate in their old home, and thought still less. The young man had been promoted from one point to another of the invalid resorts, and now remained at Cannes, which was so much brighter and less valetudinary than Mentone, simply, as the doctors said, "as a precautionary measure." Does the reader know that bright sea-margin, where the sun shines so serene and sweet, and where the color of the sea and the sky and the hills and the trees are all brightened and glorified by the fact that the grays and chills of northern Winter are still close at hand? When one has little to do, when one is fancy free, when one is young, and happiness comes natural, there is nothing more delicious than the Riviera. You are able, in such circumstances, to ignore the touching groups which encircle here and there, some of the early doomed. You are able to hope that the invalids must get better. You say to yourself, "In this air, under this sky, no one can long insist upon being ill;" and if your own invalid, in whom you are most interested, has really mended, hope for every other becomes conviction. And then there are always idlers about who are not ill, to whom life is a holiday, or seems so, and who, being impelled to amuse themselves by force of circumstances, add a pleasant movement to the beautiful scene. Without even these attractions, is not the place in which you receive back your sick as from the dead always beautiful, if it were the dirtiest seaport or deserted village? Mud and gray sky, or sands of gold and heavenly vaults of blue, what matters? That was the first time since the inspired and glorious moment at Kandersteg that Reine had felt sure of Herbert's recovery;—there was no doubting the fact now. He was even no longer an invalid, a change which at first was not nearly so delightful to his sister as she had expected. They had been all in all to each other for so long; and Reine had given up to Herbert not only willingly, but joyfully, all the delights of youth—its amusements, its companionships, everything. She had never been at a ball (grown up) in her life, though she was now over twenty. She had passed the last four years, the very quintessence of her youth, in a sick-room, or in the subdued goings out and gentle amusements suited to an invalid; and indeed, her heart and mind being fully occupied, she had desired no better. Herbert, and his comfort and his entertainment, had been the sum of all living to Reine. And now had come the time when she was emancipated, and when the young man, recovering his strength, began to think of other amusements than those which a girl could share. It was quite natural. Herbert made friends of his own, and went out with them, and made parties of pleasure, and manly expeditions in which Reine had no part. It was very foolish of her to feel it, and no critic could have been more indignant with her than she was with herself. The girl's first sensation was surprise when she found herself left out. She was bewildered by it. It had never occurred to her as likely, natural, nay, necessary—which, as soon as she recovered her breath, she assured herself it was. Poor Reine even tried to laugh at herself for her womanish folly. Was it to be expected that Herbert should continue in the same round when he got better, that he should not go out into the world like other men? On the contrary, Reine was proud and delighted to see him go; to feel that he was able to do it; to listen to his step, which was as active as any of the others, she thought, and his voice, which rang as clear and gay. It was only after he was gone that the sudden surprise I have spoken of assailed her. And if you will think of it, it was hard upon Reine. Because of her devotion to him she had made no friends for herself. She had been out of the way of wanting friends. Madame de Mirfleur's eagerness to introduce her, to find companions for her, when she paid the pair her passing visits, had always been one of the things which most offended Reine. What did she want with other companions than Herbert? She was necessary to him, and did any one suppose that she would leave him for pleasure? For pleasure! could mamma suppose it would be any pleasure to her to be separate from her brother? Thus the girl thought in her absolute way, carrying matters with a high hand as long as it was in her power to do so. But now that Herbert was well, everything was changed. He was fond of his sister, who had been so good a nurse to him; but it seemed perfectly natural that she should have been his nurse, and had she not always said she preferred it to anything else in the world? It was just the sort of thing that suited Reine—it was her way, and the way of most good girls. But it did not occur to Herbert to think that there was anything astonishing, any hardship in the matter; nor, when he went out with his new friends, did it come into his head that Reine, all alone, might be dull and miss him. Yes, miss him, that of course she must; but then it was inevitable. A young fellow enjoying his natural liberty could not by any possibility drag a girl about everywhere after him—that was out of the question, of course. At first now and then it would sometimes come into his head that his sister was alone at home, but that impression very soon wore off. She liked it. She said so; and why should she say so if it was not the case? Besides, she could of course have friends if she chose. So shy Reine, who had not been used to any friends but him, who had alienated herself from all her friends for him, stayed at home within the four rather bare walls of their sitting-room, while the sun shone outside, and even the invalids strolled about, and the soft sound of the sea upon the beach filled the air with a subdued, delicious murmur. Good François, Herbert's faithful attendant, used to entreat her to go out.

"The weather is delightful," he said. "Why will mademoiselle insist upon shutting herself up in-doors?"

"I will go out presently, François," Reine said, her pretty lips quivering a little.

But she had no one to go out with, poor child! She did not like even to go and throw herself upon the charity of one or two ladies whom she knew. She knew no one well, and how could she go and thrust herself upon them now, after having received their advances coldly while she had Herbert? So the poor child sat down and read, or tried to read, seated at the window from which she could see the sea and the people who were walking about. How lucky she was to have such a cheerful window! But when she saw the sick English girl who lived close by going out for her midday walk leaning upon her brother's arm, with her mother close by watching her, poor Reine's heart grew sick. Why was it not she who was ill? if she died, nobody would miss her much (so neglected youth always feels, with poignant self pity), whereas it was evident that the heart of that poor lady would break if her child was taken from her. The poor lady whom Reine thus noted looked up at her where she sat at the window, with a corresponding pang in her heart. Oh, why was it that other girls should be so fresh and blooming while her child was dying? But it is very hard at twenty to sit at a bright window alone, and try to read, while all the world is moving about before your eyes, and the sunshine sheds a soft intoxication of happiness into the air. The book would fall from her hands, and the young blood would tingle in her veins. No doubt, if one of the ladies whom Reine knew had called just then, the girl would have received her visitor with the utmost dignity, nor betrayed by a word, by a look, how lonely she was; for she was proud, and rather perverse and shy—shy to her very finger-tips; but in her heart I think if any one had been so boldly kind as to force her out, and take her in charge, she would have been ready to kiss that deliverer's feet, but never to own what a deliverance it was.

No one came, however, in this enterprising way. They had been in Cannes several times, the brother and sister, and Reine had been always bound to Herbert's side, finding it impossible to leave him. How could these mere acquaintances know that things were changed now? So she sat at the window most of the day, sometimes trying to make little sketches, sometimes working, but generally reading or pretending to read—not improving books, dear reader. These young people did not carry much solid literature about with them. They had poetry books—not a good selection—and a supply of the pretty Tauchnitz volumes, only limited by the extent of that enterprising firm's reprints, besides such books as were to be got at the library. Everard had shown more discrimination than was usual to him when he said that Herbert, after his long helplessness and dependence, would rush very eagerly into the enjoyments and freedom of life. It was very natural that he should do so; chained to a sick-room as he had been for so long—then indulged with invalid pleasures, invalid privileges, and gradually feeling the tide rise and the warm blood of his youth swell in his veins—the poor young fellow was greedy of freedom, of boyish company, from which he had always been shut out—of adventures innocent enough, yet to his recluse mind having all the zest of desperate risk and daring. He had no intention of doing anything wrong, or even anything unkind. But this was the very first time that he had fallen among a party of young men like himself, and the contrast being so novel, was delightful to him. And his new friends "took to him" with a flattering vehemence of liking. They came to fetch him in the morning, they involved him in a hundred little engagements. They were fond of him, he thought, and he had never known friendship before. In short, they turned Herbert's head, a thing which quite commonly happens both to girls and boys when for the first time either boy or girl falls into a merry group of his or her contemporaries, with many amusements and engagements on hand. Had one of these young fellows happened to fall in love with Reine, all would have gone well—for then, no doubt, the young lover would have devised ways and means for having her of the party. But she was not encouraging to their advances. Girls who have little outward contact with society are apt to form an uncomfortably high ideal, and Reine thought her brother's friends a pack of noisy boys quite inferior to Herbert, with no intellect, and not very much breeding. She was very dignified and reserved when they ran in and out, calling for him to come here and go there, and treated them as somehow beneath the notice of such a very mature person as herself; and the young fellows were offended, and revenged themselves by adding ten years to her age, and giving her credit for various disagreeable qualities.

"Oh, yes, he has a sister," they would say, "much older than Austin—who looks as if she would like to turn us all out, and keep her darling at her apron-string."

"You must remember she has had the nursing of him all his life," a more charitable neighbor would suggest by way of excusing the middle-aged sister.

"But women ought to know that a man is not to be always lounging about pleasing them, and not himself. Hang it all, what would they have? I wonder Austin don't send her home. It is the best place for her."

This was how the friends commented upon Reine. And Reine did not know that even to be called Austin was refreshing to the invalid lad, showing him that he was at least on equal terms with somebody; and that the sense of independence intoxicated him, so that he did not know how to enjoy it enough—to take draughts full enough and deep enough of the delightful pleasure of being his own master, of meeting the night air without a muffler, and going home late in sheer bravado, to show that he was an invalid no more.

After this first change, which chilled her and made her life so lonely, another change came upon Reine. She had been used to be anxious about Herbert all her life, and now another kind of anxiety seized her, which a great many women know very well, and which with many becomes a great and terrible passion, ravaging secretly their very lives. Fear for his health slid imperceptibly in her loneliness into fear for him. Does the reader know the difference? She was a very ignorant, foolish girl: she did not know anything about the amusements and pleasures of young men. When her brother came in slightly flushed and flighty, with some excitement in his looks, parting loudly with his friends at the door, smelling of cigars and wine, a little rough, a little noisy, poor Reine thought he was plunging into some terrible whirlpool of dissipation, such as she had read of in books; and, as she was of the kind of woman who is subject to its assaults, the vulture came down upon her, there and then, and began to gnaw at her heart. In those long evenings when she sat alone waiting for him, the legendary Spartan with the fox under his cloak was nothing to Reine. She kept quite still over her book, and read page after page, without knowing a word she was reading, but heard the pitiful little clock on the mantel-piece chime the hours, and every step and voice outside, and every sound within, with painful acuteness, as if she were all ear; and felt her heart beat all over her—in her throat, in her ears, stifling her and stopping her breath. She did not form any idea to herself of how Herbert might be passing his time; she would not let her thoughts accuse him of anything, for, indeed, she was too innocent to imagine those horrors which women often do imagine. She sat in an agony of listening, waiting for him, wondering how he would look when he returned—wondering if this was he, with a renewed crisis of excitement, this step that was coming—falling dull and dead when the step was past, rousing up again to the next, feeling herself helpless, miserable, a slave to the anguish which dominated her, and against which reason itself could make no stand. Every morning she woke saying to herself that she would not allow herself to be so miserable again, and every night fell back into the clutches of this passion, which gripped at her and consumed her. When Herbert came in early and "like himself"—that is to say, with no traces of excitement or levity—the torture would stop in a moment, and a delicious repose would come over her soul; but next night it came back again the same as ever, and poor Reine's struggles to keep mastery of herself were all in vain. There are hundreds of women who well know exactly how she felt, and what an absorbing fever it was which had seized upon her. She had more reason than she really knew for her fears, for Herbert was playing with his newly-acquired health in the rashest way, and though he was doing no great harm, had yet departed totally from that ideal which had been his, as well as his sister's, but a short time before. He had lost altogether the tender gratitude of that moment when he thought he was being cured in a half miraculous, heavenly way, and when his first simple boyish thought was how good it became him to be, to prove the thankfulness of which his heart was full. He had forgotten now about being thankful. He was glad, delighted to be well, and half believed that he had some personal credit in it. He had "cheated the doctors"—it was not they who had cured him, but presumably something great and vigorous in himself which had triumphed over all difficulties; and now he had a right to enjoy himself in proportion to—what he began to think—the self-denial of past years. Both the brother and sister had very much fallen off from that state of elevation above the world which had been temporarily theirs in that wonderful moment at Kandersteg; and they had begun to feel the effect of those drawbacks which every great change brings with it, even when the change is altogether blessed, and has been looked forward to with hope for years.

This was the position of affairs between the brother and sister when Madame de Mirfleur arrived to pay them a visit, and satisfy herself as to her son's health. She came to them in her most genial mood, happy in Herbert's recovery, and meaning to afford herself a little holiday, which was scarcely the aspect under which her former visits to her elder children had shown themselves. They had received her proposal with very dutiful readiness, but oddly enough, as one of the features of the change, it was Reine who wished for her arrival; not Herbert, though he, in former tunes, had always been the more charitable to his mother. Now his brow clouded at the prospect. His new-born independence seemed in danger. He felt as if mufflers and respirators, and all the old marks of bondage, were coming back to him in Madame de Mirfleur's trunks.

"If mamma comes with the intention of coddling me up again, and goes on about taking care," he said, "by Jove! I tell you I'll not stand it, Reine."

"Mamma will do what she thinks best," said Reine, perhaps a little coldly; "but you know I think you are wrong, Bertie, though you will not pay any attention to me."

"You are just like a girl," said Herbert, "never satisfied, never able to see the difference. What a change it is, by Jove, when a fellow gets into the world, and learns the right way of looking at things! If you go and set her on me, I'll never forgive you; as if I could not be trusted to my own guidance—as if it were not I, myself, who was most concerned!"

These speeches of her brother's cost Reine, I am afraid, some tears when he was gone, and her pride yielded to the effects of loneliness and discouragement. He was forsaking her, she thought, who had the most right to be good to her—he of whom she had boasted that he was the only being who belonged to her in the world; her very own, whom nobody could take from her. Poor Reine! it had not required very much to detach him from her. When Madame de Mirfleur arrived, however, she did not interfere with Herbert's newly-formed habits, nor attempt to put any order in his mannish ways. She scolded Reine for moping, for sitting alone and neglecting society, and instantly set about to remedy this fault; but she found Herbert's little dissipations tout simple, said not a word about a respirator, and rather encouraged him than otherwise, Reine thought. She made him give them an account of everything, where he had been, and all about his expeditions, when he came back at night, and never showed even a shadow of disapproval, laughing at the poor little jokes which Herbert reported, and making the best of his pleasure. She made him ask his friends, of whom Reine disapproved, to dinner, and was kind to them, and charmed these young men; for Madame de Mirfleur had been a beauty in her day, and kept up those arts of pleasing which her daughter disdained, and made Herbert's boyish companions half in love with her. This had the effect of restraining Herbert often, without any suspicions of restraint entering his head; and the girl, who half despised, half envied her mother's power, was not slow to perceive this, though she felt in her heart that nothing could ever qualify her to follow the example. Poor Reine looked on, disapproving her mother as usual, yet feeling less satisfied with herself than usual, and asking herself vainly if she loved Herbert as she thought she did, would not she make any sacrifice to make him happy? If this made him happy, why could not she do it? It was because his companions were his inferiors, she said to herself—companions not worthy of Herbert. How could she stoop to them? Madame de Mirfleur had not such a high standard of excellence. She exerted herself for the amusement of the young men as if they had been heroes and sages. And even Reine, though she disapproved, was happier, against her will.

"But, mon Dieu!" cried Madame de Mirfleur, "the fools that these boys are! Have you ever heard, my Reine, such bêtises as my poor Herbert takes for pleasantries? They give me mal au cœur. How they are bêtes, these boys!"

"I thought you liked them," said Reine, "you are so kind to them. You flatter them, even. Oh, does it not wound you, are you not ashamed, to see Bertie, my Bertie, prefer the noise—those scufflings? It is this that gives me mal au cœur."

"Bah! you are high-flown," said the mother. "If one took to heart all the things that men do, one would have no consolation in this world. They are all less or more, bêtes, the men. What we have to do is to ménager—to make of it the best we can. You do not expect them to understand—to be like us? Tenez, Reine; that which your brother wants is a friend. No, not thee, my child, nor me. Do not cry, chérie. It is the lot of the woman. Thou hast not known whether thou wert girl or boy, or what difference there was, in the strange life you have led; but listen, my most dear, for now you find it out. Herbert is but like others; he is no worse than the rest. He accepts from thee everything, so long as he wants thee; but now he is independent, he wants thee no more. This is a truth which every woman learns. To struggle is inutile—it does no good, and a woman who is wise accepts what must be, and does not struggle. What he wants is a friend. Where is the cousin, the Monsieur Everard, whom I left with you, who went away suddenly? You have never told me why he went away."

Reine's color rose. She grew red to the roots of her hair. It was a subject which had never been touched upon between them, and possibly it was the girl's consciousness of something which she could not put into words which made the blood flush to her face. Madame de Mirfleur had been very discreet on this subject, as she always was. She had never done anything to awaken her child's susceptibilities. And she was not ignorant of Everard's story, which Julie had entered upon in much greater detail than would have been possible to Reine. Honestly, she thought no more of Everard so far as Reine was concerned; but, for Herbert, he would be invaluable; therefore, it was with no match-making meaning that she awaited her daughter's reply.

"I told you when it happened," said Reine, in very measured tones, and with unnecessary dignity; "you have forgotten, mamma. His affairs got into disorder; he thought he had lost all his money; and he was obliged to go at a moment's notice to save himself from being ruined."

"Ah!" said Madame de Mirfleur, "I begin to recollect. Après? He was not ruined, but he did not come back?"

"He did not come back because he had to go to Jamaica—to the West Indies," said Reine, somewhat indignant, "to work hard. It is not long since he has been back in England. I had a letter—to say he thought—of coming—" Here she stopped short, and looked at her mother with a certain defiance. She had not meant to say anything of this letter, but in Everard's defence had betrayed its existence before she knew.

"Ah!" said Madame de Mirfleur, wisely showing little eagerness, "such an one as Everard would be a good companion for thy brother. He is a man, voyez-vous, not a boy. He thought—of coming?"

"Somewhere—for the Winter," said Reine, with a certain oracular vagueness, and a tremor in her voice.

"Some-vere," said Madame de Mirfleur, laughing, "that is large; and you replied, ma Reine?"

"I did not reply—I have not time," said Reine with dignity, "to answer all the idle letters that come to me. People in England seem to think one has nothing to do but to write."

"It is very true," said the mother, "they are foolish, the English, on that point. Give me thy letter, chérie, and I will answer it for thee. I can think of no one who would be so good for Herbert. Probably he will never want a good friend so much as now."

"Mamma!" cried Reine, changing from red to white, and from white to red in her dismay, "you are not going to invite Everard here?"

"Why not, my most dear? It is tout simple; unless thou hast something secret in thy heart against it, which I don't know."

"I have nothing secret in my heart," cried Reine, her heart beating loudly, her eyes filling with tears; "but don't do it—don't do it; I don't want him here."

"Très-bien, my child," said the mother calmly, "it was not for thee, but for thy brother. Is there anything against him?"

"No, no, no! There is nothing against him—nothing!"

"Then you are unreasonable, Reine," said her mother; "but I will not go against you, my child. You are excited—the tears come to you in the eyes; you are not well—you have been too much alone, ma petite Reine."

"No, no; I am quite well—I am not excited!" cried the girl.

Madame de Mirfleur kissed her, and smoothed her hair, and bid her put on her hat and come out.

"Come and listen a little to the sea," she said. "It is soft, like the wind in our trees. I love to take advantage of the air when I am by the sea."

CHAPTER XXXIV

The effect of this conversation, however, did not end as the talk itself did. Reine thought of little else all the rest of the day. When they got to the beach, Madame de Mirfleur, as was natural, met with some of her friends, and Reine, dropping behind, had leisure enough for her own thoughts. It was one of those lovely, soft, bright days which follow each other for weeks together, even though grim December, on that charmed and peaceful coast. The sea, as blue as a forget-me-not or a child's eyes—less deep in tone than the Austin eyes through which Reine gazed at it, but not less limpid and liquid-bright—played with its pebbles on the beach like a child, rolling them over playfully, and sending the softest hus-sh of delicious sound through air which was full of light and sunshine. It was not too still, but had the refreshment of a tiny breeze, just enough to ruffle the sea-surface where it was shallow, and make edges of undulating shadow upon the shining sand and stones underneath, which the sun changed to gold. The blue sky to westward was turning into a great blaze of rose, through which its native hue shone in bars and breaks, here turning to purple and crimson, here cooling down to the wistfullest shadowy green. As close to the sea as it could keep its footing, a noble stone pile stood on a little height, rising like a great stately brown pillar, to spread its shade between the young spectator and the setting sun. Behind, not a stone's throw from where she stood, rose the line of villas among their trees, and all the soft lively movement of the little town. How different from the scenes which Everard's name conjured up before Reine—the soft English landscape of Whiteladies, the snowy peaks and the wild, sweet pastures of the Alpine valleys where they had been last together!

Madame de Mirfleur felt that it would not harm her daughter to leave her time for thought. She was too far-seeing to worry her with interference, or to stop the germination of the seeds she had herself sown; and having soothed Reine by the influences of the open air and the sea, had no objection to leave her alone, and permit the something which was evidently in her mind, whatever it was, to work. Madame de Mirfleur was not only concerned about her daughter's happiness from a French point of view, feeling that the time was come when it would be right to marry her; but she was also solicitous about her condition in other ways. It might not be for Reine's happiness to continue much longer with Herbert, who was emancipating himself very quickly from his old bonds, and probably would soon find the sister who, a year ago, had been indispensable to him, to be a burden and drag upon his freedom, in the career of manhood he was entering upon so eagerly. And where was Reine to go? Madame de Mirfleur could not risk taking her to Normandy, where, delightful as that home was, her English child would not be happy; and she had a mother's natural reluctance to abandon her altogether to the old aunts at Whiteladies, who, as rival guardians to her children in their youth, had naturally taken the aspect of rivals and enemies to their mother. No; it would have been impossible in France that an affaire du cœur should have dragged on so long as that between Everard and Reine must have done, if indeed there was anything in it. But there was never any understanding those English, and if Reine's looks meant anything, surely this was what they meant. At all events, it was well that Reine should have an opportunity of thinking it well over; and if there was nothing in it, at least it would be good for Herbert to have the support and help of his cousin. Therefore, in whatever light you chose to view the subject, it was important that Everard should be here. So she left her daughter undisturbed to think, in peace, what it was best to do.

And indeed it was a sufficiently difficult question to come to any decision upon. There was no quarrel between Reine and Everard, nor any reason why they should regard each other in any but a kind and cousinly way. Such a rapprochement, and such a curious break as had occurred between them, are not at all uncommon. They had been very much thrown together, and brought insensibly to the very verge of an alliance more close and tender; but before a word had been said, before any decisive step had been taken, Fate came in suddenly and severed them, "at a moment's notice," as Reine said, leaving no time, no possibility for any explanation or any pledge. I do not know what was in Everard's heart at the moment of parting, whether he had ever fully made up his mind to make the sacrifices which would be necessary should he marry, or whether his feelings had gone beyond all such prudential considerations; but anyhow, the summons which surprised him so suddenly was of a nature which made it impossible for him in honor to do anything or say anything which should compromise Reine. For it was loss of fortune, perhaps total—the first news being exaggerated, as so often happens—with which he was threatened; and in the face of such news, honor sealed his lips, and he dared not trust himself to say a word beyond the tenderness of good-bye which his relationship permitted. He went away from her with suppressed anguish in his heart, feeling like a man who had suddenly fallen out of Paradise down, down to the commonest earth, but silenced himself, and subdued himself by hard pressure of necessity till time and the natural influences of distance and close occupation dulled the poignant feeling with which he had said that good-bye. The woman has the worst of it in such circumstances. She is left, which always seems the inferior part, and always is the hardest to bear, in the same scene, with everything to recall to her what has been, and nothing to justify her in dwelling upon the tender recollection. I do not know why it should appear to women, universally, something to be ashamed of when they give love unasked—or even when they give it in return for every kind of asking except the straightforward and final words. It is no shame to a man to do so; but these differences of sentiment are inexplicable, and will not bear accounting for. Reine felt that she had "almost" given her heart and deepest affections, without being asked for them. She had not, it is true, committed herself in words, any more than he had done; but she believed with sore shame that he knew—just as he felt sure (but without shame) that she knew; though in truth neither of them knew even their own feelings, which on both sides had changed somewhat, without undergoing any fundamental alteration.

Such meetings and partings are not uncommon. Sometimes the two thus rent asunder at the critical moment, never meet again at all, and the incipient romance dies in the bud, leaving (very often) a touch of bitterness in the woman's heart, a sense of incompleteness in the man's. Sometimes the two meet when age has developed or altered them, and when they ask themselves with horror what they could possibly have seen in that man or that woman? And sometimes they meet again voluntarily or involuntarily, and—that happens which pleases heaven; for it is impossible to predict the termination of such an interrupted tale.

Reine had not found it very easy to piece that broken bit of her life into the web again. She had never said a word to any one, never allowed herself to speak to herself of what she felt; but it had not been easy to bear. Honor, too, like everything else, takes a different aspect as it is regarded by man or woman. Everard had thought that honor absolutely sealed his lips from the moment that he knew, or rather believed, that his fortune was gone; but Reine would have been infinitely more ready to give him her fullest trust, and would have felt an absolute gratitude to him had he spoken out of his poverty, and given her the pleasure of sympathizing, of consoling, of adding her courage and constancy to his. She was too proud to have allowed herself to think that there was any want of honor in the way he left her, for Reine would have died rather than have had the pitiful tribute of a declaration made for honor's sake; but yet, had it not been her case, but a hypothetical one, she would have pronounced it to be most honorable to speak, while the man would have felt a single word inconsistent with his honor! So we must apparently go on misunderstanding each other till the end of time. It was a case in which there was a great deal to be said on both sides, the reader will perceive. But all this was over; and the two whom a word might have made one were quite free, quite independent, and might each have married some one else had they so chosen, without the other having a word to say; and yet they could not meet without a certain embarrassment, without a sense of what might have been. They were not lovers, and they were not indifferent to each other, and on both sides there was just a little wholesome bitterness. Reine, though far too proud to own it, had felt herself forsaken. Everard, since his return from the active work which had left him little time to think, had felt himself slighted. She had said that, now Herbert was better, it was not worth while writing so often! and when he had got over that unkind speech, and had written, as good as offering himself to join them, she had not replied. He had written in October, and now it was nearly Christmas, and she had never replied. So there was, the reader will perceive, a most hopeful and promising grievance on both sides. Reine turned over her part of it deeply and much in her mind that night, after the conversation with her mother which I have recorded. She asked herself, had she any right to deprive Herbert of a friend who would be of use to him for any foolish pride of hers? She could keep herself apart very easily, Reine thought, in her pride. She was no longer very necessary to Herbert. He did not want her as he used to do. She could keep apart, and trouble no one; and why should she, for any ridiculous self-consciousness, ghost of sentiment dead and gone, deprive her brother of such a friend? She said "No!" to herself vehemently, as she lay and pondered the question in the dark, when she ought to have been asleep. Everard was nothing, and could be nothing to her, but her cousin; it would be necessary to see him as such, but not to see much of him; and whatever he might be else, he was a gentleman, and would never have the bad taste to intrude upon her if he saw she did not want him. Besides, there was no likelihood that he would wish it; therefore Reine made up her mind that no exaggerated sentimentality on her part, no weak personal feeling, should interfere with Herbert's good. She would keep herself out of the way.

But the reader will scarcely require to be told that the letter written under this inspiration was not exactly the kind of letter which it flatters a young man to receive from a girl to whom he has once been so closely drawn as Everard had been to Reine, and to whom he still feels a visionary link, holding him fast in spite of himself. He received the cold epistle, in which Reine informed him simply where they were, adding a message from her brother: "If you are coming to the Continent, Herbert wishes me to say he would be glad to see you here," in a scene and on a day which was as unlike as it is possible to imagine to the soft Italian weather, and genial Southern beach, on which Reine had concocted it. As it happened, the moment was one of the most lively and successful in Everard's somewhat calm country life. He, who often felt himself insignificant, and sometimes slighted, was for that morning at least in the ascendant. Very cold weather had set in suddenly, and in cold weather Everard became a person of great importance in his neighborhood. I will tell you why. His little house, which was on the river, as I have already said, and in Summer a very fine starting-point for water-parties, possessed unusually picturesque and well-planted grounds; and in the heart of a pretty bit of plantation which belonged to him was an ornamental piece of water, very prettily surrounded by trees and sloping lawns, which froze quickly, as the water was shallow, and was the pleasantest skating ground for miles round. Need I say more to show how a frost made Everard instantly a man of consequence? On the day on which Reine's epistle arrived at Water Beeches, which was the name of his place, it was a beautiful English frost, such as we see but rarely nowadays. I do not know whether there is really any change in the climate, or whether it is only the change of one's own season from Spring to Autumn which gives an air of change even to the weather; but I do not think there are so many bright, crisp, clear frosts as there used to be. Nor, perhaps, is it much to be regretted that the intense cold—which may be as champagne to the healthy and comfortable, but is death to the sick, and misery to the poor—should be less common than formerly. It was, however, a brilliant frosty day at the Water Beeches, and a large party had come over to enjoy the pond. The sun was shining red through the leafless trees, and such of them as had not encountered his direct influence were still encased in fairy garments of rime, feathery and white to the furthest twig. The wet grass was brilliantly green, and lighted up in the sun's way sparkling water-diamonds, though in the shade it was too crisp and white with frost, and crackled under your feet. On the broad path at one end of the pond two or three older people, who did not skate, were walking briskly up and down, stamping their feet to keep them warm, and hurrying now and then in pairs to the house, which was just visible through the trees, to get warmed by the fire. But on the ice no one was cold. The girls, with their red petticoats and red feathers, and pretty faces flushed with the exercise, were, some of them, gliding about independently with their hands in their muffs, some of them being conducted about by their attendants, some dashing along in chairs wheeled by a chivalrous skater. They had just come out again, after a merry luncheon, stimulated by the best fare Everard's housekeeper could furnish, and by Everard's best champagne; and as the afternoon was now so short, and the sun sinking low, the gay little crowd was doing all it could to get an hour's pleasure out of half-an-hour's time, and the scene was one of perpetual movement, constant varying and intermingling of the bright-colored groups, and a pleasant sound of talk and laughter which rang through the clear air and the leafless trees.

The few chaperons who waited upon the pleasure of these young ladies were getting tired and chilled, and perhaps cross, as was (I think) extremely natural, and thinking of their carriages; but the girls were happy and not cross, and all of them very agreeable to Everard, who was the cause of so much pleasure. Sophy and Kate naturally took upon them to do the honors of their cousin's place. Everybody knows what a movable relationship cousinry is, and how it recedes and advances according to the inclination of the moment. To-day the Farrel-Austins felt themselves first cousins to Everard, his next-of-kin, so to speak, and comparative owners. They showed their friends the house and the grounds, and all the pretty openings and peeps of the river. "It is small, but it is a perfect little place," they said with all the pride of proprietorship. "What fun we have had here! It is delightful for boating. We have the jolliest parties!"

"In short, I don't know such a place for fun all the year round," cried Sophy.

"And of course, being so closely related, it is just like our own," said Kate. "We can bring whom we like here."

It was with the sound of all these pretty things in his ears, and all the pleasant duties of hospitality absorbing his attention, with pleasant looks, and smiles, and compliments about his house and his table coming to him on all sides, and a sense of importance thrust upon him in the most delightful way, that Everard had Reine's letter put into his hand. It was impossible that he could read about it then; he put it into his pocket with a momentary flutter and tremor of his heart, and went on with the entertainment of his guests. All the afternoon he was in motion, flying about upon the ice, where, for he was a very good skater, he was in great demand, and where his performances were received with great applause; then superintending the muster of the carriages, putting his pretty guests into them, and receiving thanks and plaudits, and gay good-byes "for the present." There was to be a dance at the Hatch that night, where most of the party were to reassemble, and Everard felt himself sure of the prettiest partners, and the fullest consideration of all his claims to notice and kindness. He had never been more pleased with himself, nor in a more agreeable state of mind toward the world in general, than when he shut the door of his cousins' carriage, which was the last to leave.

"Mind you come early. I want to settle with you about next time," said Kate.

"And Ev," cried Sophy, leaning out of the carriage, "bring me those barberries you promised me for my hair."

Everard stood smiling, waving his hand to them as they drove away. "Madcaps!" he said to himself, "always with something on hand!" as he went slowly home, watching the last red gleam of the sun disappear behind the trees. It was getting colder and colder every moment, the chilliest of December nights; but the young man, in his glow of exercise and pleasure, did not take any notice of this. He went into his cosey little library, where a bright fire was burning, and where, even there in his own particular sanctum, the disturbing presence of those gay visitors was apparent. They had taken down some of his books from his shelves, and they had scattered the cushions of his sofa round the fire, where a circle of them had evidently been seated. There is a certain amused curiosity in a young man's thoughts as to the doings and the sayings, when by themselves, of those mysterious creatures called girls. What were they talking about while they chatted round that fire, his fire, where, somehow, some subtle difference in the atmosphere betokened their recent presence? He sat down with a smile on his face, and that flattered sense of general importance and acceptability in his mind, and took Reine's letter out of his pocket. It was perhaps not the most suitable state of mind in which to read the chilly communication of Reine.

Its effect upon him, however, was not at all chilly. It made him hot with anger. He threw it down on the table when he had read it, feeling such a letter to be an insult. Go to Cannes to be of use, forsooth, to Herbert! a kind of sick-nurse, he supposed, or perhaps keeper, now that he could go out, to the inexperienced young fellow. Everard bounced up from his comfortable chair, and began to walk up and down the room in his indignation. Other people nearer home had better taste than Reine. If she thought that he was to be whistled to, like a dog when he was wanted, she was mistaken. Not even when he was wanted;—it was clear enough that she did not want him, cold, uncourteous, unfriendly as she was! Everard's mind rose like an angry sea, and swelled into such a ferment that he could not subdue himself. A mere acquaintance would have written more civilly, more kindly, would have thought it necessary at least to appear to join in the abrupt, cold, semi-invitation, which Reine transmitted as if she had nothing to do with it. Even her mother (a wise woman, with some real knowledge of the world, and who knew when a man was worth being civil to!) had perceived the coldness of the letter, and added a conciliatory postscript. Everard was wounded and humiliated in his moment of success and flattered vanity, when he was most accessible to such a wound. And he was quite incapable of divining—as probably he would have done in any one else's case, but as no man seems capable of doing in his own—that Reine's coldness was the best of all proof that she was not indifferent, and that something must lie below the studied chill of such a composition. He dressed for the party at the Hatch in a state of mind which I will not attempt to describe, but of which his servant gave a graphic account to the housekeeper.

"Summat's gone agin master," that functionary said. "He have torn those gardenias all to bits as was got for his button-hole; and the lots of ties as he've spiled is enough to bring tears to your eyes. Some o' them there young ladies has been a misconducting theirselves; or else it's the money market. But I don't think it's money," said John; "when it's money gentlemen is low, not furious, like to knock you down."

"Get along with you, do," said the housekeeper. "We don't want no ladies here!"

"That may be, or it mayn't be," said John; "but something's gone agin master. Listen! there he be, a rampaging because the dog-cart ain't come round, which I hear the wheels, and William—it's his turn, and I'll just keep out o' the way."

William was of John's opinion when they compared notes afterward. Master drove to the Hatch like mad, the groom said. He had never been seen to look so black in all his life before, for Everard was a peaceable soul in general, and rather under the dominion of his servants. He was, however, extremely gay at the Hatch, and danced more than any one, far outstripping the languid Guardsmen in his exertions, and taking all the pains in the world to convince himself that, though some people might show a want of perception of his excellences, there were others who had a great deal more discrimination. Indeed, his energy was so vehement, that two or three young ladies, including Sophy, found it necessary to pause and question themselves on the subject, wondering what sudden charm on their part had warmed him into such sudden exhibitions of feeling.

"It will not answer at all," Sophy said to her sister; "for I don't mean to marry Everard, for all the skating and all the boating in the world—not now, at least. Ten years hence, perhaps, one might feel different—but now!—and I don't want to quarrel with him either, in case—" said this far-seeing young woman.

This will show how Reine's communication excited and stimulated her cousin, though perhaps in a curious way.

CHAPTER XXXV

Everard's excited mood, however, did not last; perhaps he danced out some of his bitterness; violent exercise is good for all violent feeling, and calms it down. He came to himself with a strange shock, when—one of the latest to leave, as he had been one of the earliest to go—he came suddenly out from the lighted rooms, and noisy music, and chattering voices, to the clear cold wintry moonlight, deep in the frosty night, or rather early on the frosty morning of the next day. There are some people who take to themselves, in our minds at least, a special phase of nature, and plant their own image in the midst of it with a certain arrogance, so that we cannot dissociate the sunset from one of those usurpers, or the twilight from another. In this way Reine had taken possession of the moonlight for Everard. It was no doing of hers, nor was she aware of it; but still it was the case. He never saw the moon shining without remembering the little balcony at Kandersteg, and the whiteness with which her head rose out of the dark shadow of the rustic wooden framework. How could he help but think of her now, when worn out by a gayety which had not been quite real, he suddenly fell, as it were, into the silence, the clear white light, the frost-bound, chill, cold blue skies above him, full of frosty, yet burning stars, and the broad level shining of that ice-cold moon? Everard, like other people at his time of life, and in his somewhat unsettled condition of mind, had a way of feeling somewhat "low" after being very gay. It is generally the imaginative who do this, and is a sign, I think, of a higher nature; but Everard had the disadvantage of it without the good, for he was not of a poetical mind—though I suppose there must have been enough poetry in him to produce this reaction. When it came on, as it always did after the noisy gayety of the Hatch, he had, in general, one certain refuge to which he always betook himself. He thought of Reine—Reine, who was gay enough, had nature permitted her to have her way, but whom love had separated from everything of the kind, and transplanted into solitude and quiet, and the moonlight, which, in his mind, was dedicated to her image; this was his resource when he was "low;" and he turned to it as naturally as the flowers turn to the sun. Reine was his imagination, his land of fancy, his unseen world, to Everard; but lo! on the very threshold of this secret region of dreams, the young man felt himself pulled up and stopped short. Reine's letter rolled up before him like a black curtain shutting out his visionary refuge. Had he lost her? he asked himself, with a sudden thrill of visionary panic. Her image had embodied all poetry, all romance, to him, and had it fled from his firmament? The girls whom he had left had no images at all, so to speak; they were flesh and blood realities, pleasant enough, so long as you were with them, and often very amusing to Everard, who, after he had lingered in their society till the last moment, had that other to fall back upon—the other, whose superiority he felt as soon as he got outside the noisy circle, and whose soft influence, oddly enough, seemed to confer a superiority upon him, who had her in that private sphere to turn to, when he was tired of the rest.

Nothing could be sweeter than the sense of repose and moral elevation with which, for instance, after a gay and amusing and successful day like this, he went back into the other world, which he had the privilege of possessing, and felt once more the mountain air breathe over him, fresh with the odor of the pines, and saw the moon rising behind the snowy peaks, which were as white as her own light, and that soft, upturned face lifted to the sky, full of tender thoughts and mysteries! If Reine forsook him, what mystery would be left in the world for Everard? what shadowy world, unrealized, and sweeter for being unrealized than any fact could ever be? The poor young fellow was seized with a chill of fright, which penetrated to the marrow of his bones, and froze him doubly this cold night. What it would be to lose one's imagination! to have no dreams left, no place which they could inhabit! Poor Everard felt himself turned out of his refuge, turned out into the cold, the heavenly doors closed upon him all in a moment; and he could not bear it. William, who thought his master had gone out of his mind, or fallen asleep—for what but unconsciousness or insanity could justify the snail's pace into which they had dropped?—felt frozen on his seat behind; but he was not half so frozen as poor Everard, in his Ulster, whose heart was colder than his hands, and through whose very soul the shiverings ran.

Next morning, as was natural, Everard endeavored to make a stand against the dismay which had taken possession of him, and succeeded for a short time, as long as he was fully occupied and amused, during which time he felt himself angry, and determined that he was a very badly-used man. This struggle he kept up for about a week, and did not answer Reine's letter. But at last the conflict was too much for him. One day he rode over suddenly to Whiteladies, and informed them that he was going abroad for the rest of the Winter. He had nothing to do at Water Beeches, and country life was dull; he thought it possible that he might pass through Cannes on his way to Italy, as that was, on the whole, in Winter, the pleasantest way, and, of course, would see Herbert. But he did not mention Reine at all, nor her letter, and gave no reason for his going, except caprice, and the dulness of the country. "I have not an estate to manage like you," he said to Miss Susan; and to Augustine, expressed his grief that he could not be present at the consecration of the Austin Chantry, which he had seen on his way white and bristling with Gothic pinnacles, like a patch upon the grayness of the old church. Augustine, whom he met on the road, with her gray hood over her head, and her hands folded in her sleeves, was roused out of her abstracted calm to a half displeasure. "Mr. Farrel-Austin will be the only representative of the family except ourselves," she said; "not that I dislike them, as Susan does. I hope I do not dislike any one," said the Gray Sister. "You can tell Herbert, if you see him, that I would have put off the consecration till his return—but why should I rob the family of four months' prayers? That would be sinful waste, Everard; the time is too short—too short—to lose a day."

This was the only message he had to carry. As for Miss Susan, her chief anxiety was that he should say nothing about Giovanna. "A hundred things may happen before May," the elder sister said, with such an anxious, worried look as went to Everard's heart. "I don't conceal from you that I don't want her to stay."

"Then send her away," he said lightly. Miss Susan shook her head; she went out to the gate with him, crossing the lawn, though it was damp, to whisper once again, "Nothing about her—say nothing about her—a hundred things may happen before May."

Everard left home about ten days after the arrival of Reine's letter, which he did not answer. He could make it evident that he was offended, at least in that way; and he lingered on the road to show, if possible, that he had no eagerness in obeying the summons. His silence puzzled the household at Cannes. Madame de Mirfleur, with a twist of the circumstances, which is extremely natural, and constantly occurring among ladies, set it down as her daughter's fault. She forgave Everard, but she blamed Reine. And with much skilful questioning, which was almost entirely ineffectual, she endeavored to elicit from Herbert what the state of affairs between these two had been. Herbert, for his part, had not an idea on the subject. He could not understand how it was possible that Everard could quarrel with Reine. "She is aggravating sometimes," he allowed, "when she looks at you like this—I don't know how to describe it—as if she meant to find you out. Why should she try to find a fellow out? a man (as she ought to know) is not like a pack of girls."

"Precisely," said Madame de Mirfleur, "but perhaps that is difficult for our poor Reine—till lately thou wert a boy, and sick, mon 'Erbert; you forget. Women are dull, my son; and this is perhaps one of the things that it is most hard for them to learn."

"You may say so, indeed," said Herbert, "unintelligible beings!—till they come to your age, mamma, when you seem to begin to understand. It is all very well for girls to give an account of themselves. What I am surprised at is, that they do not perceive at once the fundamental difference. Reine is a clever girl, and it just shows the strange limitation, even of the cleverest; now I don't call myself a clever man—I have had a great many disadvantages—but I can perceive at a glance—"

Madame de Mirfleur was infinitely disposed to laugh, or to box her son's ears; but she was one of those women—of whom there are many in the world—who think it better not to attempt the use of reason, but to ménager the male creatures whom they study so curiously. Both the sexes, indeed, I think, have about the same opinion of each other, though the male portion of the community have found the means of uttering theirs sooner than the other, and got it stereotyped, so to speak. We both think each other "inaccessible to reason," and ring the changes upon humoring and coaxing the natural adversary. Madame de Mirfleur thought she knew men au fond, and it was not her practice to argue with them. She did not tell Herbert that his mental superiority was not so great as he thought it. She only smiled, and said gently, "It is much more facile to perceive the state of affairs when it is to our own advantage, mon fils. It is that which gives your eyes so much that is clear. Reine, who is a girl, who has not the same position, it is natural she should not like so much to acknowledge herself to see it. But she could not demand from Everard that he should account for himself. And she will not of you when she has better learned to know—"

"From Everard? Everard is of little importance. I was thinking of myself," cried Herbert.

"How fortunate it is for me that you have come here! I should not have believed that Reine could be sulky. I am fond of her, of course; but I cannot drag a girl everywhere about with me. Is it reasonable? Women should understand their place. I am sure you do, mamma. It is home that is a woman's sphere. She cannot move about the world, or see all kinds of life, or penetrate everywhere, like a man; and it would not suit her if she could," said Herbert, twisting the soft down of his moustache. He was of opinion that it was best for a man to take his place, and show at once that he did not intend to submit to any inquisition; and this, indeed, was what his friends advised, who warned him against petticoat government. "If you don't mind they'll make a slave of you," the young men said. And Herbert was determined to give all who had plans of this description fair notice. He would not allow himself to be made a slave.

"You express yourself with your usual good sense, my son," said Madame de Mirfleur. "Yes, the home is the woman's sphere; always I have tried to make this known to my Reine. Is it that she loves the world? I make her enter there with difficulty. No, it is you she loves, and understands not to be separated. She has given up the pleasures that are natural to young girls to be with you when you were ill; and she understands not to be separated now."

"Bah!" said Herbert, "that is the usual thing which I understand all women say to faire valoir their little services. What has she given up? They would not have been pleasures to her while I was ill; and she ought to understand. It comes back to what I said, mamma. Reine is a clever girl, as girls go—and I am not clever, that I know; but the thing which she cannot grasp is quite clear to me. It is best to say no more about it—you can understand reason, and explain to her what I mean."

"Yes, chéri," said Madame de Mirfleur, submissively; then she added, "Monsieur Everard left you at Appenzell? Was he weary of the quiet? or had he cause to go?"

"Why, he had lost his money, and had to look after it—or he thought he had lost his money. Probably, too, he found it slow. There was nobody there, and I was not good for much in those days. He had to be content with Reine. Perhaps he thought she was not much company for him," said the young man, with a sentiment not unusual in young men toward their sisters. His mother watched him with a curious expression. Madame de Mirfleur was in her way a student of human nature, and though it was her son who made these revelations, she was amused by them all the same, and rather encouraged him than otherwise to speak his mind. But if she said nothing about Reine, this did not mean that she was deceived in respect to her daughter, or with Herbert's view of the matter. But she wanted to hear all he had to say, and for the moment she looked upon him more as a typical representative of man, than as himself a creature in whose credit she, his mother, was concerned.

"It has appeared to you that this might be the reason why he went away?"

"I never thought much about it," said Herbert. "I had enough to do thinking of myself. So I have now. I don't care to go into Everard's affairs. If he likes to come, he'll come, I suppose; and if he don't like, he won't—that's all about it—that's how I would act if it were me. Hallo! why, while we're talking, here he is! Look here—in that carriage at the door!"

"Ah, make my excuses, Herbert. I go to speak to François about a room for him," said Madame de Mirfleur. What she did, in fact, was to dart into her own room, where Reine was sitting at work on some article of dress. Julie had much to do, looking after and catering for the little party, so that Reine had to make herself useful, and do things occasionally for herself.

"Chérie," said her mother, stooping over her, "thy cousin is come—he is at the door. I thought it best to tell you before you met him. For my part, I never like to be taken at the unforeseen—I prefer to be prepared."

Reine had stopped her sewing for the moment; now she resumed it—so quietly that her mother could scarcely make out whether this news was pleasant to her or not. "I have no preparation to make," she said, coldly; but her blood was not so much under mastery as her tongue, and rushed in a flood to her face; her fingers, too, stumbled, her needle pricked her, and Madame de Mirfleur, watching, learned something at last—which was that Reine was not so indifferent as she said.

"Me, I am not like you, my child," she said. "My little preparations are always necessary—for example, I cannot see the cousin in my robe de chambre. Julie! quick!—but you, as you are ready, can go and salute him. It is to-day, is it not, that we go to see milady Northcote, who will be kind to you when I am gone away? I will put on my black silk; but you, my child, you who are English, who have always your toilette made from the morning, go, if you will, and see the cousin. There is only Herbert there."

"Mamma," said Reine, "I heard Herbert say something when I passed the door a little while ago. It was something about me. What has happened to him that he speaks so?—that he thinks so? Has he changed altogether from our Herbert who loved us? Is that common? Oh, must it be? must it be?"

"Mon Dieu!" cried the mother, "can I answer for all that a foolish boy will say? Men are fools, ma Reine. They pretend to be wise, and they are fools. But we must not say this—no one says it, though we all know it in our hearts. Tranquillize thyself; when he is older he will know better. It is not worth thy while to remember what he says. Go to the cousin, ma Reine."

"I do not care for the cousin. I wish he were not here. I wish there was no one—no one but ourselves; ourselves! that does not mean anything, now," cried Reine, indignant and broken-hearted. The tears welled up into her eyes. She did not take what she had heard so calmly as her mother had done. She was sore and mortified, and wounded and cut to the heart.

"Juste ciel!" cried Madame de Mirfleur, "thy eyes! you will have red eyes if you cry. Julie, fly toward my child—think not more of me. Here is the eau de rose to bathe them; and, quick, some drops of the eau de fleur de orange. I never travel without it, as you know."

"I do not want any fleur de orange, nor eau de rose. I want to be as once we were, when we were fond of each other, when we were happy, when, if I watched him, Bertie knew it was for love, and nobody came between us," cried the girl. Impossible to tell how sore her heart was, when it thus burst forth— sore because of what she had heard, sore with neglect, and excitement, and expectation, and mortification, which, all together, were more than Reine could bear.

"You mean when your brother was sick?" said Madame de Mirfleur. "You would not like him to be ill again, chérie. They are like that, ma Reine—unkind, cruel, except when they want us, and then we must not be absent for a moment. But, Reine, I hope thou art not so foolish as to expect sense from a boy; they are not like us; they have no understanding; and if thou wouldst be a woman, not always a child, thou must learn to support it, and say nothing. Come, my most dear, my toilette is made, and thy eyes are not so red, after all—eyes of blue do not show like the others. Come, and we will say bon jour to the cousin, who will think it strange to see neither you nor me."

"Stop—stop but one moment, mamma," cried Reine. She caught her mother's dress, and her hand, and held her fast. The girl was profoundly excited, her eyes were not red, but blazing, and her tears dried. She had been tried beyond her powers of bearing. "Mamma," she cried, "I want to go home with you— take me with you! If I have been impatient, forgive me. I will try to do better, indeed I will. You love me a little—oh, I know only a little, not as I want you to love me! But I should be good; I should try to please you and—every one, ma mère! Take me home with you!"

"Reine, chérie! Yes, my most dear, if you wish it. We will talk of it after. You excite yourself; you make yourself unhappy, my child."

"No, no, no," she cried; "it is not I. I never should have dreamed of it, that Herbert could think me a burden, think me intrusive, interfering, disagreeable! I cannot bear it! Ah, perhaps it is my fault that people are so unkind! Perhaps I am what he says. But, mamma, I will be different with you. Take me with you. I will be your maid, your bonne, anything! only don't leave me here!"

"My Reine," said Madame de Mirfleur, touched, but somewhat embarrassed, "you shall go with me, do not doubt it—if it pleases you to go. You are my child as much as Babette, and I love you just the same. A mother has not one measure of love for one and another for another. Do not think it, chérie. You shall go with me if you wish it, but you must not be so angry with Herbert. What are men? I have told you often they are not like us; they seek what they like, and their own way, and their own pleasures; in short, they are fools, as the selfish always are. Herbert is ungrateful to thee for giving up thy youth to him, and thy brightest years; but he is not so unkind as he seems—that which he said is not what he thinks. You must forgive him, ma Reine; he is ungrateful—"

"Do I wish him to be grateful?" said the girl. "If one gives me a flower, I am grateful, or a glass of water; but gratitude—from Herbert—to me! Do not let us talk of it, for I cannot bear it. But since he does not want me, and finds me a trouble—mother, mother, take me home with you!"

"Yes, chérie, yes; it shall be as you will," said Madame de Mirfleur, drawing Reine's throbbing head on to her bosom, and soothing her as if she had been still a child. She consoled her with soft words, with caresses, and tender tones. Probably she thought it was a mere passing fancy, which would come to nothing; but she had never crossed any of her children, and she soothed and petted Reine instinctively, assenting to all she asked, though without attaching to what she asked any very serious meaning. She took her favorite essence of orange flowers from her dressing-case, and made the agitated girl swallow some of it, and bathed her eyes with rose-water, and kissed and comforted her. "You shall do what pleases to you, ma bien aimée," she said. "Dry thy dear eyes, my child, and let us go to salute the cousin. He will think something is wrong. He will suppose he is not welcome; and we are not like men, who are a law to themselves; we are women, and must do what is expected—what is reasonable. Come, chérie, or he will think we avoid him, and that something must have gone wrong."

Thus adjured, Reine followed her mother to the sitting-room, where Everard had exhausted everything he had to say to Herbert, and everything that Herbert had to say to him; and where the two young men were waiting very impatiently, and with a growing sense of injury, for the appearance of the ladies. · Herbert exclaimed fretfully that they had kept him waiting half the morning, as they came in. "And here is Everard, who is still more badly used," he cried; "after a long journey too. You need not have made toilettes, surely, before you came to see Everard; but ladies are all the same everywhere, I suppose!"

Reine's eyes gave forth a gleam of fire. "Everywhere!" she cried, "always troublesome, and in the way. It is better to be rid of them. I think so as well as you."

Everard, who was receiving the salutations and apologies of Madame de Mirfleur, did not hear this little speech; but he saw the fire in Reine's eyes, which lighted up her proud sensitive face. This was not his

Reine of the moonlight, whom he had comforted. And he took her look as addressed to himself, though it was not meant for him. She gave him her hand with proud reluctance. He had lost her then? it was as he thought.

CHAPTER XXXVI

Reine did not go back from her resolution; she did not change her mind, as her mother expected, and forgive Herbert's étourderie. Reine could not look upon it as étourderie, and she was too deeply wounded to recover the shock easily; but I think she had the satisfaction of giving an almost equal shock to her brother, who, though he talked so about the limitation of a girl's understanding, and the superiority of his own, was as much wounded as Reine was, when he found that his sister really meant to desert him. He did not say a word to her, but he denounced to his mother the insensibility of women, who only cared for a fellow so long as he did exactly what they wished, and could not endure him to have the least little bit of his own way. "I should never have heard anything of this if I had taken her about with me everywhere, and gone to bed at ten o'clock, as she wished," he cried, with bitterness.

"You have reason, mon 'Erbert," said Madame de Mirfleur; "had you cared for her society, she would never have left you; but it is not amusing to sit at home while les autres are amusing themselves. One would require to be an angel for this."

"I never thought Reine cared for amusement," said Herbert; "she never said so; she was always pleased to be at home; it must all have come on, her love for gayety, to spite me."

Madame de Mirfleur did not reply; she thought it wisest to say nothing in such a controversy, having, I fear, a deep-rooted contempt for the masculine understanding in such matters at least. En revanche, she professed the most unbounded reverence for it in other matters, and liked, as Miss Susan did, to consult "a man" in all difficult questions, though I fear, like Miss Susan, it was only the advice of one who agreed with her that she took. But with Herbert she was silent. What was the use? she said to herself. If he could not see that Reine's indifference to amusement arose from her affection for himself, what could she say to persuade him of it? and it was against her principles to denounce him for selfishness, as probably an English mother would have done. "Que voulez-vous? it is their nature," Madame de Mirfleur would have said, shrugging her shoulders. I am not sure, however, that this silence was much more satisfactory to Herbert than an explanation would have been. He was not really selfish, perhaps, only deceived by the perpetual homage that had been paid to him during his illness, and by the intoxicating sense of sudden emancipation now.

As for Everard, he was totally dismayed by the announcement; all the attempts at self-assertion which he had intended to make failed him. As was natural, he took this, not in the least as affecting Herbert, but only as a pointed slight addressed to himself. He had left home to please her at Christmas, of all times in the year, when everybody who has a home goes back to it, when no one is absent who can help it. And though her invitation was no invitation, and was not accompanied by one conciliating word, he had obeyed the summons, almost, he said to himself, at a moment's notice; and she for whom he came, though she had not asked him, she had withdrawn herself from the party! Everard said to himself that he would not stay, that he would push on at once to Italy, and prove to her that it was not her or her society that had tempted him. He made up his mind to this at once, but he did not do it. He lingered next day, and next day again. He thought it would be best not to commit himself to anything till he had talked to Reine; if he had but half an hour's conversation with her he would be able to see whether it was her mother's doing. A young man in such circumstances has an instinctive distrust of a mother. Probably it was one of Madame de Mirfleur's absurd French notions. Probably she thought it not entirely comme il faut that Reine, now under her brother's guardianship, should be attended by Everard. Ridiculous! but on the whole it was consolatory to think that this might be the mother's doing, and that Reine was being made a victim of like himself. But (whether this also was her mother's doing he could not tell) to get an interview with Reine was beyond his power. He had no chance of saying a word to her till he had been at least ten days in Cannes, and the time of her departure with Madame de Mirfleur was drawing near. One evening, however, he happened to come into the room when Reine had stepped out upon the balcony, and followed her there hastily, determined to seize the occasion. It was a mild evening, not moonlight, as (he felt) it ought to have been, but full of the soft lightness of stars, and the luminous reflection of the sea. Beyond her, as she stood outside the window, he saw the sweep of dim blue, with edges of white, the great Mediterranean, which forms the usual background on this coast. There was too little light for much color, only a vague blueness or grayness, against which the slim, straight figure rose. He stepped out softly not to frighten her; but even then she started, and looked about for some means of escape, when she found herself captured and in his power. Everard did not take any sudden or violent advantage of his luck. He began quite gently, with an Englishman's precaution, to talk of the weather and the beautiful night.

"It only wants a moon to be perfect," he said. "Do you remember, Reine, the balcony at Kandersteg? I always associate you with balconies and moons. And do you remember, at Appenzell—"

It was on her lips to say, "Don't talk of Appenzell!" almost angrily, but she restrained herself. "I remember most things that have happened lately," she said; "I have done nothing to make me forget."

"Have I?" said Everard, glad of the chance; for to get an opening for reproach or self-defence was exactly what he desired.

"I did not say so. I suppose we both remember all that there is to remember," said Reine, and she added hastily, "I don't mean anything more than I say."

"It almost sounds as if you did—and to see your letter," said Everard, "no one would have thought you remembered anything, or that we had ever known each other. Reine, Reine, why are you going away?"

"Why am I going away? I am not going what you call, away. I am going rather, as we should say, home— with mamma. Is it not the most natural thing to do?"

"Did you ever call Madame de Mirfleur's house home before?" said Everard; "do you mean it? Are not you coming to Whiteladies, to your own country, to the place you belong to? Reine, you frighten me. I don't understand what you mean."

"Do I belong to Whiteladies? Is England my country?" said Reine. "I am not so sure as you are. I am a Frenchwoman's daughter, and perhaps, most likely, it will turn out that mamma's house is the only one I have any right to."

Here she paused, faltering, to keep the tears out of her voice. Everard did not see that her lip was quivering, but he discovered it in the tremulous sound.

"What injustice you are doing to everybody!" he cried indignantly. "How can you treat us so?"

"Treat you? I was not thinking of you," said Reine. "Herbert will go to Whiteladies in May. It is home to him; but what is there that belongs to a girl? Supposing Herbert marries, would Whiteladies be my home? I have no right, no place anywhere. The only thing, I suppose, a girl has a right to is, perhaps, her mother. I have not even that—but mamma would give me a home. I should be sure of a home at least—"

"I do not understand you, Reine."

"It is tout simple, as mamma says; everything is tout simple," she said; "that Herbert should stand by himself, not wanting me; and that I should have nothing and nobody in the world. Tout simple. I am not complaining; I am only saying the truth. It is best that I should go to Normandy and try to please mamma. She does not belong to me, but I belong to her, in a way—and she would never be unkind to me. Well, there is nothing so very wonderful in what I say. Girls are like that; they have nothing belonging to them; they are not meant to have, mamma would say. It is tout simple; they are meant to ménager, and to cajole, and to submit; and I can do the last. That is why I say that, most likely, Normandy will be my home after all."

"You cannot mean this," said Everard, troubled. "You never could be happy there; why should you change now? Herbert and you have been together all your lives; and if he marries—" Here Everard drew a long breath and made a pause. "You could not be happy with Monsieur, your stepfather, and all the little Mirfleurs," he said.

"One can live, one can get on, without being happy," cried Reine. Then she laughed. "What is the use of talking? One has to do what one must. Let me go in, please. Balconies and moonlights are not good. To think too much, to talk folly, may be very well for you who can do what you please, but they are not good for girls. I am going in now."

"Wait one moment, Reine. Cannot you do what you please?—not only for yourself, but for others. Everything will be changed if you go; as for me, you don't care about me, what I feel—but Herbert. He has always been your charge; you have thought of him before everything—"

"And so I do now," cried the girl. Two big tears dropped out of her eyes. "So I do now! Bertie shall not think me a burden, shall not complain of me if I should die. Let me pass, please. Everard, may I not even have so much of my own will as to go out or in if I like? I do not ask much more."

Everard stood aside, but he caught the edge of her loose sleeve as she passed him, and detained her still a moment. "What are you thinking of? what have you in your mind?" he said humbly. "Have you changed, or have I changed, or what has gone wrong? I don't understand you, Reine."

She stood for a moment hesitating, as if she might have changed her tone; but what was there to say? "I am not changed that I know of; I cannot tell whether you are changed or not," she said. "Nothing is wrong; it is tout simple, as mamma says."

What was tout simple? Everard had not a notion what was in her mind, or how it was that the delicate poise had been disturbed, and Reine taught to feel the disadvantage of her womanhood. She had not been in the habit of thinking or feeling anything of the kind. She had not been aware even for years and years, as her mother had said, whether she was girl or boy. The discovery had come all at once. Everard pondered dimly and with perplexity how much he had to do with it, or what it was. But indeed he had nothing to do with it; the question between Reine and himself was a totally different question from the other which was for the moment supreme in her mind. Had she been free to think of it, I do not suppose Reine would have felt in much doubt as to her power over Everard. But it was the other phase of her life which was uppermost for the moment.

He followed her into the lighted room, where Madame de Mirfleur sat at her tapisserie in the light of the lamp. But when Reine went to the piano and began to sing "Ma Normandie," with her sweet young fresh voice, he retreated again to the balcony, irritated by the song more than by anything she had said. Madame de Mirfleur, who was a musician too, added a mellow second to the refrain of her child's song. The voices suited each other, and a prettier harmony could not have been, nor a more pleasant suggestion to any one whose mind was in tune. Indeed, it made the mother feel happy for the moment, though she was herself doubtful how far Reine's visit to the Norman château would be a success. "Je vais revoir ma Normandie," the girl sang, very sweetly; the mother joined in; mother and daughter were going together to that simple rural home, while the young men went out into the world and enjoyed themselves. What more suitable, more pleasant for all parties? But Everard felt himself grow hot and angry. His temper flamed up with unreasonable, ferocious impatience. What a farce it was, he cried bitterly to himself. What did that woman want with Reine? she had another family whom she cared for much more. She would make the poor child wretched when she got her to that detestable Normandie they were singing about with so much false sentiment. Of course it was all some ridiculous nonsense of hers about propriety, something that never could have come into Reine's poor dear little innocent head if it had not been put there. When a young man is angry with the girl he is fond of, what a blessing it is when she has a mother upon whom he can pour out his wrath! The reader knows how very little poor Madame de Mirfleur had to do with it. But though she was somewhat afraid of her daughter's visit, and anxious about its success, Reine's song was very pleasant to her, and she liked to put in that pretty second, and to feel that her child's sweet voice was in some sense an echo of her own.

"Thanks, chérie," she said when Reine closed the piano. "I love thy song, and I love thee for singing it. Tiens, my voice goes with your fresh voice well enough still."

She was pleased, poor soul; but Everard, glaring at her from the balcony, would have liked to do something to Madame de Mirfleur had the rules of society permitted. He "felt like hurling things at her," like Maria in the play.

Yet—I do not know how it came to pass, but so it was—even then Everard did not carry out his intention of making a start on his own account, and going off and leaving the little party which was just about to break up, each going his or her own way. He lingered and lingered still till the moment came when the ladies had arranged to leave. Herbert by this time had made up his mind to go on to Italy too, and Everard, in spite of himself, found that he was tacitly pledged to be his young cousin's companion, though Bertie without Reine was not particularly to his mind. Though he had been partially weaned from his noisy young friends by Everard's presence, Herbert had still made his boyish desire to emancipate himself sufficiently apparent to annoy and bore the elder man, who having long known the delights of freedom, was not so eager to claim them, nor so jealous of their infringement. Everard had no admiration for the billiard-rooms or smoking-rooms, or noisy, boyish parties which Herbert preferred so much to the society of his mother and sister. "Please yourself," he said, shrugging his shoulders, as he left the lad at the door of these brilliant centres of society; and this shrug had more effect upon Herbert's mind than dozens of moral lectures. His first doubt, indeed, as to whether the "life" which he was seeing, was not really of the most advanced and brilliant kind, was suggested to him by that contemptuous movement of his cousin's shoulders. "He is a rustic, he is a Puritan," Herbert said to himself, but quite unconsciously Everard's shrug was as a cloud over his gayety. Everard, however, shrugged his shoulders much more emphatically when he found that he was expected to act the part of guide, philosopher, and friend to the young fellow, who was no longer an invalid, and who was so anxious to see the world. Once upon a time he had been very ready to undertake the office, to give the sick lad his arm, to wheel him about in his chair, to carry him up or down stairs when that was needful.

"But you don't expect me to be Herbert's nurse all by myself," he said ruefully, just after Madame de Mirfleur had made a pretty little speech to him about the benefit which his example and his society would be to her boy. Reine was in the room too, working demurely at her mother's tapisserie, and making no sign.

"He wants no nurse," said Madame de Mirfleur, "thank God; but your society, cher Monsieur Everard, will be everything for him. It will set our minds at ease. Reine, speak for thyself, then. Do not let Monsieur Everard go away without thy word too."

Reine raised her eyes from her work, and gave a quick, sudden glance at him. Then Everard saw that her eyes were full of tears. Were they for him? were they for Herbert? were they, for herself? He could not tell. Her voice was husky and strained very different from the clear carol with which this night even, over again, she had given forth the quavering notes of "Ma Normandie." How he hated the song which she had taken to singing over and over again when nobody wanted it! But her voice just then had lost all its music, and he was glad.

"Everard knows—what I would say," said Reine. "He always was—very good to Bertie;" and here her tears fell. They were so big that they made a storm of themselves, and echoed as they fell, these two tears.

"But speak, then," said her mother, "we go to-morrow; there is no more time to say anything after to-night."

Reine's eyes had filled again. She was exercising great control over herself, and would not weep nor break down, but she could not keep the tears out of her eyes. "He is not very strong," she said, faltering, "he never was—without some one to take care of him—before. Oh! how can I speak? Perhaps I am forsaking him for my own poor pride, after all. If he got ill what should I do?"

"Chérie, if he gets ill, it will be the will of God; thou canst do no more. Tell what you wish to your cousin. Monsieur Everard is very good and kind; he will watch over him; he will take care of him—"

"I know, I know!" said Reine, under her breath, making a desperate effort to swallow down the rising sob in her throat.

Through all this Everard sat very still, with a rueful sort of smile on his face. He did not like it, but what could he say? He had no desire to watch over Herbert, to take care of him, as Madame de Mirfleur said; but he was soft-hearted, and his very soul was melted by Reine's tears, though at the same time they wounded him; for, alas! there was very little appearance of any thought for him, Everard, in all she looked and said.

And then there followed a silence in which, if he had been a brave man, he would have struck a stroke for liberty, and endeavored to get out of this thankless office; and he fully meant to do it; but sat still looking at the lamp, and said nothing, though the opportunity was afforded him. A man who has so little courage or presence of mind surely deserves all his sufferings.

CHAPTER XXXVII

Everard and Herbert made their tour through Italy without very much heart for the performance; but partly out of pride, partly because, when once started on a giro of any kind, it is easier to go on than to turn back, they accomplished it. On Herbert's part, indeed, there was occasion for a very strong backbone of pride to keep him up, for the poor young fellow, whose health was not so strong as he thought, had one or two warnings of this fact, and when shut up for a week or two in Rome or in Naples, longed unspeakably for the sister who had always been his nurse and companion. Everard was very kind, and gave up a great deal of his time to the invalid; but it was not to be expected that he should absolutely devote himself, as Reine did, thinking of nothing in the world but Herbert. He had, indeed, many other things to think of, and when the state of convalescence was reached, he left the patient to get better as he could, though he was very good to him when he was absolutely ill. What more could any one ask? But poor Herbert wanted more. He wanted Reine, and thus learned how foolish it was to throw his prop away. Reine in the meanwhile wanted him, and spent many wretched hours in the heart of that still Normandy, longing to be with the travellers, to know what they were about, and how her brother arranged his life without her. The young men arrived at the Château Mirfleur at the earliest moment permissible, getting there in the end of April, to pick up Reine; and as they had all been longing for this meeting, any clouds that had risen on the firmament dispersed at once before the sunshine.

They were so glad to be together again, that they did not ask why or how they had separated. And instead of singing "Ma Normandie," as she had done at Cannes, Reine sang "Home, sweet home," bringing tears into the eyes of the wanderers with that tender ditty. Herbert and she were indeed much excited about their home-going, as was natural. They had not been at Whiteladies for six years, a large slice out of their young lives. They had been boy and girl when they left it, and now they were man and woman. And all the responsibilities of life awaited Herbert, now three-and-twenty, in full possession of his rights. In the first tenderness of the reunion Reine and he had again many talks over this life which was now beginning—a different kind of life from that which he thought, poor boy, he was making acquaintance with in billiard-rooms, etc. I think he had ceased to confide in the billiard-room version of existence, but probably not so much from good sense or any virtue of his, as from the convincing effect of those two "attacks" which he had been assailed by at Rome and Naples, and which proved to him that he was not yet strong enough to dare vulgar excitements, and turn night into day.

As for Everard, it seemed to him that it was his fate to be left in the lurch. He had been told off to attend upon Herbert and take care of him when he had no such intention, and now, instead of rewarding him for his complaisance, Reine was intent upon cementing her own reconciliation with her brother, and making up for what she now represented to herself as her desertion of him. Poor Everard could not get a word or a look from her, but was left in a whimsical solitude to make acquaintance with Jeanot and Babette, and to be amiable to M. de Mirfleur, whom his wife's children were not fond of. Everard found him very agreeable, being driven to take refuge with the honest, homely Frenchman, who had more charity for Herbert and Reine than they had for him. M. de Mirfleur, like his wife, found many things to be tout simple which distressed and worried the others. He was not even angry with the young people for their natural reluctance to acknowledge himself, which indeed showed very advanced perceptions in a step-father, and much forbearance. He set down all their farouche characteristics to their nationality. Indeed, there was in the good man's mind, an evident feeling that the fact of being English explained everything. Everard was left to the society of M. de Mirfleur and the children, who grew very fond of him, and indeed it was he who derived the most advantage from his week in Normandy, if he had only been able to see it in that light. But I am not sure that he did not think the renewed devotion of friendship between the brother and sister excessive; for it was not until they were ploughing the stormy seas on the voyage from Havre, which was their nearest seaport, to England, that he had so much as a chance of a conversation with Reine. Herbert, bound to be well on his triumphal return home, had been persuaded to go below and escape the night air. But Reine, who was in a restless condition, full of suppressed excitement, and a tolerable sailor besides, could not keep still. She came up to the deck when the night was gathering, the dark waves running swiftly by the ship's side, the night-air blowing strong (for there was no wind, the sailors said) through the bare cordage, and carrying before it the huge black pennon of smoke from the funnel.

The sea was not rough. There was something congenial to the commotion and excitement of Reine's spirit in the throb and bound of the steamer, and in the dark waves, with their ceaseless movement, through which, stormy and black and full of mysterious life as they looked, the blacker solid hull pushed its resistless way. She liked the strong current of the air, and the sense of progress, and even the half-terror of that dark world in which this little floating world held its own between sky and sea. Everard tossed his cigar over the ship's side when he saw her, and came eagerly forward and drew her hand through his arm. It was the first time he had been able to say a word to her since they met. But even then Reine's first question was not encouraging.

"How do you think Bertie is looking?" she said.

Every man, however, be his temper ever so touchy, can be patient when the inducement is strong enough. Everard, though deeply tempted to make a churlish answer, controlled himself in a second, and replied—

"Very well, I think; not robust, perhaps, Reine; you must not expect him all at once to look robust."

"I suppose not," she said, with a sigh.

"But quite well, which is much more important. It is not the degree, but the kind, that is to be looked at," said Everard, with a great show of wisdom. "Strength is one thing, health is another; and it is not the most robustious men," he went on with a smile, "who live longest, Reine."

"I suppose not," she repeated. Then after a pause, "Do you think, from what you have seen of him, that he will be active and take up a country life? There is not much going on at Whiteladies; you say you found your life dull?"

"To excuse myself for coming when you called upon me, Reine."

"Ah! but I did not call you. I never should have ventured. Everard, you are doing me injustice. How could I have taken so much upon myself?"

"I wish you would take a great deal more upon yourself. You did, Reine. You said, 'Stand in my place.'"

"Yes, I know; my heart was breaking. Forgive me, Everard. Whom could I ask but you?"

"I will forgive you anything you like, if you say that. And I did take your place, Reine. I did not want to, mind you—I wanted to be with you, not Bertie—but I did."

"Everard, you are kind, and so cruel. Thanks! thanks a thousand times!"

"I do not want to be thanked," he said, standing over her; for she had drawn her hand from his arm, and was standing by the steep stairs which led below, ready for escape. "I don't care for thanks. I want to be rewarded. I am not one of the generous kind. I did not do it for nothing. Pay me, Reine!"

Reine looked him in the face very sedately. I do not think that his rudeness alarmed, or even annoyed her, to speak of. A gleam of malice came into her eyes; then a gleam of something else, which was, though it was hard to see it, a tear. Then she suddenly took his hand, kissed it before Everard had time to stop her, and fled below. And when she reached the safe refuge of the ladies' cabin, where no profane foot could follow her, Reine took off her hat, and shook down her hair, which was all blown about by the wind, and laughed to herself. When she turned her eyes to the dismal little swinging lamp overhead, that dolorous light reflected itself in such glimmers of sunshine as it had never seen before.

How gay the girl felt! and mischievous, like a kitten. Pay him! Reine sat down on the darksome hair-cloth sofa in the corner, with wicked smiles curling the corners of her mouth; and then she put her hands over her face, and cried. The other ladies, poor souls! were asleep or poorly, and paid no attention to all this pantomime. It was the happiest moment she had had for years, and this is how she ran away from it; but I don't think that the running away made her enjoy it the less.

As for Everard, he was left on deck feeling somewhat discomfited. It was the second time this had happened to him. She had kissed his hand before, and he had been angry and ashamed, as it was natural a man should be, of such an inappropriate homage. He had thought, to tell the truth, that his demand for payment was rather an original way of making a proposal; and he felt himself laughed at, which is, of all things in the world, the thing most trying to a lover's feelings. But after awhile, when he had lighted and smoked a cigar, and fiercely perambulated the deck for ten minutes, he calmed down, and began to enter into the spirit of the situation. Such a response, if it was intensely provoking, was not, after all, very discouraging. He went downstairs after awhile (having, as the reader will perceive, his attack of the love-sickness rather badly), and looked at Herbert, who was extended on another dismal sofa, similar to the one on which Reine indulged her malice, and spread a warm rug over him, and told him the hour, and that "we're getting on famously, old fellow!" with the utmost sweetness. But he could not himself rest in the dreary cabin, under the swinging lamp, and went back on deck, where there was something more congenial in the fresh air, the waves running high, the clouds breaking into dawn.

They arrived in the afternoon by a train which had been selected for them by instructions from Whiteladies; and no sooner had they reached the station than the evidence of a great reception made itself apparent. The very station was decorated as if for royalty. Just outside was an arch made of green branches, and sweet with white boughs of the blossomed May. Quite a crowd of people were waiting to welcome the travellers—the tenants before mentioned, not a very large band, the village people in a mass, the clergy, and several of the neighbors in their carriages, including the Farrel-Austins. Everybody who had any right to such a privilege pressed forward to shake hands with Herbert. "Welcome home!" they cried, cheering the young man, who was so much surprised and affected that he could scarcely speak to them. As for Reine, between crying and smiling, she was incapable of anything, and had to be almost lifted into the carriage. Kate and Sophy Farrel-Austin waved their handkerchiefs and their parasols, and called out, "Welcome, Bertie!" over the heads of the other people. They were all invited to a great dinner at Whiteladies on the next day, at which half the county was to be assembled; and Herbert and Reine were especially touched by the kind looks of their cousins. "I used not to like them," Reine said, when the first moment of emotion was over, and they were driving along the sunny high-road toward Whiteladies; "it shows how foolish one's judgments are;" while Herbert declared "they were always jolly girls, and, by Jove! as pretty as any he had seen for ages." Everard did not say anything; but then they had taken no notice of him. He was on the back seat, not much noticed by any one; but Herbert and Reine were the observed of all observers. There were two or three other arches along the rural road, and round each a little group of the country folks, pleased with the little show, and full of kindly welcomes. In front of the Almshouses all the old people were drawn up, and a large text, done in flowers, stretched along the front of the old red-brick building. "I cried unto the Lord, and He heard me," was the inscription; and trim old Dr. Richard, in his trim canonicals, stood at the gate in the centre of his flock when the carriage stopped.

Herbert jumped down amongst them with his heart full, and spoke to the old people; while Reine sat in the carriage, and cried, and held out her hands to her friends. Miss Augustine had wished to be there too, among the others who, she thought, had brought Herbert back to life by their prayers; but her sister had interposed strenuously, and this had been given up. When the Almshouses were passed there was another arch, the finest of all. It was built up into high columns of green on each side, and across the arch was the inscription, "As welcome as the flowers in May," curiously worked in hawthorn blossoms, with dropping ornaments of the wild blue hyacinth from each initial letter. It was so pretty that they stopped the carriage to look at it, amid the cheers of some village people who clustered round, for it was close to the village. Among them stood a tall, beautiful young woman, in a black dress, with a rosy, fair-haired boy, whose hat was decorated with the same wreath of May and hyacinth. Even in that moment of excitement, both brother and sister remarked her. "Who was that lady?—you bowed to her," said Reine, as soon as they had passed. "By Jove! how handsome she was!" said Herbert. Everard only smiled, and pointed out to them the servants about the gate of Whiteladies, and Miss Susan and Miss Augustine standing out in the sunshine in their gray gowns. The young people threw the carriage doors open at either side, and had alighted almost before it stopped. And then came that moment of inarticulate delight, when friends meet after a long parting, when questions are asked in a shower and no one answers, and the eyes that have not seen each other for so long look through and through the familiar faces, leaping to quick conclusions. Everard (whom no one took any notice of) kept still in the carriage, which had drawn up at the gate, and surveyed this scene from his elevation with a sense of disadvantage, yet superiority. He was out of all the excitement and commotion. Nobody could look at him, bronzed and strong, as if he had just come back from the edge of the grave; but from his position of vantage he saw everything. He saw Miss Susan's anxious survey of Herbert, and the solemn, simple complaisance on poor Augustine's face, who felt it was her doing—hers and that of her old feeble chorus in the Almshouses; and he saw Reine pause, with her arms round Miss Susan's neck, to look her closely in the eyes, asking, "What is it? what is it?" not in words, but with an alarmed look. Everard knew, as if he had seen into her heart, that Reine had found out something strange in Miss Susan's eyes, and thinking of only one thing that could disturb her, leaped with a pang to the conclusion that Herbert was not looking so well or so strong as she had supposed. And I think that Everard, in the curious intuition of that moment when he was nothing but an onlooker, discovered also, that though Miss Susan looked so anxiously at Herbert, she scarcely saw him, and formed no opinion about his health, having something else much more keen and close in her mind.

"And here is Everard too," Miss Susan said; "he is not such a stranger as you others. Come, Everard, and help us to welcome them; and come in, Bertie, to your own house. Oh, how glad we all are to see you here!"

"Aunt Susan," said Reine, whispering in her ear, "I see by your eyes that you think he is not strong still."

"By my eyes?" said Miss Susan, too much confused by many emotions to understand; but she made no disclaimer, only put her hand over her eyebrows, and led Herbert to the old porch, everybody following almost solemnly. Such a home-coming could scarcely fail to be somewhat solemn as well as glad. "My dear," she said, pausing on the threshold, "God bless you! God has brought you safe back when we never expected it. We should all say thank God, Bertie, when we bring you in at your own door."

And she stood with her hand on his shoulder, and stretched up to him (for he had grown tall in his illness) and kissed him, with one or two tears dropping on her cheeks. Herbert's eyes were wet too. He was very accessible to emotion; he turned round to the little group who were all so dear and familiar, with his lip quivering. "I have most reason of all to say, 'Thank God;'" the young man said, with his heart full, standing there on his own threshold, which, a little while before, no one had hoped to see him cross again.

Just then the little gate which opened into Priory Lane, and was opposite the old porch, was pushed open, and two people came in. The jar of the gate as it opened caught everybody's ear; and Herbert in particular, being somewhat excited, turned hastily to see what the interruption was. It was the lady to whom Everard had bowed, who had been standing under the triumphal arch as they passed. She approached them, crossing the lawn with a familiar, assured step, leading her child. Miss Susan, who had been standing close by him, her hand still fondly resting on Herbert's shoulder, started at sight of the new-comer, and withdrew quickly, impatiently from his side; but the young man, naturally enough, had no eyes for what his old aunt was doing, but stood quite still, unconscious, in his surprise, that he was staring at the beautiful stranger. Reine, standing just behind him, stared too, equally surprised, but searching in her more active brain what it meant. Giovanna came straight up to the group in the porch. "Madame Suzanne?" she said, with a self-possession which seemed to have deserted the others. Miss Susan obeyed the summons with tremulous haste. She came forward growing visibly pale in her excitement. "Herbert," she said, "and Reine," making a pause after the words, "this is a—lady who is staying here. This is Madame Jean Austin from Bruges, of whom you have heard—"

"And her child," said Giovanna, putting him forward.

"Madame Jean? who is Madame Jean?" said Herbert, whispering to his aunt, after he had bowed to the stranger. Giovanna was anxious about this meeting, and her ears were very sharp, and she heard the question. Her great black eyes shone, and she smiled upon the young man, who was more deeply impressed by her sudden appearance than words could say.

"Monsieur," she said with a curtsey, smiling, "it is the little child who is the person to look at, not me. Me, I am simple Giovanna, the widow of Jean; nobody; but the little boy is most to you: he is the heir."

"The heir?" said Herbert, turning a little pale. He looked round upon the others with bewilderment, asking explanations; then suddenly recollecting, said, "Ah, I understand; the next of kin that was lost. I had forgotten. Then, Aunt Susan, this is my heir?"

"Yes," she said, with blanched lips. She could not have uttered another word, had it been to deliver herself and the race from this burden forever.

Giovanna had taken the child into her arms. At this moment she swung him down lightly as a feather on to the raised floor of the porch, where they were all standing. "Jean," she cried, "ton devoir!" The baby turned his blue eyes upon her, half frightened; then looked round the strange faces about him, struggling with an inclination to cry; then, mustering his faculties, took his little cap off with the gravity of a judge, and flinging it feebly in the air, shouted out, "Vive M. 'Erbert!" "Encore," cried Giovanna. "Vive Monsieur 'Erbert!" said the little fellow loudly, with a wave of his small hand.

This little performance had a very curious effect upon the assembled party. Surprise and pleasure shone in Herbert's eyes; he was quite captivated by this last scene of his reception; and even Everard, though he knew better, was charmed by the beautiful face and beautiful attitude of the young woman, who stood animated and blooming, like the leader of an orchestra, on the lawn outside. But Reine's suspicions darted up like an army in ambush all in a moment, though she could not tell what she was suspicious of. As for Miss Susan, she stood with her arms dropped by her side, her face fallen blank. All expression seemed to have gone out from it, everything but a kind of weary pain.

"Who is she, Reine? Everard, who is she?" Herbert whispered anxiously, when, some time later, the three went off together to visit their childish haunts; the old playroom, the musicians' gallery, the ancient corridors in which they had once frolicked. Miss Susan had come upstairs with them, but had left them for the moment. "Tell me, quick, before Aunt Susan comes back."

"Ah!" cried Reine, with a laugh, though I don't think she was really merry, "this is the old time back again, indeed, when we must whisper and have secrets as soon as Aunt Susan is away."

"But who is she?" said Herbert. They had come into the gallery overlooking the hall, where the table was already spread for dinner. Giovanna was walking round it, with her child perched on her shoulder. At the sound of the steps and voices above she turned round, and waved her hand to them. "Vive Monsieur 'Erbert!" she sang, in a melodious voice which filled all the echoes. She was so strong that it was nothing to her to hold the baby poised on her shoulder, while she pointed up to the figures in the gallery and waved her hand to them. The child, bolder this time, took up his little shout with a crow of pleasure. The three ghosts in the gallery stood and looked down upon this pretty group with very mingled feelings. But Herbert, for his part, being very sensitive to all homage, felt a glow of pleasure steal over him. "When a man has a welcome like this," he said to himself, "it is very pleasant to come home!"

CHAPTER XXXVIII

"Me! I am nobody," said Giovanna. "Ces dames have been very kind to me. I was the son's widow, the left-out one at home. Does mademoiselle understand? But then you can never have been the left-out one—the one who was always wrong."

"No," said Reine. She was not, however, so much touched by this confidence as Herbert, who, though he was not addressed, was within hearing, and gave very distracted answers to Miss Susan, who was talking to him, by reason of listening to what Giovanna said.

"But I knew that the petit was not nobody, like me; and I brought him here. He is the next, till M. Herbert will marry, and have his own heirs. This is what I desire, mademoiselle, believe me—for now I love Viteladies, not for profit, but for love. It was for money I came at first," she said with a laugh, "to live; but now I have de l'amitié for every one, even this old Stefen, who do not love me nor my child."

She said this laughing, while Stevens stood before her with the tray in his hands, serving her with tea; and I leave the reader to divine the feelings of that functionary, who had to receive this direct shaft levelled at him, and make no reply. Herbert, whose attention by this time had been quite drawn away from Miss Susan, laughed too. He turned his chair round to take part in this talk, which was much more interesting than anything his aunt had to say.

"That was scarcely fair," he said; "the man hearing you; for he dared not say anything in return, you know."

"Oh, he do dare say many things!" said Giovanna. "I like to have my little revenge, me. The domestics did not like me at first, M. Herbert; I know not why. It is the nature of you other English not to love the foreigner. You are proud. You think yourselves more good than we."

"Not so, indeed!" cried Herbert, eagerly; "just the reverse, I think. Besides, we are half foreign ourselves, Reine and I."

"Whatever you may be, Herbert, I count myself pure English," said Reine, with dignity. She was suspicious and disturbed, though she could not tell why.

"Mademoiselle has reason," said Giovanna. "It is very fine to be English. One can feel so that one is more good than all the world! As soon as I can speak well enough, I shall say so too. I am of no nation at present, me—Italian born, Belge by living—and the Belges are not a people. They are a little French, a little Flemish, not one thing or another. I prefer to be English, too. I am Austin, like all you others, and Viteladies is my 'ome."

This little speech made the others look at each other, and Herbert laughed with a curious consciousness. Whiteladies was his. He had scarcely ever realized it before. He did not even feel quite sure now that he was not here on a visit, his Aunt Susan's guest. Was it the others who were his guests, all of them, from Miss Susan herself, who had always been the 'Squire, down to this piquant stranger? Herbert laughed with a sense of pleasure and strangeness, and shy, boyish wonder whether he should say something about being glad to see her there, or be silent. Happily, he decided that silence was the right thing, and nobody spoke for the moment. Giovanna, however, who seemed to have taken upon her to amuse the company, soon resumed:

"In England it is not amusing, the Winter, M. Herbert. Ah, mon Dieu! what a consolation to make the garlands to build up the arch! Figure to yourself that I was up at four o'clock this morning, and all the rooms full of those pretty aubépines, which you call May. My fingers smell of it now; and look, how they are pricked!" she said, holding them out. She had a pretty hand, large like her person, but white and shapely, and strong. There was a force about it, and about the solid round white arm with which she had tossed about the heavy child, which had impressed Herbert greatly at the time; and its beauty struck him all the more now, from the sense of strength connected with it—strength and vitality, which in his weakness seemed to him the grandest things in the world.

"Did you prick your fingers for me?" he said, quite touched by this devotion to his service; and but for his shyness, and the presence of so many people, I think he would have ventured to kiss the wounded hand. But as it was, he only looked at it, which Reine did also with a half-disdainful civility, while Everard peeped over her shoulder, half laughing. Miss Susan had pushed her chair away.

"Not for you altogether," said Giovanna, frankly, "for I did not know you, M. Herbert; but for pleasure, and to amuse myself; and perhaps a little that you and mademoiselle might have de l'amitié for me when you knew. What is de l'amitié in English? Friendship—ah, that is grand, serious, not what I mean. And we must not say love—that is too much, that is autre chose."

Herbert, charmed, looking at the beautiful speaker, thought she blushed; and this moved him mightily, for Giovanna was not like a little girl at a dance, an ingénue, who blushed for nothing. She was a woman, older than himself, and not pretty, but grand and great and beautiful; nor ignorant, but a woman who knew more of that wonderful "life" which dazzled the boy—a great deal more than he himself did, or any one here. That she should blush while she spoke to him was in some way an intoxicating compliment to Herbert's own influence and manly power.

"You mean like," said Reine, who persistently acted the part of a wet blanket. "That is what we say in English, when it means something not so serious as friendship and not so close as love—a feeling on the surface; when you would say 'Il me plait' in French, in English you say 'I like him.' It means just that, and no more."

Giovanna shrugged her shoulders with a little shiver. "Comme c'est froid, ça!" she said, snatching up Miss Susan's shawl, which lay on a chair, and winding it round her. Miss Susan half turned round, with a consciousness that something of hers was being touched, but she said nothing, and her eye was dull and veiled. Reine, who knew that her aunt did not like her properties interfered with, was more surprised than ever, and half alarmed, though she did not know why.

"Ah, yes, it is cold, very cold, you English," said Giovanna, unwinding the shawl again, and stretching it out behind her at the full extent of her white arms. How the red drapery threw out her fine head, with the close braids of black hair, wavy and abundant, twined round and round it, in defiance of fashion! Her hair was not at all the hair of the period, either in color or texture. It was black and glossy and shining, as dark hair ought to be; and she was pale, with scarcely any color about her except her lips. "Ah, how it is cold! Mademoiselle Reine, I will not say like—I will say de l'amitié! It is more sweet. And then, if it should come to be love after, it will be more natural," she said with a smile.

I do not know if it was her beauty, to which women are, I think, almost more susceptible than men, vulgar prejudice notwithstanding—or perhaps it was something ingratiating and sweet in her smile; but Reine's suspicions and her coldness quite unreasonably gave way, as they had quite unreasonably sprung up, and she drew nearer to the stranger and opened her heart unawares, while the young men struck in, and the conversation became general. Four young people chattering all together, talking a great deal of nonsense, running into wise speculations, into discussions about the meaning of words, like and love, and de l'amitié!—one knows what a pleasant jumble it is, and how the talkers enjoy it; all the more as they are continually skimming the surface of subjects which make the nerves tingle and the heart beat. The old room grew gay with the sound of their voices, soft laughter, and exclamations which gave variety to the talk. Curious! Miss Susan drew her chair a little more apart. It was she who was the one left out. In her own house, which was not her own house any longer—in the centre of the kingdom where she had been mistress so long, but was no more mistress. She said to herself, with a little natural bitterness, that perhaps it was judicious and really kind, after all, on the part of Herbert and Reine, to do it at once, to leave no doubt on the subject, to supplant her then and there, keeping up no fiction of being her guests still, or considering her the head of the house. Much better, and on the whole more kind! for of course everything else would be a fiction. Her reign had been long, but it was over. The change must be made some time, and when so well, so appropriately as now? After awhile she went softly round behind the group, and secured her shawl. She did not like her personal properties interfered with. No one had ever done it except this daring creature, and it was a thing Miss Susan was not prepared to put up with. She could bear the great downfall which was inevitable, but these small annoyances she could not bear. She secured her shawl, and brought it with her, hanging it over the back of her chair. But when she got up and when she reseated herself, no one took any notice. She was already supplanted and set aside, the very first night! It was sudden, she said to herself with a catching of the breath, but on the whole it was best.

I need not say that Reine and Herbert were totally innocent of any such intention, and that it was the inadvertence of their youth that was to blame, and nothing else. By-and-by the door opened softly, and Miss Augustine came in. She had been attending a special evening service at the Almshouses—a thanksgiving for Herbert's return. She had, a curious decoration for her, a bit of flowering May in the waistband of her dress, and she brought in the sweet freshness of the night with her, and the scent of the hawthorn, special and modest gem of the May from which it takes its name. She broke up without any hesitation the lively group, which Miss Susan, sore and sad, had withdrawn from. Augustine was a woman of one idea, and had no room in her mind for anything else. Like Monsieur and Madame de Mirfleur, though in a very different way, many things were tout simple to her, against which many less single-minded persons broke their heads, if not their hearts.

"You should have come with me, Herbert," she said, half disapproving. "You may be tired, but there could be nothing more refreshing than to give thanks. Though perhaps," she added, folding her hands, "it was better that the thanksgiving should be like the prayers, disinterested, no personal feeling mixing in. Yes, perhaps that was best. Giovanna, you should have been there."

"Ah, pardon!" said Giovanna, with a slight imperceptible yawn, "it was to welcome mademoiselle and monsieur that I stayed. Ah! the musique! Tenez! ma sœur, I will make the music with a very good heart, now."

"That is a different thing," said Miss Augustine. "They trusted to you—though to me the hymns they sing themselves are more sweet than yours. One voice may be pleasant to hear, but it is but one. When all sing, it is like heaven, where that will be our occupation night and day."

"Ah, ma sœur," said Giovanna, "but there they will sing in tune, n'est ce pas, all the old ones? Tenez! I will make the music now."

And with this she went straight to the piano, uninvited, unbidden, and began a Te Deum out of one of Mozart's masses, the glorious rolling strains of which filled not only the room, but the house. Giovanna scarcely knew how to play; her science was all of the ear. She gave the sentiment of the music, rather than its notes—a reminiscence of what she had heard—and then she sang that most magnificent of hymns, pouring it forth, I suppose, from some undeveloped instinct of art in her, with a fervency and power which the bystanders were fain to think only the highest feeling could inspire. She was not bad, though she did many wrong things with the greatest equanimity; yet we know that she was not good either, and could not by any chance have really had the feeling which seemed to swell and tremble in her song. I don't pretend to say how this was; but it is certain that stupid people, carnal and fleshly persons, sing thus often as if their whole heart, and that the heart of a seraph, was in the strain. Giovanna sang so that she brought the tears to their eyes. Reine stole away out from among the others, and put herself humbly behind the singer, and joined her soft voice, broken with tears, to hers. Together they appealed to prophets, and martyrs, and apostles, to praise the God who had wrought this deliverance, like so many others. Herbert, for whom it all was, hid his face in his clasped hands, and felt that thrill of awed humility, yet of melting, tender pride, with which the single soul recognizes itself as the hero, the object of such an offering. He could not face the light, with his eyes and his heart so full. Who was he, that so much had been done for him? And yet, poor boy, there was a soft pleased consciousness in his heart that there must be something in him, more than most, to warrant that which had been done. Augustine stood upright by the mantelpiece, with her arms folded in her sleeves, and her poor visionary soul still as usual. To her this was something like a legal acknowledgment—a receipt, so to speak, for value received. It was due to God, who, for certain inducements of prayer, had consented to do what was asked of Him. She had already thanked Him, and with all her heart; and she was glad that every one should thank Him, that there should be no stint of praise. Miss Susan was the only one who sat unmoved, and even went on with her knitting. To some people of absolute minds one little rift within the lute makes mute all the music. For my part, I think Giovanna, though her code of truth and honor was very loose, or indeed one might say non-existent—and though she had schemes in her mind which no very high-souled person could have entertained—was quite capable of being sincere in her thanksgiving, and not at all incapable of some kinds of religious feeling; and though she could commit a marked and unmistakable act of dishonesty without feeling any particular trouble in her conscience, was yet an honest soul in her way. This is one of the paradoxes of humanity, which I don't pretend to understand and cannot explain, yet believe in. But Miss Susan did not believe in it. She thought it desecration to hear those sacred words coming forth from this woman's mouth. In her heart she longed to get up in righteous wrath, and turn the deceiver out of the house. But, alas! what could she do? She too was a deceiver, more than Giovanna, and dared not interfere with Giovanna, lest she should be herself betrayed; and last of all, and, for the moment, almost bitterest of all, it was no longer her house, and she had no right to turn any one out, or take any one in, any more forever!

"Who is she? Where did they pick her up? How do they manage to keep her here, a creature like that?" said Herbert to Everard, as they lounged together for half an hour in the old playroom, which had been made into a smoking-room for the young men. Herbert was of opinion that to smoke a cigar before going to bed was a thing that every man was called upon to do. Those who did not follow this custom were boys or invalids; and though he was not fond of it, he went through the ceremony nightly. He could talk of nothing but Giovanna, and it was with difficulty that Everard prevailed upon him to go to his room after all the emotions of the day.

"I want to know how they have got her to stay," he said, trying to detain his cousin that he might go on talking on this attractive subject.

"You should ask Aunt Susan," said Everard, not shrugging his shoulders. He himself was impressed in this sort of way by Giovanna. He thought her very handsome, and very clever, giving her credit for a greater amount of wisdom than she really possessed, and setting down all she had done and all she had said to an elaborate scheme, which was scarcely true; for the dangerous point in Giovanna's wiles was that they were half nature, something spontaneous and unconscious being mixed up in every one of them. Everard resolved to warn Miss Susan, and put her on her guard, and he groaned to himself over the office of guardian and protector to this boy which had been thrust upon him. The wisest man in the world could not keep a boy of three-and-twenty out of mischief. He had done his best for him, but it was not possible to do any more.

While he was thinking thus, and Herbert was walking about his room in a pleasant ferment of excitement and pleasure, thinking over all that had happened, and the flattering attention that had been shown to him on all sides, two other scenes were going on in different rooms, which bore testimony to a kindred excitement. In the first the chief actor was Giovanna, who had gone to her chamber in a state of high delight, feeling the ball at her feet, and everything in her power. She did not object to Herbert himself; he was young and handsome, and would never have the power to coerce and control her; and she had no intention of being anything but good to him. She woke the child, to whom she had carried some sweetmeats from the dessert, and played with him and petted him—a most immoral proceeding, as any mother will allow; for by the time she was sleepy, and ready to go to bed, little Jean was broad awake, and had to be frightened and threatened with black closets and black men before he could be hushed into quiet; and the untimely bon-bons made him ill. Giovanna had not thought of all that. She wanted some one to help her to get rid of her excitement, and disturbed the baby's childish sleep, and deranged his stomach, without meaning him any harm. I am afraid, however, it made little difference to Jean that she was quite innocent of any evil intention, and indeed believed herself to be acting the part of a most kind and indulgent mother.

But while Giovanna was playing with the child, Reine stole into Miss Susan's room to disburden her soul, and seek that private delight of talking a thing over which women love. She stole in with the lightest tap, scarcely audible, noiseless, in her white dressing-gown, and light foot; and in point of fact Miss Susan did not hear that soft appeal for admission. Therefore she was taken by surprise when Reine appeared. She was seated in a curious blank and stupor, "anywhere," not on her habitual chair by the side of the bed, where her table stood with her books on it, and where her lamp was burning, but near the door, on the first chair she had come to, with that helpless forlorn air which extreme feebleness or extreme preoccupation gives. She aroused herself with a look of almost terror when she saw Reine, and started from her seat.

"How you frightened me!" she said fretfully. "I thought you had been in bed. After your journey and your fatigue, you ought to be in bed."

"I wanted to talk with you," said Reine. "Oh, Aunt Susan, it is so long—so long since we were here; and I wanted to ask you, do you think he looks well? Do you think he looks strong? You have something strange In your eyes, Aunt Susan. Oh, tell me if you are disappointed—if he does not look so well as you thought."

Miss Susan made a pause; and then she answered as if with difficulty, "Your brother? Oh, yes, I think he is looking very well—better even than I thought."

Reine came closer to her, and putting one soft arm into hers, looked at her, examining her face with wistful eyes—"Then what is it, Aunt Susan?" she said.

"What is—what? I do not understand you," cried Miss Susan, shifting her arm, and turning away her face. "You are tired, and you are fantastic, as you always were. Reine, go to bed."

"Dear Aunt Susan," cried Reine, "don't put me away. You are not vexed with us for coming back?—you are not sorry we have come? Oh, don't turn your face from me! You never used to turn from me, except when I had done wrong. Have we done wrong, Herbert or I?"

"No, child, no—no, I tell you! Oh, Reine, don't worry me now. I have enough without that—I cannot bear any more."

Miss Susan shook off the clinging hold. She roused herself and walked across the room, and put off her shawl, which she had drawn round her shoulders to come upstairs. She had not begun to undress, though Martha by this time was fast asleep. In the trouble of her mind she had sent Martha also away. She took off her few ornaments with trembling hands, and put them down on the table.

"Go to bed, Reine; I am tired too—forgive me, dear," she said with a sigh, "I cannot talk to you to-night."

"What is it, Aunt Susan?" said Reine softly, looking at her with anxious eyes.

"It is nothing—nothing! only I cannot talk to you. I am not angry; but leave me, dear child, leave me for to-night."

"Aunt Susan," said the girl, going up to her again, and once more putting an arm round her, "it is something about—that woman. If it is not us, it is her. Why does she trouble you?—why is she here? Don't send me away, but tell me about her! Dear Aunt Susan, you are ill, you are looking so strange, not like yourself. Tell me—I belong to you. I can understand you better than any one else."

"Oh, hush, hush, Reine; you don't know what you are saying. It is nothing, child, nothing! You understand me?"

"Better than any one," cried the girl, "for I belong to you. I can read what is in your face. None of the others know, but I saw it. Aunt Susan, tell me—whisper—I will keep it sacred, whatever it is, and it will do you good."

Miss Susan leaned her head upon the fragile young creature who clung to her. Reine, so slight and young, supported the stronger, older woman, with a force which was all of the heart and soul; but no words came from the sufferer's lips. She stood clasping the girl close to her, and for a moment gave way to a great sob, which shook her like a convulsion. The touch, the presence, the innocent bosom laid against her own in all that ignorant instinctive sympathy which is the great mystery of kindred, did her good. Then she kissed the girl tenderly, and sent her away.

"God bless you, darling! though I am not worthy to say it—not worthy!" said the woman, trembling, who had always seemed to Reine the very emblem of strength, authority, and steadfast power.

She stole away, quite hushed and silenced, to her room. What could this be? Not worthy! Was it some religious panic that had seized upon Miss Susan—some horror of doubt and darkness, like that which Reine herself had passed through? This was the only thing the girl could think of. Pity kept her from sleeping, and breathed a hundred prayers through her mind, as she lay and listened to the old clock, telling the hours with its familiar voice. Very familiar, and yet novel and strange—more strange than if she had never heard it before—though for many nights, year after year, it had chimed through her dreams, and woke her to many another soft May morning, more tranquil and more sweet even than this.

CHAPTER XXXIX

Next day was the day of the great dinner to which Miss Susan had invited half the county, to welcome the young master of the house, and mark the moment of her own withdrawal from her long supremacy in Whiteladies. Though she had felt with some bitterness on the previous night the supposed intention of Herbert and Reine to supplant her at once, Miss Susan was far too sensible a woman to make voluntary vexation for herself, out of an event so well known and long anticipated. That she must feel it was of course inevitable, but as she felt no real wrong in it, and had for a long time expected it, there was not, apart from the painful burden on her mind which threw a dark shadow over everything, any bitterness in the necessary and natural event. She had made all her arrangements without undue fuss or publicity, and had prepared for herself, as I have said, a house, which had providentially fallen vacant, on the other side of the village, where Augustine would still be within reach of the Almshouses. I am not sure that, so far as she was herself concerned, the sovereign of Whiteladies, now on the point of abdication, would not have preferred to be a little further off, out of daily sight of her forsaken throne; but this would have deprived Augustine of all that made life to her, and Miss Susan was too strong, too proud, and too heroic, to hesitate for a moment, or to think her own sentiment worth indulging. Perhaps, indeed, even without that powerful argument of Augustine, she would have scorned to indulge a feeling which she could not have failed to recognize as a mean and petty one. She had her faults, like most people, and she had committed a great wrong, which clouded her life, but there was nothing petty or mean about Miss Susan. After Reine had left her on the previous night, she had made a great effort, and recovered her self-command. I don't know why she had allowed herself to be so beaten down. One kind of excitement, no doubt, predisposes toward another; and after the triumph and joy of Herbert's return, her sense of the horrible cloud which hung over her personally, the revelation which Giovanna at any moment had it in her power to make, the evident intention she had of ingratiating herself with the new-comers, and the success so far of the attempt, produced a reaction which almost drove Miss Susan wild! If you will think of it, she had cause enough. She, heretofore an honorable and spotless woman, who had never feared the face of man, to lie now under the horrible risk of being found out—to be at the mercy of a passionate, impulsive creature, who could at any moment cover her with shame, and pull her down from her pedestal. I think that at such moments to have the worst happen, to be pulled down finally, to have her shame published to the world, would have been the best thing that could have happened to Miss Susan. She would then have raised up her humbled head again, and accepted her punishment, and faced the daylight, free from fear of anything that could befall her. The worst of it all now was this intolerable sense that there was something to be found out, that everything was not honest and open in her life, as it had always been. And by times this consciousness overpowered and broke her down, as it had done on the previous night. But when a vigorous soul is thus overpowered and breaks down, the moment of its utter overthrow marks a new beginning of power and endurance. The old fable of Antæus, who derived fresh strength whenever he was thrown, from contact with his mother earth, is profoundly true. Miss Susan had been thrown too, had fallen, and had rebounded with fresh force. Even Reine could scarcely see in her countenance next morning any trace of the emotion of last night. She took her place at the breakfast-table with a smile, with composure which was not feigned, putting bravely her burden behind her, and resolute to make steady head as long as she could against any storm that could threaten. Even when Herbert eluded that "business consultation," and begged to be left free to roam about the old house, and renew his acquaintance with every familiar corner, she was able to accept the postponement without pain. She watched the young people go out even with almost pleasure—the brother and sister together, and Everard—and Giovanna at the head of the troop, with little Jean perched on her shoulder. Giovanna was fond of wandering about without any covering on her head, having a complexion which I suppose would not spoil, and loving the sun. And it suited her somehow to have the child on her shoulder, to toss him about, to the terror of all the household, in her strong, beautiful arms. I rather think it was because the household generally was frightened by this rough play, that Giovanna had taken to it; for she liked to shock them, not from malice, but from a sort of school-boy mischief. Little Jean, who had got over all his dislike to her, enjoyed his perch upon her shoulder; and it is impossible to tell how Herbert admired her, her strength, her quick, swift, easy movements, the lightness and grace with which she carried the boy, and all her gambols with him, in which a certain risk always mingled. He could not keep his eyes from her, and followed wherever she led, penetrating into rooms where, in his delicate boyhood, he had never been allowed to go.

"I know myself in every part," cried Giovanna gayly. "I have all visited, all seen, even where it is not safe. It is safe here, M. Herbert. Come then and look at the carvings, all close; they are beautiful when you are near."

They followed her about within and without, as if she had been the cicerone, though they had all known Whiteladies long before she had; and even Reine's nascent suspicions were not able to stand before her frank energy and cordial ignorant talk. For she was quite ignorant, and made no attempt to conceal it.

"Me, I love not at all what is so old," she said with a laugh. "I prefer the smooth wall and the big window, and a floor well frotté, that shines. Wood that is all cut like the lace, what good does that do? and brick, that is nothing, that is common. I love stone châteaux, with much of window, and little tourelles at the top. But if you love the wood, and the brick, très bien! I know myself in all the little corners," said Giovanna. And outside and in, it was she who led the way.

Once again—and it was a thing which had repeatedly happened before this, notwithstanding the terror and oppression of her presence—Miss Susan was even grateful to Giovanna, who left her free to make all her arrangements, and amused and interested the new-comers, who were strangers in a sense, though to them belonged the house and everything in it; and I doubt if it had yet entered into her head that Giovanna's society or her beauty involved any danger to Herbert. She was older than Herbert; she was "not a lady;" she was an intruder and alien, and nothing to the young people, though she might amuse them for the moment. The only danger Miss Susan saw in her was one tragic and terrible danger to herself, which she had determined for the moment not to think of. For everybody else she was harmless. So at least Miss Susan, with an inadvertence natural to her preoccupied mind, thought.

And there were a great many arrangements to make for the great dinner, and many things besides that required looking after. However distinctly one has foreseen the necessities of a great crisis, yet it is only when it arrives that they acquire their due urgency. Miss Susan now, for almost the first time, felt the house she had secured at the other end of the village to be a reality. She felt at last that her preparations were real, that the existence in which for the last six months there had been much that was like a painful dream, had come out suddenly into the actual and certain, and that she had had a change to undergo not much unlike the change of death. Things that had been planned only, had to be done now—a difference which is wonderful—and the stir and commotion which had come into the house with the arrival of Herbert was the preface of a commotion still more serious. And as Miss Susan went about giving her orders, she tried to comfort herself with the thought that now at last Giovanna must go. There was no longer any pretence for her stay. Herbert had come home. She had and could have no claim upon Susan and Augustine Austin at the Grange, whatever claim she might have on the inmates of Whiteladies; nor could she transfer herself to the young people, and live with Herbert and Reine. Even she, though she was not reasonable, must see that now there was no further excuse for her presence—that she must go. Miss Susan settled in her mind the allowance she would offer her. It would be a kind of blackmail, blood money, the price of her secret; but better that than exposure. And then, Giovanna had not been disagreeable of late. Rather the reverse; she had tried, as she said, to show de l'amitiè. She had been friendly, cheerful, rather pleasant, in her strange way. Miss Susan, with a curious feeling for which she could not quite account, concluded with herself that she would not wish this creature, who had for so long belonged to her, as it were—who had been one of her family, though she was at the same time her enemy, her greatest trouble—to fall back unaided upon the shop at Bruges, where the people had not been kind to her. No; she would, she said to herself, be very thankful to get rid of Giovanna, but not to see her fall into misery and helplessness. She should have an income enough to keep her comfortable.

This was a luxury which Miss Susan felt she could venture to give herself. She would provide for her persecutor, and get rid of her, and be free of the panic which now was before her night and day. This thought cheered her as she went about, superintending the hanging of the tapestry in the hall, which was only put there on grand occasions, and the building up of the old silver on the great oak buffet. Everything that Whiteladies could do in the way of splendor was to be exhibited to-night. There had been no feast when Herbert came of age, for indeed it had been like enough that his birthday might be his death day also. But now all these clouds had rolled away, and his future was clear. She paid a solemn visit to the cellar with Stevens to get out the best wines, her father's old claret and Madeira, of which she had been so careful, saving it for Herbert; or if not for Herbert, for Everard, whom she had looked upon as her personal heir. Not a bottle of it should ever have gone to Farrel-Austin, the reader may be sure, though she was willing to feast him to-night, and give him of her best, to celebrate her triumph over him—a triumph which, thank heaven! was all innocent, not brought about by plotting or planning—God's doing, and not hers.

I will not attempt to describe all the company, the best people in that corner of Berkshire, who came from all points, through the roads which were white and sweet with May, to do honor to Herbert's home-coming. It is too late in this history, and there is too much of more importance to tell you, to leave me room for those excellent people. Lord Kingsborough was there, and proposed Herbert's health; and Sir Reginald Parke, and Sir Francis Rivers, and the Hon. Mr. Skindle, who married Lord Markinhead's daughter, Lady Cordelia; and all the first company in the county, down to (or up to) the great China merchant who had bought St. Dunstan's, once the property of a Howard. It is rare to see a dinner-party so large or so important, and still more rare to see such a room so filled. The old musicians' gallery was put to its proper use for the first time for years; and now and then, not too often, a soft fluting and piping and fiddling came from the partial gloom, floating over the heads of the well-dressed crowd who sat at the long, splendid table, in a blaze of light and reflection, and silver, and crystal, and flowers.

"I wish we could be in the gallery to see ourselves sitting here, in this great show," Everard whispered to Reine as he passed her to his inferior place; for it was not permitted to Everard on this great occasion to hand in the young mistress of the house, in whose favor Miss Susan intended, after this night, to abdicate. Reine looked up with soft eyes to the dim corner in which the three used to scramble and rustle, and catch the oranges, and I fear thought more of this reminiscence than of what her companion said to her, who was ignorant of the old times. But, indeed, the show was worth seeing from the gallery, where old Martha, and young Jane, and the good French Julie, who had come with Reine, clustered in the children's very corner, keeping out of sight behind the tapestry, and pointing out to each other the ladies and their fine dresses. The maids cared nothing about the gentlemen, but shook their heads over Sophy and Kate's bare shoulders, and made notes of how the dresses were made. Julie communicated her views on the subject with an authority which her auditors received without question, for was not she French?—a large word, which takes in the wilds of Normandy as well as Paris, that centre of the civilized world.

Herbert sat with his back to these eager watchers, at the foot of the table, taking his natural place for the first time, and half hidden by the voluminous robes of Lady Kingsborough and Lady Rivers. The pink gros grain of one of those ladies and the gorgeous white moire of the other dazzled the women in the gallery; but apart from such professional considerations, the scene was a charming one to look at, with the twinkle of the many lights, the brightness of the flowers and the dresses—the illuminated spot in the midst of the partial darkness of the old walls, all gorgeous with color, and movement, and the hum of sound. Miss Susan at the head of the table, in her old point lace, looked like a queen, Martha thought. It was her apotheosis, her climax, the concluding triumph—a sort of phœnix blaze with which she meant to end her life.

The dinner was a gorgeous dinner, worthy the hall and the company; the wine, as I have said, old and rare; and everything went off to perfection. The Farrel-Austins, who were only relations, and not of first importance as county people, sat about the centre of the table, which was the least important place, and opposite to them was Giovanna, who had been put under the charge of old Dr. Richard, to keep her in order, a duty to which he devoted all his faculties. Everything went on perfectly well. The dinner proceeded solemnly, grandly, to its conclusion. Grace—that curious, ill-timed, after-dinner grace which comes just at the daintiest moment of the feast—was duly said; the fruits were being served, forced fruits of every procurable kind, one of the most costly parts of the entertainment at that season; and a general bustle of expectation prepared the way for those congratulatory and friendly speeches, welcomes of his great neighbors to the young Squire, which were the real objects of the assembly. Lord Kingsborough even had cleared his throat for the first time—a signal which his wife heard at the other end, and understood as an intimation that quietness was to be enforced, to which she replied by stopping, to set a good example, in the midst of a sentence. He cleared his throat again, the great man, and was almost on his legs. He was by Miss Susan's side in the place of honor. He was a stout man, requiring some pulling up after dinner when his chair was comfortable—and he had actually put forth one foot, and made his first effort to rise, for the third time clearing his throat.

When—an interruption occurred never to be forgotten in the annals of Whiteladies. Suddenly there was heard a patter of small feet, startling the company; and suddenly a something, a pygmy, a tiny figure, made itself visible in the centre of the table. It stood up beside a great pyramid of flowers, a living decoration, with a little flushed rose-face and flaxen curls showing above the mass of greenery. The great people at the head and the foot of the table stood breathless during the commotion and half-scuffle in the centre of the room which attended this sudden apparition. "What is it?" everybody asked. After that first moment of excited curiosity, it became apparent that it was a child who had been suddenly lifted by some one into that prominent place. The little creature stood still a moment, frightened; then, audibly prompted, woke to its duty. It plucked from its small head a small velvet cap with a white feather, and gave forth its tiny shout, which rang into the echoes.

"Vive M. 'Erbert! vive M. 'Erbert!" cried little Jean, turning round and round, and waving his cap on either side of him. Vague excitement and delight, and sense of importance, and hopes of sugar-plums, inspired the child. He gave forth his little shout with his whole heart, his blue eyes dancing, his little cheeks flushed; and I leave the reader to imagine what a sensation little Jean's unexpected appearance, and still more unexpected shout, produced in the decorous splendor of the great hall.

"Who is it?" "What is it?" "What does it mean?" "Who is the child?" "What does he say?" cried everybody. There got up such a commotion and flutter as dispersed in a moment the respectful silence which had been preparing for Lord Kingsborough. Every guest appealed to his or her neighbor for information, and—except the very few too well-informed, like Dr. Richard, who guilty and self-reproachful, asking himself how he could have prevented it, and what he should say to Miss Susan, sat silent, incapable of speech—every one sent back the question. Giovanna, calm and radiant, alone replied, "It is the next who will succeed," she cried, sending little rills of knowledge on either side of her. "It is Jean Austin, the little heir."

Lord Kingsborough was taken aback, as was natural; but he was a good-natured man, and fond of children. "God bless us!" he said. "Miss Austin, you don't mean to tell me the boy's married, and that's his heir?"

"It is the next of kin," said Miss Susan, with white lips; "no more his heir than I am, but the heir, if Herbert had not lived. Lord Kingsborough, you will forgive the interruption; you will not disappoint us. He is no more Herbert's heir than I am!" again she cried, with a shiver of agitation.

It was the Hon. Mr. Skindle who supported her on the other side; and having heard that there was madness in the Austin family, that gentleman was afraid. "'Gad, she looked as if she would murder somebody," he confided afterward to the friend who drove him home.

"Not his heir, but the heir," said Lord Kingsborough, good-humoredly, "a fine distinction!" and as he was a kind soul, he made another prodigious effort, and got himself out of his seat. He made a very friendly, nice little speech, saying that the very young gentleman who preceded him had indeed taken the wind out of his sails, and forestalled what he had to say; but that, nevertheless, as an old neighbor and family friend, he desired to echo in honest English, and with every cordial sentiment, their little friend's effective speech, and to wish to Herbert Austin, now happily restored to his home in perfect health and vigor, everything, etc.

He went on to tell the assembly what they knew very well; that he had known Herbert's father and grandfather, and had the happiness of a long acquaintance with the admirable ladies who had so long represented the name of Austin among them; and to each he gave an appropriate compliment. In short, his speech composed the disturbed assembly, and brought everything back to the judicious level of a great dinner; and Herbert made his reply with modest self-possession, and the course of affairs, momentarily interrupted, flowed on again according to the programme. But in the centre of the table, where the less important people sat, Giovanna and the child were the centre of attraction. She caught every one's eye, now that attention had been called to her. After he had made the necessary sensation, she took little Jean down from the table, and set him on the carpet, where he ran from one to another, collecting the offerings which every one was ready to give him. Sophy and Kate got hold of him in succession, and crammed him with bonbons, while their father glared at the child across the table. He made his way even so far as Lord Kingsborough, who took him on his knee and patted his curly head. "But the little chap should be in bed," said the kind potentate, who had a great many of his own. Jean escaped a moment after, and ran behind the chairs in high excitement to the next who called him. It was only when the ladies left the room that Giovanna caught him, and swinging him up to her white shoulder, which was not half so much uncovered as Kate's and Sophy's, carried him away triumphant, shouting once more "Vive M. 'Erbert!" from that eminence, as he finally disappeared at the great door.

This was Giovanna's first appearance in public, but it was a memorable one. Poor old Dr. Richard, half weeping, secured Everard as soon as the ladies were gone, and poured his pitiful story into his ears.

"What could I do, Mr. Austin?" cried the poor little, pretty old gentleman. "She took him up before I could think what she was going to do; and you cannot use violence to a lady, sir, you cannot use violence, especially on a festive occasion like this. I should have been obliged to restrain her forcibly, if at all, and what could I do?"

"I am sure you did everything that was necessary," said Everard, with a smile. She was capable of setting Dr. Richard himself on the table, if it had served her purpose, instead of being restrained by him, was what he thought.

CHAPTER XL

The evening came to an end at last. The great people went first, as became them, filling the rural roads with the ponderous rumble of their great carriages and gleam of their lamps. The whole neighborhood was astir. A little crowd of village people had collected round the gates to see the ladies in their fine dresses, and to catch the distant echo of the festivities. There was quite an excitement among them, as carriage after carriage rolled away. The night was soft and warm and light, the moon invisible, but yet shedding from behind the clouds a subdued lightness into the atmosphere. As the company dwindled, and ceremony diminished, a group gradually collected in the great porch, and at last this group dwindled to the family party and the Farrel-Austins, who were the last to go away. This was by no means the desire of their father, who had derived little pleasure from the entertainment. None of those ulterior views which Kate and Sophy had discussed so freely between themselves had been communicated to their father, and he saw nothing but the celebration of his own downfall, and the funeral of his hopes, in this feast, which was all to the honor of Herbert. Consequently, he had been eager to get away at the earliest moment possible, and would even have preceded Lord Kingsborough, could he have moved his daughters, who did not share his feelings. On the contrary, the display which they had just witnessed had produced a very sensible effect upon Kate and Sophy. They were very well off, but they did not possess half the riches of Whiteladies; and the grandeur of the stately old hall, and the importance of the party, impressed these young women of the world. Sophy, who was the younger, was naturally the less affected; but Kate, now five-and-twenty, and beginning to perceive very distinctly that all is vanity, was more moved than I can say. In the intervals of livelier intercourse, and especially during that moment in the drawing-room when the gentlemen were absent—a moment pleasing in its calm to the milder portion of womankind, but which fast young ladies seldom endure with patience—Kate made pointed appeals to her sister's proper feelings.

"If you let all this slip through your fingers, I shall despise you," she said with vehemence.

"Go in for it yourself, then," whispered the bold Sophy; "I shan't object."

But even Sophy was impressed. Her first interest, Lord Alf, had disappeared long ago, and had been succeeded by others, all very willing to amuse themselves and her, as much as she pleased, but all disappearing in their turn to the regions above, or the regions below, equally out of Sophy's reach, whom circumstances shut out from the haunts of blacklegs and sporting men, as well as from the upper world, to which the Lord Alfs of creation belong by nature. Still it was not in Sophy's nature to be so wise as Kate. She was not tired of amusing herself, and had not begun yet to pursue her gayeties with a definite end. Sophy told her friends quite frankly that her sister was "on the look-out." "She has had her fun, and she wants to settle down," the younger said with admirable candor, to the delight and much amusement of her audiences from the Barracks. For this these gentlemen well knew, though both reasonable and virtuous in a man, is not so easily managed in the case of a lady. "By Jove! I shouldn't wonder if she did," was their generous comment. "She has had her fun, by Jove! and who does she suppose would have her?" Yet the best of girls, and the freshest and sweetest, do have these heroes, after a great deal more "fun" than ever could have been within the reach of Kate; for there are disabilities of women which cannot be touched by legislation, and to which the most strong-minded must submit.

However, Sophy and Kate, as I have said, were both moved to exertion by this display of all the grandeur of Whiteladies. They kept their father fuming and fretting outside, while they lingered in the porch with Reine and Herbert. The whole youthful party was there, including Everard and Giovanna, who had at last permitted poor little Jean to be put to bed, but who was still excited by her demonstration, and the splendid company of which she had formed a part.

"How they are dull, these great ladies!" she cried; "but not more dull than ces messieurs, who thought I was mad. Mon Dieu! because I was happy about M. 'Erbert, and that he had come home."

"It was very grand of you to be glad," cried Sophy. "Bertie, you have gone and put everybody out. Why did you get well, sir? Papa pretends to be pleased, too, but he would like to give you strychnine or something. Oh, it wouldn't do us any good, we are only girls; and I think you have a better right than papa."

"Thanks for taking my part," said Herbert, who was a little uncertain how to take this very frank address. A man seldom thinks his own problematical death an amusing incident; but still he felt that to laugh was the right thing to do.

"Oh, of course we take your part," cried Sophy. "We expect no end of fun from you, now you've come back. I am so sick of all those Barrack parties; but you will always have something going on, won't you? And Reine, you must ask us. How delicious a dance would be in the hall! Bertie, remember you are to go to Ascot with us; you are our cousin, not any one else's. When one is related to the hero of the moment, one is not going to let one's glory drop. Promise, Bertie! you go with us?"

"I am quite willing, if you want me," said Herbert.

"Oh, if we want you!—of course we want you—we want you always," cried Sophy. "Why, you are the lion; we are proud of you. We shall want to let everybody see that you don't despise your poor relations, that you remember we are your cousins, and used to play with you. Don't you recollect, Bertie? Kate and Reine used to be the friends always, because they were the steadiest; and you and me—we were the ones who got into scrapes," cried Sophy. This, to tell the truth, was a very rash statement; for Herbert, always delicate, had not been in the habit of getting into scrapes. But all the more for this, he was pleased with the idea.

"Yes," he said half doubtfully, "I recollect;" but his recollections were not clear enough to enter into details.

"Come, let us get into a scrape again," cried Sophy; "it is such a lovely night. Let us send the carriage on in front, and walk. Come with us, won't you? After a party, it is so pleasant to have a walk; and we have been such swells to-night. Come, Bertie, let's run on, and bring ourselves down."

"Sophy, you madcap! I daresay the night air is not good for him," said Kate.

Upon which Sophy broke forth into the merriest laughter. "As if Bertie cared for the night air! Why, he looks twice as strong as any of us. Will you come?"

"With all my heart," said Herbert; "it is the very thing after such a tremendous business as Aunt Susan's dinner. This is not the kind of entertainment I mean to give. We shall leave the swells, as you say, to take care of themselves."

"And ask me!" said bold Sophy, running out into the moonlight, which just then got free of the clouds. She was in high spirits, and pleased with the decided beginning she had made. In her white dress, with her white shoes twinkling over the dark cool greenness of the grass, she looked like a fairy broken forth from the woods. "Who will run a race with me to the end of the lane?" she cried, pirouetting round and round the lawn. How pretty she was, how gay, how light-hearted—a madcap, as her sister said, who stood in the shadow of the porch laughing, and bade Sophy recollect that she would ruin her shoes.

"And you can't run in high heels," said Kate.

"Can't I?" cried Sophy. "Come, Bertie, come." They nearly knocked down Mr. Farrel-Austin, who stood outside smoking his cigar, and swearing within himself, as they rushed out through the little gate. The carriage was proceeding abreast, its lamps making two bright lines of light along the wood, the coachman swearing internally as much as his master. The others followed more quietly—Kate, Reine, and Everard. Giovanna, yawning, had withdrawn some time before.

"Sophy, really, is too great a romp," said Kate; "she is always after some nonsense; and now we shall never be able to overtake them, to talk to Bertie about coming to the Hatch. Reine, you must settle it. We do so want you to come; consider how long it is since we have seen you, and of course everybody wants to see you; so unless we settle at once, we shall miss our chance—Everard too. We have been so long separated; and perhaps," said Kate, dropping her voice, "papa may have been disagreeable; but that don't make any difference to us. Say when you will come; we are all cousins together, and we ought to be friends. What a blessing when there are no horrible questions of property between people!" said Kate, who had so much sense. "Now it don't matter to any one, except for friendship, who is next of kin."

"Bertie has won," said Sophy, calling out to them. "Fancy! I thought I was sure, such a short distance; men can stay better than we can," said the well-informed young woman; "but for a little bit like this, the girl ought to win."

"Since you have come back, let us settle about when they are to come," said Kate; and then there ensued a lively discussion. They clustered all together at the end of the lane, in the clear space where there were no shadowing trees—the two young men acting as shadows, the girls all distinct in their pretty light dresses, which the moon whitened and brightened. The consultation was very animated, and diversified by much mirth and laughter, Sophy being wild, as she said, with excitement, with the stimulation of the race, and of the night air and the freedom. "After a grand party of swells, where one has to behave one's self," she said, "one always goes wild." And she fell to waltzing about the party. Everard was the only one of them who had any doubt as to the reality of Sophy's madcap mood; the others accepted it with the naive confidence of innocence. They said to each other, what a merry girl she was! when at last, moved by Mr. Farrel-Austin's sulks and the determination of the coachman, the girls permitted themselves to be placed in the carriage. "Recollect Friday!" they both cried, kissing Reine, and giving the most cordial pressure of the hand to Herbert. The three who were left stood and looked after the carriage as it set off along the moonlit road. Reine had taken her brother's arm. She gave Everard no opportunity to resume that interrupted conversation on board the steamboat. And Kate and Sophy had not been at all attentive to their cousin, who was quite as nearly related to them as Bertie, so that if he was slightly misanthropical and inclined to find fault, it can scarcely be said that he had no justification. They all strolled along together slowly, enjoying the soft evening and the suppressed moonlight, which was now dim again, struggling faintly through a mysterious labyrinth of cloud.

"I had forgotten what nice girls they were," said Herbert; "Sophy especially; so kind and so genial and unaffected. How foolish one is when one is young! I don't think I liked them, even, when we were last here."

"They are sometimes too kind," said Everard, shrugging his shoulders; but neither of the others took any notice of what he said.

"One is so much occupied with one's self when one is young," said middle-aged Reine, already over twenty, and feeling all the advantages which age bestows.

"Do you think it is that?" said Herbert. He was much affected by the cordiality of his cousins, and moved by many concurring causes to a certain sentimentality of mind; and he was not indisposed for a little of that semi-philosophical talk which sounds so elevating and so improving at his age.

"Yes," said Reine, with confidence; "one is so little sure of one's self, one is always afraid of having done amiss; things you say sound so silly when you think them over. I blush sometimes now when I am quite alone to think how silly I must have seemed; and that prevents you doing justice to others; but I like Kate best."

"And I like Sophy best. She has no nonsense about her; she is so frank and so simple. Which is Everard for? On the whole, there is no doubt about it, English girls have a something, a je ne sais quoi—"

"I can't give any opinion," said Everard laughing. "After your visit to the Hatch you will be able to decide. And have you thought what Aunt Susan will say, within the first week, almost before you have been seen at home?"

"By Jove! I forgot Aunt Susan!" cried Herbert with a sudden pause; then he laughed, trying to feel the exquisite fun of asking Aunt Susan's permission, while they were so independent of her; but this scarcely answered just at first. "Of course," he added, with an attempt at self-assertion, "one cannot go on consulting Aunt Susan's opinion forever."

"But the first week!" Everard had all the delight of mischief in making them feel the subordination in which they still stood in spite of themselves. He went on laughing. "I would not say anything about it to-night. She is not half pleased with Madame Jean, as they call her. I hope Madame Jean has been getting it hot. Everything went off perfectly well by a miracle, but that woman as nearly spoiled it by her nonsense and her boy—"

"Whom do you call that woman?" said Herbert coldly. "I think Madame Jean did just what a warm-hearted person would do. She did not wait for mere ceremony or congratulations prearranged. For my part," said Herbert stiffly, "I never admired any one so much. She is the most beautiful, glorious creature!"

"There was no one there so pretty," said innocent Reine.

"Pretty! she is not pretty: she is splendid! she is beautiful! By Jove! to see her with her arm raised, and that child on her shoulder—it's like a picture! If you will laugh," said Herbert pettishly, "don't laugh in that offensive way! What have they done to you, and why are you so disagreeable to-night?"

"Am I disagreeable?" said Everard laughing again. It was all he could do to keep from being angry, and he felt this was the safest way. "Perhaps it is that I am more enlightened than you youngsters. However beautiful a woman may be (and I don't deny she's very handsome), I can see when she's playing a part."

"What part is she playing?" cried Herbert hotly. Reine was half frightened by his vehemence, and provoked as he was by Everard's disdainful tone; but she pressed her brother's arm to restrain him, fearful of a quarrel, as girls are so apt to be.

"I suppose you will say we are all playing our parts; and so we are," said Reine. "Bertie, you have been the hero to-night, and we are all your satellites for the moment. Come in quick, it feels chilly. I don't suppose even Everard would say Sophy was playing a part, except her natural one," she added with a laugh.

Everard was taken by surprise. He echoed her laugh with all the imbecility of astonishment. "You believe in them too," he said to her in an aside, then added, "No, only her natural part," with a tone which Herbert found as offensive as the other. Herbert himself was in a state of flattered self-consciousness which made him look upon every word said against his worshippers as an assault upon himself. Perhaps the lad being younger than his years, was still at the age when a boy is more in love with himself than any one else, and loves others according to their appreciation of that self which bulks so largely in his own eyes. Giovanna's homage to him, and Sophy's enthusiasm of cousinship, and the flattering look in all these fine eyes, had intoxicated Herbert. He could not but feel that they were above all criticism, these young, fair women, who did such justice to his own excellences. As for any suggestion that their regard for him was not genuine, it was as great an insult to him as to them, and brought him down, in the most humbling way, from the pedestal on which they had elevated him. Reine's hand patting softly on his arm kept him silent, but he felt that he could knock down Everard with pleasure, and fumes of anger and self-exaltation mounted into his head.

"Don't quarrel, Bertie," Reine whispered in his ear.

"Quarrel! he is not worth quarrelling with. He is jealous, I suppose, because I am more important than he is," Herbert said, stalking through the long passages which were still all bright with lights and flowers.

Everard, hanging back out of hearing, followed the two young figures with his eyes through the windings of the passage. Herbert held his head high, indignant. Reine, with both her hands on his arm, soothed and calmed him. They were both resentful of his sour tone and what he had said.

"I dare say they think I am jealous," Everard said to himself with a laugh that was not merry, and went away to his own room, and beginning to arrange his things for departure, meaning to leave next day. He had no need to stay there to swell Herbert's triumph, he who had so long acted as nurse to him without fee or reward. Not quite without reward either, he thought, after all, rebuking himself, and held up his hand and looked at it intently, with a smile stealing over his face. Why should he interfere to save Herbert from his own vanity and folly? Why should he subject himself to the usual fate of Mentors, pointing out Scylla on the one side and Charybdis on the other? If the frail vessel was determined to be wrecked, what had he, Everard, to do with it? Let the boy accomplish his destiny, who cared? and then what could Reine do but take refuge with her natural champion, he whom she herself had appointed to stand in her place, and who had his own score against her still unacquitted? It was evidently to his interest to keep out of the way, to let things go as they would. "And I'll back Giovanna against Sophy," he said to himself, half jealous, half laughing, as he went to sleep.

As for Herbert, he lounged into the great hall, where some lights were still burning, with his sister, and found Miss Susan there, pale with fatigue and the excitement past but triumphant. "I hope you have not tired yourself out," she said. "It was like those girls to lead you out into the night air, to give you a chance of taking cold. Their father would like nothing better than to see you laid up again: but I don't give them credit for any scheme. They are too feather-brained for anything but folly."

"Do you mean our cousins Sophy and Kate?" said Herbert with some solemnity, and an unconscious attempt to overawe Miss Susan, who was not used to anything of this kind, and was unable to understand what he meant.

"I mean the Farrel-Austin girls," she said. "Riot and noise and nonsense are their atmosphere. I hope you do not like this kind of goings on, Reine?"

The brother and sister looked at each other. "You have always disliked the Farrel-Austins," said Herbert, bravely putting himself in the breach. "I don't know why, Aunt Susan. But we have no quarrel with the girls. They are very nice and friendly. Indeed, Reine and I have promised to go to them on Friday, for two or three days."

He was three and twenty, he was acknowledged master of the house; but Herbert felt a certain tremor steal over him, and stood up before her with a strong sense of valor and daring as he said these words.

"Going to them on Friday—to the Farrel-Austins' for three or four days! then you do not mean even to go to your own parish church on your first Sunday? Herbert," said Miss Susan, indignantly, "you will break Augustine's heart."

"No, no, we did not say three or four days. I thought of that," said Reine. "We shall return on Saturday. Don't be angry, Aunt Susan. They were very kind, and we thought it was no harm."

Herbert gave her an indignant glance. It was on his lips to say, "It does not matter whether Aunt Susan is angry or not," but looking at her, he thought better of it. "Yes," he said after a pause, "we shall return on

Saturday. They were very kind, as Reine says, and how visiting our cousins could possibly involve any harm—"

"That is your own affair," said Miss Susan; "I know what you mean, Herbert, and of course you are right, you are not children any longer, and must choose your own friends; well! Before you go, however, I should like to settle everything. To-night is my last night. Yes, it is too late to discuss that now. I don't mean to say more at present. It went off very well, very pleasantly, but for that ridiculous interruption of Giovanna's—"

"I did not think it was ridiculous," said Herbert. "It was very pretty. Does Giovanna displease you too?"

Once more Reine pressed his arm. He was not always going to be coerced like this. If Miss Susan wants to be unjust and ungenerous, he was man enough, he felt, to meet her to the face.

"It was very ridiculous, I thought," she said with a sigh, "and I told her so. I don't suppose she meant any harm. She is very ignorant, and knows nothing about the customs of society. Thank heaven, she can't stay very long now."

"Why can't she stay?" cried Herbert, alarmed. "Aunt Susan, I don't know what has come over you. You used to be so kind to everybody, but now it is the people I particularly like you are so furious against. Why? those girls, who are as pretty and as pleasant as possible, and just the kind of companions Reine wants, and Madame Jean, who is the most charming person I ever saw in this house. Ignorant! I think she is very accomplished. How she sang last night, and what an eye she has for the picturesque! I never admired Whiteladies so much as this morning, when she took us over it. Aunt Susan, don't be so cross. Are you disappointed in Reine, or in me, that you are so hard upon the people we like most?"

"The people you like most?" cried Miss Susan aghast.

"Yes, Aunt Susan, I like them too," said Reine, bravely putting herself by her brother's side. I believe they both thought it was a most chivalrous and high-spirited thing they were doing, rejecting experience and taking rashly what seemed to them the weaker side. The side of the accused against the judge, the side of the young against the old. It seemed so natural to do that. The two stood together in their foolishness in the old hall, all decorated in their honor, and confronted the dethroned queen of it with a smile. She stood baffled and thunderstruck, gazing at them, and scarcely knew what to say.

"Well, children, well," she managed to get out at last. "You are no longer under me, you must choose your own friends; but God help you, what is to become of you if these are the kind of people you like best!"

They both laughed softly; though Reine had compunctions, they were not afraid. "You must confess at least that we have good taste," said Herbert; "two very pretty people, and one beautiful. I should have been much happier with Sophy at one hand and Madame Jean on the other, instead of those two swells, as Sophy calls them."

"Sophy, as you call her, would give her head for their notice," cried Miss Susan indignant, "two of the best women in the county, and the most important families."

Herbert shrugged his shoulders. "They did not amuse me," he said, "but perhaps I am stupid. I prefer the foolish Sophy and the undaunted Madame Jean."

Miss Susan left them with a cold good-night to see all the lights put out, which was important in the old house. She was so angry that it almost eased her of her personal burden; but Reine, I confess, felt a thrill of panic as she went up the oak stairs. Scylla and Charybdis! She did not identify Herbert's danger, but in her heart there worked a vague premonition of danger, and without knowing why, she was afraid.

CHAPTER XLI

"Going away?" said Giovanna. "M. 'Erbert, you go away already? is it that Viteladies is what you call dull? You have been here so short of time, you do not yet know."

"We are going only for a day; at least not quite two days," said Reine.

"For a day! but a day, two days is long. Why go at all?" said Giovanna. "We are very well here. I will sing, if that pleases, to you. M. 'Erbert, when you are so long absent, you should not go away to-morrow, the next day. Madame Suzanne will think, 'They lofe me not.'"

"That would be nonsense," said Herbert; "besides, you know I cannot be kept in one place at my age, whatever old ladies may think."

"Ah! nor young ladies neither," said Giovanna. "You are homme, you have the freedom to do what you will, I know it. Me, I am but a woman, I can never have this freedom; but I comprehend and I admire. Yes, M. 'Erbert, that goes without saying. One does not put the eagle into a cage."

And Giovanna gave a soft little sigh. She was seated in one of her favorite easy chairs, thrown back in it in an attitude of delicious easy repose. She had no mind for the work with which Reine employed herself, and which all the women Herbert ever knew had indulged in, to his annoyance, and often envy; for an invalid's weary hours would have been the better often of such feminine solace, and the young man hated it all the more that he had often been tempted to take to it, had his pride permitted. But Giovanna had no mind for this pretty cheat, that looked like occupation. In her own room she worked hard at her own dresses and those of the child, but downstairs she sat with her large, shapely white hands in her lap, in all the luxury of doing nothing; and this peculiarity delighted Herbert. He was pleased, too, with what she said; he liked to imagine that he was an eagle who could not be shut into a cage, and to feel his immense superiority, as man, over the women who were never free to do as they liked, and for whom (he thought) such an indulgence would not be good. He drew himself up unconsciously, and felt older, taller. "No," he said, "of course it would be too foolish of Aunt Susan or any one to expect me to be guided by what she thinks right."

"Me, I do not speak for you," said Giovanna; "I speak for myself. I am disappointed, me. It will be dull when you are gone. Yes, yes, Monsieur 'Erbert, we are selfish, we other women. When you go we are dull; we think not of you, but of ourselves, n'est ce pas, Mademoiselle Reine? I am frank. I confess it. You will be very happy; you will have much pleasure; but me, I shall be dull. Voilà tout!"

I need not say that this frankness captivated Herbert. It is always more pleasant to have our absence regretted by others, selfishly, for the loss it is to them, than unselfishly on our account only; so that this profession of indifference to the pleasure of your departing friend, in consideration of the loss to yourself, is the very highest compliment you can pay him. Herbert felt this to the bottom of his heart. He was infinitely flattered and touched by the thought of a superiority so delightful, and he had not been used to it. He had been accustomed, indeed, to be in his own person the centre of a great deal of care and anxiety, everybody thinking of him for his sake; but to have it recognized that his presence or absence made a place dull or the reverse, and affected his surroundings, not for his sake but theirs, was an immense rise in the world to Herbert. He felt it necessary to be very friendly and attentive to Giovanna, by way of consoling her. "After all, it will not be very long," he said; "from Friday morning to Saturday night. I like to humor the old ladies, and they make a point of our being at home for Sunday; though I don't know how Sophy and Kate will like it, Reine."

"They will not like it at all," said Giovanna. "They want you to be to them, to amuse them, to make them happy; so do I, the same. When they come here, those young ladies, we shall not be friends; we shall fight," she said with a laugh. "Ah, they are more clever than me, they will win; though if we could fight with the hands like men, I should win. I am more strong."

"It need not come so far as that," said Herbert, complaisant and delighted. "You are all very kind, I am sure, and think more of me than I deserve."

"I am kind—to me, not to you, M. 'Erbert," said Giovanna; "when I tell you it is dull, dull à mourir the moment you go away."

"Yet you have spent a good many months here without Herbert, Madame Jean," said Reine; "if it had been so dull, you might have gone away."

"Ah, mademoiselle! where could I have gone to? I am not rich like you; I have not parents that love me. If I go home now," cried Giovanna, with a laugh, "it will be to the room behind the shop where my belle-mère sits all the day, where they cook the dinner, where I am the one that is in the way, always. I have no money, no people to care for me. Even little Jean they take from me. They say, 'Tenez Gi'vanna; she has not the ways of children.' Have not I the ways of children, M. 'Erbert? That is what they would say to me, if I went to what you call 'ome."

"Reine," said Herbert, in an undertone, "how can you be so cruel, reminding the poor thing how badly off she is? I hope you will not think of going away," he added, turning to Giovanna. "Reine and I will be too glad that you should stay; and as for your flattering appreciation of our society, I for one am very grateful," said the young fellow. "I am very happy to be able to do anything to make Whiteladies pleasant to you."

Miss Susan came in as he said this with Everard, who was going away; but she was too much preoccupied by her own cares to attend to what her nephew was saying. Everard appreciated the position more clearly. He saw the grateful look with which Giovanna turned her beautiful eyes to the young master of the house, and he saw the pleased vanity and complaisance in Herbert's face. "What an ass he is!" Everard thought to himself; and then he quoted privately with rueful comment,—

"'On him each courtier's eye was bent,
To him each lady's look was lent:'

all because the young idiot has Whiteladies, and is the head of the house. Bravo! Herbert, old boy," he said aloud, though there was nothing particularly appropriate in the speech, "you are having your innings. I hope you will make the most of them. But now that I am no longer wanted, I am going off. I suppose when it is warm enough for water parties, I shall come into fashion again; Sophy and Kate will manage that."

"Well, Everard, if I were you I should have more pride," said Miss Susan. "I would not allow myself to be taken up and thrown aside as those girls please. What you can see in them baffles me. They are not very pretty. They are very loud, and fast and noisy—"

"I think so too!" cried Giovanna, clapping her hands. "They are my enemies: they take you away, M. 'Erbert and Mademoiselle Reine. They make it dull here."

"Only for a day," said Herbert, bending over her, his eyes melting and glowing with that delightful suffusion of satisfied vanity which with so many men represents love. "I could not stay long away if I would," said the young man in a lower tone. He was quite captivated by her frank demonstrations of personal loss, and believed them to the bottom of his heart.

Miss Susan threw a curious, half-startled look at them, and Reine raised her head from her embroidery; but both of these ladies had something of their own on their minds which occupied them, and closed their eyes to other matters. Reine was secretly uneasy that Everard should go away; that there should have been no explanation between them; and that his tone had in it a certain suppressed bitterness. What had she done to him? Nothing. She had been occupied with her brother, as was natural; any one else would have been the same. Everard's turn could come at any time, she said to herself, with an unconscious arrogance not unusual with girls, when they are sure of having the upper hand. But she was uneasy that he should go away.

"I don't want to interfere with your pleasures, Herbert," said Miss Susan, "but I must settle what I am to do. Our cottage is ready for us, everything is arranged; and I want to give up my charge to you, and go away."

"To go away!" the brother and sister repeated together with dismay.

"Of course; that is what it must come to. When you were under age it was different. I was your guardian, Herbert, and you were my children."

"Aunt Susan," cried Reine, coming up to her with eager tenderness, "we are your children still."

"And I—am not at all sure whether it will suit me to take up all you have been doing," said Herbert. "It suits you, why should we change; and how could Reine manage the house? Aunt Susan, it is unkind to come down upon us like this. Leave us a little time to get used to it. What do you want with a cottage? Of course you must like Whiteladies best."

"Oh, Aunt Susan! what he says is not so selfish as it sounds," said Reine. "Why—why should you go?"

"We are all selfish," said Herbert, "as Madame Jean says. She wishes us to stay because it is dull without us ('Bien, très dull,' said Giovanna), and we want you to stay because we are not up to the work and don't understand it. Never mind the cottage; there is plenty of room in Whiteladies for all of us. Aunt Susan, why should you be disagreeable? Don't go away."

"I wish it; I wish it," she said in a low tone; "let me go!"

"But we don't wish it," cried Reine, kissing her in triumph, "and neither does Augustine. Oh, Aunt Austine, listen to her, speak for us! You don't wish to go away from Whiteladies, away from your home?"

"No," said Augustine, who had come in in her noiseless way. "I do not intend to leave Whiteladies," she went on, with serious composure; "but Herbert, I have something to say to you. It is more important than anything else. You must marry; you must marry at once; I don't wish any time to be lost. I wish you to have an heir, whom I shall bring up. I will devote myself to him. I am fifty-seven; there is no time to be lost; but with care I might live twenty years. The women of our house are long-lived. Susan is sixty, but she is as active as any one of you; and for an object like this, one would spare no pains to lengthen one's days. You must marry, Herbert. This has now become the chief object of my life."

The young members of the party, unable to restrain themselves, laughed at this solemn address. Miss Susan turned away impatient, and sitting down, pulled out the knitting of which lately she had done so little. But as for Augustine, her countenance preserved a perfect gravity. She saw nothing laughable in it. "I excuse you," she said very seriously, "for you cannot see into my heart and read what is there. Nor does Susan understand me. She is taken up with the cares of this world and the foolishness of riches. She thinks a foolish display like that of last night is more important. But, Herbert, listen to me; you and your true welfare have been my first thought and my first prayer for years, and this is my recommendation, my command to you. You must marry—and without any unnecessary delay."

"But the lady?" said Herbert, laughing and blushing; even this very odd address had a pleasurable element in it. It implied the importance of everything he did; and it pleased the young man, even after such an odd fashion, to lay this flattering unction to his soul.

"The lady!" said Miss Augustine gravely; and then she made a pause. "I have thought a great deal about that, and there is more than one whom I could suggest to you; but I have never married myself, and I might not perhaps be a good judge. It seems the general opinion that in such matters people should choose for themselves."

All this she said with so profound a gravity that the bystanders, divided between amusement and a kind of awe, held their breath and looked at each other. Miss Augustine had not sat down. She rarely did sit down in the common sitting-room; her hands were too full of occupation. Her Church services, now that the Chantry was opened, her Almshouses prayers, her charities, her universal oversight of her pensioners filled up all her time, and bound her to hours as strictly as if she had been a cotton-spinner in a mill. No cotton-spinner worked harder than did this Gray Sister; from morning to night her time was portioned out.

I do not venture to say how many miles she walked daily, rain or shine; from Whiteladies to the Almshouses, to the church, to the Almshouses again; or how many hours she spent absorbed in that strange matter-of-fact devotion which was her way of working for her family. She repeated, in her soft tones, "I do not interfere with your choice, Herbert; but what I say is very important. Marry! I wish it above everything else in life." And having said this, she went away.

"This is very solemn," said Herbert, with a laugh, but his laugh was not like the merriment into which, by-and-by, the others burst forth, and which half offended the young man. Reine, for her part, ran to the piano when Miss Augustine disappeared, and burst forth into a quaint little French ditty, sweet and simple, of old Norman rusticity.

"A chaque rose que je effeuille
Marie-toi, car il est temps,"

the girl sang. But Miss Susan did not laugh, and Herbert did not care to see anything ridiculed in which he had such an important share. After all it was natural enough, he said to himself, that such advice should be given with great gravity to one on whose acts so much depended. He did not see what there was to laugh about. Reine was absurd with her songs. There was always one of them which came in pat to the moment. Herbert almost thought that this light-minded repetition of Augustine's advice was impertinent both to her and himself. And thus a little gloom had come over his brow.

"Messieurs et mesdames," said Giovanna, suddenly, "you laugh, but, if you reflect, ma sœur has reason. She thinks, Here is Monsieur 'Erbert, young and strong, but yet there are things which happen to the strongest; and here, on the other part, is a little boy, a little, little boy, who is not English, whose mother is nothing but a foreigner, who is the heir. This gives her the panique. And for me, too, M. 'Erbert, I say with Mademoiselle Reine, 'Marie-toi, car il est temps.' Yes, truly! although little Jean is my boy, I say mariez-vous with my heart."

"How good you are! how generous you are! Strange that you should be the only one to see it," said Herbert, for the moment despising all the people belonging to him, who were so opaque, who did not perceive the necessities of the position. He himself saw those necessities well enough, and that he should marry was the first and most important. To tell the truth, he could not see even that Augustine's anxiety was of an exaggerated description. It was not a thing to make laughter, and ridiculous jokes and songs about.

Giovanna did not desert her post during that day. She did not always lead the conversation, nor make herself so important in it as she had done at first, but she was always there, putting in a word when necessary, ready to come to Herbert's assistance, to amuse him when there was occasion, to flatter him with bold, frank speeches, in which there was always a subtle compliment involved. Everard took his leave shortly after, with farewells in which there was a certain consciousness that he had not been treated quite as he ought to have been. "Till I come into fashion again," he said, with the laugh which began to sound harsh to Reine's ears, "I am better at home in my own den, where I can be as sulky as I please. When I am wanted, you know where to find me." Reine thought he looked at her when he said this with reproach in his eyes.

"I think you are wanted now," said Miss Susan; "there are many things I wished to consult you about. I wish you would not go away."

But he was obstinate. "No, no; there is nothing for me to do," he said; "no journeys to make, no troubles to encounter. You are all settled at home in safety; and when I am wanted you know where to find me," he added, this time holding out his hand to Reine, and looking at her very distinctly. Poor Reine felt herself on the edge of a very sea of troubles: everybody around her seemed to have something in their thoughts beyond her divining. Miss Susan meant more than she could fathom, and there lurked a purpose in Giovanna's beautiful eyes, which Reine began to be dimly conscious of, but could not explain to herself. How could he leave her to steer her course among these undeveloped perils? and how could she call him back when he was "wanted," as he said bitterly? She gave him her hand, turning away her head to hide a something, almost a tear, that would come into her eyes, and with a forlorn sense of desertion in her heart; but she was too proud either by look or word to bid Everard stay.

This was on Thursday, and the next day they were to go to the Hatch, so that the interval was not long. Giovanna sang for them in the evening all kinds of popular songs, which was what she knew best, old Flemish ballads, and French and Italian canzoni; those songs of which every hamlet possesses one special to itself. "For I am not educated," she said; "Mademoiselle must see that. I do all this by the ear. It is not music; it is nothing but ignorance. These are the chants du peuple, and I am nothing but one of the peuple, me. I am très-peuple. I never pretend otherwise. I do not wish to deceive you, M. 'Erbert, nor Mademoiselle."

"Deceive us!" cried Herbert. "If we could imagine such a thing, we should be dolts indeed."

Giovanna raised her head and looked at him, then turned to Miss Susan, whose knitting had dropped on her knee, and who, without thought, I think, had turned her eyes upon the group. "You are right, Monsieur 'Erbert," she said, with a strange malicious laugh, "here at least you are quite safe, though there are much of persons who are traitres in the world. No one will deceive you here."

She laughed as she spoke, and Miss Susan clutched at her knitting and buried herself in it, so to speak, not raising her head again for a full hour after, during which time Herbert and Giovanna talked a great deal to each other. And Reine sat by, with an incipient wonder in her mind which she could not quite make out, feeling as if her aunt and herself were one faction, Giovanna and Herbert another; as if there were all sorts of secret threads which she could not unravel, and intentions of which she knew nothing. The sense of strangeness grew on her so, that she could scarcely believe she was in Whiteladies, the home for which she had sighed so long. This kind of disenchantment happens often when the hoped-for becomes actual, but not always so strongly or with so bewildering a sense of something unrevealed, as that which pressed upon the very soul of Reine.

Next morning Giovanna, with her child on her shoulder, came out to the gate to see them drive away. "You will not stay more long than to-morrow," she said. "How we are going to be dull till you come back! Monsieur Herbert, Mademoiselle Reine, you promise—not more long than to-morrow! It is two great long days!" She kissed her hand to them, and little Jean waved his cap, and shouted "Vive M. 'Erbert!" as the carriage drove away.

"What a grace she has about her!" said Herbert. "I never saw a woman so graceful. After all, it is a bore to go. It is astonishing how happy one feels, after a long absence, in the mere sense of being at home. I am sorry we promised; of course we must keep our promise now."

"I like it, rather," said Reine, feeling half ashamed of herself. "Home is not what it used to be; there is something strange, something new; I can't tell what it is. After all, though, Madame Jean is very handsome, it is strange she should be there."

"Oh, you object to Madame Jean, do you?" said Herbert. "You women are all alike; Aunt Susan does not like her either, I suppose you cannot help it; the moment a woman is more attractive than others, the moment a man shows that he has got eyes in his head—But you cannot help it, I suppose. What a walk she has, and carrying the child like a feather! It is a great bore, this visit to the Hatch, and so soon."

"You were pleased with the idea; you were delighted to accept the invitation," said Reine, injudiciously, I must say.

"Bah! one's ideas change; but Sophy and Kate would have been disappointed," said Herbert, with that ineffable look of complaisance in his eyes. And thus from Scylla which he had left, he drove calmly on to Charybdis, not knowing where he went.

CHAPTER XLII

There had been great preparations made for Herbert's reception at the Hatch. I say Herbert's—for Reine, though she had been perforce included in the invitation, was not even considered any more. After the banquet at Whiteladies the sisters had many consultations on this subject, and there was indeed very little time to do anything. Sophy had been of opinion at first that the more gay his short visit could be made the better Herbert would be pleased, and had contemplated an impromptu dance, and I don't know how many other diversions; but Kate was wiser. It was one good trait in their characters, if there was not very much else, that they acted for each other with much disinterestedness, seldom or never entering into personal rivalry. "Not too much the first time," said Kate; "let him make acquaintance with us, that is the chief thing." "But he mightn't care for us," objected Sophy. "Some people have such bad taste." This was immediately after the Whiteladies dinner, after the moonlight walk and the long drive, when they were safe in the sanctuary of their own rooms. The girls were in their white dressing-gowns, with their hair about their shoulders, and were taking a light refection of cakes and chocolate before going to bed.

"If you choose to study him a little, and take a little pains, of course he will like you," said Kate. "Any man will fall in love with any woman, if she takes trouble enough."

"It is very odd to me," said Sophy, "that with those opinions you should not be married, at your age."

"My dear," said Kate seriously, "plenty of men have fallen in love with me, only they have not been the right kind of men. I have been too fond of fun; and nobody that quite suited has come in my way since I gave up amusing myself. The Barracks so near is very much in one's way," said Kate, with a sigh. "One gets used to such a lot of them about; and you can always have your fun, whatever happens; and till you are driven to it, it seems odd to make a fuss about one. But what you have got to do is easy enough. He is as innocent as a baby, and as foolish. No woman ever took the trouble, I should say, to look at him. You have it all in your own hands. As for Reine, I will look after Reine. She is a suspicious little thing, but I'll keep her out of your way."

"What a bore it is!" said Sophy, with a yawn. "Why should we be obliged to marry more than the men are. It isn't fair. Nobody finds fault with them, though they have dozens of affairs; but we're drawn over the coals for nothing, a bit of fun. I'm sure I don't want to marry Bertie, or any one. I'd a great deal rather not. So long as one has one's amusement, it's jolly enough."

"If you could always be as young as you are now," said Kate oracularly; "but even you are beginning to be passée, Sophy. It's the pace, you know, as the men say—you need not make faces. The moment you are married you will be a girl again. As for me, I feel a grandmother."

"You are old," said Sophy compassionately; "and indeed you ought to go first."

"I am just eighteen months older than you are," said Kate, rousing herself in self-defence, "and with your light hair, you'll go off sooner. Don't be afraid; as soon as I have got you off my hands I shall take care of myself. But look here! What you've got to do is to study Herbert a little. Don't take him up as if he were Jack or Tom. Study him. There is one thing you never can go wrong in with any of them," said this experienced young woman. "Look as if you thought him the cleverest fellow that ever was; make yourself as great a fool as you can in comparison. That flatters them above everything. Ask his advice you know, and that sort of thing. The greatest fool I ever knew," said Kate, reflectively, "was Fenwick, the adjutant. I made him wild about me by that."

"He would need to be a fool to think you meant it," said Sophy, scornfully; "you that have such an opinion of yourself."

"I had too good an opinion of myself to have anything to say to him, at least; but it's fun putting them in a state," said Kate, pleased with the recollection. This was a sentiment which her sister fully shared, and they amused themselves with reminiscences of several such dupes ere they separated. Perhaps even the dupes were scarcely such dupes as these young ladies thought; but anyhow, they had never been, as Kate said, "the right sort of men." Dropmore, etc., were always to the full as knowing as their pretty adversaries, and were not to be beguiled by any such specious pretences. And to tell the truth, I am doubtful how far Kate's science was genuine. I doubt whether she was unscrupulous enough and good-tempered enough to carry out her own programme; and Sophy certainly was too careless, too feather brained, for any such scheme. She meant to marry Herbert because his recommendations were great, and because he lay in her way, as it were, and it would be almost a sin not to put forth a hand to appropriate the gifts of Providence; but if it had been necessary to "study" him, as her sister enjoined, or to give great pains to his subjugation, I feel sure that Sophy's patience and resolution would have given way. The charm in the enterprise was that it seemed so easy; Whiteladies was a most desirable object; and Sophy, longing for fresh woods and pastures new, was rather attracted than repelled by the likelihood of having to spend the Winters abroad.

Mr. Farrel-Austin, for his part, received the young head of his family with anything but delight. He had been unable, in ordinary civility, to contradict the invitation his daughters had given, but took care to express his sentiments on the subject next day very distinctly—had they cared at all for those sentiments, which I don't think they did. Their schemes, of course, were quite out of his range, and were not communicated to him; nor was he such a self-denying parent as to have been much consoled for his own loss of the family property by the possibility of one of his daughters stepping into possession of it. He thought it an ill-timed exhibition of their usual love of strangers, and love of company, and growled at them all day long until the time of the arrival, when he absented himself, to their great satisfaction, though it was intended as the crowning evidence of his displeasure. "Papa has been obliged to go out; he is so sorry, but hopes you will excuse him till dinner," Kate said, when the girls came to receive their cousins at the door. "Oh, they won't mind, I am sure," said Sophy. "We shall have them all to ourselves, which will be much jollier." Herbert's brow clouded temporarily, for, though he did not love Mr. Farrel-Austin, he felt that his absence showed a want of that "proper respect" which was due to the head of the house. But under the gay influence of the girls the cloud speedily floated away.

They had gone early, by special prayer, as their stay was to be so short; and Kate had made the judicious addition of two men from the barracks to their little luncheon-party. "One for me, and one for Reine," she had said to Sophy, "which will leave you a fair field." The one whom Kate had chosen for herself was a middle-aged major, with a small property—a man who had hitherto afforded much "fun" to the party generally as a butt, but whose serious attentions Miss Farrel-Austin, at five-and-twenty, did not absolutely discourage. If nothing better came in the way, he might do, she felt. He had a comfortable income and a mild temper, and would not object to "fun." Reine's share was a foolish youth, who had not long joined the regiment; but as she was quite unconscious that he had been selected for her, Reine was happily free from all sense of being badly treated. He laughed at the jokes which Kate and Sophy made; and held his tongue otherwise—thus fulfilling all the duty for which he was told off. After this morning meal, which was so much gayer and more lively than anything at Whiteladies, the new-comers were carried off to see the house and the grounds, upon which many improvements had been made. Sophy was Herbert's guide, and ran before him through all the new rooms, showing the new library, the morning-room, and the other additions. "This is one good of an ugly modern place," she said. "You can never alter dear old Whiteladies, Bertie. If you did we should get up a crusade of all the Austins and all the antiquarians, and do something to you—kill you, I think; unless some weak-minded person like myself were to interfere."

"I shall never put myself in danger," he said, "though perhaps I am not such a fanatic about Whiteladies as you others."

"Don't!" said Sophy, raising her hand as if to stop his mouth. "If you say a word more I shall hate you. It is small, to be sure; and if you should have a very large family when you marry"—she went on, with a laugh—"but the Austins never have large families; that is one part of the curse, I suppose your Aunt Augustine would say! but for my part, I hate large families, and I think it is very grand to have a curse belonging to us. It is as good as a family ghost. What a pity that the monk and the nun don't walk! But there is something in the great staircase. Did you ever see it? I never lived in Whiteladies, or I should have tried to see what it was."

"Did you never live at Whiteladies? I thought when we were children—"

"Never for more than a day. The old ladies hate us. Ask us now, Bertie, there's a darling. Well! he will be a darling if he asks us. It is the most delightful old house in the world, and I want to go."

"Then I ask you on the spot," said Herbert. "Am I a darling now? You know," he added in a lower tone, as they went on, and separated from the others, "it was as near as possible being yours. Two years ago no one supposed I should get better. You must have felt it was your own!"

"Not once," said Sophy. "Papa's, perhaps—but what would that have done for us? Daughters marry and go away—it never would have been ours; and Mrs. Farrel-Austin won't have a son. Isn't it provoking? Oh, she is only our step-mother, you know—it does not matter what we say. Papa could beat her; but I am so glad, so glad," cried Sophy, with a glow of smiles, "that instead of papa, or that nasty little French boy, Bertie, it is you, our cousin, whom we are fond of!—I can't tell you how glad I am."

"Thanks," said Herbert, clasping the hand she held out to him, and holding it. It seemed so natural to him that she should be glad.

"Because," said Sophy, looking at him with her pretty blue eyes, "we have been sadly neglected, Kate and I. We have never had any one to advise us, or tell us what we ought to do. We both came out too young, and were thrown on the world to do what we pleased. If you see anything in us you don't like, Bertie, remember this is the reason. We never had a brother. Now, you will be as near a brother to us as any one could be. We shall be able to go and consult you, and you will help us out of our scrapes. I did so hope, before you came, that we should be friends; and now I think we shall," she said, giving a little pressure to the hand which still held hers.

Herbert was so much affected by this appeal that it brought the tears to his eyes.

"I think we shall, indeed," he said, warmly,—"nay, we are. It would be a strange fellow indeed who would not be glad to be brother, or anything else, to a girl like you."

"Brother, not anything else," said Sophy, audibly but softly. "Ah, Bertie! you can't think how glad I am. As soon as we saw you, Kate and I could not help feeling what an advantage Reine had over us. To have you to refer to always—to have you to talk to—instead of the nonsense that we girls are always chattering to each other."

"Well," said Herbert, more and more pleased, "I suppose it is an advantage; not that I feel myself particularly wise, I am sure. There is always something occurring which shows one how little one knows."

"If you feel that, imagine how we must feel," said Sophy, "who have never had any education. Oh yes, we have had just the same as other girls! but not like men—not like you, Bertie. Oh, you need not be modest. I know you haven't been at the University to waste your time and get into debt, like so many we know. But you have done a great deal better. You have read and you have thought, and Reine has had all the advantage. I almost hate Reine for being so much better off than we are."

"But, really," cried Herbert, laughing half with pleasure, half with a sense of the incongruity of the praise, "you give me a great deal more credit than I deserve. I have never been very much of a student. I don't know that I have done much for Reine—except what one can do in the way of conversation, you know," he added, after a pause, feeling that after all it must have been this improving conversation which had made his sister what she was. It had not occurred to him before, but the moment it was suggested—yes, of course, that was what it must be.

"Just what I said," cried Sophy; "and we never had that advantage. So if you find us frivolous, Bertie—"

"How could I find you frivolous? You are nothing of the sort. I shall almost think you want me to pay you compliments—to say what I think of you."

"I hate compliments," cried Sophy. "Here we are on the lawn, Bertie, and here are the others. What do you think of it? We have had such trouble with the grass—now, I think, it is rather nice. It has been rolled and watered and mown, and rolled and watered and mown again, almost every day."

"It is the best croquet-ground in the county," said the Major; "and why shouldn't we have a game? It is pleasant to be out of doors such a lovely day."

This was assented to, and the others went in-doors for their hats; but Sophy stayed. "I have got rid of any complexion I ever had," she said. "I am always out of doors. The sun must have got tired of burning me, I am so brown already," and she put up two white, pink-fingered hands to her white-and-pink cheeks. She was one of those blondes of satin-skin who are not easily affected by the elements. Herbert laughed, and with the privilege of cousinship took hold of one of the pink tips of the fingers, and looked at the hand.

"Is that what you call brown?" he said. "We have just come from the land of brown beauties, and I ought to know. It is the color of milk with roses in it," and the young man, who was not used to paying compliments, blushed as he made his essay; which was more than Sophy, experienced in the commodity, felt any occasion to do.

"Milk of roses," she said, laughing; "that is a thing for the complexion. I don't use it, Bertie; I don't use anything of the kind. Men are always so dreadfully knowing about young girls' dodges—" The word slipped out against her will, for Sophy felt that slang was not expedient, and she blushed at this slip, though she had not blushed at the compliment. Herbert did not, however, discriminate. He took the pretty suffusion to his own account, and laughed at the inadvertent word. He thought she put it in inverted commas, as a lady should; and when this is done, a word of slang is piquant now and then as a quotation. Besides, he was far from being a purist in language. Kate, however, the unselfish, thoughtful elder sister, sweetly considerate of the young beauty, brought out Sophy's hat with her own, and they began to play. Herbert and Reine were novices, unacquainted (strange as the confession must sound) with this universally popular game; and Sophy boldly stepped into the breech, and took them both on her side. "I am the best player of the lot," said Sophy calmly. "You know I am. So Bertie and Reine shall come with me; and beat us if you can!" said the young champion; and if the reader will believe me, Sophy's boast came true. Kate, indeed, made a brave stand; but the Major was middle-aged, and the young fellow was feeble, and Herbert showed an unsuspected genius for the game. He was quite pleased himself by his success; everything, indeed, seemed to conspire to make Herbert feel how clever he was, how superior he was, what an acquisition was his society; and during the former part of his life it had not been so. Like one of the great philosophers of modern times, Herbert felt that those who appreciated him so deeply must in themselves approach the sublime. Indeed, I fear it is a little mean on my part to take the example of that great philosopher, as if he were a rare instance; for is not the most foolish of us of the same opinion? "Call me wise, and I will allow you to be a judge," says an old Scotch proverb. Herbert was ready to think all these kind people very good judges who so magnified and glorified himself.

In the evening there was a very small dinner-party; again two men to balance Kate and Reine, but not the same men—persons of greater weight and standing, with Farrel-Austin himself at the foot of his own table. Mrs. Farrel-Austin was not well enough to come to dinner, but appeared in the drawing-room afterward; and when the gentlemen came upstairs, appropriated Reine. Sophy, who had a pretty little voice, had gone to the piano, and was singing to Herbert, pausing at the end of every verse to ask him, "Was it very bad? Tell me what you dislike most, my high notes or my low notes, or my execution, or what?" while Herbert, laughing and protesting, gave vehement praise to all. "I don't dislike anything. I am delighted with every word; but you must not trust to me, for indeed I am no judge of music."

"No judge of music, and yet fresh from Italy!" cried Sophy, with flattering contempt.

While this was going on Mrs. Farrel-Austin drew Reine close to her sofa. "I am very glad to see you, my dear," she said, "and so far as I am concerned I hope you will come often. You are so quiet and nice; and all I have seen of your Aunt Susan I like, though I know she does not like us. But I hope, my dear, you won't get into the racketing set our girls are so fond of. I should be very sorry for that; it would be bad for your brother. I don't mean to say anything against Kate and Sophy. They are very lively and very strong, and it suits them, though in some things I think it is bad for them too. But your brother could never stand it, my dear; I know what bad health is, and I can see that he is not strong still."

"Oh, yes," said Reine eagerly. "He has been going out in the world a great deal lately. I was frightened at first; but I assure you he is quite strong."

Mrs. Farrel-Austin shook her head. "I know what poor health is," she said, "and however strong you may get, you never can stand a racket. I don't suppose for a moment that they mean any harm, but still I should not like anything to happen in this house. People might say—and your Aunt Susan would be sure to think—It is very nice, I suppose, for young people; and of course at your age you are capable of a great deal of racketing; but I must warn you, my dear, it's ruin for the health."

"Indeed, I don't think we have any intention of racketing."

"Ah, it is not the intention that matters," said the invalid. "I only want to warn you, my dear. It is a very racketing set. You should not let yourself be drawn into it, and quietly, you know, when you have an opportunity, you might say a word to your brother. I dare say he feels the paramount value of health. Oh, what should I give now if I had only been warned when I was young! You cannot play with your health, my dear, with impunity. Even the girls, though they are so strong, have headaches and things which they oughtn't to have at their age. But I hope you will come here often, you are so nice and quiet—not like the most of those that come here."

"What is Mrs. Austin saying to you, Reine?" asked Kate.

"She told me I was nice and quiet," said Reine, thinking that in honor she was bound not to divulge the rest; and they both laughed at the moderate compliment.

"So you are," said Kate, giving her a little hug. "It is refreshing to be with any one so tranquil—and I am sure you will do us both good."

Reine was not impressed by this as Herbert was by Sophy's pretty speeches. Perhaps the praise that was given to her was not equally well chosen. The passionate little semi-French girl (who had been so ultra-English in Normandy) was scarcely flattered by being called tranquil, and did not feel that to do Sophy and Kate good by being "nice and quiet" was a lofty mission. What did a racketing set mean? she wondered. An involuntary prejudice against the house rose in her mind, and this opened her eyes to something of Sophy's tactics. It was rather hard to sit and look on and see Herbert thus fooled to the top of his bent. When she went to the piano beside them, Sophy grew more rational; but still she kept referring to Herbert, consulting him. "Is it like this they do it in Italy?" she sang, executing "a shake" with more natural sweetness than science.

"Indeed, I don't know, but it is beautiful," said Herbert. "Ask Reine."

"Oh, Reine is only a girl like myself. She will say what she thinks will please me. I have far more confidence in a gentleman," cried Sophy; "and above all in you, Bertie, who have promised to be a brother to me," she said, in a lower tone.

"Did I promise to be a brother?" said poor, foolish Herbert, his heart beating with vanity and pleasure.

And the evening passed amid these delights.

CHAPTER XLIII

I need not follow day by day the course of Herbert's life. Though the brother and sister went out a good deal together at first, being asked to all the great houses in the neighborhood, as became their position in the county and their recent arrival, yet there gradually arose a separation between Herbert and Reine. It was inevitable, and she had learned to acknowledge this, and did not rebel as at first; but a great many people shook their heads when it became apparent that, notwithstanding Mrs. Farrel-Austin's warning, Herbert had been drawn into the "racketing set" whose headquarters were at the Hatch. The young man was fond of pleasure, as well as of flattery, and it was Summer, when all the ills that flesh is heir to relax their hold a little, and dissipation is comparatively harmless. He went to Ascot with the party from the Hatch, and he went to a great many other places with them; and though the friends he made under their auspices led Herbert into places much worse both for his health and mind than any the girls could lead him to, he remained faithful, so far, to Kate and Sophy, and continued to attend them wherever they went. As for Reine, she was happy enough in the comparative quiet into which she dropped when the first outbreak of gayety was over. Miss Susan, against her will, still remained at Whiteladies; against her will—yet it may well be supposed it was no pleasure to her to separate herself from the old house in which she had been born, and from which she had never been absent for so much as six months all her life. Miss Augustine, for her part, took little or no notice of the change in the household. She went her way as usual, morning and evening, to the Almshouses. When Miss Susan spoke to her, as she did sometimes, about the cottage which stood all this time furnished and ready for instant occupation, she only shook her head. "I do not mean to leave Whiteladies," she said, calmly. Neither did Giovanna, so far as could be perceived. "You cannot remain here when we go," said Miss Susan to her.

"There is much room in the house," said Giovanna; "and when you go, Madame Suzanne, there will be still more. The little chamber for me and the child, what will that do to any one?"

"But you cannot, you must not; it will be improper—don't you understand?" cried Miss Susan.

Giovanna shook her head.

"I will speak to M. Herbert," she said, smiling in Miss Susan's face.

This then was the position of affairs. Herbert put off continually the settlement between them, begging that he might have a little holiday, that she would retain the management of the estate and of his affairs, and this with a certain generosity mingling with his inclination to avoid trouble; for in reality he loved the woman who had been in her way a mother to him, and hesitated about taking from her the occupation of her life. It was well meant; and Miss Susan felt within herself that moral cowardice which so often affects those who live in expectation of an inevitable change or catastrophe. It must come, she knew; and when the moment of departure came, she could not tell, she dared not anticipate what horrors might come with it; but she was almost glad to defer it, to consent that it should be postponed from day to day. The king in the story, however, could scarcely manage, I suppose, to be happy with that sword hanging over his head. No doubt he got used to it, poor wretch, and could eat and drink, and snatch a fearful joy from the feasting which went on around him; he might even make merry, perhaps, but he could scarcely be very happy under the shadow. So Miss Susan felt. She went on steadily, fulfilled all her duties, dispensed hospitalities, and even now and then permitted herself to be amused; but she was not happy.

Sometimes, when she said her prayers—for she did still say her prayers, notwithstanding the burden on her soul—she would breathe a sigh which was scarcely a prayer, that it might soon be over one way or another, that her sufferings might be cut short; but then she would rouse herself up, and recall that despairing sigh. Giovanna would not budge. Miss Susan made a great many appeals to her, when Reine was straying about the garden, or after she had gone to her innocent rest. She offered sums which made that young woman tremble in presence of a temptation which she could scarcely resist; but she set her white teeth firm, and conquered. It was better to have all than only a part, Giovanna thought, and she comforted herself that at the last moment, if her scheme failed, she could fall back upon and accept Miss Susan's offer. This made her very secure, through all the events that followed. When Herbert abandoned Whiteladies and was constantly at the Hatch, when he seemed to have altogether given himself over to his cousins, and a report got up through the county that "an alliance was contemplated," as the Kingsborough paper put it, grandly having a habit of royalty, so to speak—between two distinguished county families, Giovanna bore the contretemps quite calmly, feeling that Miss Susan's magnificent offer was always behind her to fall back upon, if her great personal enterprise should come to nothing. Her serenity gave her a great advantage over Herbert's feebler spirit. When he came home to Whiteladies, she regained her sway over him, and as she never indulged in a single look of reproach, such as Sophy employed freely when he left the Hatch, or was too long of returning, she gradually established for herself a superior place in the young man's mind.

As for Herbert himself, the three long months of that Summer were more to him than all the former years of his life put together. His first outburst of freedom on the Riviera, and his subsequent ramble in Italy, had been overcast by adverse circumstances. He had got his own way, but at a cost which was painful to him, and a great many annoyances and difficulties had been mingled with his pleasure. But now there was nothing to interfere with it. Reine was quiescent, presenting a smiling countenance when he saw her, not gloomy or frightened, as she had been at Cannes. She was happy enough; she was at home, with her aunts to fall back upon, and plenty of friends. And everybody and everything smiled upon Herbert. He was acting generously, he felt, to his former guardian, in leaving to her all the trouble of his affairs. He was surrounded by gay friends and unbounded amusements, amusements bounded only by the time that was occupied by them, and those human limitations which make it impossible to do two things at once. Could he have been in two places at once, enjoying two different kinds of pleasure at the same time, his engagements were sufficient to have secured for him a double enjoyment. From the highest magnates of the county, to the young soldiers of Kingsborough, his own contemporaries, everybody was willing to do him honor. The entire month of June he spent in town, where he had everything that town could give him—though their life moved rather more quickly than suited his still unconfirmed strength. Both in London and in the country he was invited into higher circles than those which the Farrel-Austins were permitted to enter; but still he remained faithful to his cousins, who gave him a homage which he could not expect elsewhere, and who had always "something going on," both in town and country, and no pause in their fast and furious gayety. They were always prepared to go with him or take him somewhere, to give him the carte du pays, to tell him all the antecedents and history of this one and that one, and to make the ignorant youth feel himself an experienced man. Then, when it pleased him to go home, he was the master, welcomed by all, and found another beautiful slave waiting serene to burn incense to him.

No wonder Herbert enjoyed himself. He had come out of his chrysalis condition altogether, and was enjoying the butterfly existence to an extent which he had never conceived of, fluttering about everywhere, sunning his fine new wings, his new energies, his manhood, and his health, and his wealth, and all the glories that were his. To do him justice, he would have brought his household up to town, in order that Reine too might have had her glimpse of the season, could he have persuaded them; but Reine, just then at a critical point of her life, declined the indulgence. Kate and Sophy, however, were fond of saying that they had never enjoyed a season so much. Opera-boxes rained upon them; they never wanted bouquets; and their parties to Richmond, to Greenwich, wherever persons of her class go, were endless. Herbert was ready for anything, and their father did decline the advantages, though he disliked the giver of them; and even when he was disagreeable, matrons were always procurable to chaperone the party, and preside over their pleasures. Everybody believed, as Sophy did, that there could be but one conclusion to so close an intimacy.

"At all events, we have had a very jolly season," said Kate, who was not so sure.

And Herbert fully echoed the words when he heard them. Yes, it had been a very jolly season. He had "spent his money free," which in the highest class, as well as in the lowest, is the most appropriate way in which a young man can make himself agreeable. He had enjoyed himself, and he had given to others a great many opportunities of enjoying themselves. Now and then he carried down a great party to Whiteladies, and introduced the beau monde to his beautiful old house, and made one of those fêtes champêtres for his friends which break so agreeably upon the toils of London pleasuring, and which supply to the highest class, always like the lowest in their peculiar rites, an elegant substitute for Cremorne and Rosherville. Miss Susan bestirred herself, and made a magnificent response to his appeals when he asked her to receive such parties, and consoled herself for the gay mob that disturbed the dignity of the old house, by the noble names of some of them, which she was too English not to be impressed by. And thus in a series of delights the Summer passed from May to August. Herbert did not go to Scotland, though he had many invitations and solicitations to do so when the season was over. He came home instead, and settled there when fashion melted away out of town; and Sophy, considering the subject, as she thought, impartially, and without any personal prejudice (she said), concluded that it must be for her sake he stayed.

"I know the Duke of Ptarmigan asked him, and Tom Heath, and Billy Trotter," she said to her sister. "Billy, they say, has the finest moors going. Why shouldn't he have gone, unless he had some motive? He can't have any shooting here till September. If it isn't that, what do you suppose it can be!"

"Well, at all events we have had a very jolly season," said Kate, not disposed to commit herself; "and what we have to do is to keep things going, and show him the country, and not be dull even now." Which admirable suggestion they carried out with all their hearts.

Herbert's thoughts, however, were not, I fear, so far advanced as Sophy supposed. It was not that he did not think of that necessity of marrying which Miss Augustine enforced upon him in precisely the same words, every time she saw him. "You are wasting time—you are wasting my time, Herbert," she said to him when he came back to Whiteladies, in July. Frankly she thought this the most important point of view. So far as he was concerned, he was young, and there was time enough; but if she, a woman of seven-and-fifty, was to bring up his heir and initiate him into her ideas, surely there was not a moment to be lost in taking the preliminary steps.

Herbert was very much amused with this view of the subject. It tickled his imagination so, that he had not been able to refrain from communicating it to several of his friends. But various of these gentlemen, after they had laughed, pronounced it to be their opinion that, by Jove, the old girl was not so far out.

"I wouldn't stand having that little brat of a child set up as the heir under my very nose; and, by Jove, Austin, I'd settle that old curmudgeon Farrel's hopes fast enough, if I were in your place," said his advisers.

Herbert was not displeased with the notion. He played with it, with a certain enjoyment. He felt that he was a prize worth anybody's pursuit, and liked to hear that such and such ladies were "after him." The Duke of Ptarmigan had a daughter or two, and Sir Billy Trotter's sister might do worse, her friends thought. Herbert smoothed an incipient moustache, late in growing, and consequently very precious, and felt a delightful complaisance steal over him. And he knew that Sophy, his cousin, did not despise him; I am not sure even that the young coxcomb was not aware that he might have the pick of either of the girls, if he chose; which also, though Kate had never thought on the subject, was true enough. She had faithfully given him over to her younger sister, and never interfered; but if Herbert had thrown his handkerchief to her, she would have thought it sinful to refuse. When he thought on the subject, which was often enough, he had a kind of lazy sense that this was what would befall him at last. He would throw his handkerchief some time when he was at the Hatch, and wheresoever the chance wind might flutter it, there would be his fate. He did not really care much whether it might happen to be Sophy or Kate.

When he came home, however, these thoughts would float away out of his mind. He did not think of marrying, though Miss Augustine spoke to him on the subject every day. He thought of something else, which yet was not so far different; he thought that nowhere, in society or out of it, had he seen any one like Giovanna.

"Did you ever see such a picture?" he would say to Reine. "Look at her! Now she's sculpture, with that child on her shoulder. If the boy was only like herself, what a group they'd make! I'd like to have Marochetti, or some of those swells, down, to make them in marble. And she'd paint just as well. By Jove, she's all the arts put together. How she does sing! Patti and the rest are nothing to her. But I don't understand how she could be the mother of that boy."

Giovanna came back across the lawn, having swung the child from her shoulder on to the fragrant grass, in time to hear this, and smiled and said, "He does not resemble me, does he? Madame Suzanne, M. Herbert remarks that the boy is not dark as me. He is another type—yes, another type, n'est ce pas!"

"Not a bit like you," said Herbert. "I don't say anything against Jean, who is a dear little fellow; but he is not like you."

"Ah! but he is the heir of M. Herbert, which is better," cried Giovanna, with a laugh, "until M. Herbert will marry. Why will not you marry and range yourself? Then the little Jean and the great Giovanna will melt away like the fogs. Ah, marry, M. Herbert! it is what you ought to do."

"Are you so anxious, then, to melt away like the fog?—like the sunshine, you mean," said the young man in a low voice. They were all in the porch, but he had gone out to meet her, on pretence of playing with little Jean.

"But no," said Giovanna, smiling, "not at all. I am very well here; but when M. Herbert will marry, then I must go away. Little Jean will be no more the heir."

"Then I shall never marry," said the young man, though still in tones so low as not to reach the ears of the others. Giovanna turned her face toward him with a mocking laugh.

"Bah! already I know Madame Herbert's name, her little name!" she cried, and picked up the boy with one vigorous, easy sweep of her beautiful arms, and carried him off, singing to him—like a goddess, Herbert thought, like the nurse of a young Apollo. He was dreadfully disconcerted with this sudden withdrawal, and when Miss Augustine, coming in, addressed him in her usual way, he turned from her pettishly, with an impatient exclamation:

"I wish you would give over," he said; "you are making a joke of a serious matter. You are putting all sorts of follies into people's heads."

It was only at Whiteladies, however, that he entertained this feeling. When he was away from home he would now and then consider the question of throwing the handkerchief, and made up his mind that there would be a kind of justice in it if the petit nom of the future Mrs. Herbert turned out to be either Sophy or Kate.

Things went on in this way until, one day in August, it was ordained that the party, with its usual military attendants, should vary its enjoyments by a day on the river. They started from Water Beeches, Everard's house, in the morning, with the intention of rowing up the river as far as Marlow, and returning in the evening to a late dinner. The party consisted of Kate and Sophy, with their father, Reine and Herbert, Everard himself, and a quantity of young soldiers, with the wife of one of them, four ladies, to wit, and an indefinite number of men. They started on a lovely morning, warm yet fresh, with a soft little breeze blowing, stirring the long flags and rushes, and floating the water-lilies that lurked among their great leaves in every corner. Reine and Everard had not seen much of each other for some time. From the day that he went off in an injured state of mind, reminding them half indignantly that they knew where to find him when he was wanted, they had met only two or three times, and never had spoken to each other alone. Everard had been in town for the greater part of the time, purposely taking himself away, sore and wounded, to have, as he thought, no notice taken of him; while Reine, on her part, was too proud to make any advances to so easily affronted a lover. This had been in her mind, restraining her from many enjoyments when both Herbert and Miss Susan thought her "quite happy". She was "quite happy," she always said; did not wish to go to town, preferred to stay at Whiteladies, had no desire to go to Court and to make her début in society, as Miss Susan felt she should. Reine resisted, being rather proud and fanciful and capricious, as the best of girls may be permitted to be under such circumstances; and she had determinedly made herself "happy" in her country life, with such gayeties and amusements as came to her naturally. I think, however, that she had looked forward to this day on the river, not without a little hope, born of weariness, that something might happen to break the ice between Everard and herself. By some freak of fortune, however, or unkind arrangement, it so happened that Reine and Everard were not even in the same boat when they started. She thought (naturally) that it was his fault, and he thought (equally naturally) that it was her fault; and each believed that the accident was a premeditated and elaborately schemed device to hold the other off. I leave the reader to guess whether this added to the pleasure of the party, in which these two, out of their different boats, watched each other when they could, and alternated between wild gayety put on when each was within sight of the other, to show how little either minded—and fits of abstraction.

The morning was beautiful; the fair river glided past them, here shining like a silver shield, there falling into heavenly coolness under the shadows, with deep liquid tones of green and brown, with glorified reflections of every branch and twig, with forests of delicious growth (called weeds) underneath its clear rippling, throwing up long blossomed boughs of starry flowers, and in the shallows masses of great cool flags and beds of water-lilies. This was not a scene for the chills and heats of a love-quarrel, or for the perversity of a voluntary separation. And I think Everard felt this, and grew impatient of the foolish caprice which he thought was Reine's, and which Reine thought was his, as so often happens. When they started in the cooler afternoon, to come down the river, he put her almost roughly into his boat.

"You are coming with me this time," he said in a half-savage tone, gripping her elbow fiercely as he caught her on her way to the other, and almost lifted her into his boat.

Reine half-resisted for the moment, her face flaming with respondent wrath, but melted somehow by his face so near her, and his imperative grasp, she allowed herself to be thrust into the little nutshell which she knew so well, and which (or its predecessors) had been called "Queen" for years, thereby acquiring for Everard a character for loyalty which Reine knew he did not deserve, though he had never told her so. The moment she had taken her place there, however, Reine justified all Everard's sulks by immediately resuming toward him the old tone. If she had not thus recovered him as her vizier and right-hand man, she would, I presume, have kept her anxiety in her own breast. As it was, he had scarcely placed her on the cushions, when suddenly, without a pause, without one special word to him, asking pardon (as she ought) for her naughtiness, Reine said suddenly, "Everard! oh, will you take care, please, that Bertie does not row?"

He looked at her wholly aggravated, but half laughing. "Is this all I am ever to be good for?" he said; "not a word for me, no interest in me. Am I to be Bertie's dry-nurse all my life? And is this all—?"

She put her hand softly on his arm, and drew him to her to whisper to him. In that moment all Reine's coldness, all her doubts of him had floated away, with a suddenness which I don't pretend to account for, but which belonged to her impulsive character (and in her heart I do not believe she had ever had the least real doubt of him, though it was a kind of dismal amusement to think she had). She put up her face to him, with her hand on his arm. "Speak low," she said. "Is there any one I could ask but you? Everard, he has done too much already to-day; don't let him row."

Everard laughed. He jumped out of his boat and spoke to the other men about, confidentially, in undertones. "Don't let him see you mean it," he said; and when he had settled this piece of diplomacy, he came back and pushed off his own boat into mid-stream. "The others had all got settled," he said. "I don't see why I should run upon your messages, and do everything you tell me, and never get anything by it. Mrs. Sellinger has gone with Kate and Sophy, who have much more need of a chaperone than you have: and for the first time I have you to myself, Reine."

Reine had the strings of the rudder in her hands, and could have driven him back, I think, had she liked, but she did not. She let herself and the boat float down the pleasanter way. "I don't mind," she said softly; "for a long time I have had no talk with you—since we came home."

"And whose fault is that, I should like to know?" cried Everard, with a few long swift strokes, carrying the boat almost out of sight of the larger one, which had not yet started. "How cruel you are, Reine! You say that as if I was to blame; when you know all the time if you had but held up a little finger—"

"Why should I hold up a little finger?" said Reine, softly, leaning back in her seat. But there was a smile on her face. It was true, she acknowledged to herself. She had known it all the time. A little finger, a look, a word would have done it, though she had made believe to be lonely and dreary and half-forsaken and angry even. At which, as the boat glided down the river in the soft shadows after sunset, in the cool grayness of the twilight, she smiled again.

But before they reached the Water Beeches, these cool soft shades had given way to a sudden cold mist, what country people call a "blight." It was only then, I think, that these two recollected themselves. They had sped down the shining stream, with a little triumph in outstripping the other and larger boat, though it had four rowers, and Everard was but one. They had gone through the locks by themselves, leaving saucy messages for their companions, and it was only when they got safely within sight of Everard's house, and felt the coldness of the "blight" stealing through them, that they recollected to wonder what had kept the others so long. Then Reine grew frightened, unreasonably, as she felt; fantastically, for was not Herbert quite well? but yet beyond her own power of control.

"Turn back, and let us meet them," she begged; and Everard, though unwilling, could not refuse to do it. They went back through the growing darkness, looking out eagerly for the party.

"That cannot be them," said Everard, as the long sweep of oars became audible. "It must be a racing boat, for I hear no voices."

They lay close by the bank and watched, Reine in an agony of anxiety, for which she could give no reason. But sure enough it was the rest of the party, rowing quickly down, very still and frightened. Herbert had insisted upon rowing, in spite of all remonstrances, and just a few minutes before had been found half fainting over his oar, shivering and breathless.

"It is nothing—it is nothing," he gasped, when he saw Reine, "and we are close at home." But his heart panted so, that this was all he could say.

CHAPTER XLIV

What a dismal conclusion it was of so merry a day! Herbert walked into the house, leaning upon Everard's arm, and when some wine had been administered to him, declared himself better, and endeavored to prove that he was quite able to join them at supper, and that it was nothing. But his pale face and panting breast belied his words, and after awhile he acknowledged that perhaps it would be best to remain on the sofa in the drawing-room, while the others had their meal. Reine took her place by him at once, though indeed Sophy, who was kind enough, was ready and even anxious to do it. But in such a case the bond of kin is always paramount. The doctor was sent for at once, and Everard went and came from his guests at the dinner-table, to his much-more-thought-of guests in the cool, silent drawing-room, where Reine sat on a low chair by the sofa, holding her brother's hand, and fanning him to give him air.

"All right, old fellow," poor Bertie said, whenever Everard's anxious face appeared; but when Reine and he were left alone, he panted forth abuse of himself and complaints of Providence. "Just as I thought I was all right—whenever I felt a little freedom, took a little liberty—"

"Oh, Bertie," said Reine, "you know you should not have done it. Dear, don't talk now, to make it worse. Lie still, and you'll be better. Oh, Bertie! have patience, have patience, dear!"

"To look like a fool!" he gasped; "never good for anything. No—more—strength than a baby! and all those follows looking on."

"Bertie, they are all very kind, they are all very sorry. Oh, how can you talk of looking like a fool?"

"I do," he said; "and the girls, too!—weaker, weaker than any of them. Sorry! I don't want them to be sorry; and old Farrel gloating over it. Oh, God! I can't bear it—I can't bear it, Reine."

"Bertie, be still—do you hear me? This is weak, if you please; this is unlike a man. You have done too much, and overtired yourself. Is this a reason to give up heart, to abuse everybody, to blaspheme—"

"It is more—than being overtired," he moaned; "feel my heart, how it goes!"

"Yes, it is a spasm," said Reine, taking upon her a composure and confidence she did not feel. "You have had the same before. If you want to be better, don't talk, oh, don't talk, Bertie! Be still, be quite still!"

And thus she sat, with his hand in hers, softly fanning him; and half in exhaustion, half soothed by her words, he kept silent. Reine had harder work when the dinner was over, and Sophy and Kate fluttered into the room, to stand by the sofa, and worry him with questions.

"How are you now? Is your breathing easier? Are you better, Bertie? oh, say you are a little better! We can never, never forgive ourselves for keeping you out so late, and for letting you tire yourself so."

"Please don't make him talk," cried Reine. "He is a little better. Oh, Bertie, Bertie, dear, be still. If he is quite quiet, it will pass off all the sooner. I am not the least frightened," she said, though her heart beat loud in her throat, belying her words; but Reine had seen Farrel-Austin's face, hungry and eager, over his daughters' shoulders. "He is not really so bad; he has had it before. Only he must, he must be still. Oh, Sophy, for the love of heaven, do not make him speak!"

"Nonsense—I am all right," he said.

"Of course he can speak," cried Sophy, triumphantly; "you are making a great deal too much fuss, Reine. Make him eat something, that will do him good. There's some grouse. Everard, fetch him some grouse—one can eat that when one can eat nothing else—and I'll run and get him a glass of champagne."

"Oh, go away—oh, keep her away!" cried Reine, joining her hands in eager supplication.

Everard, to whom she looked, shrugged his shoulders, for it was not so easy a thing to do. But by dint of patience the room was cleared at last; and though Sophy would fain have returned by the open window, "just to say good-bye," as she said, "and to cheer Bertie up, for they were all making too great a fuss about him," the whole party were finally got into their carriages, and sent away. Sophy's last words, however, though they disgusted the watchers, were balm to Herbert.

"She is a jolly girl," he said; "you are making—too—much fuss. It's—going off. I'll be—all right—directly."

And then in the grateful quiet that followed, which no one disturbed, with his two familiar nurses, who had watched him so often, by his side, the excitement really began to lessen, the palpitation to subside. Reine and Everard sat side by side, in the silence, saying nothing to each other, almost forgetting, if that were possible, what they had been saying to each other as they glided, in absolute seclusion from all other creatures, down the soft twilight river. All the recent past seemed to melt into the clouds for them, and they were again at Appenzell, at Kandersteg, returned to their familiar occupation nursing their sick together, as they had so often nursed him before.

Everard had despatched a messenger to Whiteladies, when he sent for the doctor; and Miss Susan, careful of Reine as well as of Herbert, obeyed the summons along with the anxious François, who understood the case in a moment. The doctor, on his arrival, gave also a certain consolation to the watchers. With quiet all might be well again; there was nothing immediately alarming in the attack; but he must not exert himself, and must be content for the moment at least to retire to the seclusion of an invalid. They all remained in Water Beeches for the night, but next morning were able to remove the patient to Whiteladies. In the morning, before they left, poor Everard, once more thrown into a secondary place, took possession of Reine, and led her all over his small premises. It was a misty morning, touched with the first sensation of Autumn, though Summer was all ablaze in the gardens and fields. A perfect tranquillity of repose was everywhere, and as the sun got power, and the soft white mists broke up, a soft clearness of subdued light, as dazzling almost as full sunshine, suffused the warm still atmosphere. The river glided languid under the heat, gleaming white and dark, without the magical colors of the previous day. The lazy shadows drooped over it from the leafy banks, so still that it was hard to say which was substance and which shadow.

"We are going to finish our last-night's talk," said Everard.

"Finish!" said Reine half-smiling, half-weeping, for how much had happened since that enchanted twilight! "what more is there to say?" And I don't think there was much more to say—though he kept her under the trees on the river side, and in the shady little wood by the pond where the skating had been when he received her letter—saying it; so long, that Miss Susan herself came out to look for them, wondering. As she called "Reine! Reine!" through the still air, wondering more and more, she suddenly came in sight of them turning the corner of a great clump of roses, gay in their second season of bloom. They came toward her arm-in-arm with a light on their faces which it needed no sorcerer to interpret. Miss Susan had never gone through these experiences herself, but she understood at once what this meant, and her heart gave one leap of great and deep delight. It was so long since she had felt what it was to be happy, that the sensation overpowered her. It was what she had hoped for and prayed for, so long as her hopes were worth much, or her prayers. She had lost sight of this secret longing in the dull chaos of preoccupation which had swallowed her up for so long; and now this thing for which she had never dared to scheme, and which lately she had not had the courage even to wish for, was accomplished before her eyes.

"Oh," said Miss Susan, out of the depths of an experience unknown to them, "how much better God is to us than we are to ourselves! A just desire comes to pass without any scheming." And she kissed them both with lips that trembled, and joy incredible, incomprehensible in her heart. She had ceased to hope for anything that was personally desirable to her; and, lo! here was her chief wish accomplished.

This was all Hebrew and Sanskrit to the young people, who smiled to each other in their ignorance, but were touched by her emotion, and surrounded her with their happiness and their love, a very atmosphere of tenderness and jubilation. And the sun burst forth just then, and woke up all the dormant glow of color, as if to celebrate the news now first breathed to other ears than their own; and the birds, they thought, fell a-singing all at once, in full chorus. Herbert, who lay on the sofa, languid and pale, waiting for them to start on his drive home, did not observe these phenomena, poor boy, though the windows were open. He thought they were long of coming (as indeed they were), and was fretful, feeling himself neglected, and eager to get home.

Whiteladies immediately turned itself into an enchanted palace, a castle of silence and quiet. The young master of the house was as if he had been transported suddenly into the Arabian nights. Everything was arranged for his comfort, for his amusement, to make him forget the noisier pleasures into which he had plunged with so much delight. When he had got over his sombre and painful disappointment, I don't think poor Herbert, accustomed to an invalid existence, disliked the Sybarite seclusion in which he found himself. He had the most careful and tender nurse, watching every look; and he had (which I suspect was the best of it) a Slave—an Odalisque, a creature devoted to his pleasure—his flatterer, the chief source of his amusement, his dancing-girl, his singing-woman, a whole band of entertainers in one. This I need not say was Giovanna. At last her turn had come, and she was ready to take advantage of it. She did not interfere with the nursing, having perhaps few faculties that way, or perhaps (which is more likely) feeling it wiser not to invade the province of the old servants and the anxious relatives. But she took upon her to amuse Herbert, with a success which none of the others could rival. She was never anxious; she did not look at him with those longing, eager eyes, which, even in the depths of their love, convey alarm to the mind of the sick. She was gay and bright, and took the best view of everything, feeling quite confident that all would be well; for, indeed, though she liked him well enough, there was no love in her to make her afraid. She was perfectly patient, sitting by him for hours, always ready to take any one's place, ready to sing to him, to read to him in her indifferent English, making him gay with her mistakes, and joining in the laugh against herself with unbroken good-humor. She taught little Jean tricks to amuse the invalid, and made up a whole series of gymnastic evolutions with the boy, tossing him about in her beautiful arms, a picture of elastic strength and grace. She was, in short—there was no other word for it—not Herbert's nurse or companion, but his slave; and there could be little doubt that it was the presence and ministrations of this beautiful creature which made him so patient of his confinement. And he was quite patient, as contented as in the days when he had no thought beyond his sick-room, notwithstanding that now he spoke continually of what he meant to do when he was well. Giovanna cured him of anxiety, made everything look bright to him. It was some time before Miss Susan or Reine suspected the cause of this contented state, which was so good for him, and promoted his recovery so much. A man's nearest friends are slow to recognize or believe that a stranger has more power over him than themselves; but after awhile they did perceive it with varying and not agreeable sentiments. I cannot venture to describe the thrill of horror and pain with which Miss Susan found it out.

It was while she was walking alone from the village, at the corner of Priory Lane, that the thought struck her suddenly; and she never forgot the aspect of the place, the little heaps of fallen leaves at her feet, as she stood still in her dismay, and, like a revelation, saw what was coming. Miss Susan uttered a groan so bitter, that it seemed to echo through the air, and shake the leaves from the trees, which came down about her in a shower, for it was now September. "He will marry her!" she said to herself; and the consequences of her own sin, instead of coming to an end, would be prolonged forever, and affect unborn generations. Reine naturally had no such horror in her mind; but the idea of Giovanna's ascendancy over Herbert was far from agreeable to her, as may be supposed. She struggled hard to dismiss the idea, and she tried what she could to keep her place by her brother, and so resist the growing influence. But it was too late for such an effort; and indeed, I am afraid, involved a sacrifice not only of herself, but of her pride, and of Herbert's affection, that was too much for Reine. To see his looks cloud over, to see him turn his back on her, to hear his querulous questions, "Why did not she go out? Was not Everard waiting? Could not she leave him a little freedom, a little time to himself?"—all this overcame his sister.

"He will marry Giovanna," she said, pouring her woes into the ear of her betrothed. "She must want to marry him, or she would not be there always, she would not behave as she is doing."

"He will marry whom he likes, darling, and we can't stop him," said Everard, which was poor consolation. And thus the crisis slowly drew near.

In the meantime another event utterly unexpected had followed that unlucky day on the river, and had contributed to leave the little romance of Herbert and Giovanna undisturbed. Mr. Farrel-Austin caught cold in the "blight" that fell upon the river, or in the drive home afterward; nobody could exactly tell how it was. He caught cold, which brought on congestion of the lungs, and in ten days, taking the county and all his friends utterly by surprise, and himself no less, to whom such a thing seemed incredible, was dead. Dead; not ill, nor in danger, but actually dead—a thing which the whole district gasped to hear, not finding it possible to connect the idea of Farrel-Austin with anything so solemn. The girls drove over twice to ask for Herbert, and had been admitted to the morning room, the cheerfullest room in the house, where he lay on his sofa, to see him, and had told him lightly (which was a consolation to Herbert, as showing him that he was not alone in misfortune) that papa was ill too, in bed and very bad. But Sophy and Kate were, like all the rest of the world, totally unprepared for the catastrophe which followed; and they did not come back, being suddenly plunged into all the solemn horror of an event so deeply affecting their own fortunes, as well as such affections as they possessed. Thus, there was not even the diversion of a rival to interrupt Giovanna's opportunity. Farrel-Austin's death affected Miss Susan in the most extraordinary way, so that all her friends were thunderstruck. She was overwhelmed; was it by grief for her enemy? When she received the news, she gave utterance to a wild and terrible cry, and rushed up to her own room, whence she scarcely appeared all the rest of the day. Next morning she presented to her astonished family a countenance haggard and pale, as if by years of suffering. What was the cause? Was it Susan that had loved him, and not Augustine (who took the information very calmly), or what was the secret of this impassioned emotion? No one could say. Miss Susan was like a woman distraught for some days. She would break out into moanings and weeping when she was alone, in which indulgence she was more than once surprised by the bewildered Reine. This was too extraordinary to be accounted for. Was it possible, the others asked themselves, that her enmity to Farrel-Austin had been but a perverse cloak for another sentiment?

I give these wild guesses, because they were at their wits' end, and had not the least clue to the mystery. So bewildered were they, that they could show her little sympathy, and do nothing to comfort her; for it was monstrous to see her thus afflicted. Giovanna was the only one who seemed to have any insight at this moment into the mind of Miss Susan. I think even she had but a dim realization of how it was. But she was kind, and did her best to show her kindness; a sympathy which Miss Susan revolted the rest by utter rejection of, a rejection almost fierce in its rudeness.

"Keep me free from that woman—keep her away from me!" she cried wildly.

"Aunt Susan," said Reine, not without reproach in her tone, "Giovanna wants to be kind."

"Oh, kind! What has come to us that I must put up with her kindness?" she cried, with her blue eyes aflame.

Neither Reine nor any of the others knew what to say to this strange new phase in Miss Susan's mysterious conduct. For it was apparent to all of them that some mystery had come into her life, into her character, since the innocent old days when her eyes were as clear and her brow, though so old, as unruffled as their own. Day by day Miss Susan's burden was getting heavier to bear. Farrel's death, which removed all barriers except the one she had herself put there, between Everard and the inheritance of Whiteladies; and this growing fascination of Herbert for Giovanna, which she seemed incapable of doing anything to stop, and which, she cried out to herself in the silence of the night, she never, never would permit herself to consent to, and could not bear—these two things together filled up the measure of her miseries. Day by day the skies grew blacker over her, her footsteps were hemmed in more terribly; until at last she seemed scarcely to know what she was doing. The bailiff addressed himself to Everard in a kind of despair.

"I can't get no orders," he said. "I can't get nothing reasonable out of Miss Austin; whether it's anxiousness, or what, none of us can tell." And he gave Everard an inquisitive look, as if testing him how far he might go. It was the opinion of the common people that Augustine had been mad for years; and now they thought Miss Susan was showing signs of the same malady.

"That's how things goes when it's in a family," the village said.

Thus the utmost miserable endurance, and the most foolish imbecile happiness lived together under the same roof, vaguely conscious of each other, yet neither fathoming the other's depths. Herbert, like Reine and Everard, perceived that something was wrong with Miss Susan; but being deeply occupied with his own affairs, and feeling the absolute unimportance of anything that could happen to his old aunt in comparison—was not much tempted to dwell upon the idea, or to make any great effort to penetrate the mystery; while she, still more deeply preoccupied with her wretchedness, fearing the future, yet fearing still more to betray herself, did not realize how quickly affairs were progressing, nor how far they had gone. It was not till late in September that she at last awoke to the fact. Herbert was better, almost well again, the doctor pronounced, but sadly shaken and weak. It was a damp, rainy day, with chills in it of the waning season, dreary showers of yellow leaves falling with every gust, and all the signs that an early ungenial Autumn, without those gorgeous gildings of decay which beguile us of our natural regrets, was closing in, yellow and humid, with wet mists and dreary rain. Everything dismal that can happen is more dismal on such a day, and any diversion which can be had indoors to cheat the lingering hours is a double blessing. Herbert was as usual in the morning-room, which had been given up to him as the most cheerful. Reine had been called away to see Everard, who, now that the invalid was better, insisted upon a share of her attention; and she had left the room all the more reluctantly that there was a gleam of pleasure in her brother's eye as she was summoned. "Giovanna will stay with me," he said, the color rising in his pale cheeks; and Reine fled to Everard, red with mortification and sorrow and anger, to ask him for the hundredth time, "Could nothing be done to stop it—could nothing be done?"

Miss Susan was going about the house from room to room, feverishly active in some things by way of making up, perhaps from the half-conscious failing of her powers in others. She was restless, and could not keep still to look out upon the flying leaves, the dreary blasts, the gray dismal sky; and the rain prevented her from keeping her miserable soul still by exercise out of doors, as she often did now, contrary to all use and wont. She had no intention in her mind when her restless feet turned the way of Herbert's room. She did not know that Giovanna was there, and Reine absent. She was not suspicious more than usual, neither had she the hope or fear of finding out anything. She went mechanically that way, as she might have gone mechanically through the long turnings of the passage to the porch, where Reine and Everard were looking out upon the dismal Autumn day.

When she opened the door, however, listlessly, she saw a sight which woke her up like a trumpet. Giovanna was sitting upon a stool close by Herbert's sofa. One of her hands he was holding tenderly in his; with the other she was smoothing back his hair from his forehead, caressing him with soft touches and soft words, while he gazed at her with that melting glow of sentimentality—vanity or love, or both together, in his eyes—which no spectator can ever mistake. As Miss Susan went into the room, Giovanna, who sat with her back to the door, bent over him and kissed him on the forehead, murmuring as she did so into his bewitched and delighted ear.

The looker-on was petrified for the first moment; then she threw up her hands, and startled the lovers with a wild shrill cry. I think it was heard all over the house. Giovanna jumped up from her stool, and Herbert started upright on his sofa; and Reine and Everard, alarmed, came rushing from the porch. They all gazed at Miss Susan, who stood there as pale as marble, gasping with an attempt to speak. Herbert for the moment was cowed and frightened by the sight of her; but Giovanna had perfect possession of her faculties. She faced the new-comers with a blush, which only improved her beauty, and laughed.

"Eh bien!" she cried, "you have then found out, Madame Suzanne? I am content, me. I am not fond of to deceive. Speak to her, mon 'Erbert, the word is to thee."

"Yes, Aunt Susan," he said, trying to laugh too, but blushing, a hot uneasy blush, not like Giovanna's. "I beg your pardon. Of course I ought to have spoken to you before; and equally of course now you see what has happened without requiring any explanation. Giovanna, whom you have been so kind to, is going to be my wife."

Miss Susan once more cried out wildly in her misery, "It cannot be—it shall not be! I will not have it!" she said.

Once more Giovanna laughed, not offensively, but with a good-natured sense of fun. "Mon Dieu!" she said, "what can you do? Why should not we be bons amis? You cannot do anything, Madame Suzanne. It is all fixed and settled, and if you will think, it is for the best, it will arrange all." Giovanna had a real desire to make peace, to secure de l'amitié, as she said. She went across the room toward Miss Susan, holding out her hand.

And then for a moment a mortal struggle went on in Susan Austin's soul. She repulsed wildly, but mechanically, the offered hand, and stood there motionless, her breast panting, all the powers of nature startled into intensity, and such a conflict and passion going on within her as made her blind and deaf to the world outside. Then suddenly she put her hand upon the nearest chair, and drawing it to her, sat down, opposite to Herbert, with a nervous shiver running over her frame. She put up her hand to her throat, as if to tear away something which restrained or suffocated her; and then she said, in a terrible, stifled voice, "Herbert! first you must hear what I have got to say."

CHAPTER XLV

Giovanna looked at Miss Susan with surprise, then with a little apprehension. It was her turn to be uneasy. "Que voulez-vous? que voulez-vous dire?" she said under her breath, endeavoring to catch Miss Susan's eye. Miss Susan was a great deal too impassioned and absorbed even to notice the disturbed condition of her adversary. She knew herself to be surrounded by an eager audience, but yet in her soul she was alone, insensible to everything, moved only by a passionate impulse to relieve herself, to throw off the burden which was driving her mad. She did not even see Giovanna, who after walking round behind Herbert, trying to communicate by the eyes with the woman whom all this time she had herself subdued by covert threats, sat down at last at the head of the sofa, putting her hand, which Herbert took into his, upon it. Probably this sign of kindness stimulated Miss Susan, though I doubt whether she was conscious of it, something having laid hold upon her which was beyond her power to resist.

"I have a story to tell you, children," she said, pulling instinctively with her hand at the throat of her dress, which seemed to choke her, "and a confession to make. I have been good, good enough in my way, trying to do my duty most of my life; but now at the end of it I have done wrong, great wrong, and sinned against you all. God forgive me! and I hope you'll forgive me. I've been trying to save myself from the—exposure—from the shame, God help me! I have thought of myself, when I ought to have thought of you all. Oh, I've been punished! I've been punished! But perhaps it is not yet too late. Oh, Herbert, Herbert! my dear boy, listen to me!"

"If you are going to say anything against Giovanna, you will lose your time, Aunt Susan," said Herbert; and Giovanna leaned on the arm of the sofa, and kissed his forehead again in thanks and triumph.

"What I am going to say first is against myself," said Miss Susan. "It is three years ago—a little more than three years; Farrel-Austin, who is dead, came and told me that he had found the missing people, the Austins whom you have heard of, whom I had sought for so long, and that he had made some bargain with them, that they should withdraw in his favor. You were very ill then, Herbert, thought to be dying; and Farrel-Austin—poor man, he is dead!—was our enemy. It was dreadful, dreadful to think of him coming here, being the master of the place. That was my sin to begin with. I thought I could bear anything sooner than that."

Augustine came into the room at this moment. She came and went so noiselessly that no one even heard her; and Miss Susan was too much absorbed to note anything. The new-comer stood still near the door behind her sister, at first because it was her habit, and then, I suppose, in sympathy with the motionless attention of the others, and the continuance without a pause of Miss Susan's voice.

"I meant no harm; I don't know what I meant. I went to break their bargain, to show them the picture of the house, to make them keep their rights against that man. It was wicked enough. Farrel-Austin's gone, and God knows what was between him and us; but to think of him here made me mad, and I went to try and break the bargain. I own that was what I meant. It was not, perhaps, Christian-like; not what your Aunt Augustine, who is as good as an angel, would have approved of; but it was not wicked, not wicked, if I had done no more than that!

"When I got there," said Miss Susan, drawing a long breath, "I found them willing enough; but the man was old, and his son was dead, and there was nothing but daughters left. In the room with them was a daughter, a young married woman, a young widow—"

"Yes, there was me," said Giovanna. "To what good is all this narrative, Madame Suzanne? Me, I know it before, and Monsieur 'Erbert is not amused; look, he yawns. We have assez, assez, for to-day."

"There was she; sitting in the room, a poor, melancholy, neglected creature; and there was the other young woman, Gertrude, pretty and fair, like an English girl. She was—going to have a baby," said Miss Susan, even at that moment hesitating in her old maidenliness before she said it, her old face coloring softly. "The devil put it into my head all at once. It was not premeditated; I did not make it up in my mind. All at once, all at once the devil put it into my head! I said suddenly to the old woman, to old Madame Austin, 'Your daughter-in-law is in the same condition?' She was sitting down crouched in a corner. She was said to be sick. What was more natural," cried poor Miss Susan looking round, "than to think that was the cause?"

Perhaps it was the first time she had thought of this excuse. She caught at the idea with heat and eagerness, appealing to them all. "What more natural than that I should think so? She never rose up; I could not see her. Oh, children," cried Miss Susan, wringing her hands, "I cannot tell how much or how little wickedness there was in my first thought; but answer me, wasn't it natural? The old woman took me up in a moment, took up more—yes, I am sure—more than I meant. She drew me away to her room, and there we talked of it. She did not say to me distinctly that the widow was not in that way. We settled," she said after a pause, with a shiver and gasp before the words, "that anyhow—if a boy came— it was to be Giovanna's boy and the heir."

Herbert made an effort at this moment to relinquish Giovanna's hand, which he had been holding all the time; not, I believe, because of this information, which he scarcely understood as yet, but because his arm was cramped remaining so long in the same position; but she, as was natural, understood the movement otherwise. She held him for a second, then tossed his hand away and sprang up from her chair. "Après?" she cried, with an insolent laugh. "Madame Suzanne, you radotez, you are too old. This goes without saying that the boy is Giovanna's boy."

"Yes, we know all this," said Herbert, pettishly. "Aunt Susan, I cannot imagine what you are making all this fuss and looking so excited about. What do you mean? What is all this about old women and babies? I wish you would speak out if you have anything to say. Giovanna, come here."

"Yes," she said, throwing herself on the sofa beside him; "yes, mon Herbert, mon bien-aimé. You will not abandon me, whatever any one may say?"

"Herbert," cried Miss Susan, "let her alone, let her alone, for God's sake! She is guilty, guiltier than I am. She made a pretence as her mother-in-law told her, pretended to be ill, pretended to have a child, kept up the deceit—how can I tell how long?—till now. Gertrude is innocent, whose baby was taken; she thought it died, poor thing, poor thing! but Giovanna is not innocent. All she has done, all she has said, has been lies, lies! The child is not her child; it is not the heir. She has thrust herself into this house, and done all this mischief, by a lie. She knows it; look at her. She has kept her place by threatening me, by holding my disgrace before my eyes; and now, Herbert, my poor boy, my poor boy, she will ruin you. Oh, put her away, put her away!"

Herbert rose up, trembling in his weakness. "Is this true, Giovanna?" he said, turning to her piteously. "Have you anything to say against it? Is it true?"

Reine, who had been standing behind, listening with an amazement beyond the reach of words, came to her brother's side, to support him at this terrible moment; but he put her away. Even Miss Susan, who was the chief sufferer, fell into the background. Giovanna kept her place on the sofa, defiant, while he stood before her, turning his back upon the elder offender, who felt this mark of her own unimportance, even in the fever of her excitement and passion.

"Have you nothing to say against it?" cried Herbert, with anguish in his voice. "Giovanna! Giovanna! is it true?"

Giovanna shrugged her shoulders impatiently. "Mon Dieu," she said, "I did what I was told. They said to me, 'Do this,' and I did it; was it my fault? It was the old woman who did all, as Madame Suzanne says—"

"We are all involved together, God forgive us!" cried Miss Susan, bowing her head into her hands.

Then there was a terrible pause. They were all silent, all waiting to hear what Herbert had to say, who, by reason of being most deeply involved, seemed suddenly elevated into the judge. He went away from the sofa where Giovanna was, and in front of which Miss Susan was sitting, as far away as he could get, and began to walk up and down the room in his excitement. He took no further notice of Giovanna, but after a moment, pausing in his angry march, said suddenly, "It was all on Farrel-Austin's account you plunged into crime like this? Silence, Reine! it is crime, and it is she who is to blame. What in the name of heaven had Farrel-Austin done to you that you should avenge yourself upon us all like this?"

"Forgive me, Herbert!" said Miss Susan, faintly; "he was to have married Augustine, and he forsook her, jilted her, shamed her, my only sister. How could I see him in this house?"

And then again there was a pause. Even Reine made no advance to the culprit, though her heart began to beat loudly, and her indignation was mingled with pity. Giovanna sat gloomy; drumming with her foot upon the carpet. Herbert had resumed his rapid pacing up and down. Miss Susan sat in the midst of them, hopeless, motionless, her bowed head hidden in her hands, every help and friendly prop dropped away from her, enduring to the depths the bitterness of her punishment, yet, perhaps, with a natural reaction, asking herself, was there none, none of all she had been kind to, capable of a word, a look, a touch of pity in this moment of her downfall and uttermost need? Both Everard and Reine felt upon them that strange spell which often seems to freeze all outward action in a great emergency, though their hearts were swelling. They had both made a forward step; when suddenly, the matter was taken out of their hands. Augustine, perhaps, was more slow than any of them, out of her abstraction and musing, to be roused to what was being said. But the last words had supplied a sharp sting of reality which woke her fully, and helped her to understand. As soon as she had mastered it, she went up swiftly and silently to her sister, put her arms round her, and drew away the hands in which she had buried her face.

"Susan," she said, in a voice more real and more living than had been heard from her lips for years, "I have heard everything. You have confessed your sin, and God will forgive you. Come with me."

"Austine! Austine!" cried poor Miss Susan, shrinking, dropping to the floor at the feet of the immaculate creature who was to her as a saint.

"Yes, it is I," said Augustine. "Poor Susan! and I never knew! God will forgive you. Come with me."

"Yes," said the other, the elder and stronger, with the humility of a child; and she got up from where she had thrown herself, and casting a pitiful look upon them all, turned round and gave her hand to her sister. She was weak with her excitement, and exhausted as if she had risen from a long illness. Augustine drew her sister's hand through her arm, and without another word, led her away. Reine rushed after them, weeping and anxious, the bonds loosed that seemed to have congealed her. Augustine put her back, not unkindly, but with decision. "Another time, Reine. She is going with me."

They were all so overawed by this sudden action that even Herbert stopped short in his angry march, and Everard, who opened the door for their exit, could only look at them, and could not say a word. Miss Susan hung on Augustine's arm, broken, shattered, feeble; an old woman, worn out and fainting. The recluse supporting her, with a certain air of strength and pride, strangely unlike her nature, walked on steadily and firmly, looking, as was her wont, neither to the right hand nor the left. All her life Susan had been her protector, her supporter, her stay. Now their positions had changed all in a moment. Erect and almost proud she walked out of the room, holding up the bowed-down, feeble figure upon her arm. And the young people, all so strangely, all so differently affected by this extraordinary revelation, stood blankly together and looked at each other, not knowing what to say, when the door closed. None of the three Austins spoke to or looked at Giovanna, who sat on the sofa, still drumming with her foot upon the carpet. When the first blank pause was over, Reine went up to Herbert and put her arm through his.

"Oh, forgive her, forgive her!" she cried.

"I will never forgive her," he said wildly; "she has been the cause of it all. Why did she let this go on, my God! and why did she tell me now?"

Giovanna sat still, beating her foot on the carpet, and neither moved nor spoke.

As for Susan and Augustine, no one attempted to follow them. No one thought of anything further than a withdrawal to their rooms of the two sisters, united in a tenderness of far older date than the memories of the young people could reach; and I don't even know whether the impulse that made them both turn through the long passage toward the porch was the same. I don't suppose it was. Augustine thought of leading her penitent sister to the Almshouse chapel, as she would have wished should be done to herself in any great and sudden trouble; whereas an idea of another kind entered at once into the mind of Susan, which, beaten down and shaken as it was, began already to recover a little after having thrown off the burden. She paused a moment in the hall, and took down a gray hood which was hanging there, like Augustine's, a covering which she had adopted to please her sister on her walks about the roads near home. It was the nearest thing at hand, and she caught at it, and put it on, as both together with one simultaneous impulse they bent their steps to the door. I have said that the day was damp and dismal and hopeless, one of those days which make a despairing waste of a leafy country. Now and then there would come a miserable gust of wind, carrying floods of sickly yellow leaves from all the trees, and in the intervals a small mizzling rain, not enough to wet anything, coming like spray in the wayfarers' faces, filled up the dreary moments. No one was out of doors who could be in; it was worse than a storm, bringing chill to the marrow of your bones, weighing heavy upon your soul. The two old sisters, without a word to each other, went out through the long passage, through the porch in which

Miss Susan had sat and done her knitting so many Summers through. She took no farewell look at the familiar place, made no moan as she left it. They went out clinging to each other, Augustine erect and almost proud, Susan bowed and feeble, across the sodden wet lawn, and out at the little gate in Priory Lane. They had done it a hundred and a thousand times before; they meant, or at least Miss Susan meant, to do it never again; but her mind was capable of no regret for Whiteladies. She went out mechanically, leaning on her sister, yet almost mechanically directing that sister the way Susan intended to go, not Augustine. And thus they set forth into the Autumn weather, into the mists, into the solitary world. Had the departure been made publicly with solemn farewells and leave-takings, they would have felt it far more deeply. As it was, they scarcely felt it at all, having their minds full of other things. They went along Priory Lane, wading through the yellow leaves, and along the road to the village, where Augustine would have turned to the left, the way to the Almshouses. They had not spoken a word to each other, and Miss Susan leaned almost helplessly in her exhaustion upon her sister; but nevertheless she swayed Augustine in the opposite direction across the village street. One or two women came out to the cottage doors to look after them. It was a curious sight, instead of Miss Augustine, gray and tall and noiseless, whom they were all used to watch in the other direction, to see the two gray figures going on silently, one so bowed and aged as to be unrecognizable, exactly the opposite way. "She have got another with her, an old 'un," the women said to each other, and rubbed their eyes, and were not half sure that the sight was real. They watched the two figures slowly disappearing round the corner. It came on to rain, but the wayfarers did not quicken their pace. They proceeded slowly on, neither saying a word to the other, indifferent to the rain and to the yellow leaves that tumbled on their path. So, I suppose, with their heads bowed, and no glance behind, the first pair may have gone desolate out of Paradise. But they were young, and life was before them; whereas Susan and Augustine, setting out forlorn upon their new existence, were old, and had no heart for another home and another life.

CHAPTER XLVI

When a number of people have suddenly been brought together accidentally by such an extraordinary incident as that I have attempted to describe, it is almost as difficult for them to separate, as it is to know what to do, or what to say to each other. Herbert kept walking up and down the room, dispelling, or thinking he was dispelling, his wrath and excitement in this way. Giovanna sat on the sofa motionless, except her foot, with which she kept on beating the carpet. Reine, after trying to join herself to her brother, as I have said, and console him, went back to Everard, who had gone to the window, the safest refuge for the embarrassed and disturbed. Reine went to her betrothed, finding in him that refuge which is so great a safeguard to the mind in all circumstances. She was very anxious and unhappy, but it was about others, not about herself; and though there was a cloud of disquietude and pain upon her, as she stood by Everard's side, her face turned toward the others, watching for any new event, yet Reine's mind had in itself such a consciousness of safe anchorage, and of a refuge beyond any one's power to interfere with, that the very trouble which had overtaken them, seemed to add a fresh security to her internal well-being. Nothing that any one could say, nothing that any one could do, could interfere between her and Everard; and Everard for his part, with that unconscious selfishness à deux, which is like no other kind of selfishness, was not thinking of Herbert, or Miss Susan, but only of his poor Reine, exposed to this agitation and trouble.

"Oh, if I could only carry you away from it all, my poor darling!" he said in her ear.

Reine said, "Oh, hush, Everard, do not think of me," feeling, indeed, that she was not the chief sufferer, nor deserving, in the present case, of the first place in any one's sympathy; yet she was comforted. "Why does not she go away?—oh, if she would but go away!" cried Reine, and stood thus watching, consoled by her lover, anxious and vigilant, but yet not the person most deserving of pity, as she herself felt.

While they thus remained as Miss Susan had left them, not knowing how to get themselves dispersed, there came a sudden sound of carriage wheels, and loud knocking at the great door on the other side of the house, the door by which all strangers approached.

"Oh, as if we were not bad enough already, here are visitors!" cried Reine. And even Herbert seemed to listen, irritated by the unexpected commotion. Then followed the sound of loud voices, and a confused colloquy. "I must go and receive them, whoever it is," said Reine, with a moan over her fate. After awhile steps were heard approaching, and the door was thrown open suddenly. "Not here, not here," cried Reine, running forward. "The drawing-room, Stevens."

"Beg pardon, ma'am," said Stevens, flushed and angry. "It ain't my fault. I can't help it. They won't be kep' back, Miss Reine," he cried, bending his head down over her. "Don't be frightened. It's the hold foreign gent—"

"Not here," cried Reine again. "Oh, whom did you say? Stevens, I tell you not here."

"But he is here; the hold foreign gent," said Stevens, who seemed to be suddenly pulled back from behind by somebody following him. If there had been any laughter in her, I think Reine would have laughed; but though the impulse gleamed across her distracted mind, the power was wanting. And there suddenly appeared, facing her, in the place of Stevens, two people, who took from poor Reine all inclination to laugh. One of them was an old man, spruce and dapper, in the elaborate travelling wraps of a foreigner, of the bourgeois class, with a comforter tied round his neck, and a large great coat with a hood to it. The other was a young woman, fair and full, with cheeks momentarily paled by weariness and agitation, but now and then dyed deep with rosy color. These two came to a momentary stop in their eager career, to gaze at Reine, but finally pushing past her, to her great amazement, got before her into the room which she had been defending from them.

"I seek Madame Suzanne! I seek the lady!" said the old man.

At the sound of his voice Giovanna sprang to her feet; and as soon as they got sight of her, the two strangers made a startled pause. Then the young woman rushed forward and laid hold of her by the arm.

"Mon bébé! mon enfant! donne-moi mon bébé!" she said.

"Eh bien, Gertrude! c'est toi!" cried Giovanna. She was roused in a moment from the quiescent state, sullen or stupefied, in which she had been. She seemed to rise full of sudden energy and new life. "And the bon papa, too! Tiens, this is something of extraordinary; but, unhappily, Madame Suzanne has just left us, she is not here. Suffer me to present to you my beau-père, M. Herbert; my belle-sœur Gertrude, of whom you have just heard. Give yourself the trouble to sit down, my parents. This is a pleasure very unattended. Had Madame Suzanne known—she talked of you toute à l'heure—no doubt she would have stayed—"

"Giovanna," cried the old man, trembling, "you know, you must know, why we are here. Content this poor child, and restore to her her baby. Ah, traître! her baby, not thine. How could I be so blind—how could I be so foolish, and you so criminal, Giovanna? Your poor belle-mère has been ill, has been at the point of death, and she has told us all."

"Mon enfant!" cried the young woman, clasping her hands. "My bébé, Giovanna; give me my bébé, and I pardon thee all."

"Ah! the belle-mère has made her confession, then!" said Giovanna. "C'est ça? Poor belle-mère! and poor Madame Suzanne! who has come to do the same here. But none say 'Poor Giovanna.' Me, I am criminal, va! I am the one whom all denounce; but the others, they are then my victims, not I theirs!"

"Giovanna, Giovanna, I debate not with thee," cried the old man. "We say nothing to thee, nothing; we blame not, nor punish. We say, give back the child,—ah, give back the child! Look at her, how her color changes, how she weeps! Give her her bébé. We will not blame, nor say a word to thee, never!"

"No! you will but leave me to die of hunger," said Giovanna, "to die by the roads, in the fields, qu'importe? I am out of the law, me. Yet I have done less ill than the others. They were old, they had all they desired; and I was young, and miserable, and made mad—ah, ma Gertrude! by thee, too, gentle as thou look'st, even by thee!"

"Giovanna, Giovanna!" cried Gertrude, throwing herself at her feet. Her pretty upturned face looked round and innocent, like a child's, and the big tears ran down her cheeks. "Give me my bébé, and I will ask your pardon on my knees."

Giovanna made a pause, standing upright, with this stranger clinging to her dress, and looked round upon them all with a strange mixture of scorn and defiance and emotion. "Messieurs," she said, "and mademoiselle! you see what proof the bon Dieu has sent of all Madame Suzanne said. Was it my doing? No! I was obedient, I did what I was told: but, voyons! it will be I who shall suffer. Madame Suzanne is safe. You can do nothing to her; in a little while you will lofe her again, as before. The belle-mère, who is wicked, wickedest of all, gets better, and one calls her poor bonne-maman, pauvre petite mère! But me! I am the one who shall be cast away, I am the one to be punished; here, there, everywhere, I shall be kicked like a dog—yes, like a dog! All the pardon, the miséricorde will be for them—for me the punishment. Because I am the most weak! because I am the slave of all—because I am the one who has excuse the most!"

She was so noble in her attitude, so grand in her voice and expression, that Herbert stood and gazed at her like one spellbound. But I do not think she remarked this, being for the moment transported out of herself by a passionate outburst of feeling—sense of being wronged—pity for herself, defiance of her enemies; and a courage and resolution mingling with all which, if not very elevated in their origin, were intense enough to give elevation to her looks. What an actress she would have made! Everard thought regretfully. He was already very pitiful of the forsaken creature at whom every one threw a stone.

"Giovanna, Giovanna!" cried the weeping Gertrude, clinging to her dress, "hear me! I will forgive you, I will love you. But give me my bébé, Giovanna, give me my child!"

Giovanna paused again, looking down upon the baby face, all blurred with crying. Her own face changed from its almost tragic form to a softer aspect. A kind of pity stole over it, then another and stronger sentiment. A gleam of humor came into her eyes. "Tenez," she said, "I go to have my revenge!" and drawing her dress suddenly from Gertrude's clasp, she went up to the bell, rang it sharply, and waiting, facing them all with a smile, "Monsieur Stevens," she said, with the most enchanting courtesy, when the butler appeared, "will you have the goodness to bring to me, or to send to me, my boy, the little mas-ter Jean?"

After she had given this order, she stood still waiting, all the profounder feeling of her face disappearing into an illumination of gayety and fun, which none of the spectators understood. A few minutes elapsed while this pause lasted. Martha, who thought Master Jean was being sent for to see company, hastily invested him in his best frock and ribbons. "And be sure you make your bow pretty, and say how do do," said innocent Martha, knowing nothing of the character of the visit, nor of the tragical change which had suddenly come upon the family life. The child came in with all the boldness of the household pet into the room in which so many excited people were waiting for him. His pretty fair hair was dressed according to the tradition of the British nursery, in a great flat curl on the top of his little head. He had his velvet frock on, with scarlet ribbons, and looked, as Martha proudly thought, "a little gentleman," every inch of him. He looked round him with childish complaisance as he came in, and made his little salute, as Giovanna had taught him. But when Gertrude rushed toward him, as she did at once, and throwing herself on her knees beside him, caught him in her arms and covered him with kisses, little Jean was taken violently by surprise. A year's interval is eternity to such a baby. He knew nothing about Gertrude. He cried, struggled, fought to be free, and finally struck at her with his sturdy little fists.

"Mamma, mamma!" cried little Jean, holding out appealing arms to Giovanna, who stood at a little distance, her fine nostrils expanded, a smile upon her lip, a gleam of mischief in her eyes.

"He will know me," said the old man, going to his daughter's aid. "A moment, give him a moment, Gertrude. A moi, Jeannot, à moi! Let him go, ma fille. Give him a moment to recollect himself; he has forgotten, perhaps, his language, Jeannot, my child, come to me!"

Jean paid no attention to these blandishments. When Gertrude, weeping, released, by her father's orders, her tight hold of the child, he rushed at once to Giovanna's side, and clung to her dress, and hid his face in its folds. "Mamma, mamma, take Johnny!" he said.

Giovanna stooped, lifted him like a feather, and tossed him up to her shoulder with a look of triumph. "There, thou art safe, no one can touch thee," she said; and turning upon her discomfited relations, looked down upon them both with a smile. It was her revenge, and she enjoyed it with all her heart. The child clung to her, clasping both of his arms round hers, which she had raised to hold him fast. She laughed aloud—a laugh which startled every one, and woke the echoes all about.

"Tiens!" she said, in her gay voice, "whose child is he now? Take him if you will, Gertrude, you who were always the first, who knew yourself in babies, who were more beloved than the stupid Giovanna. Take him, then, since he is to thee!"

What a picture she would have made, standing there with the child, her great eyes flashing, her bosom expanded, looking down upon the plebeian pair before her with a triumphant smile! So Everard thought, who had entirely ranged himself on Giovanna's side; and so thought poor Herbert, looking at her with his heart beating, his whole being in a ferment, his temper and his nerves worn to their utmost. He went away trembling from the sight, and beckoned Reine to him, and threw himself into a chair at the other end of the room.

"What is all this rabble to us?" he cried querulously, when his sister answered his summons. "For heaven's sake clear the house of strangers—get them away."

"All, Herbert?" said Reine, frightened.

He made no further reply, but dismissed her with an impatient wave of his hand, and taking up a book, which she saw he held upside down, and which trembled in his hand, turned his back upon the new-comers who had so strangely invaded the house.

As for these good people, they had nothing to say to this triumph of Giovanna. I suppose they had expected, as many innocent persons do, that by mere force of nature the child would turn to those who alone had a right to him. Gertrude, encumbered by her heavy travelling wraps, wearied, discouraged, and disappointed, sat down and cried, her round face getting every moment more blurred and unrecognizable. M. Guillaume, however, though tired too, and feeling this reception very different from the distinguished one which he had received on his former visit, felt it necessary to maintain the family dignity.

"I would speak with Madame Suzanne," he said, turning to Reine, who approached. "Mademoiselle does not perhaps know that I am a relation, a next-of-kin. It is I, not the poor bébé, who am the next to succeed. I am Guillaume Austin, of Bruges. I would speak with Madame Suzanne. She will know how to deal with this insensée, this woman who keeps from my daughter her child."

"My aunt is—ill," said Reine. "I don't think she is able to see you. Will you come into another room and rest? and I will speak to Giovanna. You must want to rest—a little—and—something to eat—"

So far Reine's hospitable instincts carried her; but when Stevens entered with a request from the driver of the cab which had brought the strangers hither, to know what he was to do, she could not make any reply to the look that M. Guillaume gave her. That look plainly implied a right to remain in the house, which made Reine tremble, and she pretended not to see that she was referred to. Then the old shopkeeper took it upon himself to send away the man. "Madame Suzanne would be uncontent, certainly uncontent, if I went away without to see her," he said; "dismiss him then, mon ami. I will give you to pay—" and he pulled out a purse from his pocket. What could Reine do or say? She stood trembling, wondering how it was all to be arranged, what she could do; for though she was quite unaware of the withdrawal of Miss Susan, she felt that in this case it was her duty to act for her brother and herself. She went up to Giovanna softly, and touched her on the arm.

"What are you going to do?" she said in a whisper. "Oh, Giovanna, have some pity upon us! Get them to go away. My Aunt Susan has been kind to you, and how could she see these people? Oh, get them to go away!"

Giovanna looked down upon Reine, too, with the same triumphant smile. "You come also," she said, "Mademoiselle Reine, you, too! to poor Giovanna, who was not good for anything. Bien! It cannot be for to-night, but perhaps for to-morrow, for they are fatigued—that sees itself. Gertrude, to cry will do nothing; it will frighten the child more, who is, as you perceive, to me, not to thee. Smile, then—that will be more well—and come with me, petite sotte. Though thou wert not good to Giovanna, Giovanna will be more noble, and take care of thee."

She took hold of her sister-in-law as she spoke, half dragged her off her chair, and leading her with her disengaged hand, walked out of the room with the child on her shoulder. Reine heard the sound of an impatient sigh, and hurried to her brother's side. But Herbert had his eyes firmly fixed upon the book, and when she came up to him waved her off.

"Let me alone," he said in his querulous tones, "cannot you let me alone!" Even the touch of tenderness was more than he could bear.

Then it was Everard's turn to exert himself, who had met M. Guillaume before, and with a little trouble got him to follow the others as far as the small dining-room, in which Reine had given orders for a hasty meal. M. Guillaume was not unwilling to enter into explanations. His poor wife, he said, had been ill for weeks past.

"It was some mysterious attack of the nerves; no one could tell what it was," the old man said. "I called doctor after doctor, if you will believe me, monsieur. I spared no expense. At last it was said to me, 'It is a priest that is wanted, not a doctor.' I am Protestant, monsieur," said the old shopkeeper seriously. "I replied with disdain, 'According to my faith, it is the husband, it is the father who is priest.' I go to Madame Austin's chamber. I say to her, 'My wife, speak!' Brief, monsieur, she spoke, that suffering angel, that martyr! She told us of the wickedness which Madame Suzanne and cette méchante planned, and how she was drawn to be one with them, pauvre chérie. Ah, monsieur, how women are weak! or when not weak, wicked. She told us all, monsieur, how she has been unhappy! and as soon as we could leave her, we came, Gertrude and I—for my part, I was not pressé—I said, 'Thou hast many children, my Gertrude; leave then this one to be at the expense of those who have acted so vilely.' And my poor angel said also from her sick-bed; but the young they are obstinate, they have no reason, and—behold us! We had a bad, very bad traversée; and it appears that la jeune-là, whom I know not, would willingly send us back without the repose of an hour."

"You must pardon her," said Everard. "We have been in great trouble, and she did not know even who you were."

"It seems to me," said the old man, opening his coat with a flourish of offended dignity, "that in this house, which may soon be mine, all should know me. When I say I am Guillaume Austin of Bruges, what more rests to say?"

"But, Monsieur Guillaume," said Everard, upon whom these words, "this house, which may soon be mine," made, in spite of himself, a highly disagreeable impression, "I have always heard that for yourself you cared nothing for it—would not have it indeed."

"I would not give that for it," said the old man with a snap of his fingers; "a miserable grange, a maison du campagne, a thing of wood and stone! But one has one's dignity and one's rights."

And he elevated his old head, with a snort from the Austin nose, which he possessed in its most pronounced form. Everard did not know whether to take him by the shoulders and to turn him out of the house, or to laugh; but the latter was the easiest. The old shopkeeper was like an old cock strutting about the house which he despised. "I hate your England," he said, "your rain, your Autumn, your old baraques which you call châteaux. For châteaux come to my country, come to the Pays Bas, monsieur. No, I would not change, I care not for your dirty England. But," he added, "one has one's dignity and one's rights, all the same."

He was mollified, however, when Stevens came to help him off with his coats, and when Cook sent up the best she could supply on such short notice.

"I thought perhaps, M. Austin, you would like to rest before—dinner," said Reine, trembling as she said the last word. She hoped still that he would interrupt her, and add, "before we go."

But no such thought entered into M. Guillaume's mind. He calculated on staying a few days now that he was here, as he had done before, and being made much of, as then. He inclined his head politely in answer to Reine's remark, and said, Yes, he would be pleased to rest before dinner; the journey was long and very fatiguing. He thought even that after dinner he would retire at once, that he might be remis for to-morrow. "And I hope, mademoiselle, that your villanous weather will se remettre," he added. "Bon Dieu, what it must be to live in this country! When the house comes to me, I will sell it, monsieur. The money will be more sweet elsewhere than in this vieux maison delabré, though it is so much to you."

"But you cannot sell it," said Reine, flushing crimson, "if it ever should come to you."

"Who will prevent me?" said M. Guillaume. "Ah, your maudit law of heritage! Tiens! then I will pull it down, mademoiselle," he said calmly, sipping the old claret, and making her a little bow.

The reader may judge how agreeable M. Guillaume made himself with this kind of conversation. He was a great deal more at his ease than he had ever been with Miss Susan, of whom he stood in awe.

"After this misfortune, this surprise," he went on, "which has made so much to suffer my poor wife, it goes of my honor to take myself the place of heir. I cannot more make any arrangement, any bargain, monsieur perceives, that one should be able to say Guillaume Austin of Bruges deceived the world to put in his little son, against the law, to be the heir! Oh, these women, these women, how they are weak and wicked! When I heard of it I wept. I, a man, an old! my poor angel has so much suffered; I forgave her when I heard her tale; but that méchante, that Giovanna, who was the cause of all, how could I forgive—and Madame Suzanne? Apropos, where is Madame Suzanne? She comes not, I see her not. She is afraid, then, to present herself before me."

This was more than Reine's self-denial could bear. "I do not know who you are," she cried indignantly. "I never heard there were any Austins who were not gentlemen. Do not stop me, Everard. This house is my brother's house, and I am his representative. We have nothing to do with you, heir or not heir, and know nothing about your children, or your wife, or any one belonging to you. For poor Giovanna's sake, though no doubt you have driven her to do wrong through your cruelty, you shall have what you want for to-night. Miss Susan Austin afraid of you! Everard, I cannot stay any longer to hear my family and my home insulted. See that they have what they want!" said the girl, ablaze with rage and indignation.

M. Guillaume, perhaps, had been taking too much of the old claret in his fatigue, and he did not understand English very well when delivered with such force and rapidity. He looked after her with more surprise than anger when Reine, a little too audibly in her wrath, shut behind her the heavy oak door.

"Eh bien?" he said. "Mademoiselle is irritable, n'est ce pas? And what did she mean, then, for Giovanna's sake?"

Everard held it to be needless to explain Reine's innocent flourish of trumpets in favor of the culprit. He said, "Ah, that is the question. What do you mean to do about Giovanna, M. Guillaume?"

"Do!" cried the old man, and he made a coarse but forcible gesture, as of putting something disagreeable out of his mouth, "she may die of hunger, as she said—by the road, by the fields—for anything she will get from me."

CHAPTER XLVII

I need not say that the condition of Whiteladies that evening was about as uncomfortable as could be conceived. Before dinner—a ceremonial at which Everard alone officiated, with the new-comers and Giovanna, all of whom ate a very good dinner—it had been discovered that Miss Susan had not gone to her own room, but to her new house, from which a messenger arrived for Martha in the darkening of the Winterly afternoon. The message was from Miss Augustine, written in her pointed, old-fashioned hand; and requesting that Martha would bring everything her mistress required for the night; Augustine forgot that she herself wanted anything. It was old John Simmons, from the Almshouses, who brought the note, and who told the household that Miss Augustine had been there as usual for the evening service. The intimation of this sudden removal fell like a thunderbolt upon the house. Martha, crying, packed her little box, and went off in the early darkness, not knowing, as she said, whether she was "on her head or her heels," and thinking every tree a ghost as she went along the unfamiliar road, through the misty, dreary night. Herbert had retired to his room, where he would not admit even his sister, and Reine, sad and miserable, with a headache as well as a heartache, not knowing what was the next misfortune that might happen, wandered up and down all the evening through, fretting at Everard's long absence, though she had begged him to undertake the duties of host, and longing to see Giovanna and talk to her, with a desire that was half liking and half hatred. Oh, how dared she, how dared she live among them with such a secret on her mind? Yet what was to become of her? Reine felt with a mixture of contempt and satisfaction that, so far as Herbert was concerned, Giovanna's chances were all over forever. She flitted about the house, listening with wonder and horror to the sound of voices from the dining-room, which were cheerful enough in the midst of the ruin and misery that these people had made. Reine was no more just, no more impartial, than the rest. She said to herself, "which these people had made," and pitied poor Miss Susan whose heart was broken by it, just as M. Guillaume pitied his suffering angel, his poor wife. Reine on her side threw all the guilt upon that suffering angel. Poor Giovanna had done what she was told, but it was the wretched old woman, the vulgar schemer, the wicked old Fleming who had planned the lie in all its details, and had the courage to carry it out. All Reine's heart flowed over with pity for the sinner who was her own. Poor Aunt Susan! what could she be thinking? how could she be feeling in the solitude of the strange new house! No doubt believing that the children to whom she had been so kind had abandoned her. It was all Reine could do to keep herself from going with Martha, to whom she gave a hundred messages of love. "Tell her I wanted to come with you, but could not because of the visitors. Tell her the old gentleman from Bruges—Bruges, Martha, you will not forget the name—came directly she had gone; and that I hope they are going away to-morrow, and that I will come to her at once. Give her my dear love, Martha," cried the girl, following Martha out to the porch, and standing there in the darkness watching her, while Miss Susan's maid walked out unwillingly into the night, followed by the under-gardener with her baggage. This was while the others were at dinner, and it was then that Reine saw the cheerful light through the great oriel window, and heard the voices sounding cheerful too, she thought, notwithstanding the strange scenes they had just gone through. She was so restless and so curious that she stole upstairs into the musicians' gallery, to see what they were doing. Giovanna was the mistress of the situation still; but she seemed to be using her power in a merciful way. The serious part of the dinner was concluded, and little Jean was there, whom Giovanna—throwing sweetmeats across the table to Gertrude, who sat with her eyes fixed upon her as upon a goddess—was beguiling into recollection of and friendship with the new-comers. "C'est Maman Gertrude; c'est ton autre maman," she was saying to the child. "Tiens, all the bonbons are with her. I have given all to her. Say 'Maman Gertrude,' and she will give thee some." There was a strained air of gayety and patronage about Giovanna, or so at least Reine thought, and she went away guiltily from this peep at them, feeling herself an eavesdropper, and thinking she saw Everard look up to the corner he too knew so well; and thus the evening passed, full of agitation and pain. When the strangers were got to their rooms at last, Everard found a little eager ghost, with great anxious eyes, upon the stairs waiting for him; and they had a long eager talk in whispers, as if anybody could hear them. "Giovanna is behaving like a brick," said Everard. "She is doing all she can to content the child with the new people. Poor little beggar! I don't wonder he kicks at it. She had her little triumph, poor girl, but she's acting like a hero now. What do you think, Reine? Will Herbert go on with it in spite of all?"

"If I were Herbert—" cried the girl, then stopped in her impulsive rapid outcry. "He is changed," she said, tears coming to her eyes. "He is no longer my Bertie, Everard. No, we need not vex ourselves about that; we shall never hear of it any more."

"So much the better," said Everard; "it never would have answered; though one does feel sorry for Giovanna. Reine, my darling, what a blessing that old Susan, God help her! had the courage to make a clean breast of it before these others came!"

"I never thought of that," said the girl, awestricken. "So it was, so it was! It must have been Providence that put it into her head."

"It was Herbert's madness that put it into her head. How could he be such a fool! but it is curious, you know, what set both of them on it at the same time, that horrible old woman at Bruges, and her here. It looks like what they call a brain-wave," said Everard, "though that throws a deal of light on the matter; don't it? Queenie, you are as white as the China rose on the porch. I hope Julie is there to look after you. My poor little queen! I wonder why all this trouble should fall upon you."

"Oh, what is it to me in comparison?" said the girl, almost indignant; but he was so sorry for her, and his tender pity was in itself so sweet, that I think before they separated—her head still aching, though her heart was less sore—Reine, out of sympathy for him, had begun also to entertain a little pity for herself.

The morning rose strangely on the disturbed household—rose impudently, without the least compassion for them, in a blaze of futile, too early sunshine, which faded after the first half of the day. The light seemed to look in mocking at the empty rooms in which Susan and Augustine had lived all their lives. Reine was early astir, unable to rest; and she had not been downstairs ten minutes when all sorts of references were made to her.

"I should like to know, miss, if you please, who is to give the orders, if so be as Miss Susan have gone for good," said Stevens; and Cook came up immediately after with her arms wrapped in her apron. "I won't keep you not five minutes, miss; but if Miss Susan's gone for good, I don't know as I can find it convenient to stay. Where there's gentlemen and a deal of company isn't like a lady's place, where there's a quiet life," said Cook. "Oh," said Reine, driven to her wits' end, "please, please, like good people, wait a little! How can I tell what we must do?" The old servants granted Reine the "little time" she begged, but they did it ungraciously and with a sure sense of supremacy over her. Happily she found a variety of trays with coffee going up to the strangers' rooms, and found, to her great relief, that she would escape the misery of a breakfast with them; and François brought a message from Herbert to the effect that he was quite well, but meant to stay in his room till ces gens-là were out of the house. "May I not go to him?" cried Reine. "Monsieur is quite well," François replied; "Mademoiselle may trust me. But it will be well to leave him till ce monsieur and ces dames have gone away." And François too, though he was very kind to Mademoiselle Reine, gave her to understand that she should take precautions, and that Monsieur should not be exposed to scenes so trying; so that the household, with very good intentions, was hard upon Reine. And it was nearly noon before she saw anything of the other party, about whose departure she was so anxious. At last about twelve o'clock, perilously near the time of the train, she met Giovanna on the stairs. The young woman was pale, with the gayety and the triumph gone out of her. "I go to ask that the carriage may be ready," said Giovanna. "They will go at midi, if Mademoiselle will send the carriage."

"Yes, yes," said Reine, eagerly; "but you are ill, Giovanna; you are pale." She added half timidly, after a moment, "What are you going to do?"

Giovanna smiled with something of the bravado of the previous day. "I will derange no one," she said; "Mademoiselle need not fear. I will not seek again those who have deserted me. C'est petit, ça!" she cried with a momentary outburst, waving her hand toward the door of Herbert's room. Then controlling herself, "That they should go is best, n'est ce pas? I work for that. If Mademoiselle will give the orders for the carriage—"

"Yes, yes," said Reine, and then in her pity she laid her hand on Giovanna's arm. "Giovanna, I am very sorry for you. I do not think you are the most to blame," she said.

"Blame!" said Giovanna, with a shrug of her shoulders, "I did as I was told." Then two big tears came into her eyes. She put her white, large, shapely hands on Reine's shoulders, and kissed her suddenly on both her cheeks. "You, you are good, you have a heart!" she said; "but to abandon the friends when they are in trouble, c'est petit, ça!" and with that she turned hastily and went back to her room. Reine, breathless, ran downstairs to order the carriage. She went to the door with her heart beating, and stood waiting to see what would happen, not knowing whether Giovanna's kiss was to be taken as a farewell. Presently voices were heard approaching, and the whole party came downstairs; the old man in his big coat, with his cache-nez about his neck, Gertrude pale but happy, and last of all Giovanna, in her usual household dress, with the boy on her shoulder. Gertrude carried in her hand a large packet of bon-bons, and got hastily into the carriage, while her father stood bowing and making his little farewell speeches to Reine and Everard. Giovanna coming after them with her strong light step, her head erect, and the child, in his little velvet coat with his cap and feather, seated on her shoulder, his hand twisted in her hair, interested them more than all M. Guillaume's speeches. Giovanna went past them to the carriage door; she had a flush upon her cheek which had been so pale. She put the child down upon Gertrude's lap, and kissed him. "Mamma will come to Jean presently, in a moment," she said. "Regarde donc! how much of bon-bons are in Mama Gertrude's lap. Thou wilt eat them all, petit gourmand, and save none for me."

Then with a laugh and mocking menace she stepped back into a corner, where she was invisible to the child, and stood there motionless till the old man got in beside his daughter, and the carriage drove away. A little cry, wondering and wistful, "Mamma! mamma!" was the last sound audible as the wheels crashed over the gravel. Reine turned round, holding out her hands to the forlorn creature behind her, her heart full of pity. The tears were raining down in a storm from Giovanna's eyes, but she laughed and shook them away. "Mon Dieu!" she cried, "I do not know why is this. Why should I love him? I am not his mother. But it is an attack of the nerfs—I cannot bear any more," and drawing her hands out of Reine's she fled with a strange shame and passion, through the dim passages. They heard her go upstairs, and, listening in some anxiety, after a few minutes' interval, heard her moving about her room with brisk, active steps.

"That is all right," said Everard, with a sigh of relief. "Poor Giovanna! some one must be kind to her; but come in here and rest, my queen. All this is too much for you."

"Oh, what is it to me in comparison?" cried Reine; but she suffered herself to be led into the drawing-room to be consoled and comforted, and to rest before anything more was done. She thought she kept an ear alert to listen for Giovanna's movements, but I suppose Everard was talking too close to that ear to make it so lively as it ought to have been. At least before anything was heard by either of them, Giovanna in her turn had gone away.

She came downstairs carefully, listening to make sure that no one was about. She had put up all her little possessions ready to be carried away. Pausing in the corridor above to make sure that all was quiet, she went down with her swift, light step, a step too firm and full of character to be noiseless, but too rapid at the present moment to risk awaking any spies. She went along the winding passages, and out through the great porch, and across the damp grass. The afternoon had begun to set in by this time, and the fading sunshine of the morning was over. When she had reached the outer gate she turned back to look at the house. Giovanna was not a person of taste; she thought not much more of Whiteladies than her father-in-law did. "Adieu, vieil baraque," she said, kissing the tips of her fingers; but the half-contempt of her words was scarcely carried out by her face. She was pale again, and her eyes were red. Though she had declared frankly that she saw no reason for loving little Jean, I suppose the child—whom she had determined to make fond of her, as it was not comme il faut that a mother and child should detest each other—had crept into her heart, though she professed not to know it. She had been crying, though she would not have admitted it, over his little empty bed, and those red rims to her eyes were the consequence. When she had made that farewell to the old walls she turned and went on, swiftly and lightly as a bird, skimming along the ground, her erect figure full of health and beautiful strength, vigor, and unconscious grace. She looked strong enough for anything, her firm foot ringing in perfect measure on the path, like a Roman woman in a procession, straight and noble, more vigorous, more practical, more alive than the Greek; fit to be made a statue of or a picture; to carry water-jars or grape-baskets, or children; almost to till the ground or sit upon a throne. The air cleared away the redness from her eyes, and brought color back to her cheeks. The grand air, the plein jour, words in which, for once in a way, the French excel us in the fine abundance and greatness of the ideas suggested, suited Giovanna; though she loved comfort too, and could be as indolent as heart could desire. But to-day she wanted the movement, the sense of rapid progress. She wore her usual morning-dress of heavy blue serge, so dark as to be almost black, with a kind of cloak of the same material, the end of which was thrown over the shoulder in a fashion of her own. The dress was perfectly simple, without flounce or twist of any kind in its long lines. Such a woman, so strong, so swift, so dauntless, carrying her head with such a light and noble grace, might have been a queen's messenger, bound on affairs of life and death, carrying pardon and largesse or laws and noble ordinances of state from some throned Ida, some visionary princess. Though she did not know her way, she went straight on, finding it by instinct, seeing the high roof and old red walls of the Grange ever so far off, as only her penetrating eyes and noble height could have managed to see. She recovered her spirits as she walked on, and nodded and smiled with careless good-humor to the women in the village, who came to their doors to look after her, moved by that vague consciousness which somehow gets into the very atmosphere, of something going on at Whiteladies. "Something's up," they all said; though how they knew I cannot tell, nor could they themselves have told.

The gate of the Grange, which was surrounded by shrubberies, stood open, and so did the door of the house, as generally happens when there has been a removal; for servants and workpeople have a fine sense of appropriateness, and prefer to be and to look as uncomfortable as possible at such a crisis. Giovanna went in without a moment's hesitation. The door opened into a square hall, which gave entrance to several rooms, the sitting-rooms of the house. One of these doors only was shut, and this Giovanna divined must be the one occupied. She neither paused nor knocked nor asked admittance, but went straight to it, and opening the door, walked, without a word, into the room in which, as she supposed, Miss Susan was. She was not noiseless, as I have said; there was nothing of the cat about her; her foot sounded light and regular with a frankness beyond all thought of stealth. The sound of it had already roused the lonely occupant of the room. Miss Susan was lying on a sofa, worn out with the storm of yesterday, and looking old and feeble. She raised herself on her elbow, wondering who it was; and it startled her, no doubt, to see this young woman enter, who was, I suppose, the last person in the world she expected to see.

"Giovanna, you!" she cried, and a strange shock ran through her, half of pain—for Reine might have come by this time, she could not but think—yet strangely mixed, she could not tell how, with a tinge of pleasure too.

"Madame Suzanne, yes," said Giovanna, "it is me. I know not what you will think. I come back to you, though you have cast me away. All the world also has cast me away," she added with a smile; "I have no one to whom I can go; but I am strong, I am young; I am not a lady, as you say. I know to do many things that ladies cannot do. I can frotter and brush when it is necessary. I can make the garden; I can conduct your carriage; many things more that I need not name. Even I can make the kitchen, or the robes when it is necessary. I come to say, Take me then for your butlaire, like old Stefan. I am more strong than he; I do many more things. Ecoutez, Madame Suzanne! I am alone, very alone; I know not what may come to me, but one perishes not when one can work. It is not for that I come. It is that I have de l'amitié for you."

Miss Susan made an incredulous exclamation, and shook her head; though I think there was a sentiment of a very different, and, considering all the circumstances, very strange character, rising in her heart.

"You believe me not? Bien!" said Giovanna, "nevertheless, it is true. You have not loved me—which, perhaps, it is not possible that one should love me; you have looked at me as your enemy. Yes, it was tout naturel. Notwithstanding, you were kind. You spared nothing," said the practical Giovanna. "I had to eat and to drink like you; you did not refuse the robes when I needed them. You were good, all good for me; though you did not love me. Eh bien, Madame Suzanne," she said, suddenly, the tears coming to her eyes, "I love you! You may not believe it, but it is true."

"Giovanna! I don't know what to say to you," faltered Miss Susan, feeling some moisture start into the corners of her own eyes.

"Ecoutez," she said again; "is it that you know what has happened since you went away? Madame Suzanne, it is true that I wished to be Madame Herbert, that I tried to make him love me. Was it not tout naturel? He was rich, and I had not a sou, and it is pleasant to be grande dame, great ladye, to have all that one can desire. Mon Dieu, how that is agreeable! I made great effort, I deny it not. D'ailleurs, it was very necessary that the petit should be put out of the way. Look you, that is all over. He abandons me. He regards me not, even; says not one word of pity when I had the most great need. Allez," cried Giovanna, indignantly, her eyes flashing, "c'est petit, ça!" She made a pause, with a great expansion and heave of her breast, then resumed. "But, Madame Suzanne, although it happened all like that, I am glad, glad—I thank the bon Dieu on my knees—that you did speak it then, not now, that day, not this; that you have not lose the moment, the just moment. For that I thank the bon Dieu."

"Giovanna, I hope the bon Dieu will forgive us," Miss Susan said, very humbly, putting her hands across her eyes.

"I hope so also," said Giovanna cheerfully, as if that matter were not one which disturbed her very much; "but it was good, good that you spoke the first. The belle-mère had also remorse; she had bien de quoi! She sent them to say all, to take back—the child. Madame Suzanne," cried Giovanna, "listen; I have given him back to Gertrude; I have taught him to be sage with her; I have made to smile her and the beau-père, and showed bounty to them. All that they would I have done, and asked nothing; for what? that they might go away, that they might not vex personne, that there might not be so much of talk. Tenez, Madame Suzanne! And they go when I am weary with to speak, with to smile, with to make excuse—they go, enfin! and I return to my chamber, and the little bed is empty, and the petit is gone away!"

There was no chair near her on which she could sit down, and at this point she dropped upon the floor and cried, the tears falling in a sudden storm over her cheeks. They had long been gathering, making her eyes hot and heavy. Poor Giovanna! She cried like a child with keen emotion, which found relief in that violent utterance. "N'importe!" she said, struggling against the momentary passion, forcing a tremulous smile upon the mouth which quivered, "n'importe! I shall get over it; but figure to yourself the place empty, empty! and so still! Why should I care? I am not his mother," said Giovanna; and wept as if her heart would break.

Miss Susan rose from her sofa. She was weak and tottered as she got up. She went to Giovanna's side, laid her hand on her head, and stooping over her, kissed her on the forehead. "Poor thing! poor thing!" she said, in a trembling voice, "this is my doing, too."

"It is nothing, nothing!" cried Giovanna, springing up and shaking back a loose lock of her black hair. "Now, I will go and see what is to do. Put thyself on the sofa, Madame Suzanne. Ah, pardon! I said it without thought."

Miss Susan did not understand what it was for which Giovanna begged pardon. It did not occur to her that the use of the second person could, in any case, be sin; but Giovanna, utterly shocked and appalled at her own temerity, blushed crimson, and almost forgot little Jean. She led Miss Susan back to the sofa, and placed her there with the utmost tenderness. "Madame Suzanne must not think that it was more than an inadvertence, a fault of excitement, that I could take it upon me to say thee to my superior. Oh, pardon! a thousand times. Now, I go to bring you of the thé, to shut the door close, to make quiet the people, that all shall be as Viteladies. I am Madame Suzanne's servant from this hour."

"Giovanna," said Miss Susan, who, just at this moment, was very easily agitated, and did not so easily recover herself, "I do not say no. We have done wrong together; we will try to be good together. I have made you suffer, too; but, Giovanna, remember, there must be nothing more of that. You must promise me that all shall be over between you and Herbert."

"Bah!" said Giovanna, with a gesture of disgust. "Me, I suffered, as Madame Suzanne says; and he saw, and never said a word; not so much as, 'Poor Giovanna!' Allez! c'est petit, ça!" cried the young woman, tossing her fine head aloft with a pride of nature that sat well on her. Then she turned, smiling to Miss Susan on the sofa. "Rest, my mistress," she said, softly, with quaint distinctness of pronunciation. "Mademoiselle will soon be here to talk, and make everything plain to you. I go to bring of the thé, me."

CHAPTER XLVIII

Herbert came into the drawing-room almost immediately after Giovanna left. Francis had watched the carriage go off, and I suppose he thought that Giovanna was in it with the others, and his master, feeling free and safe, went down stairs. Herbert had not been the least sufferer in that eventful day and night. He had been sadly weakened by a course of flattery, and had got to consider himself, in a sense, the centre of the world. Invalidism, by itself, is nearly enough to produce this feeling; and when, upon a long invalid life, was built the superstructure of sudden consequence and freedom, the dazzling influence of unhoped for prosperity and well-being, the worship to which every young man of wealth and position is more or less subjected, the wooing of his cousins, the downright flattery of Giovanna, the reader will easily perceive how the young man's head, was turned, not being a strong head by nature. I think (though I express the opinion with diffidence, not having studied the subject) that it is your vain man, your man whose sense of self-importance is very elevated, who feels a deception most bitterly. The more healthy soul regrets and suffers, but does not feel the same sting in the wound, that he does to whom a sin against himself is the one thing unpardonable. Herbert took the story of Giovanna's deception thus, as an offence against himself. That she should have deceived others, was little in comparison; but him! that he should be, as it were, the centre of this plot, surrounded by people who had planned and conspired in such pitiful ways! His pride was too deeply hurt, his self-importance too rudely shaken, to leave him free to any access of pity or consideration for the culprits. He was not sorry even for Miss Susan; and toward Giovanna and her strange relatives, and the hideous interruption to his comfort and calm which they produced, he had no pity. Nor was he able to discriminate between her ordinary character and this one evil which she had done. Being once lowered in his imagination, she fell altogether, his chief attraction to her, indeed, being her beauty, which heretofore had dazzled and kept him from any inquiry into her other qualities. Now he gave Giovanna no credit for any qualities at all. His wrath was hot and fierce against her. She had taken him in, defrauded him of those, tender words and caresses which he never, had he known it, would have wasted on such a woman. She had humbled him in his own opinion, had made him feel thus that he was not the great person he had supposed; for her interested motives, which were now evident, were so many detractions from his glory, which he had supposed had drawn her toward him, as flowers are drawn to the sun. He had so low an opinion of her after this discovery, that he was afraid to venture out of his room, lest he should be exposed to some encounter with her, and to the tears and prayers his embittered vanity supposed she must be waiting to address to him. This was the chief reason of his retirement, and he was so angry that Reine and Everard should still keep all their wits about them, notwithstanding that he had been thus insulted and wounded, and could show feeling for others, and put up with those detestable visitors, that he almost felt that they too must be included in the conspiracy. It was necessary, indeed, that the visitors should be looked after, and even (his reason allowed) conciliated to a certain extent, to get them away; but still, that his sister should be able to do it, irritated Herbert. He came down, accordingly, in anything but a gracious state of mind. Poor fellow! I suppose his sudden downfall from the (supposed) highest level of human importance, respected and feared and loved by everybody, to the chastened grandeur of one who was first with nobody, though master of all; and who was not of paramount personal importance to any one, had stung him almost beyond bearing. Miss Susan whom he felt he had treated generously, had deceived, then left him without a word. Reine, to whom, perhaps, he had not been kind, had stolen away, out of his power to affect her in any primary degree, had found a new refuge for herself; and Giovanna, to whom he had given that inestimable treasure of his love? Poor Herbert's heart was sore and sick, and full of mortified feeling. No wonder he was querulous and irritable. He came into the room where the lovers were, offended even by the sight of them together. When they dropped apart at his entrance, he was more angry still. Indeed, he felt angry at anything, ready to fight with a fly.

"Don't let me disturb you," he said; "though, indeed, if you don't mind, and can put up with it for a few minutes, I should be glad to speak to you together. I have been thinking that it is impossible for me to go on in this way, you know. Evidently, England will not do for me. It is not October yet, and see what weather! I cannot bear it. It is a necessity of my nature, putting health out of the question, to have sunshine and brightness. I see nothing for it but to go abroad."

Reine's heart gave a painful leap. She looked at Everard with a wistful question in her eyes. "Dear Bertie, if you think so," she said faltering, "of course I will not object to what you like best. But might we not first consult the doctors? You were so well before that night. Oh, Bertie, you know I would never set myself against what was best for you—but I should like to stay at home, just for a little; and the weather will get better. October is generally fine, is it not, Everard? You ought to know—"

"You don't understand me," said Herbert again. "You may stay at home as much as you like. You don't suppose I want you to go. Look here, I suppose I may speak plainly to two people engaged to each other, as you are. Why shouldn't you marry directly, and be done with it? Then you could live on at Whiteladies, and Everard could manage the property: he wants something to do—which would leave me free to follow my inclinations, and live abroad."

"Bertie!" cried Reine, crimson with surprise and pain.

"Well! is there anything to make a fuss about? You mean to be married, I suppose. Why wait? It might be got over, surely, in a month or so. And then, Reine being disposed of," he went on with the most curious unconsciousness, "would not need to be any burden on me; she would want no brother to look after her. I could move about as I please, which a man never can do when he has to drag a lady after him. I think my plan is a very good plan, and why you should find any fault with it, Reine—you for whose benefit it is—"

Reine said nothing. Tears of mortification different from her brother's came into her eyes. Perhaps the mortification was unreasonable; for, indeed, a sister who allows herself to be betrothed does in a way take the first step in abandoning her brother! But to be cast off in this cool and sudden way went to her heart, notwithstanding the strong moral support she had of Everard behind her. She had served, and (though he was not aware of it) protected, and guided for so long the helpless lad, whose entire comfort had depended on her. And even Everard could not console her for this sudden, almost contemptuous, almost insolent dismissal. With her face crimson and her heart beating, she turned away from her ungrateful brother.

"You ought not to speak to me so," cried the girl with bitter tears in her eyes. "You should not throw me off like an old glove; it is not your part, Bertie." And with her heart very heavy and sore, and her quick temper aflame, she hurried away out of the room, leaving them; and, like the others who had gone before, set off by the same oft-trodden road, through the village, to the Grange. Already Miss Susan's new home had become the general family refuge from all evil.

When Reine was gone, Bertie's irritation subdued itself; for one man's excited temper cannot but subdue itself speedily, when it has to beat against the blank wall of another man's indifference. Everard did not care so very much if he was angry or not. He could afford to let Herbert and all the rest of the world cool down, and take their own way. He was sorry for the poor boy, but his temper did not affect deeply the elder man; his elder in years, and twice his elder in experience. Herbert soon calmed down under this process, and then they had a long and serious conversation. Nor did Everard think the proposal at all unreasonable. From disgust, or temper, or disappointment, or for health's sake—what did it matter which?—the master of Whiteladies had determined to go abroad. And what so natural as that Reine's marriage should take place early, there being no reason whatever why they should wait; or that Everard, as her husband, and himself the heir presumptive, should manage the property, and live with his wife in the old house? The proposal had not been delicately made, but it was kind enough. Everard forgave the roughness more readily than Reine could do, and accepted the good-will heartily, taking it for granted that brotherly kindness was its chief motive. He undertook to convince Reine that nothing could be more reasonable, nothing more kind.

"It removes the only obstacle that was in our way," said Everard, grasping his cousin's hand warmly. "God bless you, Bertie. I hope you'll some time be as happy—more happy you can't be."

Poor Bertie took this salutation but grimly, wincing from every such touch, but refused at once Everard's proposal that they should follow Reine to see Miss Susan.

"You may go if you like," he said; "people feel things in different ways, some deeper, some more lightly. I don't blame you, but I can't do it. I couldn't speak to her if she were here."

"Send her a message, at least," said Everard; "one word;—that you forgive her."

"I don't forgive her!" cried the young man, hurrying back to the shelter of his room, where he shut himself up with François. "To-morrow we shall leave this cursed place," he said in his anger to that faithful servant. "I cannot bear it another day."

Everard followed Reine to the Grange, and the first sight he saw made him thank heaven that Herbert was not of the party. Giovanna opened the door, to him, smiling and at her ease. She ushered him into Miss Susan's sitting-room, then disappeared, and came back, bringing more tea, serving every one. She was thoroughly in her element, moving briskly about the old new house, arranging the furniture, which as yet was mere dead furniture without any associations, making a new Whiteladies out of the unfamiliar place.

"It is like a conte des fées, but it is true," she said. "I have always had de l'amitié for Madame Suzanne, now I shall hold the ménage, me. I shall do all things that she wishes. Tiens! it is what I was made for,

Monsieur Everard. I am not born ladye, as you say. I am peuple, très peuple. I can work. Mon Dieu, who else has been kind to me? Not one. As for persons who abandon a friend when they have great need, that for them!" said Giovanna, snapping her fingers, her eyes flashing, her face reddening. "C'est petit, ça!"

And there she remains, and has done for years. I am afraid she is not half so penitent as she ought to be for the almost crime which, in conjunction with the others, she carried out so successfully for a time. She shrugs her shoulders when by chance, in the seclusion of the family, any one refers to it; but the sin never lay very heavy on her conscience. Nor does it affect her tranquillity now. Neither is she ashamed of her pursuit of Herbert, which, so long as it lasted, seemed tout simple to the young woman. And I do not think she is at all conscious that it was he who threw her over, but rather has the satisfaction of feeling that her own disgust at his petitesse ended the matter. But while she has no such feeling as she ought to have for these enormities, she does feel deeply, and mentions sometimes with a burning blush of self-reproach, that once in an unguarded moment she addressed Miss Susan as "Thou!" This sin Giovanna will not easily forgive herself, and never, I think, will forget. So it cannot be said that she is without conscience, after all.

And a more active, notable, delightful housewife could not be. She sings about the house till the old Grange rings with her magnificent voice. She sings when there is what she calls high mass in the Chantry, so that the country people from ever so many miles off come to hear her; and just as sweetly, and with still more energy, she sings in the Almshouse chapel, delighting the poor folks. She likes the hymns which are slightly "Methody," the same ones that old Mrs. Matthews prefers, and rings the bell with her strong arm for old Tolladay when he has his rheumatism, and carries huge baskets of good things for the sick folk, and likes it. They say she is the handsomest woman in St. Austin's parish, or in the county, some people think; and it is whispered in the Almshouses that she has had very fine "offers" indeed, had she liked to take them. I myself know for a fact that the rector, a man of the finest taste, of good family, and elegant manners, and fastidious mind, laid himself and all his attributes at the feet of this Diana, but in vain. And at the first sight of her the young priest of the Chantry, Dr. Richard's nephew, gave up, without a struggle, that favorite doctrine of clerical celibacy, at which his uncle had aimed every weapon of reason and ridicule for years in vain. Giovanna slew this fashionable heresy in the curate's breast with one laughing look out of her great eyes. But she would not have him, all the same, any more than the rector, but laughed and cried out, "Toi! I will be thy mother, mon fils." Fortunately the curate knew little French, and never quite made out what she had said.

As for Miss Susan, though her health continued good, she never quite recovered her activity and vigor. She did recover her peace of mind completely, and is only entering the period of conscious old age now, after an interval of years, very contented and happy. Whiteladies, she declares, only failed her when her strength failed to manage it; and the old Grange has become the cheerfullest and brightest of homes. I am not sure even that sometimes, when her mind is a little confused, as all minds will be now and then, Miss Susan has not a moment's doubt whether the great wickedness of her life has not been one of those things which "work together for good," as Augustine says. But she feels that this is a terrible doctrine, and "will not do," opening the door to all kinds of speculations, and affording a frightful precedent. Still, but for this great sin of hers, she never would have had Giovanna's strong kind arm to lean upon, nor her cheery presence to make the house lively and sweet. Even Augustine feels a certain comfort in that cheery presence, notwithstanding that her wants are so few, and her habits so imperative, putting her life beyond the power of change or misfortune; for no change can ever deprive her of the Almshouses. Even on that exciting day when the sisters went forth from Whiteladies, like the first pair from Paradise, though affection and awakened interest brought Augustine for a moment to the head of affairs, and made her the support and stay of her stronger companion, she went to her Almshouse service all the same, after she had placed Susan on the sofa and kissed her, and written the note to Martha about her night-things. She did her duty bravely, and without shrinking;—then went to the Almshouses—and so continued all the rest of her life.

Herbert, notwithstanding his threat to leave the place next day, stayed against his will till Reine was married, which she consented to be after awhile, without unnecessary delay. He saw Miss Susan only on the wedding day, when he touched her hand coldly, and talked of la pluie et le beau temps, as if she had been a stranger. Nothing could induce him to resume the old cordial relations with one who had so deceived him; and no doubt there will be people who will think Herbert in the right. Indeed, if I did not think that Miss Susan had been very fully punished during the time when she was unsuspected, and carried her Inferno about with her in her own bosom, without any one knowing, I should be disposed to think she got off much too easily after her confession was made; for as soon as the story was told, and the wrong set right, she became comparatively happy—really happy, indeed—in the great and blessed sense of relief; and no one (except Herbert) was hard upon her. The tale scarcely crept out at all in the neighborhood. There was something curious, people said, but even the best-informed believed it to be only one of those quarrels which, alas! occur now and then even in the best-regulated families. Herbert went about the county, paying his farewell visits; and there was a fair assemblage of wealth and fashion at Reine's marriage, which was performed in the Austin Chantry, in presence of all their connections. Then Herbert went abroad, partly for his health, partly because he preferred the freer and gayer life of the Continent, to which he had been so long accustomed, people said. He does not often return, and he is rather fretful, perhaps, in his temper, and dilettante in his tastes, with the look, some ladies say, of "a confirmed bachelor." I don't know, for my part, what that look is, nor how much it is to be trusted to; but, meanwhile, it suits Everard and Reine very well to live at Whiteladies and manage the property. And Miss Augustine is already seriously preparing for the task she has so long contemplated, the education of an heir. Unfortunately, Reine has only a girl yet, which is a disappointment; but better days may come.

As for the Farrel-Austins, they sold the Hatch after their father's death, and broke up the lively society there. Kate married her middle-aged Major as soon after as decency would permit, and Sophy accompanied them to the Continent, where they met Herbert at various gay and much-frequented places. Nothing, however, came of this; but, after all, at the end of years, Lord Alf, once in the ascendant in Sophy's firmament, turned up very much out at elbows, at a German watering-place, and Sophy, who had a comfortable income, was content to buy his poor little title with it. The marriage was not very happy, but she said, and I hope thought, that he was her first love, and that this was the romance of her life. Mrs. Farrel-Austin, strange to tell, got better—quite better, as we say in Scotland—though she retained an inclination toward tonics as long as she lived.

Old M. Guillaume Austin of Bruges was gathered to his fathers last year, so that all danger from his heirship is happily over. His daughter Gertrude has so many children, that a covert proposal has been made, I understand, to Miss Susan and Giovanna to have little Jean restored to them if they wish it. But he is associated with too many painful recollections to be pleasing to Miss Susan, and Giovanna's robust organization has long ago surmounted that momentary wound of parting. Besides, is not Whiteladies close by, with little Queenie in the nursery already, and who knows what superior hopes?

Margaret Oliphant Wilson was born on April 4th, 1828 to Francis W. Wilson, a clerk, and Margaret Oliphant, at Wallyford, near Musselburgh, East Lothian.

She spent her childhood at Lasswade, near Dalkeith, Glasgow before moving to Liverpool.

Her youth was spent in establishing a writing style so much so that, in 1849, she had her first novel published: Passages in the Life of Mrs. Margaret Maitland based on the Scottish Free Church movement. It met with some success and was a good start to her career.

Two years later, in 1851, her third book Caleb Field was published. It was also now that she met the publisher William Blackwood in Edinburgh and was asked to contribute to his well-received Blackwood's Magazine. It was to be a lifetimes endeavor. Over the course of the relationship she would have well over 100 articles published.

In May 1852, Margaret married her cousin, Frank Wilson Oliphant, at Birkenhead, and they settled at Harrington Square, Camden, London. He was an artist working primarily in stained glass. With the marriage she became Margaret Oliphant Wilson Oliphant.

Their marriage produced six children but three tragically died in infancy.

When her husband developed signs of the dreaded consumption (tuberculosis) they moved, on the advice of doctors, to warmer climes. In January 1859 it was to Florence, and then to Rome where, sadly, he died.

Margaret was naturally devastated but was also now left without support and only her income from her writing. She returned to England and took up the task of supporting her three remaining children by her literary activity.

By now she was being published both as an established novelist and regularly in Blackwood's Magazine, amongst others. Her incredible and prolific work rate increased both her commercial reputation and the size of her reading audience.

Against this her domestic life continued to be tragic, full of sorrow and disappointment.

In January 1864 her only remaining daughter Maggie died and was buried in her father's grave in Rome. Her brother, who had emigrated to Canada, was shortly afterwards involved in financial ruin. Margaret generously offered a home to him and his children, adding another demand to her already heavy responsibilities.

In 1866 she settled at Windsor to be closer to her sons, who were being educated at near-by Eton School. That year, her second cousin, Annie Louisa Walker, came to live with her as a companion-housekeeper. Windsor was now to be her home for the rest of her life.

Her literary career for three decades was one of constant delivery and success. Whether she wrote historical works or across several genres in fiction: domestic realism, historical, romance or supernatural she was successful.

For more than thirty years she pursued a varied literary career but family life continued to bring problems.

The literary ambitions she wished for her sons were unfulfilled. Cyril Francis, the eldest, died in 1890, leaving a Life of Alfred de Musset, incorporated in his mother's Foreign Classics for English Readers. The younger, Francis, who she nicknamed 'Cecco', collaborated with her in the Victorian Age of English Literature and won a position at the British Museum, but was rejected by Sir Andrew Clark, a famous physician. Cecco died in 1894.

With the last of her children now lost to her, she had but little further interest in life. Her health steadily and inexorably declined.

Margaret Oliphant Wilson Oliphant died at the age of 69 in Wimbledon on 20th June 1897. She is buried in Eton beside her sons.

At her death, Margaret was still working on Annals of a Publishing House, a record of Blackwood's Magazine with which she had enjoyed such a successful relationship.

Her Autobiography and Letters, which present a thoughtful picture of her domestic anxieties, was published in 1899. Only parts were written with a wider audience in mind: she had originally intended the Autobiography for her son, but he died before she could finish it.

Opinions on Oliphant's work are split, with some critics seeing her as a 'domestic novelist', while others recognize her work as influential and important to the Victorian literature canon. Critical reception from her contemporaries is also divided. John Skelton took the view that Oliphant wrote too much and too quickly. Writing a Blackwood's article called 'A Little Chat About Mrs. Oliphant', he asked, "Had Mrs. Oliphant concentrated her powers, what might she not have done? We might have had another Charlotte Brontë or another George Eliot." However not all of the contemporary reception was negative. The esteemed M. R. James admired Oliphant's supernatural fiction, concluding that "the religious ghost story, as it may be called, was never done better than by Mrs. Oliphant in 'The Open Door' and 'A Beleaguered City'. Mary Butts lavished praise on Oliphant's ghost story 'The Library Window', describing it as "one masterpiece of sober loveliness".

More modern critics of Oliphant's work include Virginia Woolf, who asked in Three Guineas whether Oliphant's autobiography does not lead the reader "to deplore the fact that Mrs. Oliphant sold her brain, her very admirable brain, prostituted her culture and enslaved her intellectual liberty in order that she might earn her living and educate her children."

Whatever the merits of their cases Margaret Oliphant has been shamefully neglected in modern years. She is now becoming more widely recognised as a leading writer of her day.

Margaret Oliphant – A Concise Bibliography

A canon of more than 120 works, including novels, travel books, histories, and volumes of literary criticism.

Novels

Margaret Maitland (1849)
Merkland (1850)
Caleb Field (1851)
John Drayton (1851)
Adam Graeme (1852)
The Melvilles (1852)
Katie Stewart (1852)
Harry Muir (1853)
Ailieford (1853)
The Quiet Heart (1854)
Magdalen Hepburn (1854)
Zaidee (1855)
Lilliesleaf (1855)
Christian Melville (1855)
The Athelings (1857)
The Days of My Life (1857)
Orphans (1858)
The Laird of Norlaw (1858)
Agnes Hopetoun's Schools and Holidays (1859)
Lucy Crofton (1860)
The House on the Moor (1861)
The Last of the Mortimers (1862)
Heart and Cross (1863)
Salem Chapel (1863)
The Rector (1863)
Doctor's Family (1863)
The Perpetual Curate (1864)
Miss Marjoribanks (1866)
Phoebe Junior (1876)
A Son of the Soil (1865)
Agnes (1866)
Madonna Mary (1867)
Brownlows (1868)
The Minister's Wife (1869)
The Three Brothers (1870)
John: A Love Story (1870)
Squire Arden (1871)
At his Gates (1872)
Ombra (1872
May (1873)
Innocent (1873)
The Story of Valentine and his Brother (1875)
A Rose in June (1874)
For Love and Life (1874)
Whiteladies (1875)
An Odd Couple (1875)

The Curate in Charge (1876)
Carità (1877)
Young Musgrave (1877)
Mrs. Arthur (1877)
The Primrose Path (1878)
Within the Precincts (1879)
The Fugitives (1879)
A Beleaguered City (1879)
The Greatest Heiress in England (1880)
He That Will Not When He May (1880)
In Trust (1881)
Harry Joscelyn (1881)
Lady Jane (1882)
A Little Pilgrim in the Unseen (1882)
The Lady Lindores (1883)
Sir Tom (1883)
Hester (1883)
It Was a Lover and his Lass (1883)
The Lady's Walk (1883)
The Wizard's Son (1884)
Madam (1884)
The Prodigals and their Inheritance (1885)
Oliver's Bride (1885)
A Country Gentleman and his Family (1886)
A House Divided Against Itself (1886)
Effie Ogilvie (1886)
A Poor Gentleman (1886)
The Son of his Father (1886)
Joyce (1888)
Cousin Mary (1888)
The Land of Darkness (1888)
Lady Car (1889)
Kirsteen (1890)
The Mystery of Mrs. Biencarrow (1890)
Sons and Daughters (1890)
The Railway Man and his Children (1891)
The Heir Presumptive and the Heir Apparent (1891)
The Marriage of Elinor (1891)
Janet (1891)
The Cuckoo in the Nest (1892)
Diana Trelawny (1892)
The Sorceress (1893)
A House in Bloomsbury (1894)
Sir Robert's Fortune (1894)
Who Was Lost and is Found (1894)
Lady William (1894)
Two Strangers (1895)
Old Mr. Tredgold (1895)

The Unjust Steward (1896)
The Ways of Life (1897)

The Anti-Marriage League (Blackwood's Magazine, Vol. 159, 1896)

Biographies

Edward Irving (1862)
Francis of Assisi (1871)
Count de Montalembert (1872)
Dante (1877)
Cervantes (1880)
Life of Sheridan in the English Men of Letters series (1883)
John Tulloch (1888)
Laurence Oliphant (1892)

Historical & Critical Works

Historical Sketches of the Reign of George II (1869)
The Makers of Florence (1876)
A Literary History of England from 1760 to 1825 (1882)
The Makers of Venice (1887)
Royal Edinburgh (1890)
Jerusalem (1891)
The Makers of Modern Rome (1895)
William Blackwood and his Sons (1897)
The Sisters Brontë. In: Women Novelists of Queen Victoria's Reign (1897)